T0129266

GREEN
SEPTEMBER

GREEN SEPTEMBER

A Novel

Book 1 of a Trilogy

RAY VERNON

iUniverse®

GREEN SEPTEMBER
A NOVEL

iUniverse books may be ordered through booksellers or by contacting:

iUniverse
1663 Liberty Drive
Bloomington, IN 47403
www.iuniverse.com
1-800-Authors (1-800-288-4677)

ISBN: 978-1-5320-1042-2 (sc)
ISBN: 978-1-5320-1043-9 (hc)
ISBN: 978-1-5320-1044-6 (e)

Library of Congress Control Number: 2016919941

Print information available on the last page.

iUniverse rev. date: 03/20/2017

*To all the Irish Freedom Fighters who were killed in 1916
and in the years since, and to my late
mother, Netta Morrissey Vernon,
who loved them all—in particular, Michael Collins.*

Up the Rebels!
Onward and upward to a united Ireland!

*They fought with the same spirit of independence as did the Sons
of Liberty in Boston in 1776, who started
the American Revolution.*

POBLACHT NA H EIREANN.

THE PROVISIONAL GOVERNMENT
OF THE
IRISH REPUBLIC
TO THE PEOPLE OF IRELAND.

IRISHMEN AND IRISHWOMEN In the name of God and of the dead generations from which she receives her old tradition of nationhood, Ireland, through us, summons her children to her flag and strikes for her freedom.

Having organised and trained her manhood through her secret revolutionary organisation, the Irish Republican Brotherhood, and through her open military organisations, the Irish Volunteers and the Irish Citizen Army, having patiently perfected her discipline, having resolutely waited for the right moment to reveal itself, she now seizes that moment, and, supported by her exiled children in America and by gallant allies in Europe, but relying in the first on her own strength, she strikes in full confidence of victory.

We declare the right of the people of Ireland to the ownership of Ireland, and to the unfettered control of Irish destinies, to be sovereign and indefeasible. The long usurpation of that right by a foreign people and government has not extinguished the right, nor can it ever be extinguished except by the destruction of the Irish people. In every generation the Irish people have asserted their right to national freedom and sovereignty; six times during the past three hundred years they have asserted it in arms. Standing on that fundamental right and again asserting it in arms in the face of the world, we hereby proclaim the Irish Republic as a Sovereign Independent State, and we pledge our lives and the lives of our comrades-in-arms to the cause of its freedom, of its welfare, and of its exaltation among the nations.

The Irish Republic is entitled to, and hereby claims, the allegiance of every Irishman and Irishwoman. The Republic guarantees religious and civil liberty, equal rights and equal opportunities to all its citizens, and declares its resolve to pursue the happiness and prosperity of the whole nation and of all its parts, cherishing all the children of the nation equally, and oblivious of the differences carefully fostered by an alien government, which have divided a minority from the majority in the past.

Until our arms have brought the opportune moment for the establishment of a permanent National Government, representative of the whole people of Ireland and elected by the suffrages of all her men and women, the Provisional Government, hereby constituted, will administer the civil and military affairs of the Republic in trust for the people.

We place the cause of the Irish Republic under the protection of the Most High God, Whose blessing we invoke upon our arms, and we pray that no one who serves that cause will dishonour it by cowardice, inhumanity, or rapine. In this supreme hour the Irish nation must, by its valour and discipline and by the readiness of its children to sacrifice themselves for the common good, prove itself worthy of the august destiny to which it is called.

Signed on Behalf of the Provisional Government,

THOMAS J. CLARKE,

SEAN Mac DIARMADA,   THOMAS MacDONAGH,
P. H. PEARSE,   EAMONN CEANNT,
JAMES CONNOLLY.   JOSEPH PLUNKETT.

ACKNOWLEDGMENTS

MY DEEPEST APPRECIATION TO GEORGE Nedeff, my original editorial manager at iUniverse, and most recently to Sarah Disbrow, my current editorial manager, as both guided me successfully and patiently and nourished my ability in producing this book. Many thanks to you both for all your support.

My special thanks and appreciation to Melissa Watkins Starr, who, as my developmental editor, took my first novel draft and did so much to educate me in the professional craft of writing. Melissa, I owe you so much and look forward to working with you on book 2 in this trilogy.

To Alison Holen, the book jacket designer, my deepest veneration for your absolutely stunning design—your thinking "out of the box" blew me away and everyone who saw it! I so hope we can work together again on book 2.

My special thanks to a favorite Irish nephew, Darran Foster, who is a TV producer in New York and my major media consultant. Darran has given me constant support and encouragement and has promised help in promoting this book.

I would be remiss if I failed to mention six dear, lifelong friends who have always encouraged me in my writing endeavors, were constant cheerleaders, and by their achievements inspired me to pursue my dream, and so I would like to take this opportunity to thank each of them (in no particular order) for being there for me:

(1) Yasu Kizaki, owner of two renowned Japanese restaurants—Sushi Den and Izakaya Den in Denver.

(2) Ned Mansour, retired president of Mattel, Inc, in California and my favorite corporate alma mater, and also the published author of *Divided Roads* in 2002.

(3) Pam Newton, former licensing director at Paramount and Dreamworks Animation in California.

(4) Joe Miccio, retired NYFD firefighter, writer, board game designer, and 9/11 survivor on Long Island.

(5) Rick Tomasco, entrepreneur and toy-industry veteran from California.

(6) Toby Corey, entrepreneur and president of global sales and customer experience at SolarCity in California.

Last but by no means least, I want to thank my beloved wife, Cindy, who has put up with my "craziness and creative musings" for over thirty years and most importantly typed up and made sense of the first recording of this book, a habit from corporate days, and she is now very happy that I type for myself. Thank you, Cindy, for your support and encouragement and for being a constant presence in my life.

CHAPTER *1*

London, England, August 20, 1993

MAJOR KEVIN MACALLISTER BACKED HIS restored '57 Jaguar out of the garage, swinging around the front of the house. His wife, Shelia, and their dog, Max, stood by the front door, so Kevin waved as he turned right at the corner onto Willoughby Road, and then he turned left on Rosslyn Hill, shifting into top gear as he headed south toward Camden Town. He smiled as he thought about his beautiful, sexy mistress, Jenny Laster, whom he would see later in the day. Then his thoughts came back to the task in hand. He frowned in concentration as his mind ran over his carefully worked-out plans for replacing the nuclear-missile firing mechanisms with the duplicates he had made. He knew he had to be super careful so as not to arouse the slightest suspicion at the Ministry that morning.

It was only quarter to eight, so traffic was still moving steadily without too much stop and go. Kevin turned on the radio and picked up a report on BBC: "Another bomb exploded in the Lower Falls area of Belfast at 1:00 a.m. today, killing two soldiers and wounding five others. The IRA claimed responsibility in a statement reiterating their demands for the removal of all British soldiers from Northern Ireland and the reunification of the province with the Republic of Ireland."

Kevin headed down Albany Street alongside Regents Park. The news reinforced his conviction that the execution of his ultimate solution, which he planned to implement in just seventeen days, could prove to be the only way to break the cycle of violence in Northern Ireland and pave the way for a united Ireland. He felt a mixture of excitement and apprehension as the culmination of his plan to use nuclear blackmail to achieve a united Ireland drew near.

Kevin focused on the road ahead. The traffic became extremely heavy as he drove, stuck in first gear, across Euston Road and down Portland Place to Regent Street. It would now be stop and start all the way to the office. It was always like this, Kevin thought, and it had become steadily worse over the many years he had made this morning drive. Slowly rounding Piccadilly Circus and turning right on Haymarket, he reached the last bottleneck at Trafalgar Square. Picking up speed as he turned onto Whitehall, he quickly passed the Admiralty and Downing Street on his right and then turned left onto Richmond Terrace and left again down the ramp to the underground parking at Mews Park.

From the exterior, the Ministry of Defense was a massive Victorian-style structure, occupying almost an entire block overlooking the River Thames, but, in contrast, the interior had the trappings of an ultramodern military establishment with all the sophisticated computer and electronic equipment necessary to direct operations in the age of nuclear warfare.

"Good morning, sir," Corporal Jones said and saluted smartly as Kevin nodded his thank you, got out, and left Jones to park the car. Entering the lift, he punched the button for the twelfth floor.

His secretary, Margaret Bloomington, greeted him, handed him a folder, and said, "Here's the file for your meeting with Sir Ian."

"Thank you, Margaret. You're a marvel of efficiency."

"Thank you, sir," she said, a glow of pride on her face as she left the room. Kevin knew her loyalty to him was absolute, and while he always maintained a most proper relationship with Margaret, he never failed to remember her on her birthday and at Christmas and always brought her back some small token of his esteem from his many trips overseas.

Kevin quickly reviewed the contents of the folder. His familiarity with the details of the biannual military maneuvers and his role in the security and coordination of the mobile tactical nuclear weapons used in these exercises made for rapid reading of the file. It was standard Ministry procedure that the firing mechanisms, a complex microelectronic circuit board the size of a postage stamp, were removed from all the mobile missiles armed with nuclear warheads and kept at the unit bases to prevent a nuclear accident during their war games. As a further precaution, each firing mechanism was programmed to work only on the single nuclear missile to which it belonged. Kevin had personally devised this system and the backup procedure whereby an exact duplicate of all firing mechanisms were maintained in the vaults in the nuclear shelter basement of the Ministry. Of course, a complete file record indicating the missile code number and unit to which it was assigned was kept with the duplicate firing mechanism. Only two people, Sir Ian and Kevin, had direct access to them.

Margaret popped her head around the door and said, "It's five minutes to ten."

"Thanks, Margaret. I'm on my way." Kevin gathered up all his papers and put them in the folder.

Sir Ian Sinders's office was on the same floor as Kevin's but on the opposite corner of the building, where Sir Ian had a commanding view of Whitehall, Horse Guards Parade, and the entrance to Downing Street. The office was more than twice the size of Kevin's, with a large round conference table at one end where Sir Ian conducted staff meetings with the heads of all branches of the armed services. Naturally enough, Kevin was usually in attendance, as an independent nuclear deterrent was still the cornerstone of British military strategy, despite rumblings to the contrary from some Labour MPs in Westminster.

"Good morning, Jane," Kevin said to Jane Hawley, Sir Ian's confidential secretary, a rather prim and proper tall woman in her midfifties.

"Go right in, Major. Sir Ian is waiting for you."

Sir Ian sat behind his antique desk and cheerfully greeted Kevin. "Good morning, Mac. Pull up a chair. This shouldn't take long."

Kevin laid his folder on the desk, and the two men spent the next hour or so reviewing some of the final details for the upcoming military exercises. At last, Sir Ian leaned back in his chair and said, "Well, Mac, everything's in place for a productive week at Salisbury. I see from your schedule that you'll be at the Pentagon all next week getting the latest update from our American allies on their proposed further nuclear arms reduction talks with the Russians. It should be very interesting, as it's certain to have a profound effect on the nuclear arms balance in Europe, particularly for the French and ourselves. Then, as you are off for your annual week's fishing in Scotland, you can bring me up to date when we meet at Salisbury in a couple of weeks or so. Okay?"

"Absolutely, sir, and by then I should have prepared the impact report of different scenarios on our forces."

"Enjoy your trip to Scotland. I wish I could join you. Certainly, you deserve the break away from it all!"

"Yes, I'm looking forward to it. Thank you, sir. I always enjoy the remoteness I feel in Scotland. Good-bye, sir!" Kevin got up and headed out to the elevators, deciding this would be a good time to go down to the vaults in the basement.

As Kevin stepped out of the elevator on basement level four, Sergeant Jack Pedley said, "Good morning, sir," as he stood to attention behind his desk.

"At ease, Jack," Kevin said as he signed the security register and recorded the time: 11:15 a.m.

The two soldiers by the main vault entrance stood at arms ready with their eyes looking straight ahead as Kevin slipped his hand into the computer-controlled fingerprint identification reader located in the wall.

An electronic voice intoned, "You are cleared to proceed," as the door slowly opened, allowing Kevin fifteen seconds to enter before the door automatically closed behind him. This area of the vaults held top-secret documentation and other sensitive records to which as many as fourteen people in the Ministry had access. Kevin paid little attention to the rows and rows of locked filing cabinets as he walked hurriedly to the back right corner to another steel vault door with another ID reader. He repeated the procedure as before and was admitted right away. Only Kevin and Sir Ian could gain access here.

Along with the entire level-four basement area, this small, sparse room was five hundred feet underground and constructed as a nuclear bomb shelter. The level-four area was designed to be one of several command posts in the event Britain was under nuclear attack. Here on neat, high-tech plastic racks were all the duplicate firing mechanisms for Britain's entire nuclear arsenal, each with clearly marked identifying code numbers on the outside of its individual case. Kevin went straight to the Mobile Missile Launcher (MML) section and quickly located the row for field battery three of the Royal Welsh Guards Regiment. Each field battery consisted of four MMLs, and each contained two medium-range (0–1,000 miles) Penguin-class nuclear missiles. Each firing mechanism was enclosed in an airtight, clear plastic case. Kevin pulled out a sealed envelope from his left inside pocket and, carefully opening it, withdrew eight encased firing mechanisms. Quickly he inserted all eight under their correct codes in the eight empty slots. This had been one of the riskier elements of his entire plan but a calculated one, as he knew Sir Ian rarely came down here. Kevin had removed them only a week earlier to minimize the risk of discovery, but a week had been necessary for the complex task of duplication, the most critical element to the ultimate success of his plans.

Kevin was in and out of the inner vault within three minutes. Back by the elevator, Sergeant Pedley saluted smartly as Kevin signed out at 11:21 a.m.

"Cheerio, Jack, at ease!"

"Thank you, sir."

A few minutes later, Kevin was back in his office, and Margaret brought him a cup of tea and a plate of her own home-baked oatmeal biscuits, a particular favorite of Kevin's.

"You really spoil me, Margaret, but then I am rather partial to your oatmeal biscuits. Any calls?"

"No, but here are your airline tickets, and everything is checked and confirmed, including your hotel reservations."

"Thank you, Margaret," Kevin said as he took the tickets and slipped them into his left inside coat pocket with his passport. "I won't be seeing you until Monday, September 13, after the week in Salisbury. I know you'll take care of everything here with Captain Smithers. Of course, he'll be with me for the week at Salisbury."

Margaret nodded. "Don't worry, Major. Everything will run smoothly, as always, but it will be quiet without you. I hope you have a marvelous week of fishing in Scotland."

"Thank you, Margaret, and with luck I'll have a nice Scottish salmon to send you. Please have Captain Smithers come in."

Two minutes later, Captain Rodney Smithers, in uniform as usual, stood before Kevin's desk, his big mop of sandy hair combed neatly to one side of his freckled face.

"Good morning, Rodney. Have a seat."

"You know the drill while I'm away, Rodney, so no need to discuss it. I've just reviewed final details for Salisbury with Sir Ian. Here's the folder."

"Nothing to worry about, Kevin. I know Margaret can reach you wherever you are if anything should crop up. Effective at noon, the computer will have my handprint on file for emergency access to the vaults while you are away."

"Good, so everything is under control, and I'll see you on Tuesday morning, September 7, at field HQ in Salisbury."

"Have a good trip to Washington and enjoy your fishing," Rodney said, dropping his serious look and offering a boyish smile.

"Thanks, Rodney, and don't work Margaret too hard. Good-bye."

After the captain left, Kevin sat thoughtfully behind his desk as his mind again wandered back to his plans for nuclear blackmail. It was a strange feeling, knowing he would be unlikely to ever see Margaret, Rodney, Sir Ian, or any of the others again, and he certainly would never see this office again. Like any place where one spends a lot of time over the years, Kevin had grown rather fond of his office and the familiar surroundings, the view over the Thames … but he knew what lay ahead was more important than anything else.

He thought back to a gray, drizzly morning at the end of the previous November. Margaret had brought in the mail, and as usual, she had opened and sorted it in priority, so Kevin had immediately noticed the unopened airmail letter from the States sitting on top and clearly marked "Personal & Confidential." As soon as Margaret left, he had opened it carefully and quickly read the brief letter inside. It was from the New York law firm Driscoll, Hanrahan & Moynihan, and kindly requested Kevin to contact the senior partner, Mike Driscoll, at his earliest convenience in connection with the estate of the late Herbert T. S. MacAllister.

Granduncle Bertie, who was Kevin's paternal grandfather's youngest brother, had died six months earlier at the age of ninety-seven. He had been somewhat of a legend in the family, having immigrated to the States in the 1920s. Penniless and starting out as a bricklayer, he built up a very successful construction business.

Over the next four decades, Bertie had become one of the larger real estate developers between New York and Boston and reputedly amassed a considerable fortune. Kevin had many fond memories of his granduncle from his first visits when Kevin was still a teenager. Apparently Kevin's father had always been the old man's favorite nephew, and Bertie had advanced him the seed money to get started in his own small business in London. Over the years, Kevin would always make the effort to visit Granduncle Bertie at least once or twice a year when on one of his business trips to the Unites States. The old man had always seemed to relish Kevin's visits, and they would spend hour after hour talking about many things but always ended up with two favorite topics of discussion, Kevin's work in the field of nuclear weapons and Bertie's dream of a United Ireland.

As a very young man, Bertie had played a minor role in the 1916 Rising in Dublin and later was an ardent supporter of Michael Collins during the civil war. He had been disgusted with the partition of Ireland and emigrated shortly afterward. Bertie had one favorite Irish ballad that he never lost an opportunity to recite to Kevin, called "A Nation Once Again," written by the young Dublin poet Thomas Davis in the earlier part of the nineteenth century. This ballad personified Bertie's dream for Ireland.

Bertie MacAllister had never married, and he had never confided in anyone, despite his reputation as a notorious womanizer. As far as Kevin had known, he and his two cousins in Dublin were Bertie's closest relatives; however, over the years, Kevin heard vague rumors of an illegitimate son borne by one of his many fancy ladies in the 1930s. But Bertie would never talk about it. Granduncle Bertie had been a man of striking contrasts who, on one hand, would take enormous risks in his real estate business but on the other hand had an innate fear of flying and had also sworn never to set foot on a ship again after a rough passage when he first went to America. The result was that Bertie had never returned to his native land, so Kevin was the only relative he had seen in the last ten years, as Kevin's Irish cousins had never visited the States. However, Bertie had one passion, and that had been horses, and in the late forties he had bought himself an eight-acre estate called Woodlawn in Greenwich, Connecticut. Initially, he had bought the estate as a weekend retreat from the city, but lived there year-round after he finally sold off all his business interests in the late sixties. He had kept horses there right up to his death. Kevin had also grown to love the Woodlawn estate with its gorgeous late nineteenth-century classical mansion and extensive stables surrounding a cobblestone courtyard. The estate around the mansion had reminded both Bertie and Kevin of Ireland, with its undulating grasslands dotted here and there with magnificent old oak trees. Kevin had always thoroughly enjoyed the many horse rides he had taken around the estate with his granduncle.

The very next week while in Washington, DC, Kevin had flown up to New York to meet with Mike Driscoll at the law firm's office on Park Avenue. Kevin had taken an instant liking to Mike Driscoll, a man in his late fifties who was the son of one of the firm's founders, Brendan Driscoll, a lifetime friend of Bertie MacAllister. Mike had wasted no time in reading and explaining the entire contents of Kevin's late granduncle's will. The Woodlawn estate was to be preserved under a perpetual trust as a sanctuary for retired horses who had nowhere else to go and who were to be cared for until they died naturally. There was a bequest of $1 million to a certain Lawrence Rodgers located in Chicago, who Bertie acknowledged in the will as his illegitimate son; $500,000 was to go to Eleanor Woods, Bertie's nurse and companion for the last twelve years of his life; sundry other bequests were made to various charities and faithful staff members of Woodlawn; and $200,000 was to go to each of Kevin's cousins, Jim and Mary in Dublin. The balance of Bertie's estate, in cash and securities and after payment of all estate taxes, was to go to Kevin and amounted to approximately $17.5 million.

Kevin had been staggered at that amount of money coming to him with no strings attached other than his granduncle's last cryptic words in the will: "With this money I request Kevin to find a way of using a part of it to further the cause of "A Nation Once Again." Kevin knew Mike Driscoll had no idea what Bertie had meant, but Kevin had understood the old man's intent all too well. It was quickly agreed that Mike would henceforth act as Kevin's legal adviser on his vast inheritance and would act promptly on any instructions that Kevin would issue to him. Kevin had never aspired to great riches, he had always been comfortable despite his relatively modest salary at the Ministry, and a small inheritance from his parents had provided a little nest egg for a rainy day. He had fairly inexpensive tastes, though he did enjoy good food and wine; his only real indulgence was his Jaguar.

Kevin looked up and realized that Margaret was standing in front of his desk. "You looked far away, Major. Corporal Jones just called to say your car is waiting for you."

"Okay, I'm on my way, Margaret. Oh, blast, I forgot to call my wife as promised. Can you get her on the phone, please?"

Margaret dialed swiftly, knowing the number just as well as Kevin. "It's ringing, sir," she said. She handed him the phone and left the office.

"Hello, Sheila. I'm running late for my luncheon appointment, so I have to dash. My love to you and Max. I'll call tonight from New York." Max was barking in the background. Shelia had told him that Max only barked when he was on the phone.

"Have a safe trip, luv, and don't tire yourself out. I'll be thinking of you and miss you as always."

"Bye, my luv," Kevin said and hung up. He knew that, if he hurried, he'd have time to spend with his mistress before his flight.

CHAPTER 2

KEVIN SKILLFULLY MANEUVERED THROUGH THE heavy lunchtime
traffic, past the House of Parliament on his left and Westminster
Abbey on the right, with too many tourist buses slowing his
progress. Once he reached Millbank, he picked up speed and turned
up Vauxhall Bridge Road, taking a left onto Warwick Way and then
a shortcut along Pimlico Road to Sloane Street. Kevin prided himself
on his knowledge of Central London's back streets. Within fifteen
minutes of leaving his office, he arrived at the door of 25 Cadogan
Place, a typical Georgian building of six stories. Luckily, Kevin found
parking right outside, and after taking the front steps two at a time,
he quickly gave three sharp rings to the doorbell of flat number five.
Almost instantly, the front door buzzer went off. Kevin pushed the
door open and fairly bounded up the five flights of stairs to the already
opened door of number five. Standing barefoot in the doorway, Jenny
Laster, a tall, willowy American lady, called out, "Hi, Mac, darling! It's
so wonderful to see you."

Kevin was a little out of breath as he reached the doorway and
took Jenny in his arms for a long, passionate kiss. "So sorry I'm a few
minutes late, sweetheart. But you know how bad the traffic is around
Westminster at this time of year, with all the tourists in town."

"Don't fuss, Mac. You're here now, and that's all that matters.
Come in."

Kevin and Jenny went into the flat arm-in-arm and pushed the door
shut behind them as they again embraced in long, deep kisses. At least

five minutes passed before Jenny broke away from Kevin's arms and, taking his hand, led him to the stairs.

"We do have some time to kill before we leave for the airport, don't we, darling?" Jenny asked with a twinkle in her eye.

"Absolutely, sweetheart! We don't need to leave before half past two."

Jenny let go of Kevin's hand and quickly dashed up the stairs ahead of him, shouting back playfully, "C'mon, slowpoke! Catch me if you can!"

Kevin hesitated for just a moment on the first step as he looked up admiringly at his wonderful Jenny in her tight-fitting jeans. She was always so much fun. As she reached the top of the stairs, Kevin took off like a rocket and almost caught her at the double doors to her bedroom, and then, with a flying leap, he landed right in the middle of the king-sized bed just as Jenny did. Playfully, Kevin grabbed her by her wrists, and after a little mock wrestling, he had Jenny on her back as he kneeled over her. Just looking at her gorgeous, flushed face and firm, heaving breasts as she caught her breath gave Kevin intense erotic desires. He leaned down and kissed her passionately. Jenny responded with equal passion and, coming up once for air, murmured, "Darling, do take off your suit before it gets all rumpled."

Kevin was out of his suit in about ten seconds flat, and, flinging his tie at the chair beside the bed, he left the rest of his clothes on for Jenny to deal with. She had already pulled back the bedcovers and undone the top button of her jeans. Kevin willingly accepted the invitation and gently pulled the zipper down. He then helped Jenny wiggle out of them, exposing her long, shapely, tanned legs. Jenny's shirt quickly followed her jeans to the floor, and she kneeled over Kevin wearing just her lacy pink satin bra and panties. Smiling, she said, "Now it's your turn, Mac," as she leaned down and slowly unbuttoned Kevin's shirt and kissed his hairy chest, working her way down to his shorts. In no time, they were both naked. For Kevin, making love with Jenny was like a thrilling roller-coaster ride that he never wanted to end, and it was all better with Jenny on top where she could orchestrate their mounting excitement until that wonderful, fleeting moment of simultaneous climax. Kevin caressed

Jenny's gorgeous breasts and gently played with her nipples as he whispered his love in her ear.

"Oh, Mac, you make me feel so, so good … oh my God, I'm coming … Mac, come, come now …"

"Oh yes, sweetheart, oh yes, I'm coming … I'm coming too!"

Jenny collapsed in a heap on Kevin's sweaty chest.

They lay there for a good several minutes, locked together in a tight embrace. Kevin couldn't help but think how different this was compared to making love with Sheila, who had become rather frigid and mechanical in recent years. Then he felt Jenny's sparkling deep blue eyes looking into his.

"Darling, you were wonderful!" she said. "You're truly the best lover any woman could have, and I love you more than anyone in the whole world." Jenny peppered Kevin's cheeks, nose, and lips with gentle, sensuous kisses before she hopped out of bed. "It's already quarter past one, Mac, so I'm going to take a quick shower and then fix us a light lunch."

"I'll join you!"

"No, darling, let's save it for tonight in New York! You know that when we take a shower together we need all the time in the world, and we have to leave for the airport in an hour and a quarter."

"Okay, sweetheart, you're right, of course, but you certainly have a date for tonight."

Kevin lay back again on the pillow and caught a fleeting glimpse of Jenny's gorgeous naked body through the open bathroom door as she got into the shower. He thought to himself that he was indeed a very lucky man to have such a marvelous woman as his lover.

It had been almost six years since Kevin met Jenny. They were both attending a cocktail party at the US embassy in London. Kevin had been nursing a scotch and chatting quietly with a good friend, Scott Frawley, who at the time was the director of D Branch, the counterespionage arm of MI5, when a younger man and woman joined them. Scott had introduced them to Kevin as Paul Laster and his wife, Jenny. Paul headed up the CIA contingent attached to the London embassy and had wanted a private word with Scott, so Kevin had found himself left alone to chat with the very attractive Mrs. Laster. From that very first moment, he and Jenny seemed to hit it off beautifully. They had quickly found that they enjoyed many of the same interests as film buffs and lovers of live theatre, and there was clearly a mutual physical attraction. *And why not*, Kevin had thought. Jenny was an extremely attractive twenty-nine-year-old brunette whose willowy build made her look even taller than her five-foot-seven height. She had a naturally tanned complexion, high cheekbones, deep blue eyes, and a beautifully shaped small nose. Her shiny, shoulder-length hair was cut in a classical Cleopatra style that suited her perfectly. She was wearing a simple pale blue dress that fell just below the knee and displayed her slender figure to its best advantage. A single strand of pearls encircled her neck.

That first evening, Kevin had learned an awful lot about Jenny. She had been born and raised in New York in an Italian-American family, the Grinaldis, and when she was only six years old, they had moved out of the city to the small town of Bedford. However, as Jenny had always reminded him, this wasn't exactly out in the wilds, as it was still only about forty-five minutes north of Manhattan. She was the eldest of two brothers and two sisters, had done well in school, and later went to the Los Angeles School of Design to become an interior designer. While in Los Angeles, she had met and married Paul Laster, who was completing his master's in political science at UCLA. Then when Paul joined the CIA, they moved to Virginia, and Jenny landed a job at a top interior design firm in Washington, DC. Her job had flourished, but her marriage to Paul had not.

Their move to London two years earlier, to further Paul's career with the CIA, was made with the understanding between them that they would make one last major effort to save their marriage, but it hadn't worked. Jenny told him she was about to commence divorce proceedings. She had no trace of bitterness, as there was no single cause; rather she and Paul had grown apart, and the divorce was to be on the friendliest grounds of mutual incompatibility.

Kevin remembered how impressed he had been with Jenny's candor that very first evening. Now Jenny had successfully established her own interior design business in London, and she was not in any hurry to return to the States. She had a certain presence about her that was epitomized by her bright and cheerful personality.

After that first meeting, it was three months before Kevin saw Jenny again, but he had not forgotten her for one single moment; nor, apparently, had Jenny forgotten him. By then, her husband had gotten a promotion and moved back to CIA headquarters in the States. Jenny's divorce from him would be final in another nine months. It was after this second encounter that Kevin and Jenny had begun to see each other on a regular basis. Their relationship flourished, despite Kevin's marriage to someone else, and never once had Jenny hinted that perhaps he might divorce Sheila.

Kevin opened his eyes and saw Jenny standing by the bed with only a towel wrapped around her. *My God*, he thought, *she looks every bit as terrific at thirty-five as she did at twenty-nine.*

"C'mon, lazy bones, stop daydreaming! Time to get a move on."

"Okay, sweetheart, but you have to give me a kiss first!"

As Jenny leaned down to kiss him, her towel fell open, and Kevin eagerly drew her tight against his naked chest for a long, loving hug.

"That's enough, Mac darling, or you are going to get me all worked up again, and we'll surely miss the plane!"

"You're absolutely right, sweetheart," Kevin said with a big smile. He sprang out of bed, saying, "I'll just take a quick shower while you're getting dressed."

Kevin whistled softly in the shower as he thought about how excited he was at the prospect of spending a whole week with Jenny. It hadn't been possible very often in the last five years, despite the fact that she was her own boss. Of course, Jenny said she had accepted this as part of the price for her success and financial independence, both of which she enjoyed immensely.

When Kevin got out of the shower, he found Jenny had already packed everything she needed for the week in one large suitcase and was wearing comfortable baggy pants, a cotton blouse, and a light silk jacket for the plane ride. She wore very little makeup and was all set to go.

After he'd showered and dried his hair, Kevin went to the closet to get some clothes, as he always kept some at Jenny's flat. Indeed, Jenny had given him most of them, as Kevin's tastes were rather conservative, and Jenny loved to buy him more dashing casual clothes than he would buy for himself. Kevin selected a pair of pleated Ralph Lauren khaki trousers, a pale lemon-colored Polo shirt, a light beige-and-brown herringbone sports jacket, and a pair of comfortable tan casual shoes. Kevin dressed quickly, hung up his suit, ran a comb through his hair, and was down in the kitchen in five minutes flat.

"Mac, you sure are looking good. Can you get the bottle of white wine from the refrigerator, please, and take it into the dining room. I'll be right in." Kevin did as he was told, as Jenny was definitely the boss in her own kitchen.

He sauntered into the dining room end of a large open room, with the high vaulted ceilings one would expect in an old Georgian style house and the wide windows facing him as he entered. The room was elegantly furnished in a balanced blend of antiques and contemporary furnishings with pastel tones. The walls were pale peach, which gave the entire room a very light, open, and relaxed feeling. Jenny had bought this flat, which occupied the top two floors of the building, shortly after her divorce was final, and she had spent a lot of time and money remodeling it to her complete satisfaction. Everything in it reflected Jenny's excellent sense of design, color, and balance and made it easy to understand why her interior design business was so successful.

Kevin walked over to the Danish contemporary dining table and poured two glasses of wine. There was a gentle breeze coming in through the french doors, which opened onto a small brick balcony where Kevin and Jenny had whiled away many pleasant summer evenings relaxing over a glass of wine and taking in the many different scents that drifted up from the gardens below. Kevin stood for a moment by the doors and got a whiff of the lilac that grew right below the balcony.

Jenny came in carrying a loaded tray, and Kevin stepped forward to help her.

"It's not heavy, darling. Just sit down and enjoy it!"

"Jen, sweetheart, you do really spoil me. Smoked salmon and Caesar salad, two of my favorites. Besides, nobody makes a Caesar salad as good as yours."

"You're such a flatterer, Mac. I've told you a thousand times that the secret lies in the old family recipe that my mom gave me."

"Well, here's to us and to a wonderful week in the States," Kevin said and raised his glass to meet Jenny's.

Both ate with healthy appetites and chatted about the coming week. When they were finished, Kevin helped Jenny clear the table and tidy up in the kitchen. By the time they were all done, it was close to time to leave for the airport.

"Mac, I'll just run around and lock up before we leave."

"Okay, sweetheart. I've already brought your suitcase down to the hallway. Don't forget to make sure you have your tickets and passport in your purse."

"I already did! I won't be a minute, darling!"

Two minutes later, they left the flat, and Kevin carried Jenny's suitcase downstairs and out the front door to the Jag. Kevin quickly stowed it in the trunk on top of his two suitcases, and they got in and were off.

"Jen, can you just reach down under your seat and make sure my briefcase is there?"

"Yes, it is. Don't be such a worrywart, Mac."

"You want air-conditioning or the sunroof open?"

"Oh, definitely the sunroof. It's such a gorgeous, hot, balmy day for London. It would be a shame not to enjoy it."

Kevin shifted into second gear as he pressed the button for the sunroof to open. He glided up to the corner and turned right onto Pont Street, across Sloane Street and on for a few short blocks until he bore right onto Beauchamp Place. This way, he cut out the busy intersection at Knightsbridge corner but had to wait for the long stoplight at the top of Beauchamp Place before he could turn left onto Cromwell Road. Meanwhile Jenny had been playing around with the radio and found a station that featured a lot of golden oldies from the sixties. Once on Cromwell Road, they quickly passed the Victoria and Albert Museum and the exhibition halls at Earl's Court and were already on the Hammersmith Flyover when the traffic actually began to slow down somewhat.

They were already past the Great West Road and moving slowly on the Cromwell Road Extension leading to the onramp of the M4 at Chiswick. Once on the M4, traffic picked up speed again, and in twenty minutes, they were at the Heathrow exit. Fifteen minutes later, they arrived outside the ultramodern British Airways Terminal 4, having had to stop once for a brief security check on the airport access road.

Soon after they boarded their plane, a stewardess came around handing out menus. Kevin and Jenny took only a couple of minutes to make their selections, having decided beforehand they wanted to eat lightly, as they planned a nice dinner out in New York that night. While they waited for their meal, they put their seats back and reclined, relaxing with a glass of chilled white wine. They had already decided not to bother with a movie and preferred to have a nap after eating. The food was excellent, and they washed it down with some more wine.

As they settled down to their nap, others were doing the same or getting ready to watch a movie. By this time, they were two and a half hours out of London. Kevin lay there with his eyes shut, but he couldn't sleep. He got up to stretch his legs and go to the restroom. On the way back to his seat, he stopped at the galley and picked up a large Baileys Irish Cream on the rocks. He strapped himself loosely into his seat and slowly sipped his drink as he let his mind wander over the past nine months of careful planning, reliving the day he realized what was to be his destiny and the day he met the man who would help him make it happen.

January in London was always one of the dreariest, grayest months of the year, and last January had been one of the coldest in recent memory. However, despite the bitter cold, Kevin and Max had taken their morning jogs around the Heath, and their only concession to the biting cold weather was to run a little faster and not to pause for a sit-down.

One morning in mid-January as Kevin was jogging, he came to an abrupt halt, almost choking Max on the leash with the suddenness of his stop. He remembered Max looking up at him with a bewildered expression. After weeks of wrestling with the problem, in that instant, Kevin had realized exactly what he had to do and concluded that it was the only thing he could do!

For Kevin, this had been an almost terrifying moment, even at the ripe old age of forty seven. It was as if the confluence of events in his life had chosen him to be the means of striking the ultimate blow for a united Ireland, "A Nation Once Again." Kevin realized that only the very real threat of a nuclear bomb being dropped on London would be enough to strike sufficient terror in the British government and people to finally return the province of Northern Ireland to the Irish people. Kevin knew in order to succeed in the threat, he would actually have to have the means and—more importantly—demonstrate his willingness to use it. Kevin also knew that such an act of nuclear blackmail would be decried by all civilized people throughout the world as the most horrific act of terrorism ever committed. But Kevin believed that a thousand years of bloody strife and suppression in Ireland justified this ultimate act of terrorism.

Kevin realized he was the only person in Britain who could do it. Given his position at the Ministry and his inheritance, he had the critical access to the bomb, the knowledge to use it, and the money to mount a professional operation to execute the deed. Kevin knew that what he was about to embark on was a complete repudiation of everything he had stood for all his life. By any standard, he had led a comfortable middle-class lifestyle. He was politically a moderate, and given his military career, he was a supporter of the establishment. Kevin's pursuit of nuclear weaponry as his area of specialty had been in part fueled by a curious scientific brain and in part by the conviction that nuclear weapons were a necessary deterrent in the atomic age but one that would be unlikely to ever have to be used. Also, Kevin had generally condemned the acts of violence by the IRA in Northern Ireland, which had occurred with murderous frequency in the last twenty years. And yet he realized that the accumulation of all the violence that had occurred in the last thousand years of Ireland's bloody history would pale by comparison with the magnitude of what he now felt compelled to do. Kevin knew that his plan to hijack two mobile armed nuclear missiles and hold that nuclear trigger to the British government's "head" would not fail, as he had the conviction to launch a nuclear strike regardless of the consequences. He was confident that the government would back down rather than risk millions of lives.

Having come to terms with his destiny, Kevin was able to muster all the attributes of his military training and strong sense of self-discipline to approach the planning of the operation with a clear mind and a deep sense of purpose. Kevin quickly discounted enlisting the help of any current members of the IRA or the more extremist Provos, as he firmly believed that the passions of political fervor for the Irish Cause would only endanger an operation that must be carried out with professional precision and discipline. Kevin decided that what he needed was an absolutely dependable, ruthless, highly disciplined professional soldier who never failed and was motivated solely by financial gain and by a sense of pride and pleasure in exercising his skills as a soldier.

Over the next few weeks, Kevin kicked around several names in his head—names of men who could fit the profile of the mercenary he needed to execute his plan.

His good friend, Scott Frawley of MI5, had unwittingly provided Kevin with many of the names he considered, names that had come up occasionally whenever the two of them discussed certain aspects of military security. George Wilkinson's name came up more often than any others, and, in Kevin's opinion, this individual seemed to fit the requirements in every way. It was fortunate for Kevin that the Ministry records in the basement vaults included duplicate files of MI5's dossiers on all mercenaries who had previously served in the British armed forces. It had been a simple matter for Kevin to remove the Wilkinson folder overnight.

In the middle of February, Kevin had brought home the two-inch-thick Wilkinson file. After dinner, he went to his small, cozy den with Max while Sheila retired upstairs to bed to watch television. Kevin settled into his comfortable easy chair to read every detail, making relevant notes as he went along. This took him over two and half hours, and then he sat down at his desk and meticulously reorganized his notes into a coherent and concise profile of George Wilkinson.

George Wilkinson, aged forty-nine. Born in Edinburgh into a respectable, middle-class family. Father, a doctor; mother, a homemaker; and George, the only child. His schooling had been traditional public school with an average academic record, but George had excelled at sports, particularly rugby and soccer. He had never aspired to a university education and instead had enlisted in the army straight out of public school, much to the disappointment of his parents. Indeed his file noted that the young George had expressly forbidden his parents' endeavors to pull some strings and get him a commission as a junior officer. So at the age of only eighteen, George had already shown his overriding determination to be independent and to do things his own way, a characteristic he was to maintain for the rest of his life. But having joined the Royal Fusiliers regiment as a private, his natural leadership abilities, tenacity, and self-discipline propelled him to officer rank in under five years, a record-setting rate of promotions in the modern army since World War II.

George had first seen action as a subaltern in Cyprus and then extensively in British colonies in Africa, such as Kenya and Rhodesia, as these places gained independence. He had already reached the rank of captain when he did two successive tours of duty in Northern Ireland, the last in 1973. It was during that last tour of duty that, as it was reported in his records, George had seriously disagreed with his commanding officer on the role of British troops in Northern Ireland. George felt strongly that the role of the army was to carry out purely military actions and not be expected to fill the role of a police force subject to the whims of politicians. When that tour of duty was completed and George returned to England, he resigned his commission and received an honorable discharge because, though he had voiced opinions contrary to his superior officers, he had never broken any army regulations or disobeyed lawful commands. The official file described him as a tough, ruthless, independent-minded officer who demanded and got total discipline from the troops under his command and yet received complete loyalty from those same troops for his reputation as a fearless, cunning leader who had always put his own life on the line, if necessary, to save one of his own men.

After 1973, when George left the army, the records on his activities were sketchier. It was reported that he participated as a mercenary in minor wars around the globe, in Africa, Central America, and in Asia. By all accounts, he had excelled in every campaign he took on and was paid well for his exploits. He earned the reputation as a cat with nine lives who miraculously escaped any serious injuries during the course of his many campaigns. It was also reported that he had narrowly escaped a couple of assassination attempts by defeated enemies.

The file also contained other relevant pieces of information on George, reflecting the loner lifestyle he led. He never married and apparently had never formed any lasting liaisons with women, nor had he any known close friends or contact with relatives living in Britain. He kept one modest bank account at the Royal Bank in Edinburgh that he used only when in Britain, and it was supposed that the bulk of his money was in numbered bank accounts in Switzerland. As best as it could be ascertained, George Wilkinson didn't own any property, anywhere, either under his own name or under the name of George Wilson, an alias he was known to use on occasion. When he was in Britain, he appeared to observe scrupulously the laws of the land. He didn't vote in elections and generally had never been heard to utter the slightest word against the Crown or Britain. That was not to say that he hadn't been on the opposite side of British interests in various conflicts around the world, which seemed to indicate to Kevin that he was somewhat of a paradox. And clearly a man who played everything close to the chest.

Finally, Kevin carefully studied the handful of photographs of George Wilkinson so that he would have a clear image of the man in his mind. George was six foot two with wide shoulders and a lean frame and looked like a man who worked out every day to keep himself fighting fit, as was reportedly the case. From the most recent close-up color photo that Kevin found, he had been able to discern that George had sandy-colored hair, speckled with gray, thinning slightly on top and combed down over a high forehead as if to hide it. He had a rather angular, unsmiling face, with squint lines around dark green eyes and a somewhat battered-looking nose that appeared as if it had been broken many times. Kevin had gotten a distinct image in his mind of a tough, ruthless, stern man who would be unstoppable once a planned operation commenced.

The next morning, Kevin safely returned the Wilkinson file to the Ministry records, and nobody was any the wiser. Now that he had identified the man he needed to execute the plan he was masterminding, Kevin faced the next hurdle, which was to meet George Wilkinson. He realized that this would be difficult to arrange, particularly as he had no idea where to find him. The file had not been very helpful in this respect. It simply noted in chronological order what hotels Wilkinson stayed in when back in Britain for short visits and where he had rented a house when he stayed for several months at a time. What Kevin found most frustrating was that there didn't appear to be any pattern to where Wilkinson stayed. The last entry shown was for the previous October, when reportedly Wilkinson had spent a couple of weeks at a country inn in the small village of North Petherton, near Bridgwater, in Somerset. Nobody had any idea what he did there, if anything, other than relax and frequent some of the local pubs. Scott Frawley had told Kevin on many occasions that MI5 hadn't bothered putting Wilkinson under constant surveillance for the last several years, given his law-abiding status when in Britain. It proved sufficient to keep tabs on his entries and departures from the country through normal channels such as the Home Office, and to do spot checks on where he was staying.

Over the next few weeks, Kevin had patiently and discretely pumped Scott Frawley whenever he had the opportunity. But he had to be extremely careful, as Scott was a shrewd man. This Kevin knew only too well. At fifty-four, Scott Frawley was a short man with a spreading middle-age paunch and a receding hairline. In his youth, it was said that he had been a champion wrestler, and he was reputed to be very agile, still, despite his looks. Those who didn't know him would have said that he looked like everyone's idea of a jolly uncle, but behind his jovial smile there was a sharp, scheming mind that missed nothing. It was this factor that had enabled Scott Frawley to rise up through the ranks of MI5 to his position of director of D Branch with total responsibility for counterespionage.

MI5 was really the British equivalent of the FBI and was comprised of six directorates under a director-general. The gossip around Whitehall was that Scott Frawley's directorate had emerged as the most powerful of the six under his skillful leadership, and it was widely expected that he would be the next director-general when the current incumbent retired in two years. Kevin counted himself lucky to have Scott Frawley as his good friend but at the same time was increasingly frustrated that he had been unable to find out anything new about Wilkinson without arousing Scott's suspicious mind.

It was the first week of March when Kevin, while sitting at the desk in his office one afternoon reviewing some documents, was interrupted.

"Good afternoon, Mac! Can you spare a cup of tea for a weary old friend?" Scott Frawley asked. Scott had the unnerving habit of slipping right by Margaret and arriving in Kevin's office unannounced.

"Of course, Scott! What a pleasant surprise to see you," Kevin said evenly, trying to keep the genuine surprise out of his voice. He had been eagerly hoping for just such a visit. "Well, what's new in MI5?"

"Not much doing at the moment, I'm afraid. In fact, things are too bloody quiet. IRA activities in Britain these days seem to be in a lull, and I don't mind telling you that makes me nervous. It may be the lull before the storm. We have unconfirmed reports that the IRA may have received Soviet-made SAM-7 anticraft missiles with a major shipment of weaponry sent by Libya to Ireland in the last three months. If these reports turn out to be true, such surface-to-air missiles in the hands of the IRA could escalate their terrorist activities to new levels of horror. Whether directed at civilian passenger airplanes or military aircraft, the mere threat of their use would be severely disruptive. I can tell you, Sir Ian was pretty concerned when I told him just now. At least we can be damn certain that the IRA can't get their murderous hands on nuclear missiles, eh, Mac?"

Kevin had invisibly winced at Scott's last comment, and it taxed his self-control to the utmost to reply in a normal, reassuring tone, "Well, Scott, I can only speak for the security of the British nuclear arsenal, and we both know that security is airtight! I trust you and your colleagues in MI5 can prevent the IRA from ever getting nuclear weapons from foreign sources. Anyway, enough of such doomsday talk!"

"By the way, Mac, you may recall the name George Wilkinson; he's one of those mercenaries whose names I've mentioned on several occasions. Well, he turned up again a couple of weeks ago, renting a small house by the Thames down in Marlow. Apparently he signed a lease for a year with an option to buy. It's the assessment of my people that he may have decided to retire from the dangerous life of a mercenary, as, after all, he is approaching fifty. So that's probably one less we have to keep tabs on."

"That's good news, Scott. I know you always have enough on your plate and would be just as happy if all the goddamned mercenaries got killed or retired."

At that point, Scott heaved himself out of the armchair. "Well, on that happy note, ol' chum, I've got to dash. Thanks for the tea and chat." With that, Scott had gone as swiftly as he arrived.

After Frawley had left, Kevin felt elated in spite of some of the touchy areas of their conversation. In fact, at that moment, he also wondered if Scott would remember their conversation in the months ahead or conveniently choose to have forgotten it. Kevin felt a little bit annoyed that Wilkinson had already been around for a couple of weeks without him knowing it.

The next Saturday morning, Kevin had motored down the M40 to Marlow, reaching the town about eleven o'clock, pub opening time. Having found a good spot to park the Jag for a few hours, he set off at a brisk walk to tour the pubs of the town, find Wilkinson, and casually get into conversation with him. Kevin had learned from the file that Wilkinson, though not an excessive drinker, was fond of frequenting pubs and was quite a punter who liked to gamble sizable amounts on horses. Given the British penchant for betting on horses, Saturdays were always a big day for televised horse races, and most of the major meets in Britain and Ireland were covered live. Most pub lounges had color televisions that attracted large Saturday crowds who enjoyed the convivial atmosphere of the pub while watching the races. So Kevin figured his odds were better than even that he would run into Wilkinson somewhere. His bigger concern was that Wilkinson may still be under surveillance, but in view of Scott Frawley's comments a few days earlier, Kevin decided that the risk of him being spotted making contact was slim. He realized that even an apparent casual conversation between himself and Wilkinson, if reported back to MI5, would at least create some awkward questions; however, Kevin had no choice but to take the risk.

By two thirty, Kevin had covered another six pubs with no luck, and having had only a few sips of his beer in each of them, he began to feel quite sober and despondent.

Kevin then reached the Boaters Arms, the first of the two pubs that overlooked the Thames. As he entered the crowded lounge, all heads were straining toward the TV in the corner. It was apparently the last furlong of the big race of the day, the 2.45 from Epsom and the five-to-two-on favorite, Sun Dancer, was galloping neck and neck with a twenty-to-one outsider, Whispering Wind, to a photo finish. Kevin stood quietly just inside the door, watching as Sun Dancer won. A huge cheer went up from the crowd, and everyone returned to downing their drinks with a lot of boisterous backslapping.

Kevin quickly scanned the lounge and glimpsed a man who fit Wilkinson's description. He noted that the man was sitting in the far corner by the windows that ran the whole length of the lounge overlooking the river. After Kevin had bought himself a beer, he slowly and discretely worked his way through the overcrowded lounge toward that corner. This man had to be Wilkinson or an identical twin, as he matched the photographic image in Kevin's mind in exact detail except for a faint scar line over the upper lip and an almost reddish-blond mustache. Kevin strolled casually over to an empty chair and asked, "Is this chair taken, mate?"

"No, I think the chap who was sitting there left after the last race," replied the man, without even looking up at Kevin.

Kevin sat down and put his beer on the table beside the man's newspaper, which was folded open to the horse race listings.

"Do you mind if I have a quick glance at your newspaper?"

"Help yourself, mate."

Kevin distinctly noticed the somewhat neutral tone of the man, neither friendly nor unfriendly, and his first impression was of a cold personality. Kevin also picked up on the Scottish accent, though it wasn't as strong as a typical Scotsman, probably softened by years of living all over the world. Kevin scanned the racing pages of Wilkinson's newspaper for the next few minutes as if fully absorbed. Then, as Kevin neatly folded the newspaper and placed it back on the table, Wilkinson said, "See anything you fancy in the rest of today's races?"

"No, not really, but then I don't back the horses that much, usually only if I get a good tip!" Kevin answered quite truthfully.

"Well, I have a good tip for you. Flying Dutchman, a two-year-old, running in the four-thirty at Doncaster, a certainty with good odds at two-to-one."

"Thanks, mate. Maybe I will have a little flutter on him, perhaps fifty pounds each way."

"Don't be fainthearted, mate. You've got to have at least a hundred quid on to win, to make it worthwhile!"

"You're right, mate. That's what I'll do. I'm going to get myself another beer. Can I get you something?" Kevin asked him as a friendly gesture for the tip.

"That's mighty civil of you, mate. I don't mind if I do. I'll have another pint of bitter in here," Wilkinson said as he drained off his mug and handed it to Kevin.

Kevin went up to the counter and ordered a pint and a half of best bitter and then negotiated his way back through the thinning crowd with the full mugs. Taking the pint mug in his big fist, Wilkinson said, "Ta, mate. Cheers!" After downing about a quarter in one gulp, he continued, "What brings you to this neck of the woods? I haven't seen you around here before."

Kevin figured the direct approach was probably best. "Actually, I get down to Marlow occasionally, but today I came expressly to find you. You are George Wilkinson, aren't you?"

Kevin watched Wilkinson's face intently for any reaction, but the face remained impassive. Only the eyes betrayed a passing flicker of recognition. Then Wilkinson met Kevin's gaze with a penetrating look for at least a minute, before replying in an icy tone, "What if I am? What could someone like you possibly want with me?"

Despite the tone of Wilkinson's voice, Kevin decided to proceed boldly after a quick glance around to make sure there was no one within earshot. "I know all about you, Captain Wilkinson—your fifteen years in the Royal Fusiliers and your many years as a mercenary since you left the army in 1973."

"Okay, I'm George Wilkinson, and if you know as much as you claim, then your sources will also have told you that I've retired, and I have nothing else to say to you." With that, Wilkinson got up to go, leaving his beer unfinished.

Kevin also stood up and caught Wilkinson by the arm. "Please listen to what I have to say, Captain. I have a unique proposition for you, and I'm both willing and able to pay a substantial amount of money for your services. All I ask is that you hear me out. I won't take more than ten minutes of your time."

Wilkinson paused and said, "Okay, mate, I'll listen but not here. Let's take a stroll down by the river."

Kevin followed Wilkinson out of the Boaters Arms, and together they walked in silence around the back of the pub and down to the towpath by the river. Once out of sight of the pub, Kevin quickly launched into a concise overview of his proposal. "In a nutshell, I plan to hijack two armed mobile nukes and spirit them away to a remote corner of Ireland that will be extremely difficult to find. And I will threaten the destruction of London unless my demands are met."

Wilkinson listened intently without any reaction except for an almost imperceptive widening of his eyes when Kevin mentioned the nuclear missiles. The two men walked at least another hundred yards before Wilkinson said, "You've got a lot of balls to put a proposition like that to me! How do you know I won't go to the authorities and report your plan? Besides, it's the craziest idea I've ever heard!"

"First of all, I know you don't have any love for the authorities, or they for you, and they probably wouldn't believe you. Secondly, you don't know who I am or whom I represent."

Wilkinson frowned. "Maybe you're right, and maybe the idea is just so crazy that it might work. But what makes you think I'd be interested in taking part in such a plan?"

"Two reasons: one, it would represent the ultimate test of your military prowess, and two, money."

Wilkinson seemed to weigh up these two points carefully. Finally, Wilkinson turned to Kevin, as if testing him, and said, "I just might consider it, but it is going to take an awful lot of money for me to give it serious thought. At least a few million dollars."

Kevin didn't flinch at the amount and boldly met Wilkinson's stare. "That can be arranged. How long do you need to think it over?"

"A week should be enough. As you have apparently done good research on me, you must also know that MI5 occasionally have me under surveillance. I usually know when they are watching me, but in any case, we mustn't meet again in Marlow. I suggest we meet next Saturday afternoon at two o'clock by the main entrance to the Royal Pavilion in Brighton, and I'll give you my decision."

"I'll be there."

Kevin readily agreed to this second meeting because he realized even a man like Wilkinson would need some time to think over such an audacious undertaking.

At that point, Wilkinson said he must be on his way, but after he had gone a few yards, he turned back toward Kevin and yelled, "Don't forget, Flying Dutchman in the four-thirty at Doncaster! Don't be shy. Put at least a hundred on him, mate!"

With that, Wilkinson abruptly turned heel again and with long strides quickly disappeared into the distance. Kevin stood there a while, gazing after him thoughtfully, and wondered if he would ever see him again. All in all, that first meeting had gone just about as Kevin had expected.

Kevin made his way back toward the center of town and on impulse went into a Ladbrook's bookmaker he was passing and placed a one-hundred-pound bet on Flying Dutchman. It was about twenty past four, and, feeling tired and drained from his encounter with Wilkinson, he decided to pop into the pub next door to the bookmakers and have a stiff drink. He ordered a double scotch on the rocks and sat down near the television to watch the four-thirty from Doncaster. As if a good omen for his future relationship with Wilkinson, Flying Dutchman romped home to win by an easy length and a half. Kevin thought that was a fitting end to a great day. After picking up his winnings, Kevin walked to his car and headed back to London.

The next week passed quickly, and Kevin had been busy enough in the office to keep his mind off the upcoming meeting with Wilkinson. However, he made the time to phone Mike Driscoll in New York and let him know that he would be instructing him to transfer $2 million to a numbered account in Switzerland within the next two weeks. Kevin realized this action implied he had a high degree of confidence that Wilkinson had risen to the bait, but he also considered the other possibilities—that Wilkinson might simply not show up, indicating he was not interested or, worst of all, he might even tip off MI5 anonymously so that they would be waiting for Kevin. This last possibility filled Kevin with sheer dread, because the consequences could be just as severe as if he succeeded in his plans.

That Saturday morning, arriving in Brighton about five minutes past one, Kevin easily found parking near the oceanfront. The winds blowing in off the channel were almost gale force and made the drizzle seem more like a downpour, but Kevin gamely left the dry comfort of his Jag to walk the long block to the Royal Pavilion to reconnoiter the area around the main entrance. The whole area was deserted, which hadn't surprised Kevin, who, by then, was already getting soaked, despite the trench coat buttoned up to his neck. His umbrella had been utterly useless in the high winds. Having seen nobody hanging about, Kevin ducked into the nearest pub, the Royal Sussex Arms. There was a nice fire going in the small lounge, which was deserted except for a couple of locals sitting at the counter, so Kevin had drawn up a chair by the fire, draping his coat over another chair to drip-dry. He ordered a piping hot bowl of their oxtail soup with french bread and a half of bitter and settled down to while away the time until two o'clock.

At seven minutes to two, Kevin stood and pulled on his trench coat again. He felt a shiver as apprehension gripped him. What if MI5 agents were there waiting for him, or what if Wilkinson didn't show up? He went outside, bracing himself against the wind and rain, and reached the main entrance to the Royal Pavilion at exactly two o'clock. The place was deserted. Kevin waited nervously a full five minutes when a bus full of tourists arrived. Their tour guides quickly ushered them inside as Kevin paced around as inconspicuously as possible. Suddenly, a voice from just behind Kevin nearly made him jump out of his skin. "Good afternoon, mate! I hope you made a few quid on Flying Dutchman!"

Kevin wheeled around and with a flood of relief saw Wilkinson, dressed in a tan mackintosh with a dark brown trilby pulled down over his eyes. "Oh, good afternoon, Captain! How nice to see you again. Yes, thanks, I did pick up a couple hundred on Flying Dutchman, but let's not hang about in the rain. Why don't we go to the pub up the street a ways. It's cozy and quiet there."

Wilkinson nodded agreement, and Kevin led the way back to the Royal Sussex Arms. While walking briskly, the rain and wind at their backs, Kevin learned that Wilkinson had joined a day tour to Brighton from London and had already eaten lunch with the tour party at a country inn on the South Downs, just before they got into Brighton. Wilkinson explained that the tour was a convenient cover to get him down to Brighton without attracting any attention and that he would rejoin the tour party at about four thirty for afternoon tea at the Grand Hotel, from where the bus would return to London.

When they were settled in the pub, Wilkinson downed a good third of his beer in one gulp and, wiping the froth off his lips with the back of his hand, looked across at Kevin and said, "Well, let's get down to business. Obviously, I've made my decision, or I wouldn't be here. But first, I need to know exactly who you are and who you represent. Naturally, I did some discreet research on you during the last week, but I came up empty."

Kevin glanced around one more time before he proceeded to give Wilkinson a concise account of himself and his position at the Ministry. He had decided that he would tell Wilkinson only what he absolutely needed to know to carry out his part of the operation. However, he mentioned some details of his inheritance from his granduncle Bertie to explain how he was able to fund the project, and he clarified that he was acting entirely alone and quite independent of any group such as the IRA or the Provos, emphasizing that he wanted to mount a completely professional operation. Kevin concluded by explaining why he hadn't been in the least surprised that Wilkinson had been unable to get any leads on his identity; his position as head of the highly secret Section Q11 or BAFNP Group was only known to the very highest levels of military and government circles and, of course, to MI5.

Wilkinson's face betrayed nothing of what he was thinking, though he appeared to listen with rapt attention. When Kevin finished, Wilkinson sat staring into the fire for several minutes before he said a word.

"Mac, if I may call you that? But it's certainly better than calling you Major." Kevin nodded before Wilkinson went on. "And do call me George rather than Captain. Now that I know who you are and your position at the Ministry, everything begins to fall into place. I completely take back my original reaction that the idea is crazy. I believe the operation can be carried out successfully with military precision. Whether or not it will have the political results you desire remains to be seen. I'm not much interested in politics myself, but I wouldn't be at all surprised if we get what you want."

They spent the next couple of hours discussing and refining Kevin's plan, and Kevin was very impressed. "You know, George, your great suggestion about how to get the nukes to the ferry is so spot-on—that's exactly how we will do it."

They had become so engrossed in their discussion that Kevin made only one trip back up to the counter for refills. "Just so you know," Kevin said when he came back, "I've named the operation Green September to represent the final greening of the map of a united Ireland."

"I like that a lot, particularly now that we have set September 6 as D-day for our operation."

At that point, there had been only two issues left to discuss, money and ongoing contact. It had already been agreed that Wilkinson would handle the recruitment and training of the men needed to execute the plan, as well as the procurement of all vehicles and safe houses.

"Okay, Mac, the plan looks solid, and I'll stake my life and reputation on its success. But success doesn't come cheap. It'll still cost you $2 million up front, plus another million for expenses in recruiting and supplies, and a final $2 million to me three days before D-day, a grand total of $5 million."

Kevin felt this was an insignificant price to pay if their plan succeeded in reuniting Ireland after almost eight decades of painful division. "You have a deal, George. Just tell me where and how you want the money delivered and I will transfer $2 million next week, another million the following week, and the final $2 million three days before D-day."

Wilkinson gave Kevin the numbers of two bank accounts in Switzerland, one specifically for himself and the other for a half million of expense money. For the final half million of the expense money, Wilkinson gave a corporate account number at a bank in the Grand Cayman Islands. This really intrigued Kevin, but he made no comment.

"Now that's settled, Mac, I believe the best way to keep contact is for me to make a fifteen-second call to your home or mobile and give you the phone number of a public phone booth and two alternative times to call. That way we will avoid any possible eavesdropping monitoring of your home or mobile phones by MI5, and you'll have two shots of finding a suitable public phone box to call me from. Agreed?"

Kevin readily agreed, knowing all too well that his phones were randomly monitored by MI5 on a routine basis because of his high security clearance at the Ministry. Kevin also knew that it took twenty-five seconds before he would hear the almost indiscernible click of MI5's monitoring equipment. "Well, George, I think that concludes a very productive afternoon's work. Would you like a last scotch for the road?"

"I don't mind if I do!"

While Kevin was buying the drinks, Wilkinson slipped on his coat. They were still all alone in the lounge as Kevin handed Wilkinson a glass. They raised their glasses in a toast to Green September.

The months had gone by quickly. Kevin and Wilkinson didn't meet again until the middle of August in Chelmsford, when Kevin passed the all-important nuclear missile electronic firing mechanisms to Wilkinson for duplication. That meeting was brief. Then, the day before Kevin left for the States, they had their final and briefest meeting, in London, so that Kevin could retrieve the now duplicated firing mechanisms to return to the Ministry vaults before they were discovered missing. To that point, everything had gone smoothly, but Kevin knew the most critical part of all was rapidly drawing closer.

Kevin woke with a start when the pilot's voice came over the intercom. "Good evening, ladies and gentlemen, this is your captain speaking. Welcome to New York! The time is exactly 7:41, the temperature outside is seventy-nine degrees Fahrenheit with 82 percent humidity and a gentle breeze of eight miles per hour out of the southeast. Please remain in your seats until we come to …"

Kevin tuned out the rest of the announcement because he had heard it so many times before. First-class passengers were first off the plane, and they didn't have to wait more than ten minutes to retrieve their bags. They got through customs and immigration equally quickly, and by ten minutes past eight, Kevin and Jenny were aboard a helicopter bound for the Eastside Heliport in Midtown Manhattan. Kevin nearly always took the helicopter service to save time. At the heliport, they got a cab right away, and by 8:35 they were at the Grand Hyatt Hotel, checking in. This hotel held many fond memories for them, as this was where they stayed whenever they managed to get to New York together. More often that not, Sir Ian readily allowed Kevin to add on a day or two of holiday time to his overseas trips on behalf of the Ministry, which Kevin deeply appreciated.

CHAPTER 3

ONCE IN THEIR ROOM, THEY decided to take very quick showers, without dallying, before they changed for dinner. While Jenny showered, he made a quick phone call to his wife to let her know he'd arrived safely. He'd barely hung up when Jenny called from the bathroom, "Darling, what time is our reservation at Le Cirque?"

"Nine fifteen, so we're in good time, sweetheart!"

Kevin wore his navy pinstripe suit, a white shirt, and a navy tie with red diamond design for a dash of color. Jenny wore an equally conservative black silk dress with small white polka dots, which had antique lace around the neckline and three-quarter-length sleeves. With a single strand of pearls around her neck and a wide black belt sitting loosely around her perfect waistline, Kevin thought she looked simply divine and so elegant and sexy that it crossed his mind for a moment to forget about dinner.

The cab took them speedily up Park Avenue to the restaurant at the southwest corner of Park and Sixty-Fifth Street. Kevin had eaten there twice before and loved the food and ambiance, but it was Jenny's first time, and he knew she was looking forward to it immensely, as she enjoyed fine cuisine just as much as Kevin did. They arrived punctually for their reservation and were immediately shown to their table.

Le Cirque was a luxuriously styled establishment that boasted one of the finest French chefs in all of New York. It was definitely a place where people came to see and be seen while enjoying the most elegantly prepared French cuisine in town. Jenny seemed in her element, as they had been given a table in the corner at which they sat facing outward, giving them a commanding view of the surrounding diners. As they studied the menu, Jenny whispered, "Look, there's Jerry Seinfeld." Kevin glanced up; she was right. At another table, they spotted the author Stephen King. Kevin ordered a bottle of California zinfandel from the small Stag's Leap winery, which was one of Jenny's favorites. Jenny started out with the Maine lobster, while Kevin had the quail. They shared succulent rack of lamb, done to perfection and served with crispy vegetables, followed by Le Cirque's famous and sinfully rich dessert, the chocolate soufflé smothered in fresh cream so incredibly delicious that they ate every last bit of it although they were already quite full. Kevin ordered each of them a large brandy to sit and relax over while Jenny lavished her praise on the excellent dinner.

When they left Le Cirque, it was close to midnight and still pleasantly warm with a hint of a fresh breeze. They decided to take a leisurely stroll back to their hotel to help work off the fabulous dinner and recover from the plane ride, so they headed over toward Central Park and down Fifth Avenue to Forty-Second Street.

It was about twelve thirty when they reached their hotel room, and they both felt revived after their walk. Kevin slipped the do-not-disturb sign over the outside doorknob before closing and bolting the door for the night. They would be in no hurry in the morning. The maid had already been in and had turned down the king-size bed and left on just one bedside lamp, which cast a soft glow over the whole room. Just inside the door, Kevin took Jenny in his arms and kissed her passionately; she responded eagerly. Kevin simply loved Jenny's enthusiasm about everything from fine food to wonderful sex, and, as he kissed her neck and nibbled her ear, the delicious scent of her body intermingled with lingering traces of her Cartier perfume excited his senses. They were so perfectly attuned to each other that as Kevin impatiently tugged at the zipper down the back of Jenny's dress, she was quickly undoing his tie and trouser belt. Almost simultaneously, they were down to their underwear as they threw the rest of their clothes in an unruly pile on the floor. They were almost halfway to the bathroom when they fused together again in a passionate embrace. Kevin was growing excited as he felt Jenny's nearly naked body hug tightly to his own, and he knew she must have felt his growing excitement between her legs. As they reached the bathroom, Kevin almost stumbled out of his shorts and tugged Jenny's panties down to her ankles so she could kick them aside. Then, while Jenny reached in to turn on the shower, Kevin unsnapped the back of her bra, revealing her firm breasts in their beautiful nakedness. They stepped into the warm shower together, kissing yet again. They reveled in feeling and touching every nook and cranny of each other's bodies as the warm water cascaded all over them. Kevin felt exhilarated and slowly began to kiss every square inch that was Jenny, working his way down her neck to her breasts with hardening nipples and lingering there as he sucked them gently. He moved on to her smooth, firm tummy, kneeling down in the shower until he reached his goal. Jenny was the only woman in his entire life with whom Kevin could truthfully say he thoroughly enjoyed being intimate in this way. He could tell from her reaction that his tongue gently probing and licking her most private parts gave Jenny the utmost pleasure. In turn, Kevin licked her more hungrily as he felt Jenny's passion mount to her climax. As Kevin savored her love juices in his mouth, he felt her knees buckle as she moaned in sheer pleasure and struggled not to collapse to the marble floor of the shower.

It was a few minutes before Jenny recovered her composure. Kevin cradled her in his arms with loving kisses. As Jenny revived, she looked straight into Kevin's eyes and said, "You naughty, wonderful man! You give me more pleasure than you can possibly imagine, my darling. Now it's my turn to make you feel good. If I can make you feel even half as good as you made me feel, it will be terrific!"

"Oh, my sweetheart, you do excite me so. Every single time, you make me feel incredible!"

"Okay, darling, do stand up while I kneel and give you a treat!"

Kevin needed no second bidding as his already steely erection felt like a dog straining on his leash, wanting to bust free. As Jenny took him in her hands and gently pulled the foreskin back and forth, Kevin felt an electric charge surge through his body. He knew that with the way he was feeling tonight, he wouldn't be able to hold himself back for long. Kevin then felt the warm moistness of Jenny's tongue licking him faster and faster. The sensations were terrific! She then took him in her mouth, and to Kevin, it felt like his erection was being swallowed up by a hot, soft, vibrating pouch. Every time Jenny did this for him, Kevin was amazed that he never felt her teeth; it was almost as if they withdrew inside her gums. She certainly had the knack like no other woman Kevin had ever known. As Kevin looked down adoringly at Jenny's head, it reminded him of how his homemade boats made of bottle corks would bob up and down on the ripples of the pond on Clapham Common, where he played as a small child. Kevin began to feel a huge surge well up through his whole body, and instinctively his hands pressed Jenny's head closer to him as he felt spurt after spurt dissipate into Jenny's mouth and down her throat. Kevin just stood there, trembling with emotion while Jenny continued to gently lick up every last drop from his waning erection.

Jenny stood up, her face flushed, and Kevin held her in his arms for a long time without a word, both still oblivious to the water running down their bodies. Kevin kissed her long and hard as if he couldn't get enough of her. Knowing what he had to do in just seventeen days made Kevin treat every precious moment with Jenny as if it were his last. He realized that even if he didn't die doing what he must do, this was definitely the last week he would ever spend with Jenny. Kevin knew for certain that after September 6 all links with his current life would be broken forever.

Kevin finally let go of Jenny, and looking straight into her eyes, he said, "You're a wonderful woman, Jen, and no matter what happens, I'll always love you in a very special way."

"Kevin, my darling man, you're a diehard romantic. It must be your Irish heritage, but you know, I believe you, because I can feel the depth of your love in every fiber of my body, and I can see it in your eyes every time I look into them. And the love I feel for you is also very special, and I know I have never felt this way with any other man—nor could I ever again. What we have together, my darling, comes only once in a lifetime!"

"My sweetheart, you always have a way with words and manage to express what I feel, so much better than I can myself."

"C'mon, you ol' flatterer, soap me down!" Jenny said teasingly.

Kevin grabbed the soap and lathered Jenny up nicely, and she did the same for him. They shampooed their own hair and then took turns rinsing off under the showerhead. They dried quickly, and then Jenny got playful again as she raced for the bed and stretched out, naked on top of the covers, sexily beckoning him to join her. Before doing so, Kevin turned down the air-conditioning to low for the night and made a quick call to the operator for a ten o'clock wake-up call, just in case they overslept, and asked that any incoming calls be held until that time.

Kevin rolled over on the bed beside Jenny and began kissing her, lightly at first. He enjoyed lingering over every touch and working Jenny up very slowly while restraining his own passion until Jenny was well and truly ready for him. They enjoyed exploring each other's bodies with gentle caresses and soft kisses. It was at intimate times like this that Kevin wondered what Jenny would think about what he was going to do. How would she react to such an act of terrorism by the man she loved so much? Or worse still, she might even be killed by his action. This had been Kevin's private nightmare during the past several months as his mind grappled with finding a way of ensuring that Jenny was out of London on September 7 and 8. But there was no way of warning his beloved Jenny without jeopardizing his plans, and he could only trust that fate would deal a kind hand, which wasn't too far-fetched since Jenny was often away from London on business.

Kevin realized that if he should live and Jenny die, he would be paying the maximum personal price for the unification of Ireland. As he followed this train of thought, an idea flashed into his brain that would fulfill one of Jenny's travel dreams—a luxurious first-class round trip to Rio De Janeiro and a penthouse suite in the Rio Palace Hotel on Copacabana Beach to enjoy their world famous five-day super spa session for ladies only. He would book it for the five days from September 5 to September 10 and give it to her as a thank-you gift for this wonderful time in New York.

He held Jenny tightly in his arms for a few moments longer before he lay on top of her, and they joined in another beautiful round of lovemaking. It was already past three o'clock in the morning when they finally fell asleep, exhausted, in each other's arms.

Kevin awoke a little before nine thirty. Jenny was still fast asleep, close to him, with her arm hung loosely across his chest and her legs entwined with his. Slowly, he maneuvered himself out of bed without disturbing her and went straight to the bathroom. He used the phone in there to cancel the wake-up call and order breakfast. Kevin then shaved and showered and emerged in a hotel robe with another robe over his arm for Jenny. She was already awake and got up right away, slipping on the robe while Kevin drew back the curtains. The bright sunshine streamed in through the windows, and as Kevin looked down at the Saturday shoppers scurrying around far below on Forty-Second Street, he noticed the sidewalks were still darkened with rain. While shaving, he had heard on the bathroom radio that the weather forecast for the weekend was excellent—predictions of warm, sunny days and relatively low humidity after a thunderstorm during the night had cleared the air. He and Jenny had slept right through the whole thing.

Jenny came out of the bathroom, having just washed her face and brushed her hair. Kevin was struck at just how beautiful she looked without a hint of makeup. Her face and eyes seemed to radiate happiness.

"Did you sleep well, sweetheart?"

"Like a babe, darling. It looks like you got an earlier start."

Jenny gave Kevin a hug as she ran her hands over his smoothly shaven face.

"I've ordered breakfast, and it should be here in a few minutes, Jen. I know you want to do a little shopping before we catch the train up to your parents' place. Oh, better remove the do-not-disturb sign from the doorknob or we may get no breakfast!"

Kevin was just in time, for a waiter was already coming down the corridor toward their room with a breakfast cart. Kevin waited for him by the open door, and the waiter set up breakfast for them by the window and was on his way. He also left a copy of the *New York Times*.

"Kevin, darling, you're a thoughtful man! I don't need to go shopping; it's just that I love to browse around the stores on Fifth Avenue and perhaps pick up a couple of odds and ends that I mightn't find in London so easily. Boy, this breakfast looks yummy! Let's eat before it gets cold."

Kevin and Jenny sat down opposite each other and tucked in on a hearty breakfast of bacon and eggs, toast, coffee, and delicious fresh-squeezed orange juice. Both of them had healthy appetites after the previous night's activities, and Jenny chatted away about her family and childhood home. Kevin had met her parents several times before on previous trips to New York for dinner or to see a show on Broadway, but he had never visited their home or met any other members of her family.

After breakfast, while Jenny showered and got ready to go out, Kevin glanced through the *Times* and had a last cup of coffee before he got dressed. They both wore jeans, T-shirts, and sneakers and had their bags repacked and ready to go just before eleven. They planned to return about twelve fifteen and check out in time to catch the 12:48 to Mount Kisco, where Jenny's sister would pick them up. As they left the room, Kevin couldn't help admiring how good Jenny looked in tight jeans and how her gorgeous, firm boobs seemed to stand at attention even in a very loose T-shirt. She was one helluva good-looking woman no matter what she wore, Kevin thought, and once again he reminded himself how lucky he was to have her as his lover. At moments like this, he thought he really must be crazy to be about to give it all up.

Kevin and Jenny left the hotel arm-in-arm, donned sunglasses, and turned right on Forty-Second Street toward Fifth Avenue. The sidewalks were crowded with colorfully dressed Saturday morning shoppers, and they strolled along among the excited chatter of tourists in French, German, Spanish, Japanese, and other languages Kevin didn't recognize. Jenny was in high spirits and dragged Kevin in and out of several stores along the way. Kevin wasn't exactly a big shopper and usually found shopping tiresome, but Jenny's enthusiasm was infectious, and the time passed quickly. Jenny's sole purchase was a silk scarf with an unusual Navajo design, and she was delighted with her find, which was Kevin's treat.

They made it to the train about twelve forty, and Jenny led the way to the almost deserted front carriage. The train departed Grand Central Station exactly on time, and the trip passed quickly as the first stop was White Plains, and then it was only seven more stops to Mount Kisco. The changing scenery reminded Kevin a lot of childhood train rides from London to Brighton, as the big city changed to middle-class suburbia, and after, White Plains gave way to rocky woodlands and rugged countryside, dotted here and there with magnificent custom-designed homes. They reached Mount Kisco right on schedule at one forty-five. As Kevin gathered their bags on the platform, a young woman strode up to meet them and immediately threw her arms around Jenny and hugged her. Jenny turned to Kevin and said, "Darling, this is my kid sister, Nancy."

"Very pleased to meet you at last, Nancy. Jenny has told me rather a lot about you."

"Hi, Kevin! I'm delighted to meet you too, and I've heard so much about you. For once Jenny didn't exaggerate!" Nancy said as she gave Kevin a friendly hug.

"C'mon, Nance, don't embarrass me! Give us a hand with the bags and let's go to the car," Jenny said affectionately.

Kevin liked Nancy instantly. Nancy was a lot fairer and looked quite different from Jenny but was also rather attractive. Nancy was about an inch shorter than her sister and certainly had a somewhat fuller figure, but she wasn't what he considered fat. The most striking things about Nancy were her gorgeous natural red hair, which tumbled to her shoulders in big curls, and her bright, shining green eyes. Jenny had explained that Nancy's coloring was a throwback to some of their fairer-skinned paternal ancestors from Northern Italy. At twenty-three, Nancy was the baby in Jenny's family, and after graduating from college the previous year, she had returned to live at home with her parents and commute to her job at an advertising agency in Manhattan. Nancy was wearing a tight-fitting tank top and shorts, and Kevin couldn't help but notice her shapely legs as she led the way to the car.

Nancy had borrowed her mother's big old station wagon to pick them up, and Kevin quickly loaded up all their bags into the rear of the wagon. All three of them decided to ride together on the spacious front bench seat, and Kevin sat back with his arm out the open window while Jenny and Nancy talked thirteen to the dozen. Kevin was quite content to listen while the sisters brought each other up to date on their respective lives, although Nancy was doing most of the talking to give Jenny all the latest family news. On the fifteen-minute ride to the house, Kevin learned that Jenny's dad would be retiring early the following year on his sixty-third birthday, as the major computer company where he had worked for thirty-eight years was restructuring and encouraging early retirement for many of its senior executives. As a result, Jenny's parents were considering selling the family home and retiring to either California or Arizona to be near their grandchildren. Apparently both Jenny's brothers were married and living on the West Coast.

Nancy appeared to be a good driver, and she got them through the town of Mount Kisco and onto Route 172 in no time at all. It was only a couple of miles down this road when they took a sharp turn to the right onto Old Wagon Road and went all the way to the end, where the Grinaldi family had a beautiful old Colonial style house sitting on four acres, overlooking the small, pretty Howlands Lake to the west and a nature conservancy to the south. As they drove up the winding driveway to the front of the house, Kevin noticed a paddock to his right and commented on it to Nancy. She told him that she used to have a horse when she was a teenager, but she had to give him up when she went away to college. On learning of Nancy's love of horses, Kevin invited her to join Jenny and himself on a visit to Woodlawn in Greenwich the next day. When Kevin explained what Woodlawn was all about, Nancy said to count her in.

As they drew up to the front door, Jenny's parents came out to greet them. Her father, John Grinaldi, was a handsome man of about six feet, well built and fit looking. He had the same tanned complexion and high cheekbones as Jenny but a rather large patrician nose and a receding hairline. At sixty-two, his hair was still jet black with just a hint of gray at the temples, and he wore the relaxed expression of a man who was content with his life. Kevin always thought that Jenny had a lot of her father in her, ever since the first time he'd met her father several years earlier. Jenny's mother, Maria, on the other hand, bore a closer resemblance to Nancy, at least in shape. Her hair had been brunette like Jenny's but was now rapidly turning silver gray, which looked becoming on her. She had a more rounded face than the rest of the Grinaldis and a small nose like Jenny. Kevin could clearly see that she had been an attractive woman when she was younger and at fifty-nine was wearing her age well. What Kevin thought was most remarkable about both Jenny's parents was the absence of age lines on their faces, apart from a few smile lines around their mouths. Kevin liked them both very much.

As the car came to a stop, the family dog, Jeepers, came flying out the front door, barking excitedly and determined to preempt everyone in greeting the new arrivals. Knowing how much Kevin loved dogs and particularly his Max, Jenny had told him all about Jeepers, who was a sprightly nine-year-old male Shetland sheepdog. Jeepers bounded straight up to the open window of the car on Kevin's side, placed his front paws on Kevin's arm, and licked his face lavishly in welcome. Kevin stroked his head in return, and Jeepers responded with a bushy tail that wagged furiously.

Jenny's dad walked over and said, "Welcome, Kevin! It's great to see you again; it's been too long! You know, Kevin, Jeepers's greeting is quite a compliment, as Jeepers is usually quite standoffish with strangers."

Meanwhile, Jeepers had bounded around the other side of the car to greet Nancy, who had just gotten out, so Kevin could now safely open the car door to get out himself. Jenny slid across the seat right after him and gave her dad a big hug and then hugged her mom, who had walked over to join them.

"It's so wonderful to see you both," her mother said. "You're looking terrific, Jen. You've got quite a glow! We're so pleased, Kevin, that you could finally come and stay for a night. We only wish it could be for longer!" And with that, Jenny's mom gave Kevin a hug as if he were one of the family.

"It's great to be here and so wonderful to see you both again. And I'm so pleased to finally meet Nancy," Kevin said with warm sincerity as he caught a sideways glance of the big smile on Nancy's face.

Nancy had already unloaded their bags and along with her dad gave Kevin a hand to carry them into the house and upstairs while Jenny walked off to the kitchen with her mom, Jeepers at their heels. Kevin was shown into a large bedroom with a queen-size bed and its own adjoining bathroom. It was at a back corner of the house and had a great view over the lake to the west.

Like many families, the Grinaldis often gathered in the kitchen for family get-togethers, and it made Kevin feel good to be treated just like them. Jenny's mom had already laid out quite a spread of rolls, cold cuts, and cheeses on the kitchen table while her dad offered glasses of chilled California blush wine, which Kevin found very light and exceptionally palatable. There was a festive mood about the gathering, and not being one to be left out, particularly when there was food around, Jeepers roved around like a vacuum cleaner scooping up the slightest crumb that fell on the floor. Nancy and Jenny both fed him little pieces of cheese from their hands, and when Jeepers had exhausted their kindness, he went and sat at attention at Kevin's feet, looking up at him with imploring eyes just like Max would do. Of course, Kevin couldn't resist such a look, and several tasty morsels found their way into Jeepers's tummy. Jeepers almost wafted the food from his hand, so gently that it also reminded him of his beloved Max.

The rest of the afternoon was spent relaxing around the family swimming pool and chatting. Jenny and Nancy had put on their bathing suits to take advantage of the strong afternoon sunshine, and when they went swimming, they insisted that Kevin join them. Kevin didn't have any bathing trunks with him, so Jenny's dad kindly lent him a pair, and both men joined the girls in the pool while Jenny's mom went to see about dinner.

For Kevin, the evening went by all too quickly. Jenny's parents had invited their good friends Danny and Julia Duncan over for dinner, and Nancy had invited her current boyfriend, Tom Birch, who, at twenty-eight, had already successfully established his own software company in nearby Armonk. Jenny's mom served a delicious dinner of veal piccata, several different pasta dishes, and Caesar salad, followed by fresh strawberries and cream. The California chardonnay wine was excellent, and the conversation flowed freely. Kevin did notice that Jenny's dad frequently referred to him as "Jenny's British major friend" who held an important post at the British Ministry of Defense, which required Kevin to visit their Pentagon several times a year. "Very hush-hush," he would say. Kevin was rather amused by this, as Jenny had explained to him before that her dad was all the more intrigued with Kevin's job because Kevin couldn't talk about it (just like his ex-son-in-law's position in the CIA). In fact, it was a kind of family joke that Jenny always seemed to manage to pick men who did secret work for their governments.

Kevin and Jenny were quite tired when they went to bed after midnight but not too tired for each other. Kevin was driven by an overwhelming urge not to waste a single precious moment of the time remaining to him with Jenny.

The next morning, Kevin took the whole family out to brunch at a local restaurant after Jenny's parents got back from Sunday Mass. In the afternoon, Nancy drove Kevin and Jenny to Greenwich to visit the Woodlawn estate, which turned out to be only about a half hour's drive from the house. The entrance to Woodlawn was through an enormous wrought-iron and granite-pillared gateway and up a straight tree-lined half-mile-long driveway to the main house, a late nineteenth-century mansion in the classical style. As they drove up, Kevin was pleased to notice that there were plenty of horses grazing on the grasslands to each side of the driveway, so it appeared that Granduncle Bertie's last wishes had already been implemented.

When they went into the house and Kevin introduced himself to the man in charge, they were all made very welcome and were invited to take a ride around the estate on three of Granduncle Bertie's own horses that Kevin knew by name. These horses were considerably younger than many of the horses now living on the estate. Once they had saddled up, they spent an enjoyable couple of hours riding around the estate, which was bordered by the Audubon Center of Greenwich to the west, the New York and Connecticut state line to the north, and Round Hill Road to the east, with the estate entrance to the south on John Street. All three of them loved every minute of it, even Jenny, who had not done a lot of riding in her life. Nancy, of course, was in her element and totally fell in love with the place. Before they left the estate, Kevin was easily able to make arrangements with the chief custodian for Nancy to be allowed to come there at any time to ride or simply to visit the horses as she wished. When Kevin told Nancy about what he had arranged, she was absolutely thrilled and gave him a big hug, and so did Jenny.

Nancy decided to take them home a different way, through the quaint village of Armonk, where she suggested they stop at the famous Schultz's Cider Mill to get some refreshments. Nancy explained to Kevin that if only he could stick around for another two or three weeks, it would be the start of cider season, and Schultz's fresh cider was renowned throughout the region. Kevin laughed and said he truly wished he could. Jenny, of course, also knew the cider mill very well and suggested to Kevin that they buy her mom some corn and fruit, as Schultz's was equally renowned for its fresh fruit and vegetables. Jenny said that Shultz's corn was a particular favorite of her dad's. Having made their purchases, they were on their way and then home in about twenty minutes.

Jenny's parents decided to treat Kevin to a traditional American cookout for dinner before he and Jenny left for their 7:30 p.m. flight to Washington, DC, so when they got home about a quarter after five, Jenny's dad was busy at the barbecue cooking big hunks of steak and huge Vidalia onions wrapped in foil while her Mom was busy in the kitchen putting the finishing touches to homemade potato salad. They ate at a picnic table in the backyard and washed down the delicious food with beer. Kevin particularly liked the onions, which after an hour and a half of slow cooking tasted more like baked apples. Kevin had never tasted anything like them before, and they proved to be a perfect complement to the tasty steak. All through the dinner, Jeepers attached himself to Kevin's side, as if he knew Kevin would soon be leaving, and much to the amusement of the rest of the family, who realized that the smart Jeepers's devotion to Kevin was amply rewarded with several juicy pieces of steak.

As Kevin sat back after the magnificent meal and gazed at the reddening sun moving like a giant fireball toward the horizon beyond the lake, he felt rooted to the spot and found himself wishing time could stand still. But Kevin knew that time waits for no man, and the clock was ticking inexorably to his date with destiny. Kevin realized these last couple of days with Jenny and meeting her charming family were among the happiest in his entire life, but he felt very sad, knowing that this would be the last weekend he would ever spend with Jenny. Kevin could feel tears well up in his eyes and had to choke them back.

"A penny for your thoughts, darling!" Jenny had come up behind Kevin and startled him a little.

"I was just thinking what a perfect weekend this has been, and I wish it could last forever."

"Yes, it has been rather special, my darling. And you know, my mom and dad are becoming awfully fond of you. As for Nancy, well, if we were staying around much longer, you'd probably have to fight her off! Your easy Irish charm certainly wasn't lost on her, darling."

"You know, sweetheart, you have one terrific family, and this is such a gorgeous place where you grew up. It all helps me understand even more why I love you so much."

"C'mon, darling, we do have a plane to catch, and if you go on like that, you're going to make me cry. I'm so happy."

Jenny took Kevin by the arm and walked him into the house. Jenny's dad and Nancy had already loaded their bags into the back of the station wagon, and Jeepers was hanging around, looking subdued, as if sensing their imminent departure. As Nancy had a date with Tom that evening, Jenny's dad was driving them to the airport, but Jenny's mom wasn't going in the car with them, as she hated airport farewells. After teary-eyed good-byes and thanks all around, Kevin and Jenny got into the front with her dad, but Jeepers was nowhere in sight. Just as they were about to leave, he came tearing around the side of the house, and Kevin opened the door so that he and Jenny could give him a hug good-bye. To everyone's surprise, Jeepers jumped into the wagon and sat himself down between Kevin and Jenny and seemed to be grinning ear to ear as he panted. This amusing action by Jeepers brought comic relief to the sad departure.

John Grinaldi took the faster and more direct highway routes to the country back roads, and he soon had them traveling south on the nearby Interstate 684. As they sped along, Jenny suddenly remembered with an exclamation that she had completely forgotten to give her mom and dad their gifts of J&B scotch and Harrod's biscuits that she had bought for them at London airport. So, on impulse, she scrambled over to the backseat to reach her bag and retrieve them. To Kevin's amazement, both Jenny's dad and Jeepers remained perfectly calm while all the commotion was going on.

They reached the Westchester County Airport at exactly seven o'clock, just twenty minutes after leaving the house. As it was Sunday evening and there were only a couple of more flights out of there, the tiny airport was almost deserted. Kevin had never flown out of there before and was not too impressed with the World War II vintage Quonset hut that served as the airport's only terminal. But Jenny had pointed out that it would be a lot more convenient from her parents' house than going all the way to LaGuardia, despite having to change planes in Philadelphia and fly in small Beech 1900 commuter planes, which actually made Jenny even more nervous than large jets.

Kevin and Jenny said their farewells to the rascally Jeepers who stayed behind in the station wagon. With the place so empty, they had found parking right outside the main entrance. Jenny's dad helped them carry their bags into the terminal, and before they went inside, Kevin took a last glance back at Jeepers, who was sitting on the front seat with his head pressed against the passenger side window, staring intently after them as if watching with disapproval every step they took. Kevin gave Jeepers a last wave good-bye but got no reaction other than a continuing stare. Inside was equally deserted, and check-in took less than a minute. They could see the small plane already outside on the tarmac and waiting for the handful of passengers. They decided to board right away rather than stand around the almost empty terminal. Jenny gave her dad a last long hug good-bye.

"Thanks for everything, Dad! We had a wonderful visit but much too short."

"We loved having you and Kevin, and we all wished you could have stayed longer, but it's only four months until Christmas, and then you'll be with us longer. I don't know if your mother told you, but both your brothers and their families will be coming for what may be our last Christmas all together in that house. Is there any chance you might be able to come for Christmas, Kevin?"

"At this point, I doubt it, John. I would love nothing better than to spend Christmas with you all, but we'll see. Thanks again for all your hospitality and for making me feel so much at home. I had a truly wonderful, relaxing time. Good-bye, John, and my best wishes to Maria and Nancy!"

Kevin shook hands warmly with John Grinaldi and then took Jenny's arm and walked out to the plane. As they looked back to give a last wave at the foot of the short stairs up to the plane, Jenny's dad yelled, "Fly safe, you two! And, Jenny, thanks again for my favorite scotch! I know your mother will love the fancy Harrod's biscuits. Bye!"

The plane left on time with only three other people on board the nineteen-seater, whose only crew were a pilot and a copilot, who happened to be a woman. Kevin found the bucket-type seats in a single row on each side of the aisle to be somewhat cramped. Jenny sat across the narrow aisle from him, and they held hands. Kevin always thought of these types of planes as puddle jumpers, as it seemed they were no sooner up and level when the plane started to descend again. Jenny remained pretty quiet and tense for the twin hops to Washington, with her only respite in Philadelphia while they changed planes.

They arrived at Washington National Airport a few minutes after ten, and it was still warm and muggy out. Once they got their bags, they took a cab straight to their hotel on Massachusetts Avenue NW. Kevin always stayed at the Ritz-Carlton Hotel, as he liked its traditional style and elegance and its convenient location, a five-minute cab ride from the British embassy. Kevin always personally paid for any upgrades to his travel arrangements that exceeded Ministry guidelines.

Check-in at the hotel was typically slow for a Sunday night, with many people arriving around the same time for their week's business in Washington. Kevin and Jenny were both relieved but tired when they finally got to their room about eleven. They decided to settle for a nightcap from their room's minibar before turning in for the night, rather than wait for room service. Jenny was quickly asleep in Kevin's arms, and he wasn't far behind her. As he drifted off, Kevin thought, *Only fifteen days to go. Hope this week will go by quickly, except for my precious time with Jenny.*

The next morning, Kevin was up at seven, feeling refreshed and ready for work. Colonel Gary Marshall was sending a car over to pick him up at eight thirty and take him to the Pentagon, so Kevin had plenty of time to get ready while Jenny slept. After shaving and showering, Kevin got dressed in his uniform, spent a short time going through some papers from his briefcase, and even remembered to put in the bottle of brandy for Gary. A few minutes before eight, Kevin woke up Jenny with a kiss and told her he had ordered a light breakfast in their room for eight so that she could join him before he had to leave for the day. Jenny was her usual bubbly self. After the room service waiter left, they sat down together at the table set by the corner windows to enjoy a light breakfast of coffee, toast, and orange juice.

"Well, sweetheart, what have you planned for today?" he asked.

"Nothing yet. I'll probably spend the morning on the phone catching up with some old friends and see what arrangements I can make for the rest of the week. And this afternoon, I'll probably go down to the Mall and see what's new in a couple of the galleries of the Smithsonian. I wish you could come with me, as I know you enjoy strolling around the art galleries as much as I do!"

Jenny was right, of course. Kevin enjoyed doing many things with Jenny, such as visiting art galleries and museums and going to the theater and good movies.

"Yes, I'd love to come, sweetheart, but I'm afraid it's a working week for me. Anyway, you can tell me all about anything new you see. And you won't forget that we're having dinner tonight at eight with Gary and Diane Marshall, and unfortunately, on Wednesday night I have that damn dress uniform affair at the embassy that I have to attend alone."

Kevin frowned, trying to think if there was any possible way he could get out of going to the embassy function on Wednesday, as he really would prefer to spend his last evening in Washington with Jenny. Jenny gave Kevin an incredulous look, which he took seriously.

"You do know that I would much prefer to be with you, don't you?"

"Oh, darling, don't look so serious. I'm only teasing you! Of course, I understand. I know you're only going because you have to. Besides, even if I were invited, I don't think I'd want to go. The military attaché at the embassy is such a boring stuffed shirt! And I hope you haven't forgotten, my darling, that tomorrow night we're going to the Henderson's dinner party at their home in Georgetown. You remember Bob and Joan, don't you? He's the California congressman I've known since my Los Angeles days—you met him and his wife a couple of years ago at the John F. Kennedy Center for the Performing Arts."

"Yes, I do remember Bob. Pretty savvy about foreign affairs, I seem to recall, and a nice chap too, but I can't remember his wife."

"Well, you did meet her, and you will certainly remember her when you see her again. She's a dazzling blonde and a former Miss California! Ah, now you remember, darling. Don't blush! Though you did comment at the time that she was quite a knockout! Anyway, the Hendersons always have very interesting people at their dinner parties, so it should be fun. For Wednesday night, I think I'll try to arrange to have dinner with my dear old friend Helen Jaffe. You remember, I told you all about her before; she was my mentor when I worked at the interior design firm here in Washington. Anyway, she has had her own firm for several years now and just got divorced after seventeen years of marriage, and we have a lot of news and gossip to catch up on."

"Well, I hope you can set it up. I'm absolutely sure you'll have a much better time than I'll have at the embassy. Perhaps I'll be able to slip away early enough to join you both for an after-dinner drink or two. I would like to meet Helen, finally, after hearing so much about her!"

"Oh, darling, do you really think you might? That would be terrific, as Helen knew my ex and always felt he wasn't quite right for me. I know she'd love to meet you. Which reminds me, I do have to meet Paul one day while I'm here to wrap up one final loose end on the townhouse we used to own here in Arlington years ago—some legal technicality, I believe. Anyway, it won't be any big deal! By the way, did I mention to you that I heard from a mutual friend a couple of weeks ago that Paul has remarried?"

"Yes, I believe you did. By the way, is he still based at CIA headquarters in Langley?"

"I think so. He'd better be, or I won't know where to contact him, as that's the only phone number I have for him."

"And then we have our nine o'clock flight back to London on Thursday night from JFK, so all in all I think the next four days are going to be pretty hectic! Oh my word, it's eight twenty-five already! I'd better get ready to go."

When he came back, Jenny had his uniform jacket off the clothes hanger and was ready to help him on with it. She helped him to button up his uniform and handed Kevin his hat, which he nearly always just carried with his briefcase, as he hated to wear hats. When he was ready to go, she stood back as if to inspect him and said, "Major, you pass inspection, sir!" Then she said, "And this lady here wishes you could cancel all appointments for the morning and take care of her."

Seeing that definite twinkle in Jenny's eyes again, he truly wished he could stay, but duty called.

"You are such a tease, sweetheart! But watch out tonight, we'll have to feign tiredness, jet lag, or something, to the Marshalls after dinner so we can get away early! Now I've got to dash, or I'll be late. I should be back about five thirty or a quarter to six. I hope you have a fun day!"

Kevin kissed Jenny full on the lips and said, "Cheerio."

"Bye, darling! Hope you have an interesting day," and with that, Kevin was gone.

He reached the lobby door just as a car with discreet military markings drew up. The car stopped right in front of Kevin, and a big black man in US Army sergeant's uniform got out and stepped up to Kevin, saluting smartly, and said, "Would you be Major MacAllister from London, sir?"

"Yes, I am."

"Sergeant Partellow at your service, sir! Colonel Marshall gave me instructions to pick you up at 0830 and take you straight to his office at the Pentagon, sir!"

"Thank you, Sergeant. At ease. Shall we go then?"

Partellow opened the door for Kevin to the roomy, air-conditioned passenger section of the car and then jumped in front. Having left the engine running, Partellow quickly maneuvered the car back into the morning rush-hour traffic and expertly headed south on Twenty-Third Street, past Washington Circle and onto the congested E Street

Expressway to take the Theodore Roosevelt Bridge across the Potomac River. Kevin knew the route so well. He sat back and relaxed, picking up a copy of the *Washington Post* that someone had thoughtfully left for him on the backseat. Partellow wasn't very talkative but did occasionally point out something new here and there. Kevin rather liked his southern accent and learned that the sergeant once did a tour of duty in England, which he really enjoyed.

When Kevin looked out again, they were already speeding southward along the highway on the west bank of the Potomac. It was about nine o'clock when they arrived at the Pentagon and Sergeant Partellow pulled up outside the main entrance. A soldier waiting by the steps opened the door for Kevin and saluted. Sergeant Partellow told the soldier to park the car and escorted Kevin into the building, efficiently ushering him through all the security checkpoints. Kevin was issued a special security visitor's pass that would get him in and out over the next four days with a minimum of fuss. Kevin knew the procedure well after the countless visits he had made to the Pentagon over the years. Partellow took him straight up to Colonel Marshall's office on the third floor.

Colonel Gary Marshall, a West Point graduate and career officer in the US Army, held a similar position to Kevin's on the US general staff, with responsibility for coordination of the vast US nuclear arsenal. Unlike Kevin, he did not have a technical background but had a reputation as a superb tactician. Gary had first seen action in Vietnam as a young combat officer and later served on General Westmoreland's staff during the last phase of the Vietnam War, earning high marks for his skills in difficult circumstances. He had held his current position for seven years and also played the role of chief military adviser to the US negotiating team in Vienna in their ongoing nuclear arms reduction talks with the Russians. Gary had also won a lot of plaudits from both his military superiors and politicians for the deft way in which he handled questioning in Congress when summoned to testify at periodic hearings on Russian proposals for nuclear arms reduction.

Kevin was shown into Colonel Marshall's office right away, and Sergeant Partellow withdrew. Gary Marshall got up from behind his huge, cluttered desk and came around to greet Kevin, pumping his hand vigorously in welcome. Six feet three and brawny, Gary towered over Kevin, but he had a genial face and was surprisingly soft-spoken for such a big man. Gary's disarming manner belied his shrewd mind and would easily mislead those who didn't know him as well as Kevin did. At fifty-seven, with silvery gray hair, Gary was ten years older than Kevin and on track to make general by the time he was sixty. From their first encounter seven years earlier, Kevin and Gary had become firm friends with nothing but mutual respect and admiration for each other's abilities and strengths. As he sat down across the desk from Gary, it crossed Kevin's mind that his good friend the colonel would be deeply shocked if he knew what Kevin planned to do in just fourteen days.

Gary offered Kevin English tea, which he gratefully accepted, and Kevin gave Gary the bottle of brandy that he had brought from London. Gary was delighted and jokingly suggested they should have a drop to get the day rolling. The two men quickly dispensed with the preliminaries and got straight down to business. Because of the special relationship between the United States and Britain, Kevin was accorded the highest level of security clearance given to any US ally and certainly greater than that given to other NATO members. So Gary was able to be a lot more frank in his discussions with Kevin than he would be if other NATO representatives were present. The day went quickly, and Kevin was both intrigued and impressed by the radical nature of some of the new American proposals on nuclear arms reduction that were under consideration for presentation to the Russians. They would represent a dramatic departure from the past and certainly put the sincerity of the Russians to the test. Kevin now clearly understood America's revised targets and finally spoke up.

"Gary, I totally get it and will be happy to bring your new proposals home with me."

"So, are you pretty confident that you and Sir Ian will get the British government to agree to our revised levels of nuclear weaponry?"

"Listen, Sir Ian relies on me 100 percent to understand and analyze all your proposals, and in turn, he has the total trust of the government."

"You know, our goal is to sit down with the Ruskies in Geneva before Christmas and have a new treaty in place for the New Year."

"Yes, and you can absolutely rely on us Brits to support you."

Gary promised Kevin even more startling proposals under consideration over the next few days. By the end of the day, Kevin felt invigorated—the discussions managed to distract him from his own preoccupation. Sergeant Partellow was assigned to Kevin for his entire four-day visit, and the efficient sergeant had Kevin back at his hotel by twenty minutes to six, with a promise to pick him up the next morning at eight thirty.

When Kevin got to their room, Jenny, who had got back just ten minutes earlier, was already undressed and in her robe, just waiting for Kevin to join her for a long, leisurely shower before they dressed for dinner with the Marshalls. They had a fun evening with Gary and Diane and got back to the hotel later than they would have liked but still managed another memorable night.

Tuesday went by just as fast, and that evening, Kevin and Jenny arrived at the Hendersons' dinner party about seven thirty.

Bob and Joan Henderson were the quintessential Washington host and hostess, and the dozen people invited that evening were all "somebodies" in their respective fields. There was a famous heart surgeon, a leading Californian businessman, an avant-garde architect, a popular novelist, and a couple of foreigners, including Kevin. All came with partners, either wives or girlfriends; it didn't seem to matter to the Hendersons. And like Jenny, many of the women had prominent careers of their own. Most of those at the party were unknown to Kevin and Jenny, but as they both enjoyed meeting new people, they mingled freely.

On Wednesday night, Kevin was true to his word and did manage to slip away early from the boring embassy function. He joined Jenny and her good friend about ten thirty at the Jockey Club, a fine French restaurant in their hotel. As Kevin walked into the crowded restaurant, Jenny waved to him from a table in the far corner. After he made his way over to join the two ladies, Jenny did the introductions, and it was obvious that Helen took to him immediately without reservation. Kevin also liked the older woman, who clearly was very fond of Jenny. The ladies were just finishing dessert when Kevin arrived, so he ordered coffee and brandy for the three of them. Helen was a very outgoing woman in her midfifties with a gravelly voice and infectious laugh, whose one foible was that she enjoyed a good cigar after dinner, which didn't bother Kevin or Jenny in the slightest.

Kevin and Jenny didn't make it to bed until after one in the morning, but neither of them felt sleepy, realizing it was their last night alone together for some time. Only Kevin knew it was probably their last night together ever, and he wanted to make every moment count. Jenny finally fell asleep in his arms about three thirty, utterly exhausted. Kevin remained awake most of the night, cradling Jenny in his arms and thinking of what lay ahead, now only twelve days away.

Thursday was a short day. Kevin didn't meet with Gary Marshall until eleven, and they wrapped up their discussions by four. Kevin had made careful notes about the new US nuclear arms reduction proposals during each of the four days of meetings, which he would use as the basis for his final report to Sir Ian, which he still planned to leave at Salisbury. While Kevin was with Gary, Jenny did finally manage to meet with her ex-husband, Paul, and clear up the last legal wrinkle of their divorce. She also learned that Paul Laster had recently been promoted to chief of the European Sector for CIA operations, which Kevin was very interested to hear.

That evening, Sergeant Partellow drove Kevin and Jenny to National Airport in time to catch the six thirty shuttle flight up to La Guardia, which allowed them plenty of time to transfer to JFK to catch the nine o'clock British Airways overnight flight 176 to London. Kevin was tired and depressed as he said his last farewells to his second and third favorite cities, but he feigned cheerfulness for Jenny's sake. Jenny was equally tired, and they both slept for most of the long flight home.

CHAPTER 4

EVIN AND JENNY LANDED ON schedule at Heathrow at 8:40 on
Friday morning, feeling somewhat refreshed after their short
night's sleep. As Kevin glanced at his watch and saw 3:40 a.m.,
he realized he had forgotten to put his watch forward before they left
New York. Several transatlantic flights had all arrived within twenty
minutes of one another, so there was a real bottleneck at HM customs
and passport control. Kevin hated the wait in long lines, and even his
diplomatic passport didn't help much when it was this busy.

It was ten o'clock by the time they got outside the terminal, and
judging by the wet pavement and the black, heavy clouds rolling away
quickly to the west, they had just missed one of those nasty, fast and
furious summer thunderstorms that often hit the London area in
August. The sun had already come out and reflected off the wet ground
the clearing blue skies from the east. Kevin asked Jenny to stay curbside
with their bags while he went to get the car.

Kevin quickly reached the secured section reserved for the Ministry
of Defense and flashed his credentials to one of the two soldiers on
duty. The soldier saluted and waved Kevin on to his car. The Jag was
gleaming, and Kevin thanked the soldiers for cleaning off all the airport
grime that had accumulated from sitting there for a week. He got in,
and the engine roared to life with the first turn of the key. Three minutes
later, he was outside the terminal and picking up Jenny and the bags.
It still took the usual fifteen minutes to get out of the vicinity of the
airport and onto the M4 toward Central London.

Kevin was thankful that the delays at the airport at least caused them to miss the worst of the morning rush-hour traffic, and he was able to do sixty most of the way into town. Neither Kevin nor Jenny was feeling very talkative; they both felt kind of down knowing that a wonderful week together was rapidly drawing to a close. Kevin was careful to mask the mixed emotions he was feeling: on the one hand, his heart felt like it was slowly breaking in half at the thought of never seeing Jenny again; and on the other, he felt a growing sense of excitement and anticipation as September 6 drew nearer. Jenny had popped in a CD of some mellow classics, but Kevin scarcely noticed the music he was so lost in his own thoughts.

They reached Knightsbridge in a record twenty-five minutes, and a couple of minutes later Kevin pulled up outside Jenny's flat at Cadogan Place. Kevin got out Jenny's bags while she searched for her keys. When they got to the flat, Kevin took her bags upstairs to the bedroom while Jenny went into the kitchen. Jenny had done some shopping in Washington and hadn't been able to fit everything in her suitcase, which Kevin put down by the closet. The shopping bags he put on the chaise lounge by the big window. He stood there for a couple of minutes just looking slowly around the room, taking in every detail, almost sensing and smelling Jenny's presence in everything he laid eyes on and remembering the countless happy and fun times he had spent with Jenny in this room … and in this bed.

"A penny for your thoughts, darling!"

Kevin was startled, as he hadn't heard Jenny come up the stairs or enter the room. She came over to him, and Kevin took her in his arms and hugged her tightly.

"I was just thinking how much I'm going to miss you over the next couple of weeks when I'm in Scotland and then down in Salisbury, my sweetheart."

"Your stint in Salisbury is over on Friday evening, isn't it? But then I'll still be at the lovely spa resort for pampering, which is such a thoughtful gift, darling. Let's plan to meet the instant I get back."

"That's a super idea, sweetheart. Let's plan on it," Kevin said it with more enthusiastic conviction than he felt, knowing that he might be dead by then. And of course, if he lived, he might be anywhere but certainly not in London, which might no longer exist.

"How about I give Sheila a call right now and say there were long delays at the airport, and I have to make a stop on the way home for business? Then we could spend some time together now. It's just gone eleven o'clock, so maybe we could have a couple of hours or so. When did you plan to go to your showroom?"

"I told Carol I would be in a little after twelve, but I'll give her a quick call and tell her it won't be till about one thirty."

Kevin made his call to Sheila first and said he would be home around two. Sheila said she would have some lunch ready for him. It sounded to Kevin as if he had woken Sheila up, and he wondered why she would be still in bed. He speculated that perhaps she had been hitting the bottle again, but he hoped not. He was relieved to hear Max barking in the background. Jenny then gave Carol a quick call, and as she hung up, Kevin came up behind her and started kissing the back of her neck as he brought his hands around her and began gently rubbing her breasts, feeling her nipples harden and stretch the fabric of her tight blouse. They tumbled onto the bed.

It was already quarter to one, and Kevin lay there caressing Jenny's face and holding her close as if he never wanted to let her go. He looked into her deep blue sparkling eyes, seeing nothing but love and happiness. He felt miserable inside. This was his very last time with her, and Kevin couldn't put off the inevitable any longer. It was time to get going before he broke down and told Jenny everything. Jenny was the first to speak.

"Mac darling, you're wonderful! You always make me feel so contented and relaxed that I don't want to move, but I must, and so should you. I'll just take a very quick shower to freshen up before I go down to my office. Don't look so glum! We'll be together again soon!"

Jenny sounded so cheerful as she skipped off to the bathroom and luckily didn't look back to see the expression on Kevin's face. Kevin had a quick shower right after her and put on the shirt and suit he had left there the previous Friday. They went out to the street together, but Jenny insisted she wanted to walk to her office, as she needed the exercise, so they said their farewells on the steps. Kevin sat in his Jag and watched Jenny until she disappeared around the corner with a last wave good-bye.

Kevin felt absolutely miserable and depressed as he started up the car. He drove by sheer instinct and noticed nothing along the way until he turned into the cobblestoned street of Rudall Mews and was home.

Kevin put the car in the garage and was getting his bags out of the trunk when Sheila came out to meet him with Max prancing at her side. Sheila looked as if she had made a real effort to spruce herself up for Kevin's homecoming. She was wearing a light mauve summer dress with flowery prints, and her long auburn hair was pulled back into a loose braid. Sheila was only a couple of inches smaller than Jenny, but her appreciably plumper figure made her appear considerably shorter. Her freshly applied makeup and lipstick couldn't disguise the sallowness of her complexion, and her pale green eyes still looked a little bloodshot, but Kevin pretended not to notice. Though only forty-three, Sheila looked older, almost matronly, but remarkably had no gray hairs, and Kevin thought, *What a shame she's let herself go downhill.* He remembered how attractive she was before, with a much slimmer figure, a fresh complexion, and more spark to her personality, but the death of their son, Owen, at age three, years ago, had really taken a toll on her. Their son had run across a street and been run over by a bus. As he looked at Shelia now, he realized his love for her had long since turned to pity, and he stayed with her because she depended on him, and he hadn't the heart to abandon her, but now he finally would. Sheila came up to him and gave him a kiss on the cheek.

"Welcome home, Kevin! Max and I missed you. Did you have a good trip?"

"Yes, thanks, luv, but rather tiring, so it's good to be home." Kevin turned to the impatient Max, who was rubbing against his leg for attention.

"Well, ol' fella, how have you been? Miss me, eh?" Max needed no further encouragement as he jumped up and put his front paws in Kevin's outstretched hands and gave Kevin lots of licks and slurps all over his face. Max was clearly delighted to have his master home, and Kevin knew Sheila was glad too, as she got lonely when he was away.

The three of them went into the house, and Sheila had a nice ham salad ready for lunch. During lunch, she mentioned that Kevin had gotten a phone call about an hour earlier—no name, just a number to call back about four o'clock, which she had written down on the message pad by the kitchen phone. Kevin gave no reaction, as he knew it could only be George Wilkinson, probably wanting to confirm Monday's meeting in Scotland. Kevin gave Sheila an edited account of his trip, which always seemed to please her. After lunch, Kevin went out into the garden to relax in the sunshine and look through the week's mail, which contained nothing interesting. Max lay beside him in the shade of his chair, and Kevin was absentmindedly stroking him and thinking how remarkable it was that whenever he got back from a trip, Max stuck with him like glue and wouldn't let him out of his sight.

Kevin nodded off, as he really was tired, but woke up around three thirty and decided to go for a jog on the Heath with Max, who was beside himself with excitement when he saw Kevin changing into his jogging gear. Kevin knew that while he was away Sheila would walk Max in the morning and evening but nothing like the several-mile run he would get with Kevin—he was sure Max missed those long runs. As Kevin left the house, he stuffed the phone message in his pocket along with some loose change.

When Kevin reached the Heath, he could feel the excitement of Max straining on his leash, so they broke into a fast run up the hill to Kenwood House where Kevin knew there were several public pay phones. It was just on four o'clock, and luckily there was no one about. Kevin was a little out of breath as he lifted the first pay phone he reached. It wasn't working. The phone box had been vandalized, and Kevin swore out loud. He went to the next one and found it worked. He lined up the coins on top of the phone, and reading from the crumpled piece of paper, Kevin quickly dialed the number. It seemed to ring for ages, and Kevin glanced at his watch: three minutes past four. *Surely Wilkinson would wait a few minutes,* Kevin thought impatiently. Finally the ringing stopped, and Kevin heard the voice at the other end. Kevin spoke quickly after he inserted all the coins he was instructed to by the computerized voice. The connection was lousy. He gave Wilkinson the phone number of the booth he was in, asked him to call right back, and hung up just as the computerized voice cut in requesting more money to continue the call. Public phones irritated Kevin, as it was difficult to have a long-distance call with the constant interruptions to insert more money. Kevin waited for the phone to ring. Max was sitting patiently beside him and still panting from their hot run up the hill. The phone had barely rung when Kevin grabbed it.

"Hello, Mac! Thought you would be home this morning. No problems, I hope?"

"No, just a delay at the airport. Everything okay at your end?"

"Yes, everything is on track, and the men are ready. Just wanted to confirm our meeting on Monday morning at ten. You have the directions. It should be easy to find, as you know the area. See you then."

"Okay, George. Till Monday." Kevin hung up the phone.

Still holding the leash, Kevin walked slowly over to a park bench about fifty yards away and sat down. Max stretched out on the grass at his feet. Kevin gazed out over London. The day had really cleared up after the morning thunderstorm, and the late-afternoon sky was a hazy blue. He did feel tired after his uphill run and a little unfit after his week in the States, where he hadn't found time for his daily jog. The anxiety he felt before talking to George had disappeared. He was relieved everything was on track, and his anticipation was growing. Just ten days to go!

Kevin didn't sit for too long. He decided to do about another four miles before going home. This time he and Max jogged at a comfortable pace. The breeze coming up felt good, and there was no sense of urgency, nothing to rush home for.

After an early dinner, Kevin went into his small den, having decided to write up his final report for Sir Ian and get a few personal things taken care of for his trip to Scotland. Sheila went on up to the bedroom to watch television, like always. It took him about two hours to finalize his report. Kevin then began to review the mental checklist of his personal affairs, which he had spent the summer putting in order. He had left a simple will with his London firm of solicitors, Hardy & Jones, naming his best friend, Peter Royston, as his executor and the bulk of his British assets left to Sheila, which would take care of her for the rest of her life. Over the last several months, he had converted all his inheritance from Granduncle Bertie to cash by a series of instructions to Mike Driscoll in New York and had transferred the whole proceeds into a numbered Swiss bank account, which, if he lived, he could access from anywhere in the world. He had left a will with Mike Driscoll covering this money with Jenny, his main beneficiary, and some minor bequests to his cousins Jim and Mary in Dublin and to Peter Royston's children, Angela and Ross. This will was placed in a safety deposit box in a New York bank and the key given to Mike Driscoll, with strict instructions for it to be kept in a safe place in his home. Kevin was satisfied with these arrangements.

Next, Kevin went through his wallet to clear out unnecessary clutter. He went through an old family photo album and carefully selected three photos of his parents, one of which included Granduncle Bertie, which Kevin remembered being taken on one of their visits to the States when he was a teenager. He also took out a couple of childhood photos of himself. Everything in the desk was in order, with absolutely nothing to hint at his plans. There was no need to leave any kind of message for Sheila, as Kevin was confident that Peter would take care of everything as his executor.

As he glanced around his den, Kevin found it hard to believe that these were the last couple of days he would ever spend in this house. He couldn't think of anything he'd overlooked; everything seemed in order on the home front.

Kevin went up to bed and found Sheila asleep with the television still on. He wasn't at all surprised, but as he turned it off, he wondered who would do it when he was gone for good. Max was already stretched out comfortably on his bed. Kevin opened the window wide to let the night breeze blow through, and he put out the lights. As he slipped into his bed, Max sort of half woke up and rolled over a bit to give Kevin more room, looking bleary-eyed at his master. Kevin figured Max must be as tired as he was; neither of them had so much exercise and fresh air for a week.

It was about a year after Owen was killed that Sheila suggested they replace their double bed with two singles so that she wouldn't keep him awake when she couldn't sleep. Kevin knew it had been more than that, but given her state of mind then, he had agreed without argument. The separate beds had stayed until it didn't matter to Kevin anymore and were now symbolic of their relationship. It was barely eleven thirty, and Kevin was very tired, but his orderly mind was at rest. All his plans were in place, and all he had to do was execute them. He drifted off to sleep quickly and had his best night's sleep in months.

Next morning, even though it was Saturday, Kevin and Max were up at the crack of dawn, just as if Kevin had never been away. They followed their usual morning routine, and Kevin was glad to get his five-mile jog in early, as he could tell the weather was getting muggy again. After breakfast, Kevin spent the morning getting his fishing gear ready for Scotland. He planned to do a little lake trout fishing and fish the local rivers for salmon and pike. He sat at the kitchen table and meticulously sorted out the best fishing flies for both trout and salmon. He mounted them on his fishing hat carefully, putting the flies for the trout on the left side of the hat and the ones for salmon on the right. Then he polished the bright, shiny metal baits for the pike and organized them neatly in his tackle box. Lastly, he checked out his fishing rods and reels and packed each of them carefully in their own cases. When he was done, he loaded all his fishing paraphernalia into the trunk of the car. It was at this point that Max figured out what was going on. Kevin believed Max was a very smart dog who knew that fishing rods in the trunk of the car meant that he and his master were going on a fishing trip. This year was no exception, and early on, Kevin had explained this to Wilkinson, as every year Max went to Scotland with him and often on to Salisbury. To do otherwise would arouse suspicion.

Around lunchtime, Sir Ian called Kevin for a short chat from his country residence in Kent. Kevin wasn't perturbed, as Sir Ian often did that when Kevin got back from a trip to the States. After he hung up, Kevin remembered to call Peter. He got through to Lois, as Peter was out. She said Peter had made reservations for the four of them for eight that night at the new Italian restaurant, La Triestina, in Golders Green. It was agreed that Peter and Lois would pick up Kevin and Sheila around seven thirty, as they knew Kevin would have his car all loaded up for Scotland by then. Kevin was really looking forward to this last evening out with his dearest friends but also felt a little sad.

Sheila had taken two of his regular uniforms to the cleaners and picked them up that morning. She spent the afternoon helping Kevin get packed. The afternoon flew by. Kevin's last preparation for the trip was to gather what Max would need for the next two weeks—a large bag of his favorite kibble, his special treats, and water dishes, including Max's own traveling water flask, which held a half gallon of water and ice and had a wide screw-on lid that doubled as a drinking dish whenever they would stop at the side of the road for an exercise break. Kevin was pleased when everything was in the car and ready for an early morning start the next day. Of course, by that time there was no mistaking Max's mounting excitement. Kevin thought it was funny the way Max would race around the house and in and out of the backyard like a little kid having a mad half hour. Sheila didn't see the funny side and would look disapprovingly at the dirt Max's paws might bring into the house.

Right on the dot of seven thirty, Lois and Peter arrived, and Kevin invited them in for a quick drink, as the restaurant was only about ten minutes away and Sheila wasn't quite ready. By then, Max had calmed down and was his usual social self to Lois and Peter. Kevin and Peter were both wearing navy blazers and casual pants with open-neck shirts. The restaurant was very informal and didn't require collar and tie—just the sort of place Kevin liked best. Kevin thought Lois looked radiant and rather sexy in a pale peach summer dress with ruffled sleeves and high neckline.

La Triestina had earned quite a reputation locally for its fine northern Italian cuisine. All four of them thoroughly enjoyed their dinner and agreed the reputation was well deserved. After dinner, they decided to adjourn to their favorite pub, the Spaniards, on top of Hampstead Heath.

It was a lovely evening all-around, and everyone seemed to be in top form, particularly Kevin, who was determined that this last evening with his dearest friends would be nothing short of marvelous. It was. Kevin had to raise his voice frequently over the noise of the busy pub to be heard.

"So, Pete, did I hear you right? You and Lois are driving the kids back to boarding school in Devon next Saturday?"

"That's right, and on Sunday we'll be flying out from Gatwick to our villa in Portugal for two weeks as usual, and as always, you and Sheila are welcome to join us."

Sheila said with a slight slur, "That's always lovely, you two. You know we have a grand ol' time when we join you there, but Kevin has military duty that first week down in Salisbury or somewhere like that—boys' war games or some such nonsense." Sheila burped and added, "Oops, I'm not supposed to mention that!"

"It's okay, luv. Lois and Pete would never breathe a word."

Lois nodded agreement with a twinkle in her eyes but said, "Maybe you could both fly down and join us for the second week?"

"No can do this year, as I have other Ministry business on my schedule that week also. Maybe next year again for sure," Kevin said. "Time to hit the road?"

Pete drained down his drink and stood up. "Yep, time to head home!"

It was around midnight when Lois and Peter dropped Sheila and Kevin at home, and as it was a dark, moonless night, Kevin figured nobody could see the sadness on his face as he said his farewells. As he gave Lois a friendly good-night kiss, Kevin lingered a moment too long, but nobody seemed to notice, except maybe Lois, but she said nothing. Kevin knew each of them had quite a bit to drink, and while none of them were drunk, they were certainly feeling no pain.

As their dear friends sped away, Kevin locked up as usual and followed Sheila up the stairs and into their bedroom.

"Why don't I sleep with you tonight, my luv, as it is my last night at home for a couple of weeks or so and I have to be up super early in the morning?"

"That would be lovely, Kev, but I'm not up to much anymore, as you know, and tonight I am really tired. All the wine I suppose." She then collapsed on the bed and started snoring.

Gently Kevin undressed her down to her underwear and with some difficulty managed to get her under the covers.

As Kevin got into bed beside her, she snuggled up to him, murmuring sleepily, "You feel so nice." Then she drifted off, asleep again.

That night Kevin slept with Sheila and actually felt a certain closeness to her. Maybe it was the drink, or maybe he just felt sorry for the woman in his arms who had never really recovered from the loss of their son. Either way, Kevin was glad that he was spending his last night in the house this way.

On Sunday morning, Kevin woke up to the sound of the alarm clock at five, an hour earlier than he and Max would normally wake up, but he had a long drive ahead of him and wanted to be on the road no later than six. Max looked a little bewildered as Kevin shook him awake, but he soon caught on and dutifully followed Kevin downstairs. By ten to six, Kevin was ready to leave and quietly went up to say good-bye to the still-sleeping Sheila, who barely opened her eyes as Kevin leaned down to give her a kiss on the cheek. He paused at the bedroom door on the way out and stole a last glance at Sheila's peaceful, sleeping face. That was one of the memories of her that he would carry with him, and he consoled himself that no matter what happened to him, Sheila would continue to live with her tortured memories in her own world … or mercifully would die instantly in the nuclear annihilation of London.

Kevin didn't waste any more time in getting on the road. He draped Max's car rug over the front passenger seat of the Jag, knowing Max preferred to sit up front with him rather than on the roomier backseat. Kevin reversed out of the garage, closed the door after him, and drove out of Rudall Mews for the last time. It was still dark out, and the streets were deserted at that ungodly hour on a Sunday morning as he drove through North London to the M1 motorway.

By the time Kevin was on the M1, it was about quarter past six, and the dawn was slowly streaking in from the east, the sun rising behind scattered clouds. The average driving time to Glasgow was about nine hours in normal weekday traffic, but Kevin knew he would do it in eight hours or less on a Sunday and so decided to allow himself a half hour for breakfast and an hour or so for lunch along the way. Kevin figured that would put him in the vicinity of Glasgow around three thirty that afternoon and would leave just ninety miles to Oban, where he would be staying. That last stretch would probably take two to two and a half hours, as the motorway ended at Glasgow, and then he would be traveling on secondary roads, which would become increasingly mountainous. Kevin set his goal to reach Oban no later than six thirty that evening, around dusk.

CHAPTER 5

KEVIN CRESTED THE LAST MOUNTAIN and began the long, winding descent to the small town of Oban, nestled tightly along the rugged shoreline of the Firth of Lorne, which separated Oban from the island of Mull. Beyond the island of Mull and a scattering of smaller islands farther out lay the gray vastness of the North Atlantic. On a clear day, Kevin loved this view, but on this late August Sunday evening, in the midst of a thunderstorm and driving rain, all he could think of was getting down to the town as quickly as possible. His beloved Max lay cowering on the seat beside him, wrapped around himself in a tight ball. *Poor Max*, Kevin thought; the only things in the whole world that he seemed to fear were thunder and lightning. In the car, there was nowhere for him to hide. Kevin concentrated on safely negotiating the twisting road. Visibility was down to zero as the rain came down in solid sheets, and every sharp bend tested all Kevin's driving skills to keep the car on the road. The gathering dusk and black clouds made it seem like nighttime, except for the occasional flashes of lightning, which lit up the sky like fireworks and made Max cringe even more. Finally, the road leveled off and got straighter; Kevin knew he must be close to the town. After a few minutes, Kevin noticed more and more houses alongside the road and then realized he was on the east end of the main street, which ran all the way through the town, down to the oceanfront.

When Kevin reached the oceanfront, he turned right along the esplanade and drove about a quarter of a mile until he came to the sign that said "Thistle House Bed-and-Breakfast." Kevin could hardly read the sign with the driving rain beating against it, but by instinct, he knew he had reached his destination, having come here for eight years out of the last ten. Thistle House had only a small front yard and no driveway, so Kevin parked on the street outside the front gate. As Kevin turned off the engine of the Jag, a light came on over the front doorway, and the familiar figure of Mrs. Dorrie MacPhee opened the door. Kevin got his mackintosh off the backseat and, slipping it on, buttoned it all the way up to his neck. He quickly got out of the car and went around to the passenger door to get Max. He decided the easiest thing to do would be to bundle the trembling Max up in the car rug and dash with him into the house. Dorrie MacPhee held the door open.

"Welcome, Major! What an awful evening for your arrival. Anyway, it's grand to see you again. Well, whatever have you there? My, my, why if it isn't Max, all wrapped up like an overgrown baby!"

"Thank you, Dorrie. It's great to be back again. I just wish the storm had held off for another half an hour; we would have made it here nice and dry. I think you know how Max is about thunderstorms, and he's certainly no featherweight to carry at seventy pounds."

Kevin quickly unwrapped Max and let him down in the hallway, and Max looked at him with an expression as if to say that he was highly indignant to be treated like a baby, particularly in front of Mrs. MacPhee. Max went over and licked Mrs. MacPhee's hand. Kevin thought to himself that Max was as wily as a fox, because he knew that every year when they stayed at Thistle House, Mrs. MacPhee was the person who fed him and took care of him, and once he recognized where he was, he was quick to play up to the lady of the house. Mrs. MacPhee, the owner and landlady of Thistle House, was a small, wiry woman in her early sixties, with steely gray hair pulled back in a tight bun. She wore horn-rimmed glasses that emphasized the severity of her gaunt face. She had a sharp tongue on occasion, and over the years Kevin had witnessed its impact on some of the local girls whom she employed to help in the dining room and to clean the bedrooms, if they had the misfortune to do anything that displeased her. Kevin knew that life had been hard on Dorrie MacPhee, having been widowed about twenty years earlier when her husband lost his life in a boating accident out on the nearby Atlantic. She had successfully finished the raising of two children who, when they graduated from the university, to her dismay, moved south of the border, and she didn't see them very often. Thistle House was one of twenty-odd Victorian-style terraced houses that ran along the esplanade overlooking the ocean. When her husband died, Dorrie MacPhee had turned it into a bed-and-breakfast to help make ends meet. She was so successful at it that over the years she managed to buy the adjoining two houses and could now accommodate over thirty people a night in the twenty bedrooms she had available. She was usually pretty full throughout the season, as Oban was the first major stopping point for the Scottish Highlands and islands. In the Highlands, spring arrived late, and fall came early, so the season was short, running from May through September. Kevin knew that Dorrie MacPhee must make a good living out of her bed-and-breakfast business, but she was a thrifty woman, and to look at her, you would never suspect that she had money, as she always seemed to wear the same few skirts and sweaters. Thistle House was primarily a bed-and-breakfast; however, with advance notice, one could get dinner in the evenings between six thirty and seven thirty. But, unlike a regular hotel, there was no bar on the premises. Despite her tough exterior and unbending manner, Dorrie had quite a soft spot for Kevin and Max, and over the years, he had grown quite fond of this lonely woman. At times, Kevin felt that Dorrie treated him almost like a long-lost son.

"You have your usual room, Major—number seven with the bay window overlooking the ocean. I think you shouldn't fetch your bags until the storm passes. So why don't you go upstairs to freshen up a little bit, and I'll have some hot dinner for you in about fifteen minutes. I'll take Max into the kitchen and rustle up something for him."

"That'll be perfect, Dorrie. I'll be down in ten minutes."

Kevin went upstairs to his room. Thistle House, like most bed-and-breakfasts, did have hot and cold running water in the room but no bathroom. Guests from four or five bedrooms had to share the one bathroom down the hallway, but Kevin never minded this minor inconvenience. What Kevin loved most of all about Thistle House was the view from his bedroom window. The wide, curving window commanded a panoramic view of the Firth, the island of Mull, and the small islands beyond, to the wide-open North Atlantic. Over the years, Kevin had frequently enjoyed sitting by the window and watching magnificent suns slip into the ocean behind the islands. Kevin stood by the window for a few minutes, reminiscing. The storm was heading out over the ocean as the thunder grew fainter and the lightning less frequent.

Down in the dining room, Kevin enjoyed a hearty meal of Scottish stew and lots of fresh, home-baked bread. He ate alone, although there were a few people scattered around at other tables. But Max was not allowed in the dining room. After dinner, the rain had settled down to just a light drizzle, and Kevin brought everything in from the car and up to the room. He then decided to take Max and go for a long walk along the esplanade toward the point on the north side of town.

Kevin and Max walked for a good hour and a half and, despite the lingering rain, thoroughly enjoyed themselves. For both of them, it was an opportunity to become familiar again with the sights and sounds of Oban. Back in the B&B, Kevin gave the wet Max a good rubdown with a towel, which he loved. And although as a general rule Dorrie MacPhee didn't allow pets in the bedrooms, she made an exception for Max and the major. Kevin turned in early, as he was tired after the long drive and wanted a clear head for the next day.

The next morning, Kevin and Max were up at the crack of dawn and went out jogging for an hour, just like at home. After a hearty breakfast, Kevin put his fishing gear in the car and, leaving Max in the care of Mrs. MacPhee, set off toward Glencoe. All traces of the previous evening's storm were gone, and although somewhat cooler, the skies were clear, and it looked like it would be a beautiful day. Kevin felt refreshed and clearheaded, and his mind focused on only one thing: what lay ahead on the following Monday.

The road to Glencoe was narrow and weaved around every inlet of the jagged shoreline, but Kevin had allowed himself plenty of time for the thirty-odd-mile drive, and so he relaxed and enjoyed the spectacular scenery along the way. Kevin reached the village of Glencoe around a quarter to ten, and with the clear directions he had from George Wilkinson, he easily found the Lismore House estate a couple of miles west of the village on the southern shore of Loch Leven. Kevin came to a stop at the closed main gates of Lismore House. The massive wrought-iron gates were attached on each side to stone turrets that stood like silent sentries guarding the entrance. Kevin got out of the car and went over to the intercom built discreetly into the side of the right-hand turret. When he announced who he was, the gates were opened electrically from the house. As Kevin passed through the gateway, the gates automatically closed behind him, and it was almost another two miles before he came to the actual house. Lismore House was like a castle, with turrets at each of the four corners of the mansion. And it had a long and colorful history. At various times it had been owned by the Clan MacDonald, then by the Campbell Clan, and again in the hands of the MacDonalds. The current owner of Lismore House was a wealthy London businessman who, when he wasn't using the estate for himself, would rent it out in August and September for the grouse shooting season. George Wilkinson had rented the estate on that pretext for the months of August and September, which provided excellent cover for his real purposes. The sporting rich, who generally rented Lismore House, would normally bring their own servants. George had no need for any servants, and he had picked Lismore House for that very reason and for its remote location.

The estate of Lismore House embraced most of Glencoe, also known as the Glen of Weeping. The glen was frequently shrouded in mist like a veil of melancholy, for though it was a beautiful spot, it had a murderous history. It was in this very glen that King William III, acting on a treacherous charge that the MacDonalds had not sworn allegiance to him, ordered his troops, who happened to be mostly Campbells, to act. The Campbells first accepted the hospitality of the MacDonalds and then slaughtered thirty-eight MacDonald men, women, and children. Legend had it that the order for the massacre was written on a nine of diamonds, which, as most card players know, earned the nickname of "the curse of Scotland." For Kevin, the setting and atmosphere of this remote glen conjured up a poignant reminder of the days when clans ruled the Highlands.

As Kevin finally pulled up outside the large double doors of the house, George Wilkinson came down the steps to meet him. The first thing Kevin noticed was that George had shaved off his mustache; otherwise, George looked just the same as when Kevin had last seen him. Kevin got out of the car, and the two men shook hands firmly.

"Right on the dot, Mac. You found your way here easily then?"

"No trouble at all, George. Your directions were crystal clear—thanks. This is quite a place you found here. Of course, over the years I've heard quite a lot of stories about Lismore House, but I have never been beyond the front gates before."

"Yes, it's rather an interesting place. The house itself is a lot larger than we needed, but the main reason I rented the place was for the remoteness of the grounds and the complete privacy it afforded us. Besides, it is rather deserted hereabouts."

"Well, I think you picked a perfect location. It is convenient to where I have always stayed over the years, and nobody could ever possibly suspect what is going on behind these gates. And the grouse-shooting season is perfect cover for any gunfire. In any case, I knew I could leave all the details safely in your hands."

"I'm glad you're pleased, Mac, but let's go on into the house, and we can get down to business in comfort."

The two men went into the house. The entry hall was vast, as was typical of these old mansions. The centerpiece was a broad, sweeping stairway to the second level, with beautiful hand carving on the wooden rails. There were several doorways on each side of the entry hall, and George Wilkinson led the way to the last door on the left. Kevin followed him into a large library that George had clearly turned into his main operations room. A library was a standard feature in all the older mansions in the country, and this one was typical. Three of the four walls were lined with handsome leather-bound books that looked dusty and undisturbed for years. Along one wall, there were two standing easels with flip charts, which George had obviously been using to lay out parts of the plan. In front of the window at the far side of the room, there was an antique desk that George was using as his work area. George was a neat man, and careful, and the desktop was clear except for a tidy stack of folders on one side. George sat down in the high-back chair behind the desk and offered Kevin a comfortable armchair alongside.

"We won't be disturbed here; the men are down at the other end of the glen, training. Before we get started, Mac, would you like a cup of tea or coffee or something?"

"A cup of tea would be good, thank you."

"Okay, I'll go take care of that. But while I'm gone, why don't you get started by reading up on the backgrounds of the men I have selected as our team. Here is a folder with a profile sheet on each of the five."

George handed Kevin the folder and left the room. Kevin sat there for a moment, thinking. He had certainly made a wise choice in selecting George Wilkinson; he was always efficient and businesslike. From where he was sitting, Kevin could just catch a faint glimmer of the shimmering surface of Loch Leven in the distance. The strong morning sunlight was shining in through the east-facing leaded panes of the library windows and gave a dappled effect to everything in the room. Kevin opened the folder and settled down to read. The profile sheets were handwritten in a neat, clear style by George Wilkinson himself. The first profile sheet was headed up:

Ned O'Sullivan

Ned is in his early forties, about 5'8" with a stocky build. He has black hair, thinning on top, and a well-tanned complexion with an old scar on his left cheek. He is a man of few words but bright enough. He is a first-class mechanic and driver and can fix absolutely anything with a motor. He was born and raised in the south of Ireland, in Kinsale, County Cork. He is self-educated to a degree, having finished formal education at the age of fifteen. He served ten years in the Irish Army, in the 1960s, rising to the rank of sergeant. While serving in the Irish Army, Ned got his first taste of overseas action and was part of the Irish peacekeeping forces that served in both the Belgian Congo and Cyprus troubles, when troops from the Irish Army served under the United Nations banner. I first got to know Ned in Cyprus, and when, after ten years with the Irish Army, he quit, he got in touch with me to see if there would be opportunities for him as a mercenary in foreign parts. Ned was something of an adventurer, and a restless person who wanted to see more action overseas and get paid well for it. I first employed him as a mercenary in Africa in the 1970s, where Ned proved to be loyal, capable, and very useful. Not only was he a first-class mechanic, he also turned out to be able to procure anything we might need that was difficult to obtain, and he could even cook very decently.

Our plan calls for the use of several different vehicles that must be absolutely reliable, due to our timing constraints. It's my opinion that Ned will ensure this part of our plan. I have also made him my second in command, and under my direction, he is training the other four men to play their roles as British soldiers flawlessly. He is the only one of the five whom I know firsthand and can trust implicitly.

On the personal level, he has never married but wanted to do one last major job to have enough money to fulfill his lifelong dream of finally retiring to his native Kinsale and buying a house by the sea. He is certainly not a ladies' man, but I know he harbors a desire to marry a lady who he always refers to as "the widow Flanagan," whom he has known since his childhood. I am paying Ned more than I am paying any of the other men; Ned knows this, and it buys his absolute loyalty.

Kevin liked what he read, and it struck him that, in ways, this Ned O'Sullivan was not unlike George Wilkinson himself. Clearly, Ned was not endowed with George's training and leadership abilities, but there were certain similarities, and Kevin's impression was that Ned was a tough, resourceful loner. A good choice, Kevin thought, and he flipped over to the next sheet.

Pat Feeney

Pat is a Dubliner in his early thirties who was, until recently, working in Leeds in the building trades, in order to support his wife and four children who live in public housing in Cabra West, in Dublin. He is 5'10", slight build, with dark brown hair and light brown eyes and a sallow complexion. He is both an explosives expert and a small weapons specialist. I realize we do not need his explosives expertise, but his other attributes make him suitable for our plan.

I first came across him while I was doing service in Northern Ireland. At that time, Pat was in his early twenties, having joined the IRA in his teens; he had proved himself to be a cold-blooded and ruthless killer. After one particular bombing incident, he got caught in a sweep by British troops and was interned for three years at the Maze prison camp, without trial, and subject to constant questioning. In all that time, Pat never broke or pointed the finger at anyone, despite the constant interrogations. However, when he was finally released, he was a bitter man who felt abandoned by his former IRA comrades and deeply resentful of the treatment he had received in the Maze. Totally disillusioned, Pat moved to England and took any jobs, wherever he could find them, to support his family back in Dublin, whom I learned he only visited on rare occasions. Pat became an atheist and craved obscurity.

I managed to track him down and sign him up for this operation. His motivation is mostly money, but I did detect that he saw the operation as a way of obtaining revenge on the IRA, with whom he was so totally disillusioned. He wants the money for two purposes: one, to leave a good sum with his wife in Dublin and finalize his obligations to her; the balance he intends to use to buy himself a new identity and slip in the back door to the United States and simply disappear.

As Kevin finished reading about Pat Feeney, he felt a little disturbed. He wasn't sure that it was such a good idea to have anyone on this operation who had any connections with the IRA whatsoever, no matter how far back they had been. Kevin made a mental note that he wanted to talk further with George about this one. He decided to read on.

Tom Fallon

Tom is in his late twenties and comes from Belfast. He is six feet tall, well built, with unruly fair hair and blue-gray eyes, and would be regarded by many as a handsome young man. Tom is a communications and computer expert and has considerable experience in jamming radio signals and an uncanny ability to distort the sources of both radio signals and electronic impulses, such as computer transmissions. He worked for a small computer-programming firm in Belfast and, as a Catholic, was a natural sympathizer with the IRA. On occasion, he helped them with communication and computer problems. Though never an active IRA member, his close association with them made things hot for him in Belfast, and he decided to move to Liverpool.

He has lived in Liverpool for the last several years and has worked quietly for a major electronics company there. He has no current record and apparently has had no links with the IRA since leaving Belfast. Tom is not married and has a reputation as somewhat of a womanizer. It is believed that he has no strong attachments to anyone. I learned about him through some contacts, who also indicated that Tom had a big ambition to found his own software company but needed capital to do it. I later confirmed his need for money, and he agreed to be a part of this operation.

Kevin thought to himself, *This Tom Fallon might be bloody useful in handling the computers on the missiles.* He might also be helpful with some ideas Kevin had about distorting sources. Kevin's only real concern about this man was the fact that he was a womanizer, and he made a mental note to discuss that aspect later with George. Kevin turned to the next sheet to see who George had selected to be the fourth member of his team.

Sean Morrissey

Sean is twenty-seven years old and recently got an honorable discharge from the Irish Army after seven years of service. He is 5'10" with a solid build, light brown hair, hazel eyes, a ruddy complexion, and a rather somber expression. Sean comes from Banagher in County Offaly, right in the middle of Ireland, where his widowed mother has a small farm. Sean is unmarried and absolutely devoted to his mother. He desperately wants and needs a lot of money to help his mother, who recently developed a rare form of thyroid cancer that can be best treated in the Mayo Clinic in the United States. He would die for his mother, according to Ned O'Sullivan, who located him for me.

Ned had come across him some years earlier and knew him to be a well-disciplined man with a reputation as a superb marksman with either a rifle or a handgun.

Kevin liked this Sean Morrissey, on paper anyway; he appeared cleaner than the others and certainly had one of the best motives. No sign of George yet with the tea, so Kevin turned to the last sheet.

Terry O'Neill

At only twenty-five, Terry is the youngest of the team, and his main attributes are that he has a photographic memory, is extremely articulate, and has a strong Derry accent. I selected him to handle all our telephone communications with the world, after we have the missiles. He is about 5'11" with fairly reddish hair, pale blue eyes like a cat, a boyish, innocent-looking face, and a good, athletic build.

He is single, and both his parents are dead. Tom Fallon was the one who recommended Terry. He said their paths crossed several years earlier at Queens University in Belfast, and Tom liked Terry. Like many young Catholics in Derry, Terry was an IRA sympathizer, but unlike most of them, he had no desire to participate in the violence. In fact, his only desire was to have enough money to immigrate to Canada and start a new life for himself, far away from the troubles of Northern Ireland.

Kevin closed the folder and sat thinking for a few moments. George had certainly assembled a team of very different people, and Kevin hoped that by now they had been molded into a military team that would act together effectively. At that point, George came back into the room carrying a tray with a teapot, two mugs, and a small jug of milk.

"My apologies, Mac. It took a little longer than I expected."

"Don't worry, George. It gave me time to read these interesting profiles you prepared on our team. But it did raise some questions I'd like to discuss."

George put the tray on the desk and poured each of them a mug of strong, brewed tea and then added milk. Kevin took a couple of mouthfuls before he continued.

"I guess my biggest concern is with Pat Feeney and Tom Fallon, both who had strong IRA connections. Is there any likelihood that they could be spotted, particularly Pat Feeney who was an active member of the IRA and interned?"

"No chance, Mac. I've done some checking on my own, through my own channels, and there are no longer any official records on Tom Fallon. In the case of Pat Feeney, his records are in the inactive file, and I am reliably informed that the most recent file photograph of him is at least six years old, and he has changed considerably in that time. At this point, I doubt if even Pat Feeney's old comrades in the IRA would recognize him."

"Okay, that clears up that concern, but it does bring to mind something else. Mentioning photos on file, all the photos that MI5 have of you show you clean-shaven. So, I was thinking it might be a damn good idea if you grew back your mustache over this next week. If nothing else, it will make it a little more difficult for the authorities to tie in your description with their records after Salisbury. I guess the only other concern I had was the relative youthfulness and total inexperience of Terry O'Neill."

"You don't have to worry about Terry, Mac. He proved to be very tough and determined during the training period. Besides, his determination is driven by a burning desire to get out of the hellhole of Derry. I'm confident Terry is going to carry out his part of the operation exactly as instructed. Actually, the only one of the five I have some concern about is Sean Morrissey. I'm afraid that if he were to get any bad news about his mother next week, he might bolt. But I have taken the precaution that once we are in Ireland, he'll never be out of Ned's sight, so there's no possible way for him to get any news about his mother. With that risk eliminated, I believe Sean will do fine. He has the grit and experience that counts."

"It looks like you've thought of all the angles."

"That's what you're paying me for, Mac. Besides, money is a more reliable motivation than patriotism. You know my dictum: patriots blinded with zeal make mistakes; paid professionals don't, or it's their last. Over the last several weeks of training, I've carefully instilled in each and every one of them that I demand total discipline and won't tolerate any breaches. By now, each of them realizes they are in this thing 110 percent and there is no turning back. Any mistakes or last-minute second thoughts, and they know I'll shoot them without hesitation."

Kevin noticed a steely glint to George Wilkinson's eyes and the harsh note of his voice, and there was no doubt in his mind that George was perfectly capable of killing anyone who interfered with his plans. At that moment, Kevin also realized that if it ever came down to a choice between his own life and that of George Wilkinson, George wouldn't hesitate to kill him.

"Let's hope it never comes to that, George. I take it all other aspects of our operation are on track?"

"Yes, everything has been taken care of, with the exception of the Royal Welsh Guards uniforms. But tomorrow I'll be driving down myself to Edinburgh to pick them up. They're ready. However, I've made one small change, or addition if you like, to our plans after Salisbury. Just in case the Ministry or MI5 have an eye on you, and you know how your height and military bearing can make you stand out on your own, I decided to make your crossing on the ferry from Fishguard to Rosslare less conspicuous. I've made arrangements for a thirty-one-year-old woman and her ten-month-old baby to accompany you. I believe this will enable you to blend in with all the other passengers. I trust you'll agree?"

"That's a marvelous idea, George! I wouldn't have thought of that myself. You leave little or nothing to chance."

"You're right. I prefer to leave nothing to chance. I like to operate on the basis of calculated risks. Speaking of which, you should know, Mac, that as of right now only Ned knows all the details of the entire operation. And even he doesn't yet know your true identity. Just like in the army, I'm operating on the time-honored principle that you know very well of telling the men only what they need to know."

Kevin nodded. He knew only too well, as he was applying the same principle to his dealings with George Wilkinson. Kevin was feeling very pleased and confident that, barring any unforeseen events, his planned operation would indeed be carried out successfully. Whether his political objectives would be met remained in the laps of the gods.

"Well, George, when do you think I should finally meet our men?"

"I think Thursday will be good, if that's okay with you? But I want you to meet Ned today. He'll be bringing the men back to the house at noon for chow, and I've asked him to join us here."

"Good, I'm looking forward to meeting Ned, and Thursday will be fine. I'll also bring Max along with me so he can become familiar with the men and feel comfortable around them."

George then got out a couple of maps from the desk drawer. First, he spread out the map of southern England and Wales. He pointed out to Kevin the exact location of the house and barn he had rented near Salisbury Plain and showed the proposed route to Fishguard. Kevin nodded his concurrence. Next, George got out the map of Ireland, on which he highlighted the route they would follow from Rosslare to the Dingle Peninsula. George also outlined to Kevin the kinds of vehicles they planned to use to transport the missiles and the location of each transfer point. George had just put the maps away when there was a knock at the door.

"Come in!"

Ned O'Sullivan entered the library. He was wearing a black beret and an army camouflage jacket pulled tightly over his broad, stocky frame, along with a pair of regular jeans and black army boots. Ned strode up to the desk, and as he came within the bright light of the windows, Kevin noticed the pronounced scar on his left cheek and wondered how he had gotten it. He would ask George about it. Ned addressed Wilkinson but was looking intently at Kevin.

"Reporting as requested, Captain!"

"Thanks for coming in, Ned. I wanted you to meet the major."

Kevin shook hands with Ned, and the three men sat down. Kevin noticed how George didn't give Ned his last name, proving yet again that George Wilkinson was not a man who gave out unnecessary information.

"Well, Ned, I'd like you to tell the major how the men are doing."

"They're a good bunch o' lads, Major, sir, and myself and the captain here have whipped them into a crack platoon. They're certainly ready for this operation, and we're going to be damn successful too."

When Ned first spoke, Kevin thought his voice sounded just like that of Sergeant Pedley back at the Ministry, or like any other sergeant's for that matter, but after he spoke a little more and relaxed, Kevin could clearly detect the unmistakable lilt of Ned's original Cork accent. The three men spent the next half hour or so discussing key elements of the planned operation.

Ned said, "The way I see it, there are three vulnerable points in our operation—"

Before he could continue, Kevin said, "I agree, and the first and most critical is that we must execute flawlessly our plan to get the nukes to the barn."

George quickly interjected, "And the other two are getting on and off the ferry. If we carry out all three operations to perfection, and I'm 100 percent confident we will, then we're on our way."

At that point, George suggested to Ned that he rustle up a little lunch for himself and the major. While Ned went out to see about lunch, Kevin took that opportunity to ask George about Ned's scar.

"Actually, Mac, Ned didn't get that scar in battle. He got it in a pub brawl in Rhodesia." George was laughing as he told Kevin the story. Apparently Ned was pretty drunk one night when he got into a silly argument with two white Rhodesians and ended up getting a glass shoved in his face. Ned needed twenty-six stitches; it would have required some skin grafting and plastic surgery to completely remove the scar. Ned had never bothered about it and over the years had actually managed to take delight in his scar and in telling people he had gotten it in a fierce battle in Zambia.

Ned came back a short time later, bringing Kevin and George a makeshift lunch of bread, cheese, and two mugs of beer. Ned explained that he couldn't stay, as he wanted to get back to the men and continue with the afternoon's mountain climbing that he had planned.

"Where are you taking them, Ned?" George asked.

"Over to those peaks the other side of the lake." And turning to Kevin, he said, "Nice to have met you, Major. We'll see you on Thursday then?"

"It was good to meet you, Ned. I'd heard a lot about you. Yes, I'll see you on Thursday and meet all the men."

When Ned was gone, the two men chatted some more while having their lunch. When they finished eating, George suggested to Kevin that he had a good afternoon to get in some fishing, unless there was anything else he wanted to discuss with him. Kevin was satisfied that everything seemed under control and decided it would be best if he did spend the afternoon fishing. After all, he did not want to return to Thistle House empty-handed and arouse Mrs. MacPhee's suspicions. It was agreed there was no need for Kevin to come back until Thursday, unless some emergency should arise.

Kevin decided to take advantage of being on the grounds of Lismore House and planned to do some trout fishing on Loch Leven for the afternoon. He got his fishing gear out of the trunk of the car and walked around the side of the house down through the woods to Loch Leven. There were a couple of rowboats pulled up on the shore of the lake; Kevin took one and rowed himself out to the middle of the lake and started casting his flies. He spent all afternoon on the lake and never saw another soul. He felt relaxed and thoroughly enjoyed his afternoon, catching eight good-sized trout. At about five o'clock, he decided to call it quits, and when he got back to his car at the front of the house, seeing nobody about, he left.

Kevin got back to Thistle House a little after six and presented Mrs. McPhee with his catch. Mrs. McPhee was delighted and of course suggested that Kevin might like a couple of them broiled for his dinner, which he readily agreed to. Max was clearly delighted to have his master home again, and after dinner, Kevin took Max for a long walk all around the vicinity of Oban, and they ended up at the old fort overlooking the town, watching the moon rise over the mountains. It was a beautiful, starry night, with just the slight chill of early fall in the air, but it felt wonderful after the previous night's storm.

It was after nine thirty when Kevin and Max got back to Thistle House. And even though he didn't have a strenuous day, Kevin felt tired; besides, for this week he had set himself a regimen of getting to bed early each night and conserving his energy so that he would be well rested for the challenges of the following week.

The next couple of days passed quickly, and it was Wednesday night after dinner, just before he and Max went out for a walk, that Kevin got a call from London. There were no telephones in the rooms at Thistle House, and as he went downstairs to take the call in the phone box in the hall, he was thinking it must be Jenny. It was hardly likely to be Sheila, because since Sunday afternoon she had been on her retreat at the Dominican Friary in Hampstead and never called him while he was away in Scotland. Kevin closed the door of the phone box as he picked up the receiver and was delighted to find it was his adorable Jenny on the other end of the line.

"Hello? Jenny sweetheart! How terrific to hear from you! What's new?"

"Mac darling, you sound so relaxed but far away. I just wanted to call and tell you how much I love you and miss you. And I wanted to tell you I got this fabulous new assignment from an American lady, a Mrs. Lyndhurst, who has just bought a big country estate outside Norwich. Apparently, Helen Jaffe recommended me to her. You remember; you just met her last week in Washington. Anyway, she wants me to help her do over the whole interior of this big mansion. Do you mind if I reschedule my trip to the spa? I'm going to be spending all of next week up there going over all the plans with her."

"That's absolutely marvelous, sweetheart! I'm so terribly thrilled for you. I'm sure you'll enjoy the challenge immensely, and of course, you can reschedule the trip to the spa."

Kevin felt even happier and more delighted than he could ever pretend to Jenny. He felt totally relieved that Jenny would be out of London all of next week. He felt it was a good luck omen that everything was going to go right the following week.

"I'll be going up there on Monday morning and coming back to London on Friday afternoon. So, are our plans still on for Friday night?"

"You bet, sweetheart. I've squared everything away with Sheila, and she isn't expecting me home until early on that Saturday afternoon."

Kevin felt awful having to lie to his beloved Jenny, but at the same time, this was nothing compared to how he felt before he knew Jenny would be out of London all of next week. His relief at that fact far outweighed anything else.

"That's great, Mac! I'm looking forward to it already. Anyway, how's the fishing up there?"

"The fishing's been good; the first couple of days I just did some trout fishing in nearby lakes. But today I went salmon fishing and had a good catch. In fact, I sent one down to you tonight on the overnight train, along with one to the Roystons and one to Margaret at the office. I know how much you like fresh Scotch salmon. I do wish you were here with me, sweetheart; it would make this place absolutely perfect."

"I wish I were there too, Mac, but at least you have Max."

"Well, I guess Max is some consolation. Actually, he's pacing up and down the hallway right now, expecting to be taken for a walk. I've taken him out with me fishing the past couple of days, and he is so funny the way he'll sit and watch as I play the fish into the boat. It's almost like he's mesmerized by them, but as you know, he hates to eat fish."

"Well, Mac, I'd better say good-bye. Just wanted to let you know I miss you and love you, and to tell you my news. You'd better go and take Max for his walk."

"Yes, I had better go before Max wears out Mrs. McPhee's hallway carpet!"

"Bye, Mac darling." And Jenny was gone.

Kevin hung up the phone and opened the door to the phone box, to be greeted by the impatient Max. Kevin bent down to pick up Max's leash, which was trailing on the floor, and Max gave him a nice friendly lick on the face. That night, as Kevin walked with Max, he felt almost elated at Jenny's news. For now, all those nearest and dearest to him, with the exception of Sheila, would be out of London the following week. Part of him felt sorry that Sheila would be there, but another part of him knew that if the end were to come for Sheila, it would be fast and merciful, and after her retreat this week, he knew she would be close to her God and probably would be better off in the next life than in this one. That night, as Kevin drifted off to sleep, he felt a renewed sense of purpose. For the first time since he began planning this operation, he could finally focus on what lay ahead with a clear mind and without feeling any guilt.

The next morning, Thursday, September 2, Kevin left Oban before dawn, taking Max in the car with him. When he had arrived in Oban the previous Sunday evening, he had deliberately left the suitcase with his uniforms in the trunk of his car. He wanted to reach Lismore House by seven thirty so that he could change into his uniform there and conduct the first review of his men. It was a foggy morning, and the going was slow along the winding coast road to Glencoe. Kevin finally reached the gates of Lismore House at twenty minutes to eight. Wilkinson himself answered the intercom, and the gates were opened for Kevin immediately. Five minutes later, he was at the house and hurriedly changing into his uniform. Wilkinson was already wearing a captain's uniform with the markings of the Royal Welsh Guards when he arrived. George explained to Kevin that the plans didn't call for Ned O'Sullivan to wear a uniform, as he would not be coming into contact with the British Army.

Kevin accompanied George to a courtyard at the back of the house. There, Ned, wearing the same outfit that Kevin had seen him in on Monday, had assembled the four men dressed in uniforms of the Royal Welsh Guards. Having studied their profiles, Kevin could easily identify each of the four men. Pat Feeney was wearing a corporal's uniform, as he could muster the best British accent. The other three had such distinctive Irish accents that they would have been too difficult to disguise, and dressed in the ordinary uniforms of regular soldiers, there would be little reason for them to speak in the presence of anyone other than their own group. Kevin was introduced to the men by Ned simply as "the major"—again, no last name. Kevin realized that the red flashings on his uniform would clearly signify his standing as a senior staff officer of the British Army. On a nod from George, Ned then put the men through their paces so that Kevin could see that they would easily pass muster as British soldiers. George had thought of every detail, down to regulation haircuts for the men. After half an hour, Ned dismissed the men and adjourned to the library with George and Kevin. In the library, the three men reviewed some last details of the operation until Kevin pronounced himself fully satisfied with the plan. At that point, Ned left the two men alone after saying to Kevin that he would see him on Monday night.

George told Kevin that on Saturday he and the five men would be driving down to Sherborne Farm, which he had rented in Devizes, at the north end of the Salisbury Plain, near where the biannual military maneuvers would be held. They would leave very early in the morning and should get there by nightfall. George explained to Kevin that they planned to spend Sunday getting everything ready for the start of the operation on Monday evening, and on Monday they would rest up and lay low. Kevin said he would drive down and join them at the house on Sunday night, and on Monday afternoon, he would check in with the barracks in Warminster, where he was expected.

Kevin changed out of his uniform and then went in search of Max, whom he had left with the men. When Kevin eventually located them at the back of the house, he found that his dog was reluctant to leave; he was so enjoying all the attention. Kevin took his leave of everybody, and putting Max on the leash, escorted him around at the front of the house to the car. As Kevin drove away from Lismore House, he looked back ruefully, thinking that this was yet another place he would never see again.

Kevin spent the rest of that Thursday fishing at one of his favorite spots up at Loch Eli, near Fort William. Friday he spent salmon fishing on the Orchy River. On Saturday, Kevin chartered a boat to do some deep-sea fishing off the island of Iona, which was just west of the island of Mull. Kevin had a marvelous day and caught several large bass. That evening as he headed back to Oban and had reeled in his fishing lines for the last time, Kevin stood quietly on the deck watching a magnificent sunset on the Atlantic. He felt sad at all he was going to be leaving behind.

Sunday morning, September 5, Kevin was up when it was still dark outside. He had packed up the car the night before so that he could leave immediately after breakfast. Mrs. McPhee was up, wearing just an old woolen robe, and she prepared a big breakfast of bacon, eggs, and sausages for Kevin. She even cooked a couple of extra sausages to chop up and put in Max's kibble as a treat. After breakfast, Kevin settled his bill for the week with Dorrie and included a very generous tip as always but particularly because Dorrie took such good care of Max. Dorrie McPhee certainly appeared to be sorry to see them leaving as she went to the front door to see them off. Kevin gave the older woman a friendly hug good-bye, and not to be outdone, Max gave her hand a good licking in farewell.

Following directions from George Wilkinson, Kevin left the M-4 near Chippenham. It was slow-going on the country roads, but Devizes lay only ten miles south of Chippenham, and Kevin reached the small town at about a quarter to five. Kevin easily found the main Trowbridge Road and about a mile out of the town found the turnoff to Sherborne Farm. George had picked Sherborne Farm for its quiet location on the northern end of the Salisbury Plain and even more for the fact that it had a large empty barn. In fact, Sherborne Farm was a misnomer, as apparently all the farmland had been long since sold off, and all that remained was an old country house and a big barn surrounded by an acre of gardens. The current owners were overseas for six months and had decided to rent out the property on a short-term basis. Kevin turned into the broken gateway of Sherborne Farm and up a short driveway to an old rambling Tudor-style farmhouse. He thought it was certainly different from Lismore House in Scotland, but then, what did it matter—they only needed it for a couple of days.

As Kevin came to a stop in front of the house, George Wilkinson came out of the front door, which was almost hidden by overgrown ivy, to meet him. When Kevin let Max out of the car, Max took off for the trees at the side of the house, sniffing and exploring. Kevin and George greeted each other warmly and with a firm handshake. Over the last week, Kevin felt that a certain bond had developed between himself and

Wilkinson—one that went a little beyond the ties of professionalism and money.

"Welcome to Sherborne Farm, Mac. Not quite as large or as grand as Lismore House, but it will suit our purposes perfectly. Anyway, I trust you had a good drive down?"

"Oh it was fine, pretty uneventful. Once I got on the motorway at Carlisle, it was plain sailing. Well, George, just twenty-four hours to go. Oh, while I think of it, I did make that transfer on Friday—the last $2 million owed to you, into your account in the Grand Cayman Islands. So, for my part, everything is set for tomorrow. Everything okay from your end?"

"Everything is set and ready to go. Before we go into the house, why don't I take you over to the barn and show you what we have rigged up for the missile carrier."

George Wilkinson unlocked a large padlock on the door of the barn and pulled the doors wide open. Inside were two cars and a large furniture mover's truck. It was a big dark brown truck, and on each side of the truck and on the rear double doors were the words "Evesham & Sons—Furniture and Home Removals Our Specialty—Swindon, established 1947." A large unpainted wooden ramp, which looked like it had just been constructed, was placed behind the back doors of the truck. George led the way up the ramp and opened the doors of the truck. As Kevin peered into the dark interior, he at first couldn't see anything. Then, as his eyes grew accustomed to the darkness, he could just make out the outline of two odd-shaped wooden contraptions that looked like an organ split in half, lying on each side of the truck.

"So, George, what I am looking at here? Are these two odd contraptions what I think they are?"

"Right on the money, Mac. These two odd-looking pieces have been constructed exactly to your specs of the mobile missile carrier, and when we have it, we'll roll it into the truck, and these two pieces will join in the middle right over it, completely hiding it."

"Truly ingenious, George, and a masterpiece of construction!" Kevin said with a huge grin.

"Thanks, Mac. The odd pieces of furniture that you noticed

standing around the interior of the barn will be packed around the supposed organ and the whole back of the truck filled up, so that it looks like a typical household being moved."

"Brilliant, George. Just about perfect."

George further explained to Kevin that a manifest had been prepared that listed every bit of furniture, including the organ, that would be loaded into the truck, and it could be shown to customs in Fishguard and Rosslare. Kevin was very impressed and felt sure that with this cover they would certainly get the missiles to Ireland, undetected, barring any unforeseen circumstances. As they left the barn, which George locked up again, he explained to Kevin that the men had constructed the ramp that very morning. The mock organ had been built elsewhere to specifications, and George himself had brought it there several weeks earlier. The truck had been legally purchased, and Ned had done the lettering on the sides and back.

As Kevin and George walked toward the front door of the house, Max came racing out of nowhere to join them, looking frisky and pleased with himself. The three of them went into the house.

That night, all seven men sat down together to a delicious dinner of steak and kidney pie with all the trimmings, which somehow the versatile Ned had managed to dish up. There was lots of wine and beer, though Kevin and George were the only ones to prefer wine, as the rest of the lads much preferred their beer. Kevin sat at the head of the table with George on his right and Ned to his left, and as he looked around the table at the six men sitting there, he thought about Granduncle Bertie's legacy and the twists of fate that had brought them all together. They were indeed an odd bunch of men, each with his own motive for being there and now united with a common bond. The conversation during dinner barely touched on the next day's operation, and there was almost a forced joviality about the gathering, helped a little by the drink. Kevin thought the scene was no different from many others down through the years of military history, when men gathered the night before a major battle. For in a way, Kevin considered the operation they were about to embark on as the last battle in a thousand-year war for the ultimate freedom of Ireland. It was about nine o'clock when Kevin decided it was time to bring a close to the evening, because everyone would need a clear head for the next day.

Kevin stood up with a glass of brandy in his hand and asked each of the men to join him in a toast. There was a shuffling and scratching of chairs as each of them stood up with a glass in hand and looked at Kevin, and silence fell on the group.

"To Green September! To a united Ireland!"

There was a general clinking of glasses, and every man knocked back the last drop of drink in his glass. After that, everyone drifted off to bed. Sleeping accommodations for the night were somewhat makeshift, but nobody cared. As Kevin fell asleep that night with Max curled up on the pallet beside him, he lay there wondering nothing more than when he would next sleep in a real bed, if ever.

CHAPTER 6

M ONDAY MORNING, SEPTEMBER 6, KEVIN was awake a few minutes
before six. *D-day*, he thought to himself. *This is it!* It sent a shiver
down his spine, and he wasn't sure if it was just from excitement
or part fear. He got up immediately; Kevin was never a man who liked
to lie in bed once he was awake, and today of all days, he felt, should be
a day of action and not one in which to dwell on his thoughts too long.
As he pulled on a shirt and trousers, Kevin felt a great sense of purpose
and was full of confidence, for everything had been planned down to
the tiniest detail. Now was the time to spring into action.

It wasn't light out yet, and the house was quiet and dark as Kevin
made his way, softly in his stocking feet, with Max at his side, downstairs
to the kitchen at the back of the house. He needed a nice strong cup
of tea to get him going for the day. When he entered the kitchen,
Kevin was surprised to see Ned O'Sullivan standing there by the radio,
listening to the weather report, with a mug of tea in his hand.

"Good morning, Ned. I thought I was the first up this morning,
but I guess you beat me to it."

"Good morning, Major, sir! I've been up for about an hour now. I'm
not one for much sleep at the best of times, and particularly the night
before an operation. Can I fix you some tea, sir?"

"That would be super, Ned."

While Ned was pouring out a mug of tea for him, Kevin noticed the
burly arms of the man and realized he had the look of a wrestler. Ned

was still in his undershirt, with his trousers loosely belted. Kevin took the mug of piping hot tea from Ned and took a few sips.

"Thanks, Ned. So, have you heard the forecast for today?"

"Indeed I did, sir. I caught the five-thirty detailed area forecast on the British Home Service. It looks like we're going to have perfect weather for our plans; the local forecast calls for a cloudy day and a cloudy evening, which will block out the moonlight. I also caught the regional shipping forecasts, and no storms are predicted in the Irish Sea tonight. And so, all ferries from Fishguard and Holyhead in Wales to Ireland should be running as scheduled."

"That's just perfect. We couldn't have wished for more! And by the way, Ned, you needn't address me as sir; Major will do just fine."

"Okay, sir—beggin' your pardon, I mean Major. You don't mind if I smoke, do you, Major?"

"No, go right ahead; it doesn't bother me at all. I used to be a heavy smoker, but I quit about ten years ago. Health reasons, you know."

Ned took a cigarette out of his pack of John Players sitting on the counter and lit up. Kevin had noticed the previous night that Ned was quite a heavy smoker; he was a little surprised, as he had not seen him smoke up in Scotland. But then he remembered that when he himself used to smoke, he always smoked a lot more when he was nervous. Kevin thought it interesting that, out of the seven of them, only Ned and Pat Feeney smoked, as far as he knew. Just then, Max came pushing in the back door, which Kevin had left ajar when he let him out on first coming down to the kitchen. Kevin was certainly pleased how Max had befriended all the men, and Max sure seemed happy with all the attention he was getting. Ned got Max's dish off the floor and began to put some fresh water in it.

"Believe it or not, Ned, if there's enough of it there, Max actually prefers milk."

"We've lots! We might as well give him whatever he likes best. He's really a nice dog, sir—sorry, I mean Major."

"Yes, he is. He's certainly my most loyal companion."

George Wilkinson joined them in the kitchen. He also was only partly dressed and unshaven. He accepted the mug of tea that Ned offered him.

"Well, I trust you gentlemen had a good night's sleep."

"Max and I slept pretty well."

"You know me, Captain. I'm never one to sleep too good the night before."

"Not much left to do today, George?"

"No, Mac. I expect the men will do some last-minute polishing up of buttons, making sure their uniforms and boots are absolutely spiffy. And I expect Ned here will probably do a little tinkering with the truck and the cars to make sure that everything is in tip-top shape. And yourself, Major?"

"I'll just try to relax for the morning, perhaps take a long walk with Max. Then about midafternoon, I'll put on my uniform and drive over to the base."

"By the way, Mac, I have been using the name Wrixon over the last several months, and so I will assume the name of Captain Wrixon this evening. Only Ned and you know my real name, and I don't see any reason for the rest of the men to know it."

Kevin left George and Ned alone in the kitchen, and Max chose to stay with them while he went upstairs to shave and shower. The other four men didn't appear to be up yet, and the house was still very quiet. Now that he had been up for an hour and was wide awake, Kevin began to get a nervous feeling in the pit of his stomach. He began to consider all the possible things that could go wrong. But even as he did so, he discounted them one by one as very slim possibilities. He really had made the perfect selection in choosing George Wilkinson to organize the operation, as anything that Kevin might have failed to consider, George always managed to think of. By nine thirty, everyone was up, and Ned had managed to put together a darn good breakfast. Kevin noticed that the mood at breakfast was in sharp contrast to the previous night's joviality. There was a certain tension in the air, like a coiled spring ready to be released. Even Max appeared to sense the tension and did his begging for food more discreetly and quietly than usual.

After breakfast, Kevin and Max left the house and went out for a walk. As he walked, Kevin thought about many things, but most of all he thought about Jenny. With only a few hours to go, he felt tense and realized it would take a superb effort on his part to appear absolutely his usual self when he arrived at the barracks in Warminster. Kevin was relieved that for once the weather forecast appeared to be correct. It was a mild, cloudy day, but it certainly didn't look like it would rain.

By the time Kevin got back to the house, everyone seemed to be in a state of preparation, and Pat Feeney was already in uniform with his corporal's tunic still unbuttoned. Ned was apparently out in the barn tinkering with the truck. George was nowhere about. Kevin decided to go into the living room and read the newspaper until it was time for him to get ready. There were cold cuts and bread out in the kitchen for anyone who felt like some lunch, with only tea, coffee, or milk to drink, as Wilkinson had made sure there would be no beer available that day. He wanted all the men to be stone-cold sober.

At about four o'clock, Kevin, in uniform, left the house with Max, got into his Jag, and drove off toward Warminster. Leaving Sherborne Farm, Kevin took a right onto the Trowbridge Road and, as he drove along, noticed the red warning flags were already up on the side roads, indicating that military exercises would be in progress. Kevin knew the actual exercises weren't scheduled to begin until the next morning, but they always put the red flags up a couple of days beforehand as the various regiments and battalions took up positions around the perimeter of the northern end of the Salisbury Plain. It was only about twenty-four miles to Warminster from Devizes, but Kevin decided to take a shortcut through Westbury, in any case.

When he took the turnoff just before Trowbridge, he had to pass through an army checkpoint. Half an hour later, he reached the main barracks in Warminster, and the sentries at the gate, recognizing him immediately, waved him through. Kevin drove straight over to the visiting officers' quarters. He parked alongside the end bungalow in which he normally stayed, and which happened to be next door to the one Sir Ian Sinders would occupy. He had only brought the one suitcase with him, which contained his spare uniforms and army shirts; the other suitcase, which had his civvies in it, he left at Sherborne

Farm for the trip to Ireland. Nobody questioned Max's presence at the barracks, because over the years he had become a familiar figure with the major, and, indeed, if he weren't there, Kevin would probably get a lot of questions about the dog's whereabouts. Kevin settled into the bungalow, unpacking, hanging up his uniforms, and making everything look like he intended to stay the week, as normal. He also rang through to the office of the CO, Colonel Barnes, to announce his arrival and to inquire when Sir Ian Sinders was expected to arrive. Kevin also arranged with the colonel to have the use of an army Land Rover, as he planned to tour some of the units that evening. Colonel Barnes was most accommodating and said he would have one delivered to Kevin's bungalow right away and would be happy to supply a driver. Kevin thanked him but politely and firmly refused his offer of a driver, saying that he would prefer to drive on his own. Ten minutes later, the Land Rover arrived out front, and a soldier brought the keys to the door. At ten minutes to six, Kevin was ready to leave. He took a last glance around the room to make sure everything looked as if he had moved in as normal. Then he double-checked his inside pocket to check that he had the envelope with the all-important firing mechanisms. Kevin deliberately left the folder containing his Washington trip report for Sir Ian sitting on top of his briefcase on the table by the window, knowing it would be found there in the morning.

The Land Rover was roughly the equivalent of the American Jeep, and in addition to the driver and one passenger in front, it could carry six soldiers in the back. But unlike the American Jeep, the Land Rover had a hard shell over the rear and a back door that gave access to two benches, one on each side. Most important of all, all the army Land Rovers came equipped with a tow bar for pulling military equipment. Kevin put Max in the back and then drove off. When he left the barracks, he took the same route by which he had come and once again passed through the checkpoint just south of Trowbridge. It was dusk, and Kevin passed quite a few other military vehicles. It was perfect; Kevin had known there would be a fair amount of military traffic in the area, and nobody would pay attention to one more military vehicle. When Kevin reached the main Trowbridge Road, he turned right and went about a mile, then turned left onto Horseshoe Lane, a deserted country road. It was now dark, and Kevin had driven only about a hundred yards when a car's headlights flashed on before him, from under some trees at the side of the road. Kevin flashed the Land Rover's headlights twice in response and drove beyond the car to turn around and park in front of the car.

He got out, leaving the engine running. He walked back to the car just as George Wilkinson got out of the passenger seat and the four men got out of the back. Ned sat grim-faced behind the wheel of the car. Then, without a word to anyone, Ned took off and headed back in the direction of Sherborne Farm. Silently, Pat Feeney and the three others got into the back of the Land Rover with Max, while George got in behind the steering wheel and Kevin got in on the passenger's side. George shifted into gear and headed back in the direction from which Kevin had just arrived. Kevin glanced at his watch. It was exactly sixteen minutes past six; they were right on schedule. They traveled back about half a mile along the Trowbridge Road and turned left down an unpaved country lane with no name, with red warning flags flying on each side of the road.

About a quarter of a mile down the lane, they came to an army checkpoint for the encampment of the third battalion of the Royal Welsh Guards. Kevin showed his credentials, and the crossbar was lifted to allow them to pass through. On Kevin's instructions, George brought the Land Rover to a halt outside an army tent, which was serving as field HQ for the third battalion. Only Kevin and George got out of the Land Rover and pulled back the flap of the tent. Inside, a young lieutenant sat behind a fold-up table with a field telephone on it. The lieutenant looked up from some paperwork and immediately jumped up and stood at attention.

"At ease, Lieutenant. I'm Major MacAllister from the general's staff, and I would like you to take Captain Wrixon here and his squad of men to Field Battery Three, where they are going to hitch up one of the mobile missile launchers to move to another location. Your name, Lieutenant?"

"First Lieutenant Ridley at your service, sir! Major, I have had no instructions about any transfer of an MML. Perhaps I should call up my CO who is over in the mess at Warminster Barracks and won't be back for another hour?"

"That won't be necessary, Lieutenant Ridley. In case you are unaware of it, I'm the officer in charge of planning these military exercises, and I've made some last-minute changes to the plans. Please be good enough to show the captain and his men to the MML right away."

"Right away, sir!"

Kevin noticed that the young lieutenant was somewhat red in the face as he saluted smartly and led George out of the tent. Kevin paced up and down nervously as he heard the doors of the Land Rover slam and the engine roar into life. In any case, Kevin was relieved that the awkward moment had passed without any problems. As he paced, he wondered whether the young lieutenant would try to engage George in conversation to ascertain where he stood in the regiment rankings. But hopefully Kevin had intimidated him enough, and they would move so quickly in the dark that Lieutenant Ridley wouldn't notice much. Five minutes later, Kevin heard the Land Rover pull up outside the tent once again and doors slam, but the engine was left running. Lieutenant Ridley came in alone, looking flushed, and brought himself to attention smartly in front of Kevin.

"One MML from Field Battery Three now attached to your Land Rover, Major!"

"Thank you, Lieutenant. The prompt way in which you have carried out my orders is commendable. I will certainly be keeping an eye out for you during the week's exercises. Good luck tomorrow!"

"Thank you, sir. Good night."

"Good night, Lieutenant Ridley."

Kevin went out of the tent and was relieved to see the MML securely attached to the tow bar at the rear of the Land Rover. He got in beside George. Kevin and George exchanged glances without a word and were on their way. They were waved right through the checkpoint and didn't even have to stop. Both men were quiet until they again reached the Trowbridge Road and turned toward Sherborne Farm and Devizes. George Wilkinson was the first to break the silence.

"Well, Mac, that completes phase one successfully. Who would ever believe it could be so bloody easy to hijack a couple of nuclear missiles! Though, I will admit it was an awkward moment when the young lieutenant wanted to call his CO. However, your rank as a senior staff officer solved that problem quickly."

"You're sure it's one of the four allocated to the Field Battery Three of the Royal Welsh Guards Regiment, aren't you?"

"Of course, Mac. We checked the markings on it against your list."

"There's one thing that bothers me, George. What if his CO does come back in an hour and questions the lieutenant about my orders? Then, if his CO isn't entirely satisfied, he may do some calling around to the other battalions or, worse still, call the barracks and ask to speak to me. If that happens, the balloon will go up tonight rather than tomorrow morning, and we won't have the head start we thought we had."

There was silence again while George Wilkinson mulled over what Kevin had just said. "You know, as well as I do, Mac, that most officers in the army don't want to rock the boat. Besides, I'm sure young Ridley's CO knows exactly who you are and will figure that you've made some change in the plans for the field exercises, or just added a new wrinkle, and he'll probably figure it's not his position to question why. At least, let's hope so!"

"I pray that's the case, George. Then there should be no general alarm until I fail to turn up for my seven-thirty meeting with Sir Ian in the morning, unless by a bad stroke of luck Sir Ian seeks me out tonight, or Colonel Barnes learns I haven't returned with the Land Rover. Anyway, there's no point in speculating anymore; we must move quickly now to phase two."

The two men lapsed into silence for the last couple of miles to Sherborne Farm. Kevin sat there, stealing an occasional glance in the wing mirror at what they were towing behind, noticing just the dark outline of the MML as it swayed gently to and fro. In the darkness of the night, Kevin thought it could look as if they were towing a speedboat rather than one of the most lethal weapons on earth.

In the short drive, they encountered little traffic, only two other military vehicles and one private car. Luckily, as they made the turn into the gateway of Sherborne Farm, there was no other vehicle in sight. George drove straight to the barn where Ned had the doors open and was waiting by the ramp to the truck.

Just before the ramp, George locked the Land Rover hard to the left, leaving the MML positioned at the bottom of the ramp. George turned off the engine of the Land Rover, and the four men behind, plus Max, clambered out quickly. George and Kevin followed. Two of the men pulled the barn doors shut, putting a crossbar on the middle to make sure nobody could get in. The other two men were disengaging the MML from the tow bar. Max pranced around excitably and barked at all the activity, but Kevin quickly silenced him. At this point, Kevin double-checked the markings and serial numbers on the MML against his master list. Feeling relieved, he said, "Everything's in order, George, so proceed!"

Under George's direction, the four men had now positioned themselves on each side of the MML, with Ned taking up the rear, and they began pushing the MML slowly up the ramp and onto the truck. Once they were level on the bed of the truck, George and Ned maneuvered it to the back of the truck and positioned the two halves of the dummy organ over it, while the others went to get ready to load furniture. The two halves came together and fitted like a glove. As Kevin watched, he was very impressed with how the finished dummy organ completely concealed the MML. George pressed a concealed button, and a cassette player hidden inside the organ began to play organ music, and the keys began to move up and down as if they really worked.

"Well, what do you think, Mac?"

"Absolutely perfect, George. You really think of everything."

Kevin was pleased. It was now exactly five minutes past seven, and from the moment he had met them, it had taken only fifty minutes to get the MML and have it securely hidden. George and Ned got out of the truck to make way for the other four men who had already stripped off their tunics and were busy moving furniture into the back of the truck. Next, they had to dispose of the Land Rover.

George, still in his uniform, got into the Land Rover, and Ned got into one of the cars. Kevin opened the doors of the barn, and George led the way out with Ned close behind. As they drove off, Kevin closed the doors of the barn and went into the house with Max to get out of his uniform. Ten minutes later, George and Ned returned in the car, and Ned entered the barn to join the others. Then George came into the house to take off his uniform. Kevin, already changed into a fresh shirt, sports jacket, and pants, greeted George in the hallway.

"No problems?"

"No, everything went smoothly. There's a disused quarry about two miles north of here, only reachable by an old dirt track; we ditched the Land Rover there and camouflaged it as best we could. It's unlikely to be found there for some time."

"Excellent, George. Why don't you get out of your uniform while I go out and join the men in the barn? I'll leave Max here with you so he'll be out of the way."

When Kevin got to the barn, the truck was already three-quarters full, and the organ was barely visible at the back. The men looked hot and sweaty as they worked quickly and efficiently to fill up the truck. They had used old furniture that the owners of Sherborne Farm had stored in the barn, along with a few additional pieces from the house, enough to fill up the truck. With Ned's brute strength lending a hand, the truck was soon full, and the rear doors were closed and locked, with Ned pocketing the key. Ned sent the four men to the house to get out of their uniforms and told them not to forget their tunics, as he didn't want any traces of the uniforms left in the barn. Kevin watched as Ned diligently checked out the vehicles one last time, and he himself scanned the barn to make sure there was no evidence left lying around. When they were both satisfied that everything was in order, Kevin and Ned followed the men into the house.

Kevin joined the others in the living room while Ned went quickly to wash up. All five men were now in civilian clothes, and there were two suitcases on the floor containing all the uniforms, including Kevin's. The game plan was for George, Pat Feeney, and Tom Fallon to travel together in the black Rover 3000, posing as three men going on a fishing holiday in Ireland. These three were dressed in appropriate casual clothes. The two younger men, Sean Morrissey and Terry O'Neill, were dressed in working clothes and would be traveling in the cab of the truck with Ned, posing as his helpers. Kevin was to leave first in the old gray Vauxhall with Max, followed at five-minute intervals by Ned and the two men in the truck, and then by George and the other two in the Rover 3000. It was 186 miles to the port of Fishguard from Devizes, and George had estimated that their traveling time should be four hours exactly, allowing for the fact that just north of Swansea, the Motorway ended and the last sixty miles would be on a secondary road.

George's idea, also, was that no one should exceed the speed limit and attract any attention; this would also allow the truck to move at an average speed of fifty miles per hour. George had arranged that Kevin would pick up Betty Moriarity at the last motorway truck and rest stop at Pontardulais, just northwest of Swansea. After meeting Betty there, Kevin was to wait until both the truck and the Rover had caught up with him, and then he would leave for Fishguard with the others following, again at five-minute intervals. George had estimated their time of arrival in Fishguard at no later than fifteen minutes before midnight, in plenty of time to get on the 1:00 a.m. ferry to Rosslare. George had also planned that the two suitcases with the uniforms would be disposed of in the River Avon between Pontardulais and Fishguard. George had personally timed everything, and this was the schedule he set; their departure from Sherborne Farm was to be at 7:45 p.m.

George didn't overlook the slightest detail, and the Rover 3000 was already loaded up with luggage and enough fishing equipment for the three men traveling in it. The three men in the truck were each allowed one small bag with a change of clothes. All their weapons were carefully concealed in a hidden compartment built into the floor of the truck and totally invisible from either underneath or above. This was something that George and Ned had worked on alone.

Ned came back into the room, dressed in a brown corduroy jacket and tattered old cap that looked suitable for the driver of a furniture moving van. It was exactly twenty minutes to eight, and George seemed pleased that everything was running on schedule, so with five minutes to spare, he ran through phase three of the plan one more time, for everyone's benefit.

"Mac, you go first with Max in the Vauxhall and pick up Betty at the last motorway truck stop. And remember, act like you know her well and do nothing that would attract any attention."

"Check, all clear!"

Turning to Ned, George said, "Five minutes after the major leaves, you, Sean, and Terry take off in the truck—and remember, keep to the speed limit. We wouldn't want you attracting any attention from the motorway police, would we?"

Making a mock salute, Ned said, "No worries, Cap'n. Understood."

Now laughing a little, George turned to Pat and Tom and said, "Right, lads, we leave last and all set for our fishing holiday in Ireland. Congrats, those clothes make you both look the part!"

When George was finished, Ned went out to the barn and brought the old Vauxhall to the front of the house for Kevin. During all of this, Max was hovering at Kevin's side. Ned came back and said, "It's all set for you, Major, and you should have absolutely no problems. Don't be deceived by the old, battered look of the car. I have it running beautifully. And your suitcase is in the trunk. All papers for the car are in the glove box, and I left the engine running. Good luck!"

George accompanied Kevin and Max out to the car. "Okay, Mac, it's exactly 7:45; you're on your way. And don't forget, if by any chance you do have a breakdown, just pull over on the hard shoulder and don't put on your emergency flashers until you see Ned's truck in your rearview mirror. But that's unlikely, so don't worry. I won't talk to you again until we all meet at the house outside Rosslare. Good luck, and I'm sure you'll find Betty Moriarity a pleasant traveling companion. You know the drill when you dock, right?"

"Yes, I do. And I'm sure Betty will be fine, so I'll be on my way."

"Okay, Mac. One last thing, you do have the UK driver's license in the name of Kevin Moriarity in your wallet, don't you?"

"Yes. I'm off." As Kevin went out the gateway of Sherborne and turned toward Devizes, Max had already settled down comfortably in the passenger's seat.

Kevin reached the M-4 motorway, going west toward Bristol, having safely passed through Devizes and Chippenham. He wasn't enjoying driving the old, beat-up Vauxhall; even though the engine sounded good and was powerful enough, it didn't compare to the feel and smooth ride of his Jag. But he thought, *This isn't a bloody pleasure trip, so I'd best ignore it.* The car was a necessary cover for a poor workingman taking his wife and baby over to Ireland to visit their family. As he drove along, Kevin was thinking about what the truck just five minutes behind him was carrying. But he knew that nobody could ever guess that a furniture removal truck would be carrying such deadly cargo as two nuclear missiles.

After Kevin passed the interchange with the M-5, the traffic got heavier as he headed over the vast span of the Severn Bridge, the main gateway from the south of England to the industrial south of Wales, which carried all the traffic from London and Bristol. Once he passed the major Welsh City of Cardiff, the traffic thinned out once more, and Kevin found his thoughts creeping back again to the missiles in the truck behind. He kept wondering if it had gotten over the Severn Bridge safely with no mishaps along the way. By five minutes to ten, Kevin was passing Swansea to his south, and by five minutes past ten, he had pulled up at the truck stop at Pontardulais a few minutes ahead of schedule. Kevin went inside the roadside cafe where he was to meet Betty Moriarity.

Inside, it was pretty crowded with truckers and travelers, many of whom were probably heading toward the ferry at the port of Fishguard. Kevin knew he was looking for a woman of thirty-one with auburn hair and a fresh Irish complexion, about five feet seven inches tall with a stocky build, quite similar to his wife Sheila. She was supposed to be wearing a bright red coat and have a ten-month-old baby girl with her, dressed in a pink romper. Kevin looked around the whole place, but it was hard to see everyone, so he began walking down the aisle between the window-side booths and the tables in the middle. Then he spotted a woman and baby fitting the descriptions, in a middle booth by the side windows. He made his way over to her table, and, seeing the seat opposite to her empty, he politely asked if he could sit down. The woman nodded. Kevin slid in on the seat.

"By any chance, are you Betty Moriarity?"

The woman was cooing to her baby, sort of jiggling her up and down to keep her happy. She answered in a strong Irish accent.

"I am indeed Betty. And you wouldn't happen to be Kevin, would you?"

"I am indeed." Kevin smiled at her.

Betty Moriarity returned his smile and said, "Good, now that's settled. Would you like a cup of tea? I ordered two just a few minutes ago, as I was expecting you. And by the way, this is little Mary." Betty turned sideways to show Kevin the baby, who smiled shyly at him.

Kevin drank his tea and then made a quick visit to the bathroom. When he came back to the table, he left some money to cover the check and then suggested to Betty that they should be getting on their way. Kevin picked up Betty's suitcase and brought it out to the car with them. When they reached the car, Kevin let Max out on the nearby grass to take care of himself and then put him in the backseat. "You'll have to share the backseat," he told Max as he pulled a baby car seat from the floorboard. He then asked Betty to sit in front as he buckled Mary into the car seat George had provided. Then Kevin got in on the driver's side. Max was showing a lot of curiosity toward Betty and particularly toward the baby. Kevin sat for a minute or two while he looked over the parking lot. When he spotted the furniture van and saw Ned wave, he started the car and got back on the road to Fishguard.

Betty was a pleasant companion, though a little on the talkative side for Kevin's liking, and the baby was good, sleeping most of the way. Kevin noticed that Betty was not unattractive, and she wore a bright red clip that almost matched her overcoat and held her hair back on one side. As they drove along, Kevin learned that Betty's husband, Joe, had dropped her off at the roadside cafe at about ten o'clock and that Joe was a good friend of Pat Feeney, the two men having worked together in Birmingham. Betty was almost apologetic when she explained why she was willing to do this; she needed the money. But despite her talkativeness, Kevin saw that she was smart enough not to ask any probing questions, and Kevin didn't volunteer any information about himself. All Betty Moriarity knew about him was his first name, Kevin.

The time passed quickly, with Betty talking away about her husband and her family in Ireland. They reached Fishguard at about twenty minutes to twelve, five minutes ahead of schedule, but Kevin went ahead anyway down to the port area and joined the line of cars waiting to board the ferry. The formalities for crossing on the ferry to Ireland were exceedingly simple, usually only a cursory customs inspection at each end and no passport control. Kevin thought it was lucky for them. Over the years, he had never ceased to be amazed that despite all the recent troubles in both Northern Ireland and England, England had continued to maintain completely open ports with Ireland. In fact, it was easier to cross between England and Ireland than between the north and south of Ireland.

The line was moving briskly, and first an official from the ferry came and inspected their tickets for the passage. Shortly after that, a customs officer poked his head in Kevin's window and asked if they had anything to declare and the purpose of their visit to Ireland. Kevin answered, saying they were just going to visit his wife's family for the week. While sitting in the line and, luckily for Kevin, even while dealing with the customs inspector, little baby Mary, as if on cue, kept saying "Mama, Dada," the only two words the little girl knew how to say. The customs inspector then asked him to open the trunk of the car, which Kevin gladly got out to do. The inspector looked briefly, didn't even ask to open the suitcases, and waved them on. Kevin nosed onto the upper car deck and parked the car. Kevin then suggested to Betty that they go upstairs to the passenger lounge, and Kevin left Max in the car with the windows open a little so he would be comfortable. Kevin knew that as soon as Max got bored, he would curl up and sleep for the trip. On the top deck, the passenger lounge was already quite full, but Kevin and Betty did manage to find a couple of seats by a table. Betty Moriarity made a little bed of blankets for baby Mary and laid her out there to sleep. Once they were settled, Kevin asked her if she would mind if he left her for a while to go up on deck. There weren't too many people about as, at that time of the morning, there was a definite chill to the September air, so he easily made his way to the rear of the ferry and stood at the rail overlooking the loading area.

It was already a quarter after midnight, and Kevin scanned the lines until he could clearly see the furniture truck, over to the left, in line with several other trucks. Farther back to the right in the car line, he spotted the Rover 3000 and George behind the steering wheel. *At least they're here on time, without mishap,* Kevin thought. But he kept worrying how thorough the customs inspection of a furniture removal van would be. He suspected that they might be a little more curious than they were with a passenger car. Kevin stood there a long time just watching the boarding procedure as the two lines of cars and the line of trucks seemed to inch forward and disappear into the bowels of the ferry. Then it came the turn of the brown furniture truck to be inspected by customs, and Kevin gripped the rail tensely. He could clearly see Ned handing the customs inspector the manifest listing the contents of the truck. The inspector seemed to be asking Ned several questions and was apparently getting satisfactory answers. Ned got out of the cab and followed the customs inspector to the rear, where Ned undid the padlock on the double doors and opened them. Kevin watched as the customs inspector took a big flashlight and shone it inside for what seemed like an age. Eventually, the inspector turned off his flashlight, Ned locked the back of the truck, and the customs inspector stamped the manifest and handed it back to Ned. The inspector went to the next truck, and Ned got back in his cab. Kevin let out a long sigh of relief.

Not having anything better to do, Kevin continued to hang about, idly watching the cars drive onto the ferry, until finally it was the Rover 3000's turn. Kevin wasn't concerned, as George and the other two certainly looked like three regular people going on a fishing trip. Nothing uncommon about that. Kevin was right, and soon the Rover 3000 disappeared into the ship beneath him, having easily passed inspection. Nonetheless, Kevin was worried, as he felt things were going almost too smoothly.

At this point, he expected any moment to see flashing blue lights coming down the quay toward the ferry, indicating that somehow the authorities had discovered the missiles were missing and had found their way to Fishguard. At the same time, Kevin knew he was being ridiculous, because at this point, even if the missiles had been found missing, nobody could have any possible idea that they were now on board the ferry in Fishguard bound for Rosslare in Ireland. Yet something kept Kevin rooted to that spot until finally it was one in the morning, all cars and trucks were loaded, and the ferry's whistle gave several loud blasts indicating its departure from the dock. Finally, as the ferry headed out of the harbor and into the open Irish Sea, Kevin decided to go and join Betty Moriarity and baby Mary.

When Kevin got back down to the passenger lounge, it was a good deal more crowded than when he had left, but he found Betty and her baby in the same spot, and, indeed, she had even saved his seat for him. The buffet and bar were now open, and Kevin asked if there was anything he could get for Betty or the baby. Betty said she would have a glass of Guinness and nothing for the baby. Kevin fought his way through the crowd now milling around the bar and eventually managed to get the glass of Guinness and a pint of beer for himself. As he made his way back to the table where Betty was waiting, he noticed George and the two others out of the corner of his eye, but they showed no recognition, nor did Kevin. When Kevin got back to the table with the drinks, Betty became quite talkative again as she sipped her Guinness, and Kevin sat there patiently with a smile, but his mind was elsewhere. Eventually, Kevin dozed off for a while.

When he awoke, it was already nearly four in the morning, and most people in the lounge were sleeping in their chairs or just sitting quietly. It was a smooth crossing, just the normal ocean breezes with hardly a ripple of a wave. Betty was awake and giving a bottle to little Mary. Betty Moriarity had come well prepared, for there was a battery-operated bottle warmer sitting on the table and a bag of diapers sitting alongside.

"Did you sleep at all, Betty?"

"No, not really, Kevin. Just shut the eyes a little now and then. Had to keep one eye on the little one here. But then, I'll have a good sleep when I get home tonight."

"Well, I would guess we're just about an hour out of Rosslare by now, if we're on schedule. If it's okay with you, Betty, I think we should go down and get in the car at about twenty minutes before five. That way, we'll avoid the last-minute scramble as people go down for their cars."

"That'll be grand, Kevin. But crowds never bother me anyway." Betty was then interrupted by little Mary burping up some of her bottle. Kevin was impressed that she seemed a good-humored baby, and traveling on a ship certainly didn't seem to bother her. He began thinking about Max, sleeping in the car, and wondered if he was okay. But it wasn't the first time he'd left Max to sleep in the car on a ferry. Shortly after four thirty, there was an announcement over the intercom that they would be docking in Rosslare Harbor at five in the morning and a request that people please be patient and wait their turn to disembark. Shortly after that, Kevin helped Betty to gather up all her belongings, and they went down to the car deck and found the car with Max still fast asleep inside, obviously lulled into a deep sleep by the gentle motion of the ship. Kevin tapped the window of the car with his knuckle, and Max woke up, looking startled at first, until he realized it was his master. Kevin buckled baby Mary, who was still asleep, into the car seat while Betty settled herself into the front passenger's seat. Kevin didn't want to let Max out of the car because he knew that after sleeping for half the night, he would immediately trot off and relieve himself, probably on someone else's car. He would just have to hold it until after they docked. Kevin got in on the driver's side and closed the door as gently as he could, so as not to awaken the baby.

Kevin looked around to see if he could locate the black Rover 3000, but he couldn't, so he figured it must be on the lower deck with all the trucks. Kevin had only once before taken this particular ferry to Ireland; normally when he went on visits, he took the Holyhead ferry to Dun Laoghaire, so he wasn't that familiar with the town of Rosslare. He ran George's directions through his mind once more so that he would know clearly where he needed to go when they docked. The first thing he had to do after he left the dock area in Rosslare was to drop Betty and the baby off at the train station so that she could catch the 6:00 a.m. train to Dublin and then take the ferry from Dun Laoghaire over to Holyhead and a train to her home in Birmingham. Then he had to find Garryrhu House, which George told him was about three miles north of Rosslare Harbor on the Wexford Road and about one mile before the village of Killinick.

George had told Kevin that Garryrhu House was owned by a German industrialist who usually rented out the house for a month at a time between mid-May and mid-September. George had rented the place from mid-August through mid-September. What appealed to George was that the German usually brought his own staff whenever he stayed at Garryrhu House, and when he was not in residence, there was only a caretaker living in the cottage by the main gate. George had cleverly arranged for the caretaker to be in Dublin from Monday, September 6 through Wednesday, September 8 on the pretext of locating some particular items for George, and he had paid the man handsomely. In that way, he insured that Garryrhu House would be totally deserted when they arrived early in the morning on Tuesday.

As Kevin was thinking these things over, he stole a glance at Betty Moriarity. Her face looked a little pinched with fatigue, and she was finally rather quiet. Kevin took two envelopes from the inside pocket of his jacket, and after carefully checking the one that contained the firing mechanisms, which he had transferred from his uniform pocket, he immediately returned that to his inside pocket. The other envelope contained five thousand pounds in cash, which George had given him to give to Betty Moriarity after they docked in Rosslare. The five thousand pounds was in an assortment of British five- and ten-pound notes. Kevin stuck this envelope in his outside right-hand pocket.

Kevin glanced at his watch; it was five minutes to five. He knew they must be docking, as he could hear the loud reverberations of the ferry's engine screws going into reverse so that the ferry could back up to the unloading dock. A few minutes later, the engines of the ferry fell silent, and Kevin heard the scurry of the merchant seamen as they threw the ropes to the dock to be secured to the bulwarks. Then there was the announcement that disembarkation would commence. Only one lane of cars was allowed off at a time, and Kevin had to sit patiently, awaiting their turn. When it finally came, Kevin turned the key in the ignition, the old Vauxhall started up immediately, and they rolled off slowly in first gear.

As Kevin waited in the line for customs inspection, he was relieved to notice that there didn't appear to be any undue activity around the dock. He felt pretty confident that this early in the morning there wouldn't be any problems. Little baby Mary finally woke up but was good-humoredly chatting, "Mama, Dada, Mama, Dada," and Max appeared to be watching the little baby in total fascination. A young Irish customs inspector came to the car window, which Kevin had rolled down. He looked rather sleepy-eyed, and his questions were even more cursory than those asked at Fishguard; he didn't even ask Kevin to open the trunk.

Kevin easily found the train station, which was less than half a mile from the dock. It was almost deserted at this hour, so he was able to pull up right outside the main entrance. Nobody was around, not even a porter, to take any notice of them. So Kevin shut off the engine, and leaving Max in the car, he got out Betty's suitcase and carried it onto the station platform for her. Even the buffet on the platform wasn't open yet, so he settled Betty and the baby on a bench with their bags alongside. Kevin handed her the envelope with her payment, thanked her for her help, and wished her a safe trip back to England, saying his good-byes. When he glanced back as he left the station, Betty smiled and took the little hand of baby Mary to wave to him. He felt she richly deserved the money. Kevin smiled as he got back in the car, seeing that Max had resumed his old spot in the front passenger's seat.

Kevin easily found the north road to Wexford out of the small town of Rosslare Harbor. It was just past five thirty in the morning and still pitch-black out. There were just a few cars on the road, and Kevin suspected that most of them were either coming from or going to the ferry. After going about two and three-quarters miles, Kevin slowed down and began straining his eyes to find the entrance to Garryrhu House, which George had told him would be on the left-hand side. Finally, he reached it; there was no actual gate, only a low, curved wall on each side of two broken-down pillars, and he could just make out the name etched in the stonework. He passed between the pillars and saw the caretaker's cottage on the right. The driveway to the house was almost like a tunnel, as the old trees on each side had gradually grown together overhead. After a half mile later, he came to a big circular gravel driveway in front of the house. Everything was dark, but best as Kevin could make out from the lights of the car, the house was clearly in need of repair.

Kevin drew up by the front door and parked. He got out of the car and went to get the key, which the caretaker was supposed to have left under the doormat for him. He pulled up the mat, felt around, and realized he had no key to Garryrhu House. He walked up the steps and tried the front door, just in case, but it was securely locked.

Kevin felt a shiver down his spine, and he realized that the damp air with a trace of mist in it made it feel chillier than it really was. He went to the trunk of the car, opened his suitcase, and groped around in the dark until he found a light overcoat, and slipped it on. He thought there was no point to sitting in the bloody car any longer, so he got Max's leash and decided they should take a walk together. Kevin was not a man who was generally afraid of the dark, but the tall old trees that surrounded Garryrhu House and the trace of mist in the air gave the whole place a cold, almost ghostlike, foreboding air. Max immediately relieved himself on a clump of bushes near the front doorsteps. After that, Kevin kept him on a short leash and decided to stick to the gravel area for their walk and not go wandering off into the dark woods. It was already ten minutes to six, and Kevin wondered how long he would have to wait before the others arrived.

Though it was hard to see in the dark, Kevin followed the gravel driveway off to the left side of the house and came to some outhouses that appeared to be mostly stables converted to garages. There was no sign of life or lights here either, but Kevin did find a side door into the house and tried it anyway; it was also locked. There was another doorway in a high wall to the back of the yard that, as far as Kevin could make out, was probably into a walled-in garden at the back of the house. He decided not to venture any farther; tugging Max to come on, he walked back to the front of the house and the car. Then he thought that maybe Ned had put a flashlight somewhere in the car. So to kill time, Kevin began looking for one—nothing in the trunk, nothing around the back of the car, and just as he put his hand under the front passenger seat, he grasped what certainly felt like a flashlight. Kevin pulled it out and clicked it on; it worked and cast a powerful beam of light across the gravel driveway. Kevin looked at his watch; two minutes past six. He was beginning to feel anxious.

Armed with the flashlight, Kevin decided to take another look at the outhouses on the side. He felt a little more relaxed with the comforting light from the flashlight and relaxed his grip on Max's leash. They walked slowly so that Max could enjoy giving everything a good sniff in this unfamiliar territory. Kevin walked down the row of converted stables, shining the light in the windows and trying the doors; everything was locked, and with the reflection of the light off the glass, he really couldn't see much but did notice a vague outline of vehicles in a couple of garages. He had just reached the end of the row of stables when he heard the distant roar of a truck's laboring engine. He turned off the flashlight and tightened his grip on Max's leash, drawing the dog closer to him, and stood there quietly in the dark, his ears straining. Yes, it was definitely a truck engine; whether it was the right one or not, Kevin couldn't be sure. He wasn't very good at distinguishing engine noises, but it was definitely drawing closer.

He started back toward the front of the house, keeping the flashlight off. The engine noise got closer and closer. Then he saw a glimmer of lights coming from the tunneled driveway. He hoped the truck wasn't too tall for the trees that grew over the driveway. Kevin felt cold again as he began to imagine maybe it wasn't a furniture truck, maybe it was an army truck. But then he thought, why the hell, if the authorities knew anything, would they send a truck? They wouldn't, Kevin thought. He had to get a grip and stop letting his imagination run wild. At that moment, the truck came into view, and Kevin felt a flood of relief when he saw that it was the brown furniture removal truck, with Ned behind the wheel. The truck appeared to be listing slightly to one side, and Kevin wondered what the hell had happened—or was it still his imagination playing tricks on him? The truck came to a stop, and it was then Kevin noticed that the black Rover was right behind it.

Kevin flashed his flashlight on and off a couple of times to signal that he was there and walked over toward the Rover just as George was getting out. Feeling immense relief, Kevin was the first to speak.

"Thank God you made it, George! I had begun to get anxious, as you are late. What was the problem?"

"Nothing disastrous. Just that about a mile down the road, the truck got a flat tire, and I came upon them a few minutes later stopped at the side of the road. The truck was too heavy, fully loaded, to change the tire; and as we were so near to Garryrhu House, I decided to proceed very slowly, even though continually shredding the tire, and for the last half mile, that wheel was driving on the rim. You may have noticed that the truck was lopsided. We were only able to go about five miles an hour. But if it had to happen, it was lucky that it was so close to here and not at the docks. So, at worst, we've lost ten to fifteen minutes on the road and may lose another ten minutes changing the tire when the truck is unloaded. By the way, Mac, how come you didn't go into the house?"

"The caretaker didn't leave me a key, George. I hope you have one."

"Sure. Here it is," George said, handing a key to Kevin.

"Anyway, at least you're all here, safe and sound. We'd better get cracking and try to make up some time. No problems at customs, then?"

"No, at least we were very lucky in that respect. Even for the truck, passing through Irish customs turned out to be a piece of cake. I'm sorry I didn't give you a key, Mac; that was an oversight on my part. Anyway, here's one now. Perhaps you wouldn't mind putting some water on the boil for tea. I think everyone could use something hot to drink. And while you're doing that, I'll get all the men working at double pace to unload the truck and get the MML off and into the smaller truck for the next leg of our trip. Thanks, Mac."

"Okay, George. I'll join you and the others in the yard in a few minutes."

Kevin went on into the house while George had Ned drive the truck around to the side yard, reversing it up near the garage where the smaller truck was. Kevin discovered that the somewhat dilapidated state of the exterior was deceptive, for inside, everything was in tip-top shape, tastefully furnished, and the kitchen beautifully modernized with every convenience.

Once he had the kettle on for hot water and had given Max some kibble, Kevin found his way out the side door and into the yard. The yard was now almost as bright as day, with four spotlights at each corner of the yard shining brightly on a scene of intense activity. Even George himself was working feverishly with the other men and already had the big truck unloaded of the furniture, which was left standing around the yard. A couple of the garages had been unlocked, and the black Rover was parked in one, and a much smaller truck, painted dark green, was sitting in another with its back doors already open and a makeshift ramp placed up against it.

Kevin wandered over toward the small green truck, as he was curious what cover George had picked for this. The lettering on the side of the truck was somewhat faded, but Kevin could make out that it said "The Kilkenny Music Company," and underneath, "Piano and Organ Sales and Repairs." *Just perfect,* Kevin thought. *High marks for George again.*

Meanwhile, under George's direction, the men were now positioning the MML, with its mock organ cover removed and ready for loading, into the music truck. The MML was now placed at the base of the ramp into the truck. Kevin went over and joined George.

"Hey, George, you sure got another piece of ingenious cover here with this truck. But I'm a little concerned if it'll be able to take the weight of the MML, as it's a lot smaller than the other truck."

"No worries, Mac. When Ned and I were over here a few weeks ago getting everything ready, we reinforced the bed of this truck with a couple of steel girders that could carry a battleship."

Kevin and George watched as the four men, with Ned taking up the rear, maneuvered the MML slowly up the makeshift ramp and into the truck. At one point, Kevin thought the ramp was going to collapse, as it appeared to be groaning under the weight of the MML. But finally the MML was safely on the bed of the truck, and the men were quickly bringing the sham organ halves to cover it once more. The men then loaded in two upright pianos that were standing nearby. One had come in the other truck from England, and the second one, Kevin learned, had been bought secondhand by George when he'd bought the green truck. Tom Fallon then closed the rear door of the truck and put a padlock on it while the three other men went out in the yard to help Ned, who was already busy taking the flat tire off the big truck in the yard.

Max, who had come out from the kitchen after finishing his kibble, had learned his lesson at Sherborne Farm and was quietly sticking close to Kevin's side. Terry O'Neill was busy inside the back of the now empty big truck, recovering all their weapons: three Uzi machine guns, five automatic rifles, seven handguns, and many rounds of ammunition. Each man would now carry his own handgun in a shoulder holster, and the rifles and machine guns would be hidden in the trunks of the two cars.

George's planning was meticulous, so Kevin was not surprised to learn that George already had two different cars, which they would drive to their next stop, waiting in garages there. The black Rover and the old Vauxhall would be left locked up in their places, out of sight. Kevin asked George, "Why are they bothering to change the wheel on the big truck?"

"Well, Mac, there was no barn or outhouse big enough to hide the big brown truck from England. So my plan was to have the truck driven to the high cliffs between Carnsore Point and Kilmore Quay and dumped into the ocean, deep enough at that point to hide it from view forever. I'd wanted to get the truck to the cliffs in darkness, but now we're running twenty minutes behind schedule, and dawn will be breaking in about half an hour, so we have to hurry." By the time George got through explaining this to Kevin, the spare wheel had already been put on the truck, and the men were quickly reloading it with the furniture, which had been standing around the yard. George and Kevin joined the others to speed up the job.

By the time the truck was reloaded, it was only twenty minutes before dawn, and it was a good fifteen-minute-drive to the cliffs. Ned was already in the cab and starting up the engine when Sean Morrissey got in beside him. Pat Feeney had already taken the Ford car out of one of the other garages and was ready to follow them. Kevin and the others stood for a few minutes watching the truck, followed by the car, disappear quickly down the driveway. Terry O'Neill turned off all the yard lights, though it was unlikely anyone would have noticed with all the trees around, and besides, there were no other houses close by. Weary and sweating, they all traipsed into the house and went to the kitchen to wash up and have steaming mugs of tea and some toast. No one seemed to be in a mood to talk.

George kept glancing nervously at his watch every few minutes, but, almost to the dot, a half an hour after they had left, Ned, Pat, and Sean returned in the car and joined them in the kitchen with big smiles. A gray, misty dawn had broken the night sky about ten minutes earlier. The smiles sent a ripple of relief around the room, even before Ned said, "Mission accomplished, Major! Nobody's gonna find that truck in a million years, or at least for a few days."

"Well done, lads," Kevin said.

And George added, "And you are absolutely sure, Ned, that no one saw you ditch the truck over the cliffs?"

"There wasn't a soul stirring, Captain. There was a faint twinkle of lights from a couple of fishing trawlers way out at sea, but with the mist, there was no way they could have seen anything."

"Okay, men, it looks like phase three is successfully completed," George announced proudly.

Kevin nodded his agreement and told Ned and the other two to help themselves to tea and toast, as none of them could be sure when they would have their next bite to eat. When everyone was done, they left the kitchen as they had found it, put out the lights, and all seven men went out the side door into the yard, locking the door after them.

A late-model, light blue Ford was left parked in front of the house, and Ned backed out the small dark green truck from the garage and drove it around to behind the car. George went and got the old dark gray station wagon out of another garage and parked it behind the truck. All garages were now locked up, with the two cars from England in two of them and all traces of their presence cleared up. With everything checked out and ready to go, George's plan now called for Kevin to ride in front in the blue Ford, with Terry O'Neill for company. Ned and Sean Morrissey would follow in the dark green truck. And George would drive the station wagon with Pat Feeney and Tom Fallon. Again, they were all going to follow the same route for this last leg of their journey and leave at five-minute intervals. Kevin noticed that all three vehicles had local Irish license plates, so no one was likely to take a blind bit of notice of them.

It was exactly ten minutes to eight as Kevin and Terry set off in the lead car with Max on the backseat. They waved good-bye to the others. The next stop would be their final destination. As they headed down the tunneled driveway, Kevin wondered what was going on now on the other side of the Irish Sea.

CHAPTER 7

I T WAS WELL AFTER EIGHT o'clock, and Sir Ian Sinders was eating breakfast because he hated being angry on an empty stomach. He looked up quizzically at Captain Smithers, whom he'd sent to search for Kevin, as he came in.

"Well, Captain? Speak up, man!"

"Well, sir, I can't find any trace of Major MacAllister. Colonel Barnes is already out in the field, and I learned from his office that the major did check in yesterday evening and, at a little before six, left in a Land Rover for some last-minute inspections. I then went to his bungalow, and when there was no answer to my knocks, finding the door open, I ventured in and had a look around. It certainly looks as if he has moved in. His briefcase was still sitting there along with his Washington trip report, which I know he had planned to give you this morning. Everything appeared normal, sir. I really don't know what to make of it, sir!"

"Okay, Captain, you did what you could. But I can't wait around here all morning. I have to get over to field GHQ right after breakfast. In the meantime, I'd like you to track down Colonel Barnes and find out what you can and then try to track Major MacAllister's movements yesterday evening and find out who spoke with him last. None of this makes any sense, so I want you to get to the bottom of it as quickly as possible. And, Captain, as soon as you have anything to report, please come over, in person, to field GHQ."

"Yes, sir!"

Twenty minutes later, Smithers arrived at field GHQ and approached Sir Ian. "Sir, Colonel Barnes said MacAllister visited the Third Battalion of the Royal Welsh Guards regiment sometime yesterday evening and moved an MML to another location for today's exercises. I then spoke with Captain Craig, who said he removed one of the four MMLs from our field battery, telling Lieutenant Ridley that he had made some last-minute changes to the plans for today's exercises. Craig said he figured since the major is in charge of all these things, he must know what he's doing, so he didn't think any more about it."

Sir Ian interrupted him. "And they have no idea where the major took the MML?"

Smithers shook his head. "No, absolutely no idea. Lieutenant Ridley didn't think it was his place to ask the major. However, he said the major had a captain with him from our own Royal Welsh Guard regiment and four soldiers, one of whom was a corporal."

Sir Ian felt his stomach lurch slightly. "Did Lieutenant Ridley recognize this captain or notice anything else?"

"No, he didn't. He just assumed the captain was from another battalion in our regiment. I called the COs of the other battalions and asked them about the major, but they said they hadn't seen him, and none of them mentioned that he had borrowed a captain and soldiers from his battalion."

Sir Ian sighed. He stood abruptly and said, "Have my staff contact the colonel of every regiment participating in the exercises and find out which MML was removed and who last saw Major MacAllister."

"Yes, sir. Anything else?"

Sir Ian left Smithers standing there while he sat thinking, *This is serious, very serious, and I'd better do something.* He wondered if the major had been kidnapped. *If so, that means the MML is also missing. I'd better call the minister of defense.* He turned to Smithers and said, "Captain Smithers, could you be so good as to send in my adjutant, Captain Harscombe, and leave this matter with me? You can get on with your other duties."

"Certainly, sir."

When Harscombe came ambling into field GHQ a few minutes

later, Sir Ian was irritated by his leisurely pace. "Don't dither about, man! Sit down! We've got a major problem on our hands, which may have serious ramifications. You're probably aware by now that Major MacAllister seems to have disappeared. Given his key position on my staff, that's pretty damn serious, and I fear he may have met with an accident, or even worse, he may have been kidnapped. But potentially even more serious is the possibility that one of our MMLs may be missing. Last night, the major removed one from the Third Battalion of the Royal Welsh Guards, and we haven't been able to track it down since. In view of this, I've made a decision to immediately halt our entire military exercises until the missing MML is accounted for. Please have all regimental COs notified of my orders right away, with instructions to account for and cross-check the location of all MMLs, and to report their findings back here no later than 1100 hours."

Captain Harscombe made a move to get out of his chair.

"Don't leave yet, Captain. I'm not through. After you have issued those instructions, please contact the minister of defense's office in London and find out what his schedule is for today. If at all possible, I'd like to meet with him at 12:15 at the Ministry. He should be available, as I believe he was scheduled to speak in the House of Commons this morning. Once you have that set up, arrange to have a helicopter standing by at 11:15 a.m. to take me to London. That will be all for now. Please report back to me as soon as everything is in place."

"Yes, sir! I'll see to it right now."

Right on the dot of 11:00 a.m., Captain Harscombe reported back to Sir Ian that nobody had seen Major MacAllister and there was no trace of the missing MML. "Okay, Harscombe," said Sir Ian, "the facts look grim, but until we can find out more, we have to deal with what we have. I want an immediate and thorough search of the entire area in and around the northern end of Salisbury Plain. I want photographs of Major MacAllister released to the local police. Heaven knows we have enough troops concentrated here to search every square inch of the area. The local police are to be told nothing of the missing MML, only that we need their assistance in locating Major MacAllister, but no facts about the major's role in the Ministry. And they are to be warned that no information whatsoever is to be given to the press. Only our own troops will be given the task of searching for the missing MML. But I want you to stress to all regimental COs that there is to be absolutely no leak about the missing MML by any soldier, as this information will be covered under the Official Secrets Act. Is all of that clear, Harscombe?"

"Yes, Sir Ian, crystal clear."

"Right, that's that. Now, have you made an appointment for me with the minister and is the helicopter ready?"

"Yes, sir. You'll be meeting with the Right Honorable Gordon Hargreaves at 12:15 p.m. in his office at the Ministry, and the helicopter is standing by for you right now."

"Good job, Harscombe. I'm leaving you to coordinate events at this end. Please tell Captain Smithers to join me at the helicopter, as I will need him in London. One other important issue. Please ask all regimental COs to account for the firing mechanisms to all the nuclear MMLs assigned to their regiments, including that for the missing MML. Everything clear?"

"Yes, sir. I'll get everything under control at this end."

"Excellent. I'll leave in two minutes. Please make sure the helicopter is ready to lift off and that Captain Smithers is there waiting for me."

When Sir Ian got out to the waiting helicopter, Captain Smithers was already there, and they boarded immediately. Sir Ian was preoccupied with thoughts about the meeting with the minister. The Right Honorable Gordon Hargreaves, who liked to be called Gordy by his friends and associates, was a difficult man to deal with. Hargreaves had only become minister of defense six months earlier when a Labor/ Liberal Party coalition had come to power after fifteen years of Tory rule. Sir Ian didn't like the brusque manner of Hargreaves and also felt that the new minister deliberately kept him off balance by not giving him clear indications of his own position on major issues facing the British Armed Forces. And most important of all, Sir Ian had not been able to get a firm reading on Hargreaves's stand on Britain's independent nuclear deterrent. It was six years since Sir Ian had become the head of the joint chiefs of staff. The first chief of the RAF to reach that position, he had grown accustomed to dealing with Tory ministers of defense, two in that period, who had treated him with respect and had valued his judgment. And indeed, Sir Ian felt comfortable with them and certainly dealt with them as his equals.

Though not allowed to openly admit it, Sir Ian was definitely a Tory supporter and didn't have time for a lot of the socialist ideas that the Labor Party subscribed to. Given this state of affairs, Sir Ian knew that his meeting with the minister about the disappearance of both a nuclear MML and the chief coordinator of Britain's nuclear arsenal would not be a pleasant one. And Sir Ian didn't feel any degree of confidence that the minister would support him.

When they were only about seven minutes from the Ministry, Sir Ian finally said to Captain Smithers, "When we get to the Ministry, I want you to go immediately to the vaults and check that no firing mechanisms are missing. Check every single one for every regiment, and for every battery in each regiment, and report back to me the minute you are through."

"Yes, I will, sir."

"And, Captain, were you able to find out if Major MacAllister had his dog with him at Warminster? He usually does, doesn't he?"

"As a matter of fact, sir, yes. It was reported that when the major arrived at Warminster yesterday evening, the dog was sitting in the front seat beside him. Also, when he left, the guard at the front gate is almost sure that he noticed a dog in the back of the Land Rover."

"Good, I thought he might have his dog with him. Then, Captain, take a minute before you go to the vaults and give Harscombe a quick call at field GHQ and advise him of that fact. It may help him get some leads as to what happened to the major. Max is the major's dog's name, isn't it? Tell Harscombe that also."

"Yes, I will, sir."

The helicopter landed on the roof of the Ministry, and Sir Ian and Captain Smithers got out, clutching their hats as the rotor blades were still kicking up a hell of a wind. Once inside the Ministry, Sir Ian went down to his office, as he had a few minutes before he would meet Hargreaves.

At 12:15 exactly, Sir Ian presented himself to Gordon Hargreaves, his boss and the current minister of defense. They were meeting in the minister's office, which was on the floor above Sir Ian's. The burly man was in his midfifties and had started out in life as a Yorkshire coal miner and an ardent socialist. Hargreaves had made a name for himself with the coal miner's union and was first elected to Parliament in the sixties as a Labor MP for his Yorkshire constituency under the Wilson Labor government. He had quickly learned to master the ins and outs of parliamentary procedure and to use them to his best advantage; so he attracted attention from the party leadership, but only in the later years of the Wilson government, and had no opportunity to serve at the ministerial level. Hargreaves had proved to be a quick learner at whatever he turned his hand to, and through a series of positions in the party hierarchy, he had eventually emerged as the Labor Party spokesman on defense matters. For the last several years under the Tory government, Hargreaves had been the Labor Party spokesman for defense in the shadow cabinet in Parliament and now seemed to revel in the fact that his party was in power and he had become minister of defense. Not only was Sir Ian, who came from a noble family that had long served the Crown in military capacities, from a very different family background than Gordon Hargreaves, but also the two men were stark contrasts in styles and looks. Gordon Hargreaves's jet-black hair, bushy eyebrows, and rough-and-ready facial features were in sharp contrast to Sir Ian with his silver-white hair and tall, patrician good looks. While Sir Ian was a prompt and courteous man, Gordon Hargreaves tended to be blunt and often liked to keep people waiting.

Sir Ian had to wait a good five minutes while Gordon Hargreaves chatted on the telephone. By the time he got in to see him, Sir Ian was quietly fuming but knew he had to keep it to himself in front of his political master. Sir Ian felt he looked imposing and impeccable in his light blue RAF uniform, compared to Hargreaves in a rumpled, dark gray suit and a red tie that was twisted sideways along his white shirt. He sat down without being asked and, putting his best foot forward, adopted a most cordial tone of voice. "How very good of you to see me on such short notice, Minister."

"Not at all, Sir Ian. It is always a pleasure to see my head of the joint chiefs of staff."

Sir Ian hardly failed to detect the slight note of sarcasm in the minister's voice, but he chose to ignore it before going on.

"Well, Minister, I won't beat about the bush. I requested this meeting because I'm afraid a very grave problem has arisen, and under the circumstances, I felt it was imperative to inform you, myself, right away."

Gordon Hargreaves visibly straightened in his chair. "So, please, do go on. You have my undivided attention."

"Well, Minister, you do know who Major MacAllister is, don't you?"

"Yes, yes, of course. Isn't he the chap on your staff who is head of Section Q11 and responsible for coordination of our nuclear weapons? Do go on, Sir Ian."

"The fact is the major has disappeared. He was last seen last night. It's my belief he may have been kidnapped, but we have no confirmation of that yet. But that isn't the worst of it. Apparently, a nuclear MML that he was transferring from one battalion to another has also disappeared."

Sir Ian paused to let the full effect of what he had said sink in, scrutinizing the minister's face for some reaction, but his scrutiny was met with a poker face. There was a long silence before Hargreaves said, "You were absolutely right to advise me of this situation right away. A kidnapping we can deal with, but a nuclear accident would be very tricky. I assume, of course, that the nuclear warheads on the twin missiles were unarmed and that normal security measures were in place for the firing mechanisms?"

Sir Ian was on his guard and wary that whatever he might say could have repercussions down the road. In the last six months, he had learned all too well that Hargreaves was, first and last, a politician and saw his job as minister of defense purely as a stepping stone along the path of his political career. Sir Ian knew this was not the time to admit that he had Captain Smithers checking the firing mechanisms in the vault at that very moment and decided to go on, evasively.

"Yes, of course, Minister. All normal security measures are in force, and the firing mechanisms remained at regimental headquarters with the duplicates here at the Ministry. So if anyone has kidnapped the major and hijacked the MML, there is no way they can activate the nuclear warhead."

"That's good, Sir Ian, I'm glad to hear you say that. So, what steps have you taken to find the major and the MML?"

"I have halted the military exercises as of ten o'clock this morning, and now all troops are searching the entire area for both the major and the MML; local police stations have been furnished with a photograph of the major and advised that he is missing. But they were not told anything about the MML; right now that is purely a military matter, and I have informed all my COs that any mention of it to anyone outside the military will be treated as a breach of the Official Secrets Act. Naturally, Minister, you are the first to be advised of this whole affair."

Hargreaves was quiet again for a moment or two before he went on rather briskly, "That's as it should be. I suppose that what you've done so far is certainly adequate. With so many troops in the field for the exercises on Salisbury Plain, I believe a thorough search should be completed within a couple of hours. I'll give you until three o'clock to report back to me, and if no trace of the major or the MML has been found, I believe we should call in MI5 to expand the search nationwide. As our domestic intelligence service, they have far more sources and informants than local police forces, and in these circumstances, they're essential. In the meantime, I'll advise the prime minister on a confidential basis and will keep her informed of any progress."

"That should be sufficient time to conclude the search, and I do agree that if we haven't found anything by three o'clock, we should certainly call in MI5."

Hargreaves smiled and said, "I'm pleased you agree, Sir Ian, but now I have things to do, and so do you. Just keep me advised if anything breaks before three o'clock. Otherwise, let's meet again here at that time."

In his typically abrupt fashion, Hargreaves took some papers out of his ministerial folder to indicate the end of the meeting. Sir Ian got up without another word and left, thinking, *God, how that man rattles me.* He hurried back to his office, where he found Captain Smithers waiting for him.

"Well, Captain, I trust you found everything was in order in the vaults?"

"Yes, sir, all firing mechanisms were present and intact. Sir, there was one other small matter bothering me. I ran into the major's secretary in the halls, and she seemed surprised to see me, but I cut and ran. Do you think I can tell her anything? And also, I was wondering whether the major's wife should be informed that he is missing."

"Why don't you let me take care of it, Captain? It will be best if I speak to Margaret. And I'll also give the major's wife a call, as I have known her for a number of years. Meanwhile, please call Captain Harscombe at the field GHQ and find out if there have been any developments. That will be all for now, Captain."

Once Smithers left, Sir Ian had his secretary, Jane Hawley, fetch Margaret, and he informed both women about the major's disappearance. He didn't insult either of them by warning them not to discuss it with anybody, as he was well aware of their long records of service to the Ministry and that each of them had a high level of security clearance. After he dismissed Margaret and Jane, he made his call to Sheila MacAllister.

"Hello, Sheila. Ian Sinders here. Just wondering if you heard from Kevin since he got to Salisbury?"

"Oh, Sir Ian, how lovely to hear from you! No, I didn't, but then he usually doesn't call when he's away on department business. Why, is anything the matter?"

He sensed the rising anxiety in Sheila's voice and said, "We seem to have lost track of Kevin in Salisbury, but don't worry, we have a search underway, and we're sure there's a simple explanation. I'll call you just as soon as I hear anything. Bye for now, Sheila."

Sir Ian felt relieved after he had completed his brief call. It was already past one o'clock, and he felt a bit helpless. There was nothing else he could do until he got some reports in from field GHQ. So he asked Jane to bring him in some lunch, as he had no idea when he would next have a chance to eat. Within minutes, she brought him a plate of baked chicken, grilled mixed vegetables, and rice with gravy and a steaming cup of tea.

He had just finished lunch when Captain Smithers reported that there were still no new developments from Salisbury Plain. As he sat there, Sir Ian had a nagging feeling that this affair could turn out to be the worst crisis of his whole career. But for now, there was nothing he could do but wait.

At about twenty minutes past two, Sir Ian got a call from Captain Harscombe, who said, "Sir, the Land Rover Major MacAllister drove last night was found intact in a quarry between Trowbridge and Devizes. It was camouflaged and had been wiped clean of any prints. There was no trace of the MML."

"No other evidence found at the scene?"

"None, sir."

Sir Ian mulled over this latest development—the only bright spot was that his troops had found the Land Rover, not the local police. In all other respects, the news was terrible, because there was absolutely no trace of the major, his dog, or the nuclear MML. For the life of him, Sir Ian couldn't figure who would have pinpointed the major, as he knew Major MacAllister had always maintained a very low profile due to his position at the Ministry. He was well aware that only a handful of people in the entire country knew that the major was the chief of Section Q11. He wondered who could have kidnapped him, as there were so many terrorist groups in the world, and many of them had an ax to grind against Britain for one reason or another, either imagined or real. He speculated it could be the IRA, the Libyans, the PLO, or any number of active extremist groups in Europe. It could be just about anyone. Besides, Sir Ian was genuinely fond of Major MacAllister and on several occasions had invited the major and his wife down to his country house for the weekend. So he felt a deep personal concern on top of his professional concerns for both the major's safety and that of the country.

At ten minutes to three, Sir Ian called through to Captain Harscombe to inquire if there were any further developments, as he would have to meet the minister again shortly. There were none. So, realizing that it could no longer remain purely a military matter and that MI5 would have to take over, Sir Ian gave Captain Harscombe instructions that the military exercises were to resume and continue as planned over the next several days but with double security on the movement of all MMLs in the area.

After he hung up, Sir Ian felt that this was the only decision he could have made in the circumstances, as not to continue the exercises would undoubtedly have raised the curiosity of the media, which could be very awkward. With a sinking feeling, Sir Ian went up to rejoin the minister and apprise him of the latest development. Sir Ian realized that the total disappearance of the MML was just about the most major breach of national security that could occur, and the whole affair would now escalate to the level of the prime minister. The only saving grace was that without the firing mechanisms, the missing nuclear missiles were inoperable. But despite that, Sir Ian also realized that his career could come to a sudden end if the MML was not quickly located and recovered.

This time, when Sir Ian entered Gordon Hargreaves's office, he noticed that for once, the minister was ready and waiting for him and almost seemed too cordial, which immediately put him on his guard. He sat down and tried warily to size up the real meaning of the minister's attentiveness.

"Well, Sir Ian, what new developments have we?"

"The latest report is that the Land Rover that Major MacAllister was using last night has been found in an old quarry. Luckily, it was found by our own troops and not by local police. However, there were absolutely no fingerprints or any signs left on the Land Rover to give us any clue as to what may have happened to the major. Also, unfortunately, there is no trace of the missing MML, but the missiles are totally inoperable, as all firing mechanisms have been checked and accounted for."

"So it does appear that your theory may well be correct and that indeed the major may have been kidnapped. But for what purpose? And what good would the missiles be to a terrorist group without the firing mechanisms?"

"Yes, it certainly does look like kidnapping. As for what purpose, I don't know. I can only speculate. Without knowing what group may be behind the kidnapping, it's hard to establish a motive. As for the purpose of obtaining the uranium in the nuclear warheads, I really don't have any answers at this point. I believe our first priority must be to locate the major, and that should lead us to the MML."

"I agree. But how do we go about finding the major without enlisting the help of all the police and security forces throughout the country? And what story do we give them without any mention of the nuclear missiles? It's of the utmost importance that not a single word leak out about the missing missiles."

Sir Ian mulled over these questions, and he did have some ideas, but he wasn't quite ready to put all his cards on the table. He would prefer to let the minister suggest what should be done.

At last, Hargreaves said, "Well, perhaps we shouldn't attempt to answer those questions here and now on our own. I've arranged for us to meet with the prime minister and the home secretary at 10 Downing Street at 3:45 p.m., and I think that would be the best forum in which to decide what to do next. Wouldn't you agree?"

"Yes, that would be best."

Sir Ian knew that with Downing Street involved, they would arrive at a more balanced decision as to what to do next. But at the same time, he knew his own position would be more exposed, and he was quite certain he couldn't rely on Gordon Hargreaves for any support. But no matter how he looked at it, he would be the only professional military man in a den of politicians.

Hargreaves broke in on his thoughts, saying, "By the way, I think you did the correct thing in recommencing the military exercises, as no doubt to have suspended them indefinitely would have raised awkward questions. I suppose there's no need for me to ask that security has been doubled on all other MML units."

"Thank you, and yes, I have given explicit instructions to beef up all security on the MMLs."

"Okay, there's nothing more we can solve here. Why don't you meet me downstairs in the lobby in about ten minutes, and we can stroll across together to Downing Street."

"Fine, Minister. I'll be there."

Sir Ian got up and went back to his office. He got Harscombe on the line, but there was no news—only that the military exercises were once again in full swing, and he was thankful for that. Sir Ian also telephoned Captain Smithers and told him to stick around his office until he was needed, since there was no point in his returning to Salisbury Plain that afternoon, when he might be needed in London.

He sat there quietly for a few more minutes, trying to collect his thoughts. It really was one hellish situation. He then gathered up a few papers and stuck them in his leather folder. Taking a light overcoat from the coat rack, he slipped it on. It was a nice, mild, sunny September day, but he felt it would be advisable to cover up his RAF uniform as he strolled over to Downing Street with the minister. On his way out of the office, he asked his secretary to stay around, and he caught the elevator down to the lobby. The lobby clock said 3:35 p.m.; needless to say, the minister had not yet arrived. Sir Ian paced until five minutes later when Gordon Hargreaves finally joined him. The two men set off at a brisk walk, across Whitehall, and down to 10 Downing Street.

A uniformed policeman opened the door for the two men. Inside, they were shown into a small waiting room adjoining the cabinet room. Sir Ian was pleased to note that the clock on the mantelpiece said exactly a quarter to four and that they were on time, despite the minister having kept them waiting. Neither man spoke, and Sir Ian was thinking that this was his first time at 10 Downing Street since the current government had come into power the previous March. He now felt very uncomfortable at the circumstances for his first visit to 10 Downing Street with a socialist prime minister. At that point, Sir Ian's thoughts were interrupted by Jack Larson, confidential secretary to the prime minister. "Gordy, Sir Ian, the PM is now ready to see you!"

Gordon Hargreaves and Sir Ian followed Jack Larson into the prime minister's private office, which also had a door at the right that opened into the cabinet meeting room. The prime minister, Muriel Hobson, was sitting behind her large antique desk, with glasses perched on the end of her nose. She was flanked by Ernest Brooking, the home secretary, on one side, and Charles Mills, the secretary of state for foreign affairs, on the other. Also present were Scott Frawley from MI5 and Sir Hugh Blake, the permanent cabinet secretary and a senior career civil servant who, like Sir Ian, had served successive governments. There were two empty chairs in front of the desk for Gordon Hargreaves and Sir Ian.

Muriel Hobson was in her late fifties, with steely gray hair tied back behind her ears. She had a rather pleasant smile, but, as many politicians knew, that smile masked a tough, ruthless woman who had survived a lot of party infighting to emerge as the first-ever woman leader of the British Labor Party and the first woman prime minister. Muriel Hobson had politics in her blood and was indeed the granddaughter of Lloyd George, who had served as prime minister from 1916 through the early 1920s. She was the member of Parliament for an industrial area of Manchester, which had returned her to Parliament with increasing majorities in the last seven general elections, thus giving her one of the safest Labor seats of any member of Parliament. And Sir Ian knew that each minister sitting in the room had been hand-chosen by Muriel Hobson for his skills, his toughness, and above all, his personal loyalty to her. Muriel Hobson was well known not to tolerate anyone in the party who defied her wishes.

As Sir Ian looked around the room, he knew he didn't have any friends there, except perhaps Sir Hugh Blake, who had as long and distinguished a career in the civil service as Sir Ian had had in the RAF. And perhaps Scott Frawley, with whom Sir Ian believed he had a very good working relationship, but as an intelligence man, Sir Ian never quite trusted him 100 percent. Sir Ian wondered why Charles Mills was at this session and, at the same time, why Sir Harold Gilbert, the director general of British Intelligence Services, was not present. So even before the prime minister spoke, Sir Ian could sense that this was not going to be a very pleasant meeting.

"Well, Gordy, have you and Sir Ian come up with anything?"

"Since I spoke to you earlier, Muriel, the Land Rover that Major MacAllister was driving last night has been found but with no traces of a struggle and no fingerprints. There is absolutely no trace of the mobile missile launcher and its twin nuclear missiles. Sir Ian and I have agreed that the first priority is to find the major, which in turn may lead us to the MML. But we did want to hear your opinion and that of Ernest here, as to how we should proceed with that search."

"Actually, Gordy, I've had some discussion on this topic with both Ernest and Charles before you joined us. We have decided that the best approach to take would be to issue a statement to the press to the effect that we believe Major MacAllister has had an accident and may be suffering from amnesia. And to ask the media to splash his photograph across the newspapers and on TV this evening on the six o'clock news and on all later news bulletins. Obviously, we must make no mention of the missing MML. So, what do you think, Gordy?"

"That's a terrific idea, Muriel."

"And you, Sir Ian, what do you think?"

"Prime Minister, I believe you have found an excellent solution to our dilemma."

Muriel Hobson's face creased into a smile. "Okay, if we are all in agreement, then …" All the men in the room nodded. "Then, Jack, please draft up a suitable statement for the press, and I believe it should be your responsibility, Gordy, to meet with the press and to issue the statement."

"Certainly, Muriel. I'll be happy to do that. But obviously, the major's true position at the Ministry should not be mentioned. I'll simply state that he's a serving senior officer."

"Now that's settled; let's get on to the next topic. Is it possible, Gordy, that the MML could be activated, and could it be removed from the country?"

"On your first point, Muriel, Sir Ian has assured me that the twin missiles on the MML are totally inoperative without their own unique, coded firing mechanisms, and the mechanisms for those particular missiles have been accounted for. That would appear to eliminate that particular danger. As for your second point, I don't really know how easy it would be to disguise the MML and to get it out of the country, but perhaps Sir Ian can elaborate on this."

"Certainly, Prime Minister. It would be extremely difficult to disguise the MML in as much as it is a seven-foot-long by five-foot-wide vehicle, with two six-foot-long missiles perched on top of it. However, as apparently the MML disappeared last night along with the major, then it is conceivable that whoever hijacked the missiles has had plenty of time to disguise it and possibly has already taken it out of the country. So, while it is possible, at this point, we have no reason to believe that the MML has left the country."

"So in other words, Sir Ian, we have no guarantees that the MML hasn't already left the country." She paused and glanced around the room. "Gentlemen, as you all know, Sir Harold Gilbert, our director general of intelligence services, is away on private holiday in the outback of Australia and cannot be reached. So I have asked Scott Frawley as director of MI5 to coordinate all efforts by both MI5 and our foreign intelligence service, MI6, to track down the major, and, most importantly, the MML. I asked Charles here to be at this meeting in the event that we find out that the MML has left the country; then, clearly, we'll have a need for discussions with foreign governments."

Very discreetly, Sir Ian glanced around at everyone else in the room and knew that each had the same thing on his mind, and he knew no one wanted to actually say it: if indeed the MML had ended up outside Britain, this whole affair could escalate into a major international crisis. Sir Ian was also very much aware of the look of contentment on Scott Frawley's face, like that of the cat who got all the cream. For it looked as though this whole affair may play right into his hands in his quest to be the next director general of the intelligence services. But Sir Ian did admit to himself that the cover story to be used to explain Major MacAllister's disappearance was quite clever and could only help flush out someone, somewhere, who saw something. And if they saw the major, hopefully the MML would not be too far away.

The prime minister said, "Okay, now that that's settled, I believe we don't need you anymore, Sir Ian, or you, Sir Hugh. And please remember, Sir Hugh, at this point I don't want this affair to go beyond the people in this room. It is not yet a matter for the full cabinet."

Both Sir Ian and Sir Hugh took their somewhat abrupt dismissal by their political master very graciously and left the room. They chatted for a couple of minutes in the waiting room, when Scott Frawley joined them. Obviously he, too, had been dismissed. Clearly, Muriel Hobson wanted to be alone with her closest and most trusted political associates.

"Sorry to interrupt, Sir Hugh, but, Sir Ian, will you be available later at your office at the Ministry?"

"I certainly will, Scott; in fact I'll probably spend the night at the Ministry to keep close to events." Scott Frawley left them, and a few minutes later, Sir Ian bid farewell to Sir Hugh and went out in the hallway to slip on his coat. He put both his RAF hat and his leather folder under his arm and left 10 Downing Street to walk back to the Ministry.

When Sir Ian reached Richmond Terrace, rather than going back into the Ministry, he decided he needed a walk to clear his head and do some thinking. So he turned left at the corner of the Ministry building onto Victoria Embankment and slowly strolled alongside the River Thames toward the RAF Memorial. He stood proudly and silently before the memorial, as if seeking inspiration. None came, only the desolate feeling that he might well be the first member of his family to end his career ignominiously, after so many generations of his family had given such distinguished service in various branches of the British Armed Services. A chilly breeze began to blow in off the river, and Sir Ian pulled up the collar of his overcoat and decided it was time to go back to his office. It was already a quarter to five when he got back, and he decided to call his wife, who was spending the week at their country house, Bramble Hall, in Kent.

He knew she had assumed he would be in Warminster and Salisbury Plain all week. Sir Ian told his wife about Major MacAllister's disappearance and little else, but he did say that due to the crisis, he would most likely be spending the night at the Ministry if she should need to contact him for any reason. He hung up, as he really wasn't in a mood to talk anymore. Time was hanging heavy on his hands, as this was one of the few occasions in his life that he didn't quite know what he should do next. Even the press release about the major's disappearance would be handled by the minister's office and was scheduled for five thirty in the evening. Sir Ian thought at least he could watch the six o'clock news on the television in his office to see how the media carried the story. He knew he would hear from Captain Smithers and Captain Harscombe if they had anything new to report. *Maybe Scott Frawley will have turned up something by the time he drops in on me,* Sir Ian thought. To help keep his mind occupied, he reviewed the revised appropriations for naval spending, as he was the man who had to balance the requests from each branch of the armed services against total appropriations. But try as he may, Sir Ian's mind kept wandering back to Major MacAllister.

CHAPTER 8

KEVIN AND TERRY O'NEILL IN the old blue Ford were the first to reach their destination; it had taken them almost five and half hours to travel the two hundred miles from Rosslare. It was only one thirty in the afternoon, but the mist rolling in off Dingle Bay blocked out the sunshine, and it almost appeared like dusk. Just before reaching the little ocean-side village of Glenbeigh, Kevin pulled off onto a small side road and went about half a mile where he stopped under a clump of trees. Kevin and Terry had taken turns driving, and now both were tired and hungry, as they had only made a couple of quick stops to let Max out for a run. They were to wait there until the others arrived, as it had been agreed before they left Garryrhu House that George, Pat, and Tom, who were traveling last in the old station wagon, would make a couple of stops along the way and stock up on food. They did not want to be seen together at any restaurants along the route. Kevin turned to Terry and said, "I think I'll take Max for a walk. Would you care to join me, Terry?"

"Sure I would, Major, but maybe I'd better wait here in the car in case you aren't back when the others arrive. They might worry if they don't see us here."

"Well, I may as well go off. I'll probably head in the direction toward the mountains, just to scout ahead a little, as it were."

Kevin loved this part of Ireland, and he embraced the mist and soaked up the smell of the heather as if he couldn't get enough of it. He remembered many happy summer days spent with his cousins, Jim and Mary, when he visited this part of the country as a child. They had loved rock climbing in this region, which contained most of the highest mountain peaks in all of Ireland. The area was pretty deserted except for a few coastal resorts and fishing villages along Dingle Bay and the Atlantic. The land wasn't good enough to farm, and even the mountains in many places were too steep to allow sheep to graze. Kevin knew he had picked the right spot for the missiles, and Ned, who knew the area best of all, had picked the perfect location high in the mountains. Kevin's once-sharp memories of every nook and cranny of the area had grown dim over the years, and he regretted that he hadn't come back here more often as an adult.

As he walked with Max trotting along excitedly at his side, Kevin couldn't help thinking what must be going on over in London. He figured that Sir Ian and Captain Smithers must be in a rare flap, as he realized that by now they would have confirmed that not only was he missing but also the MML. Having known Sir Ian for a long time, he felt almost sure that it would be assumed he was kidnapped and the MML hijacked. But he also knew they would be very puzzled about how it had happened, and he wondered if they had even yet found the Land Rover. As he soaked up the wonderful scenery, Kevin knew that these might well be his last days alive. But even knowing that, he felt more exhilarated than at any time in his life; he had been chosen by fate to help achieve the unification of Ireland, once and for all time. Checking his watch, Kevin decided it was time to walk back to the car.

As he rounded the last bend in the laneway, he saw that the small green truck had pulled in behind the car, and Terry O'Neill was standing there talking to Ned and Sean Morrissey. Ned waved when he saw Kevin, and as Max got excited when he saw the others, Kevin let him off the leash to run up to the men.

"Glad to see you finally made it, Ned. No problems along the way, I trust?"

"No, Major. Everything went without a hitch. So you found the spot without any trouble then."

"Yeah, Ned, you gave good directions. I wonder where George and the others are. I hope they'll get here before too long."

"Oh, don't you be worrying yourself, Major. I'm sure they'll be along shortly. Remember they were going to make a couple of stops for food."

"Don't be reminding me about food, Ned. I don't know about you and Sean, but Terry and I are feeling pretty damn hungry. Which reminds me, no need for Max to starve—I have his food in the trunk, so maybe I'll give him a dish of kibble now."

Max's ears pricked up like antennae. It seemed as if he recognized the word and was close on Kevin's heels when he went to the car. Kevin had begun to feel that Max was their good luck mascot, and besides, Max was always well worth taking care of. Just as the dog was tucking into the kibble in his dish, the four men turned their heads to look down the laneway toward an approaching station wagon. As it came fully into view, they saw with relief that it was George and the other two. George pulled in behind the truck, and the three men got out.

"Well, George, we're all certainly relieved to see you three, and in more ways than one. It so happens we're all rather hungry, so we hope you have lots of food in the wagon."

George, Pat, and Tom broke out laughing as if at a private joke. "No worries, Mac," George said. "Actually I had a bet on with the lads here that once we arrived, one of the first things you all would be asking about was food. We've got enough to feed us for more than a week. So how long have you been waiting, Mac?"

"Oh, Terry and I got here about one thirty, and Ned and Sean arrived about twenty minutes later, so we're not in bad shape. I'm pleased that the mist has rolled in early, as that will send the few tourists who are about back to their hotels."

"Well, from here on, Mac, I'm going to have to rely on you and Ned, as this is your territory."

"I'm afraid my memory of the area is a little vague, so I think I'll defer to Ned to get us to our final hiding place. But first, if Ned feels we're not likely to be spotted here, perhaps we should have a quick bite to eat to give us all some energy for the last couple of miles, which will be mostly an uphill climb."

"Oh, we should be fine here, Major," Ned said. "We're well off the beaten track, and this laneway just peters out about a mile farther in. There used to be a farm nearby, but it's long since closed down. So there's nobody living hereabouts."

Everyone enjoyed a quick lunch of bread, cheese, and milk, and Max paraded around looking for odd scraps as if he hadn't been fed. When they were done, Ned suggested that they get moving, and this time, he led the way in the green truck while the others followed in the car and station wagon. After following Ned for about a mile, they came to the end of the laneway with the deserted farmhouse and barns he had mentioned, off to the left overlooking Lough Caragh. Here Ned said the car and the station wagon could be well hidden in one of the old barns, and after they got the MML out of the truck, they would dump the truck in Lough Caragh, which was very deep.

Once the MML was out of the truck, Kevin demonstrated to Ned and George how to lower the MML's own tracks over its wheels and to start its electric engine. Sean took care of ditching the truck in the lake, and the others took out the guns, food, and anything else they needed from the car and station wagon. When everyone was all set to go, Kevin said that the guns and any bags that could fit could be put on top of the MML. He would sit on the small seat inside the MML and drive it on its battery motors, which at all times held enough charge to drive at an average of twenty-five miles an hour for up to six hours. It was about twenty minutes to three when they were all ready to leave the deserted farm. Ned led the way up a rough track by the side of the lake, followed by Kevin in the MML and George and the others on foot behind.

They soon left the lake behind them and were now following a path along the banks of the River Caragh, climbing steadily. The mist got thicker as they climbed into the upper reaches of Ireland's highest mountain range, the MacGillycuddy's Reeks. Kevin drove the MML very carefully, but he was confident that it could make it, even as the pathway narrowed to about the same width as the MML, which had been designed to be able to handle such terrain. Ned advised Kevin that they were heading for one particular part of the mountain range called Skregmore, which contained several caves and that, Ned assured Kevin and George, was not well known even among rock climbers. They were now at about 2,200 feet above sea level on Mount Skregmore, and the last few hundred feet had been difficult going for the MML, as the pathway got narrower and narrower. Ned indicated for them to go around the bend. No one could even see the cave until Ned moved some wild bushes out of the way and exposed the entrance. Ned had the men set about cutting a wide enough gap with their knives to let the MML into the cave. When they were done, Kevin very carefully maneuvered the MML up over a slight ridge and down a slope to the floor of the cave. Kevin was impressed. It was perfect. As he maneuvered the MML around so that the missiles were facing outward, he would be able to set them on a perfect trajectory. Ned also explained to Kevin that the cave went right through to the other side of the mountain, which was about a quarter of a mile away.

All the bags of food and other equipment were unloaded from the MML. George came into his own again as he unpacked one suitcase that Kevin hadn't noticed before. It contained four walkie-talkies, two field telephones, a powerful portable radio receiver, and a large supply of spare batteries for all the equipment. George explained that they would keep one field telephone here in the cave with them while the other would be used halfway down the mountain at the first lookout point; from there on, the walkie-talkies would be used to communicate with Terry and the others at the deserted farm. The radio had a powerful antenna that could be rigged up outside the mouth of the cave, and as George explained, it would be critical that they be able to listen in to all BBC news broadcasts.

Finally, George got out the last piece of equipment from the suitcase, which to Kevin looked like a cross between a radio and some sort of radar device; he asked Tom Fallon to explain it to Kevin, as Tom had devised it. Tom called it a distorter. It would enable him to throw off the signals from both the field telephone and the walkie-talkies, to confuse anyone trying to pick up the signals as to their exact location. Tom explained to Kevin that it had a distortion ratio of three to one and a range of up to fifteen miles, which should be adequate. Tom went on to explain that this technology could not distort the satellite-driven GPS in mobile phones and early on had suggested to George and Kevin that mobile phones be banned from the last stage of the operation. Every single phone had been ditched in the Avon Gorge along with the uniforms.

Again, George had thought of everything. Though certainly, Ned had made his contribution by picking such a perfect cave. Kevin could tell the way the cave slanted downward and with the undergrowth around the mouth of the cave, they would be almost invisible even from the air, even though from inside Kevin had a good view of the skies above.

Lastly, George explained to Kevin the role that each man would play at this point in the operation. Ned was to man the first lookout point halfway down the mountain. He would have the field telephone there and a walkie-talkie to communicate with the next man in the chain. Ned would be armed with a rifle and one of the submachine guns. Sean Morrissey was to man the next lookout point in a suitable spot about halfway between Ned and the deserted farmhouse. Sean would also have a walkie-talkie and would be similarly armed. The last point in the chain would be the farmhouse, which would be manned by Pat Feeney with a walkie-talkie, a rifle, and a machine gun. He would liaise with Terry O'Neill, who was handling telephone communications with London. Tom Fallon was to remain in the cave with George and Kevin and could assist Kevin in handling the computer on the MML while at the same time using the distorter whenever there were communications between themselves. Those in the cave would be armed with rifles and handguns.

It was now five o'clock, and everything had been organized in the cave to go into action. George issued final instructions to the men and then sent Ned, Pat, and Sean off to their respective lookout points, armed and each with a supply of food. All men were now wearing civilian clothes, combinations of tweed jackets, sweaters, and jeans so that any of them would easily pass for a local farmer or fisherman, or even a lost tourist.

As the three men set off down the mountain, George told Tom and Terry to remain on lookout at the mouth of the cave and to man the field telephone. Then George beckoned to Kevin to follow him to the other end of the cave. Both men carried flashlights as they slowly made their way through the cave, the ceiling of which seemed to be gradually sloping downward all the time. Kevin began to feel claustrophobic in the damp, smelly cave that at times was so low that they had to almost crawl to pass through. Ned was right—after about a quarter mile, they came to the other side of the mountain. The entrance was a lot smaller than at the other side; there was barely enough room for a man to wriggle through, out into some scrub growing on the side of the mountain. Kevin followed George out through the hole. The two men lay there, crouching, with their heads just above the low-lying bushes scattered around the cave's exit. This side of the mountain wasn't quite as steep as the side they had climbed up, and there was dense undergrowth rolling all the way down to the ocean below. It appeared that the only approach to this side of the mountain would be from the ocean.

"Mac, I wanted you to come with me to reconnoiter this end of the cave so that I could explain to you, in private, the contingency escape plan I developed. Only Ned is aware of it, as he helped me to plan it. I know that you may be willing to give your life for a united Ireland, but if I can help it, I would like to go on living when this is over. I developed this plan not just for Ned and me but also with you in mind. Do you see that cove way down to the right, as the mountain curves out into a headland into the ocean?"

Kevin's glance followed in the direction that George was pointing, but with the swirling mist, he could barely make out where George meant. As his eyes searched, he finally focused on the cove that he thought George was pointing to.

"I think I see it now, George. Is it that point over there?"

"Exactly, Mac. That's the place. Well, with Ned's help, I have hidden a small but powerful motor launch stocked with extra supplies of gasoline, water, and a small amount of food. It's in a small cave to the left of the cove, and there's a narrow chasm down through the rocks, which we can reach from the bottom of this side of the mountain. I wanted you to know this, Mac; in the event that I don't make it, but you can, you have got to get down there and get the hell away from this mountain."

"If anyone deserves to get away, George, it's you. Without you, this entire operation would have been impossible. And your planning of every detail has been first-class."

The two men looked at each other, and the unspoken bond that had grown between them in the last six months appeared to be confirmed. With that, they squeezed their way back into the cave, which Kevin found a good deal more difficult than coming out. Twenty minutes later, they were back with Tom and Terry at the other end of the cave and got a big greeting from Max, who had remained with the two men. Terry was due to leave in a few minutes, so with Kevin's agreement, George wanted to run through his instructions to Terry one more time.

"Right, Terry. You have your Irish driver's license and, in your pocket, the car registration in your own name for the old blue Ford. And I believe you and Kevin filled up the car with petrol in Killorglin on the way here. You've got Sir Ian Sinders's private number at the British Ministry of Defense written down and in your pocket? You know that you place the call to Sir Ian at exactly 6:15 p.m. And you're clear on the wording, or let's go through it one last time."

Terry repeated the precise wording of the message to be given to Sir Ian for the British government when he answered his phone. "Just shut up and listen. We've got your major and your missiles. Stand by at this number tomorrow morning at seven o'clock, and we will give you our demands."

Kevin was impressed as he watched, and Terry's strong Derry accent was guaranteed to send shivers down Sir Ian's spine.

George said, "Very good, Terry. You have the wording perfect. It should take you approximately twenty-five minutes to make it to the farmhouse and Pat, and remember to leave him your handgun and holster. No weapons beyond the farmhouse. It should then take you only fifteen minutes, tops, to drive into Killorglin, which I estimate you should reach by about five minutes past six. That leaves you plenty of time to find a telephone kiosk from which to make the call. And you have plenty of loose change. Right? And remember, Terry, no drinking and no chatting with the locals, unless you can't avoid it. Your accent could well attract some attention."

"Don't worry, Captain. I'll carry out my instructions to the letter.

You can rely on me. I should be back at a little past seven, all going well. So, I'll be off now."

It was exactly twenty-five minutes past five as George and Kevin stood by the mouth of the cave and watched Terry O'Neill begin his descent of the mountain.

As they settled down to wait, Tom Fallon was already fiddling around with the radio receiver, having rigged the aerial when George and Kevin had gone to the other end of the cave. This far away from London, it was difficult to fine-tune the station, but Tom finally did, just as the last of the beeps trailed away: "This is the British Home Service at 5:30 p.m., Tuesday, September 7. Here are the latest news headlines. In Brussels today at a meeting of the EEC ministers, it was agreed to accept Britain's proposed changes to the Common Agricultural Policy. This represents the successful culmination of many years of talks to alter the Common Market Agricultural Policy. In Washington, it was announced today that a tentative accord has been reached between the US and Britain whereby British technology would be used in the development of the Star Wars program. Here in London this evening, many train commuters on British Rail's Southern Region remain stranded as a result of the unofficial one-day strike by railway men. A news release issued by the Ministry of Defense just moments ago states that a senior officer, Major Kevin MacAllister, was reported missing this morning after his Land Rover was found after an apparent accident. It is believed that the major may be suffering from amnesia, and anyone who sees him is requested to contact the military authorities or their local police station. Photos were issued to the television and newspaper media. Here is a description of the missing man ..."

The three men gathered around the radio exchanged glances. Kevin sat there quietly, wondering how his beloved Jenny would react when she heard the news. Kevin assumed that his wife would have been notified in advance, most likely by Sir Ian himself, who knew her. George was the first to break the silence.

"Well, Mac, at least the cat's out of the bag now. Obviously no mention of the MML; they wouldn't bloody dare! Quite a good ruse, don't you think, saying that you were in an accident and must be suffering from amnesia? Probably the only way they could have announced your disappearance and released pictures. Makes me wonder how long they'll genuinely believe that you were actually kidnapped, Mac."

"Oh, I don't know, George. They've no reason to believe anything other than that. And Sir Ian, in particular, will be convinced of it. Anyway, Terry's call at six fifteen will help reinforce it, but I doubt we'll ever hear anything about the phone call on the news."

Fallon, having lowered the volume on the radio earlier, now switched it off altogether; no point in wasting the batteries needlessly. The three men again lapsed into silence and settled down to wait.

CHAPTER 9

SCOTT FRAWLEY WAS FEELING EXCITED as he left 10 Downing Street after his meeting with the prime minister, Sir Ian, and the other ministers. He paused on the bottom step and stretched out his chest; it was only twenty past four, and he had a lot to do. He was very pleased that this crisis had arisen while the director general, Sir Harold Gilbert, was away in Australia. And even though he knew he was likely to be the next director general when Sir Harold retired in two years, he would certainly be very happy not to have to wait that long for a promotion he felt he deserved. The prime minister had made it quite clear to everyone in the room that he was now in charge of resolving this crisis. It was the sort of challenge that he reveled in.

He set off toward Whitehall and the couple of blocks to his office. At fifty-four, he was a shortish man with a middle-age paunch and a receding hairline, but in his youth he had been a wrestler and still kept reasonably fit. He was the type of man who always seemed to glide along rather than walk, and he had a habit of coming up on people without being heard. He enjoyed misleading people, and his jovial smile masked a sharp, scheming mind that missed nothing. MI5 and MI6 had just recently moved to new offices in a government office building on King Charles Street; in fact, his new office had a good view of both the Foreign Office and the Home Office on the opposite side of King Charles Street. Across Parliament Street, he could see a corner of the Ministry of Defense Building. Scott Frawley still had fond memories of Leconfield House, where he had started his career with MI5. Then, in the 1970s, they had moved to offices at the top of Curzon Street, which he didn't care for as much. But he was immensely pleased with the location of his new offices, so close to the center of power. He was a man who enjoyed power. By four thirty, he was back in his office on the fourteenth floor. Frawley sat down behind his desk for a few minutes to plan his next move.

Events were moving fast; he hadn't been aware of any of this until he got the call from Gordon Hargreaves some time after three o'clock. He had immediately called up Major Kevin MacAllister's file from records and had sent two of his own people down to the Trowbridge area to examine the recovered Land Rover. At three thirty, he had gotten the call to attend the meeting in the prime minster's office. He had already gone through the MacAllister file once, but nothing had struck him right between the eyes yet. However, Scott Frawley had a suspicious mind, and even though he had been on very friendly terms with Kevin MacAllister over the years, his golden rule was to assume everyone guilty first, until he could prove their innocence. Therefore, his devious mind was already entertaining dark possibilities that he wasn't quite ready to admit even to himself.

As he sat there, Frawley recalled that it was he who had introduced Kevin MacAllister to Jenny Laster while she was still married to Paul Laster of the CIA. In fact, Scott Frawley had such a memory for detail that he could even remember the occasion: a reception at the American embassy about five years earlier, and Frawley was well aware of Kevin's ongoing affair with her ever since. He had even made a note of it in the MacAllister file. However, he decided he would not contact Jenny Laster until after the news was released to the media. Then he would call her out of friendly concern as he tried to pump her for information, knowing full well that she may or may not be shocked at the news.

He had decided on his first plan of action—that he would personally go and see Sheila MacAllister right away and play on her shock value, as he knew that Sir Ian had already advised her that Kevin was missing. He called Mrs. MacAllister briefly to advise her that he would be up to see her shortly. Next, he called Captain Smithers at the Ministry and asked him to make arrangements to have Lieutenant Ridley at the Ministry no later than six o'clock that evening. Frawley wanted to interview him, as he was still apparently the last person known to have seen and spoken to Major Kevin MacAllister.

By twenty minutes to five, he was driving his car out of the underground garage and joining the rush hour traffic as he headed to north London to see Sheila MacAllister in Hampstead. Even when it came to driving, he knew every trick in the book, and despite the heavy evening traffic, he made it to the MacAllister house in Rudall Mews in Hampstead by five fifteen. He had to ring the doorbell several times before the door was finally opened. Sheila MacAllister stood there wearing only a housecoat, her hair tied back, her eyes bloodshot, her cheeks tearstained.

"Good afternoon, Mrs. MacAllister. I'm Scott Frawley. I just called you a little while ago."

"Yes, of course, Mr. Frawley, please do come in."

Scott followed Sheila down the hallway and into the living room on the right.

"Please sit down. Can I get you something to drink?"

"No, thank you. I don't think I'll have anything to drink now, but thank you anyway."

"Well, I hope you won't mind if I do. I need one."

She left the room, presumably to go to the kitchen to fix herself another drink. Scott thought that she had probably already had a few, but he considered that might actually make this interview a little easier. As he sat waiting for her to return, he scanned the room and quickly took in everything that was there. He noted with particular interest prominent photographs of the MacAllister's young son, Owen, who, Scott knew from his files, had been killed when only three years old. There were also some old photographs that appeared to be of Kevin MacAllister when he was a kid, taken on fishing trips in what looked like Scotland or Ireland. That possibility caused Scott Frawley to pause. There was another framed photograph on the mantelpiece that showed Kevin as a teenager on a horse with an elderly man standing close by but with no indication of where it had been taken. Sheila came back into

Ray Vernon

the room with a glass of gin and flopped into the armchair on the other side of the fireplace, opposite Frawley. She took a deep gulp of her drink.

"Well, sir, what can I do for you? You know, I do vaguely remember your name, not that Kevin ever mentions very much about the people he works with."

"Well, I believe Sir Ian told you the truth in that it looks like your husband was kidnapped. We're not sure yet who may be behind the kidnapping or why. But you do know, of course, that he has the highest security clearance at the Ministry of Defense, and we suspect that he's been kidnapped, as he has considerable knowledge of affairs of state that are of the utmost importance. Of course, as I work closely with Kevin, and we have become good friends over the years, I'm personally deeply concerned at his disappearance and would like to ask you a few questions that may help us in locating him."

"Well, of course. I'll gladly help you in any way I can, as I'm most anxious for Kevin to be found safe and sound."

Scott could hardly fail to notice the slight slurring of her words, and he figured she had probably been drinking since she'd gotten the news from Sir Ian. He decided he'd better keep his questions short and to the point, or he would risk losing her attention completely.

"Have you noticed anything odd about your husband's behavior or manner recently?"

Sheila frowned into her glass and appeared to be desperately trying to focus her mind on something before she answered. "Not really. Kevin has seemed about the same recently as he always is. He's a pretty even man, you know … but then, you would know that if you're his close friend. He's never discussed any of his work with me and has never displayed any ups and downs due to his job. There really isn't anything I can think of that might help."

"Were there any odd phone calls or letters, perhaps, that you noticed recently that may have any bearing on his disappearance? Anything of that nature that you can think of?"

"Uh, no, nothing there either. All our mail, I often saw before Kevin saw it. I never noticed anything odd there. As for phone calls, just the usual, from friends—things like that. Wait a moment. Now

152

that I think of it, I do seem to remember a call the morning he got back from the States, and the man, whom I didn't recognize, just left a number for Kevin to call that afternoon. The odd thing about it was that the man wanted him to call back at a specific time. Now that I think of it, I can't remember if Kevin ever did call him back, but then it was probably something to do with his work, and he never discussed that with me at all. Anyway, I'm sure that hasn't anything to do with this."

Scott thought there just might be something here, and he knew he could easily check to see if Kevin had received any calls from the Ministry that day.

"Can you tell me how your husband was that last weekend at home before he left for his fishing trip to Scotland?"

"He seemed in fine form, but then Kevin is usually a pretty even sort of man, as I said before, and more often up than down. I would say he seemed just like himself."

Scott Frawley knew he was probably going to elicit very little else from Sheila MacAllister, but he was curious to have a look around at Kevin's personal belongings, just in case his trained eye spotted something that might be meaningless to Kevin's wife.

"I guess that's about all the questions I have for you, Mrs. MacAllister. By the way, please don't talk with anyone about Kevin's disappearance or about the nature of his position at the Ministry, as much as you know about it. If you have any phone calls from anyone other than friends, I would be very pleased if you could let me know right away. Here's my card with the phone number in case you should need anything or you wish to call me. And by the way, don't be alarmed at the news bulletins you see, as it will be reported that we believe Kevin to be suffering from amnesia after an accident. We don't want to raise unnecessary questions. We simply want to find him as soon as possible. Oh, one last thing before I go. Would you mind if I had a look at some of your husband's personal belongings?"

"No, of course not. I don't think you'll find anything of any importance, in any case. But please help yourself. The small library, opposite, Kevin used as a den—that's where his desk is. If you want to look elsewhere, just let me know. I'll be happy to show you. I'll be in the kitchen if you need anything."

Scott Frawley took her at her word and immediately went into Kevin's den. He rapidly went through the desk with the eye of one trained to be speedy and neat. He uncovered nothing of any relevance. And before leaving the den, he took a quick look around to make sure he hadn't missed anything important. There was nothing.

He went out to the kitchen and asked Mrs. MacAllister if he could have a look at Kevin's things in their bedroom. She told him to go right ahead. Scott Frawley was very fast upstairs, making a mental note of the separate beds. He had quickly gone through Kevin's drawers of clothes and his closet, when a pile of jogging shorts and sweats on the floor caught his eye. He checked the pockets and found a crumpled piece of paper with a phone number on it in the pocket of a pair of shorts. He stuffed the paper into his own pocket and left the room. There didn't appear to be anything else.

Downstairs, he popped his head into the kitchen doorway and quickly took his leave from Sheila MacAllister, seeing himself out. The entire visit had lasted only twenty minutes, and as he checked his watch, he decided he would now head straight down to the Ministry of Defense and first interview Lieutenant Ridley and then drop in on Sir Ian. When he got into his car, he took out the crumpled piece of paper and looked at the phone number again. He wasn't sure, but he thought the area code was for somewhere in Scotland. He looked at it for a few seconds, wondering what could be the significance of it. Probably nothing, perhaps just a hotel where the major would be staying on his fishing trip. He folded the paper neatly and put it back in his pocket. He would run it through the computer later and find out exactly where it was. He started the car and headed back to central London.

His return drive to the Ministry took him only twenty-five minutes, as by then most of the traffic was leaving the city. So at a couple of minutes past six he arrived at the Ministry and immediately went upstairs to interview Lieutenant Ridley in Captain Smithers's office. Scott Frawley thanked the captain for getting Lieutenant Ridley there so promptly and asked if he would mind leaving for a while, as he wished to talk to the young lieutenant alone. Once they were alone, the lieutenant appeared to be rather uneasy, so Scott Frawley deliberately omitted any mention of his connection with MI5.

"My name is Scott Frawley, and I'm handling the government's investigation of Major MacAllister's disappearance and the missing MML. I do appreciate your being available so promptly. This shouldn't take too long, but I do need to ask you some questions, as apparently you may have been the last person to see the major."

Lieutenant Ridley nervously fingered the hat on his lap and appeared somewhat hesitant when he answered, "I'll be glad to help any way I can, sir, but I don't know what I can add to what I've already told everyone."

Scott Frawley flashed him one of his benevolent smiles to make the young lieutenant more relaxed and got him to repeat everything about his conversation with Major MacAllister the previous evening, and anything and everything he'd noticed about the captain and the other soldiers with him. But Frawley didn't learn anything new, and so he wrapped up his questions with Lieutenant Ridley for the time being.

"Oh, one last thing, Lieutenant Ridley. I'd like you to look over some photographs a little later this evening at my office. I trust you'll be available?"

"Certainly, sir, I'll be happy to." Lieutenant Ridley seemed relieved that his latest round of questioning was at an end, and Scott thought that maybe Ridley would be able to pick someone out of the photographs.

"Good. That will be most helpful. I'll have Captain Smithers bring you over to my office a little later. It's only a couple of blocks from here. That'll be all for now, Lieutenant, and thank you."

Scott Frawley left Lieutenant Ridley sitting in Captain Smithers's office and on his way out found the captain in the outer office. He asked him to bring the lieutenant over to his office when he called him later. In the hallway, an idea struck Scott Frawley, and instead of going in to see Sir Ian Sinders right away, he punched the elevator button and went down to the vaults. He went to Vault Level Four where the duplicate firing mechanisms for all of Britain's nuclear arsenal were kept. But that wasn't exactly what he was interested in, as they had already been thoroughly checked. He was more interested in the register that recorded the comings and goings of everyone who had access to the vault. A Sergeant Middleton was on duty at the desk, as he normally took over from Sergeant Pedley at five thirty in the evening. When Scott Frawley presented his credentials, the sergeant immediately passed over the register. Scott quickly reviewed it, looking most closely at the entries during the last four weeks. He took out his notebook and pen and neatly entered the exact times, days, and dates that Major MacAllister had accessed the vault over the last several months. He returned the register to the sergeant, thanked him, and left. Taking the elevator back upstairs, he kicked around some vague ideas in his mind, but he wasn't sure yet what they might lead him to.

It was just coming up to six thirty when Scott Frawley walked straight into Sir Ian Sinders's office. Apparently, he had already sent home his secretary, so Scott arrived unannounced. He found Sir Ian pacing by the windows, clearly in a state of great agitation. Realizing that Sir Ian hadn't heard him come in, Scott Frawley cleared his throat loudly before he spoke.

"Good evening, Sir Ian. What appears to be the matter?"

Sir Ian spun around sharply and looked startled, and then regained his composure before replying, "I didn't hear you come in, Scott. I'll tell you what's the matter. Just fifteen minutes ago, at 6:15 precisely, I got a call on my private line from the people who have kidnapped the major and who apparently also have the MML with the two missiles."

The two men sat down as Sir Ian quoted the exact words from the telephone call; Scott carefully wrote everything down in his little notebook.

"Now, Sir Ian, you say it was definitely a Northern Ireland accent on the other end of the phone. Could you possibly distinguish which part of Northern Ireland, such as a Belfast accent as opposed to a Derry accent, for example?"

"No, I couldn't tell—how the hell would I know? Either way, it would now appear to point to the IRA as the kidnappers and hijackers. Is there much difference?"

"No, there really isn't much difference between a Derry accent and a

Belfast one, except to those used to listening to both accents. The main reason I asked is that it could give a clue as to which branch of the IRA is involved. A Belfast accent could indicate that maybe it was the old IRA, whereas Derry is the home base for the Provos or, as you would know them, the Provisional IRA. Anyway, there appears to be little to go on at this point, until we get the call with their demands at seven o'clock tomorrow morning. I will send one of my men over here later, if you don't mind, to rig up a recording device to your phone. We'll also put a tap on the line to see if we can trace where the call comes from. If it's within Britain, we need only forty seconds to trace the call. If by some chance they're already outside the country, then it can take as much as ninety seconds or longer to get a fix on the origin of the call. We may be dealing with very smart people here who will have all that figured out, so we certainly can't rely on being able to trace the call."

"Of course, Scott, have your people do anything they want with my phone. My first concern is to get the major back—and then the missiles."

Scott Frawley was silent for a minute or two, and one of those vague ideas in the back of his mind raised its ugly head again and prompted his next question.

"Sir Ian, I'm just a little bit curious. If it were possible to actually remove one of the firing mechanisms and have it duplicated, is the duplication process difficult and would it take a long time?"

"Well, Scott, as you know, this whole system was actually Major MacAllister's brainchild. If he were here, he'd be able to give you the best answer. But as far as I understand, very specialized computer equipment was needed to do the duplication, and it takes several days to complete. I do recall him mentioning once that there were maybe only half a dozen facilities in the world that were properly equipped to carry out this precise task. I don't know if that helps you much."

Scott touched his face and asked, "You haven't told the minister yet about this call, have you?"

"No, I didn't. I knew you were going to be dropping by my office very shortly, so I decided it could wait until you and I had an opportunity to discuss it."

Scott Frawley didn't miss much, and he definitely noticed the sharp tone that Sir Ian used when he said he hadn't yet told the minister. Scott made a mental note of it and then, as if to placate Sir Ian's sensitivities about the minister, he proceeded very diplomatically.

"Why don't you let me take care of it then, as the prime minister has put me in charge of investigating this case?"

Sir Ian looked relieved, and Scott Frawley knew that this would ensure that he retained control of all information and developments on the case. He was sure now that Sir Ian was more than happy to let him deal with both the minister of defense and the prime minister.

"Are you spending the night here at the Ministry?"

"Yes, I am, but I think I'll go out shortly to my club for dinner. Would you care to join me?"

"Uh, no thanks, I'm afraid I'll have to pass. I have a lot of things to do yet. Will it be okay if my people come over to work on your phone while you're out, or would you prefer they wait until you're back?"

"It doesn't matter to me, whatever works out best for you."

"That's fine, sir. I really do appreciate your cooperation. I'll be on my way now. I'll call you later if there are any developments. I'll also be spending the night at my office across the way, so you know where to reach me. If we don't talk tonight, I'll be here tomorrow morning no later than six thirty so that I can be with you when you get the call from the kidnappers or terrorists."

"Okay, that'll be fine. I'll see you in the morning."

"Good night, sir. Cheerio."

Scott Frawley left as quietly and quickly as he had arrived and took the elevator straight downstairs, deciding to leave his car in the Ministry garage and walk the two short blocks to his own office. While he had been in the Ministry, it had gotten dark, and when he went outside, he noticed that it was also considerably chillier. He had no overcoat with him, so he walked very briskly to his office.

Once settled behind his desk, Scott Frawley sprang into action. First, he arranged for the recording and tapping equipment to be put on Sir Ian's private line. Plus, he gave the phone number he had found at Kevin MacAllister's house to another member of his staff to run through the computers. Then he called the prime minister and passed on the information about the call regarding the major and the missiles. He informed the prime minister that it was too early to say if it was, indeed, any of the known IRA groups. But he promised to keep her informed as his investigation developed and certainly after he had an opportunity, the next morning, to hear what the terrorists' demands would be. To play it safe, he also managed to locate the minister of defense, Gordy Hargreaves, and relayed much of the same information to him. Next, he placed a call to Jenny Laster's showroom. Even though he knew she wouldn't be there, he hoped the answering machine would give him a number where he could reach her. He was given a number up in Norwich, where an older American woman answered. Not even bothering to ask her name, he simply asked if he could speak with Jenny Laster. After a few moments, Jenny came on the line.

"Hello, Jenny? It's Scott Frawley, here. You remember me? I work closely with Kevin and used to know your ex-husband rather well. I know it's been some time since we met. Did you happen to see the news on television this evening?"

"Yes, I did, and I've been going frantic since. I'm so glad you called, Scott; maybe you can tell me what the hell's going on?"

"Okay, Jenny, I can tell you a little more than you heard on the news. But you have to understand that whatever I tell you must stay completely in your confidence. I know you know about these things, as your ex-husband is in the CIA, and you know that I'm with MI5, and we are all subject to the Official Secrets Act. I'm sorry if I sound a bit of a heavyweight on this, Jenny, my dear, but I really must insist that anything we discuss must not go beyond either of us, as it could imperil Kevin's life. I know that's the last thing you would want."

Scott paused for effect and could almost hear Jenny gulp. He went on, "Kevin is indeed missing, but it was no accident, and as far as we know, he's certainly not suffering from amnesia. I'll be brutally frank, Jenny. It appears he's been kidnapped by terrorists, along with some crucial military hardware." Scott Frawley paused again, as he wanted to give Jenny time to take in what he had said.

Jenny's voice came over the line, sounding rather strained. "Are you absolutely sure of this, Scott? Or is this just speculation at this point?"

"I'm afraid not, Jenny, my dear. We've already been contacted by the kidnappers, saying they have him and the hardware. Jenny, I wanted to ask you if you noticed anything odd, or anything troubling Kevin, the last time you saw him or spent time with him."

"No, I can't say that I did. I thought everything seemed fine with him. In fact, he's been in particularly good form lately, now that I come to think of it."

"Do you know why that might be?" There was a silence at the other end of the line for a couple of moments, and Scott Frawley believed that Jenny was genuinely trying to think over what he'd asked.

"Well, now that you mention it, he did say something about an inheritance from a granduncle in the States, not all that much, I believe, but he did feel good about it."

Scott thought, *Aha! Maybe something interesting here ... but maybe not.* He didn't recall reading anything in Kevin's file that suggested he had rich American relatives.

"Well, Jenny, I don't think I can tell you much more at this point, but if you think of anything, please give me a call at this number."

Frawley gave her his private number.

"Thanks, Scott. And I really would appreciate you letting me know right away, the moment you know that Kevin is okay. It really is very worrisome, and I don't understand why someone should kidnap him."

Frawley thought, *Bloody right, lady—you shouldn't know, not unless Kevin was indiscreet and discussed his job with you, but I doubt that.* The Kevin MacAllister that Scott Frawley knew so well was much too sensible and shrewd to discuss his Ministry work with either his wife or his lover.

"I will, Jenny, and be sure to let me know if you think of anything else out of the ordinary that might have some bearing on his kidnapping. Chin up, Jenny, we'll find him okay, and thanks for your help."

"Okay, Scott, and I do appreciate your telling me what you have. I know Kevin will be all right. Good-bye and good luck."

After Jenny Laster hung up and Scott Frawley had put his phone back in the cradle, he sat there thinking. Again, he had another new piece of the puzzle to add to the other vague ideas floating around in his mind. Scott considered that what he had just learned from Jenny Laster could warrant a quick phone call to Sheila MacAllister, and perhaps one to Kevin's secretary, Margaret Bloomington. Just then, one of his staff, John Miles, brought in information on the phone number that Scott had asked him to trace. It turned out to be a public phone kiosk in the small village of Glencoe, Scotland. Scott thanked John and dismissed him. It didn't make sense. Scott wondered why Kevin MacAllister would be calling a public phone box in a small village in Scotland. It wasn't even in the town of Oban, where he knew Kevin stayed almost every year on his fishing trips. Once again, Scott had another new piece of information to add to the growing puzzle in his mind, and like the others, right now it didn't fit. He called down to records and asked them to dig out all photo files on known members of the IRA, and then, just before hanging up and almost on impulse, he asked that the photo records of mercenaries be brought up along with the IRA files. Next, he called Captain Smithers and asked him to bring young Lieutenant Ridley over to his office as soon as possible. Smithers told him that they would be over in about ten minutes.

Scott put a call through to Sheila MacAllister and very tactfully inquired into her husband's recent inheritance from a granduncle in America. She explained that she really left all financial matters to Kevin, but she knew that Kevin had inherited some money from his granduncle Bertie in the States, whom she had never actually met. Frawley then asked her if she would know where he might find out more about the inheritance, stressing that money might have been the motive behind Kevin's kidnapping. There was a long silence, and Scott realized that Sheila had probably been drinking steadily since he'd left her house and was struggling to collect her thoughts. Finally, she said she remembered Kevin having mentioned a lawyer by the name of Mike Driscoll, but, she added, all Kevin's correspondence with him had been through his office, and she really didn't know anything else about it. Frawley thanked her and hung up.

Then, quickly looking up Margaret Bloomington's number, he

called her. He reached her at her flat in Muswell Hill, and Frawley was quick to notice Margaret's surprise at being called at home. He knew, of course, that she was well aware of who he was, so he came straight to the point. He explained to Margaret that he was simply trying to verify some information and asked her if she could recall a lawyer named Driscoll in America, and did she know the name of the firm he was with? Scott was hopeful, as he knew Margaret was a fine secretary with an incredible memory. He didn't have to wait long for an answer. Margaret said yes, she could remember some correspondence from a New York law firm the previous November or December, and, best as she could remember, the name of the firm was Driscoll, Hanrahan, and Moynihan. Frawley thanked her and praised her admirable memory, but before he could hang up, Margaret inquired whether there was any further news about the major. Scott reassured her that he was doing everything possible to find Kevin, and as soon as he had any concrete news, he would let her know. Margaret Bloomington seemed satisfied with that, and Scott was glad to get off the phone.

There was a knock at his office door, and John Miles came in followed by two young chaps, each carrying a big box. John explained to his boss that one box contained all photographic records that MI5 had on known IRA members, while the other, somewhat smaller box held photographic records of known mercenaries who were ex-British Army. John Miles and the two young men had just left his office when Captain Smithers arrived with Lieutenant Ridley in tow.

As John Miles had already laid out the IRA photos on the conference table in the corner of the office, Frawley wasted no time before he gave Lieutenant Ridley the task of going through every single photograph, under Captain Smithers's supervision. While Ridley was going through the photos, Scott sat at his desk and once again began to review Kevin MacAllister's file, making some notes of what he had already learned that afternoon. He reviewed the detail in the major's file, which covered virtually the entire span of Kevin's life. From his birth in Clapham to his brilliant university career and his rise at the Ministry to head of Section Q11 with total responsibility for the coordination of Britain's nuclear arsenal, he realized that everyone, including Scott Frawley himself, thought of MacAllister as British. But as Scott looked at the file in front of him, it gradually dawned on him that everyone had always overlooked the fact that Kevin's parents, even though they had lived in London for so many years, were both Irish-born. The file did indicate that both Kevin's parents had been checked out when Kevin joined the British Army as a nuclear expert, and they had proved to be clean of connections with anything illegal whatsoever. Frawley's instincts told him there was something here in Kevin's Irish heritage, but he couldn't quite put his finger on it yet. He made another entry on his notepad. This could be the key to pulling together other pieces of the puzzle, but he wasn't sure. He needed to find out more, particularly about Kevin's American inheritance.

By then, Ridley had looked through all the photos of known IRA and Provo terrorists and had found none he recognized. Scott then had him look at the known active mercenaries' photographs; the result was the same. Frawley felt discouraged, but at that moment, John Miles came in carrying a folder, which he explained contained the photographic records of mercenaries whom the department had classified as "no longer active." John Miles suggested that maybe Scott would like the lieutenant to look at them. Frawley wasn't hopeful, but he felt the lieutenant should have a look. While Ridley was reviewing this new batch of photos, Scott Frawley went back to thinking about what he knew at that point. He was making an effort to piece together the various fragments of the puzzle but without success. Suddenly his thoughts were interrupted by an exclamation from Ridley. Ridley and Smithers brought over a photograph and fact sheet to Scott at his desk.

"Sir, I do believe that this man is the same man as the captain, Captain Wrixon, who accompanied Major MacAllister into my tent last night. The only difference is that Captain Wrixon had a mustache; otherwise, this man is the spitting image of him. I would stake my life on it."

Scott Frawley was inclined to believe him, as the young lieutenant seemed so definite and looked to be almost glowing after spending so long fruitlessly looking at hundreds of photographs.

"Are you absolutely sure that this is the same man you saw last night?"

"Absolutely, sir. May I take your pencil for a moment and mark on this photograph?"

Scott Frawley handed him the pencil, nodding his head. Ridley penciled in a thin mustache on the photograph of George Wilkinson. Frawley said nothing as Ridley passed him back the photograph.

"Now that I have added the mustache, I would swear that this is the captain who accompanied Major MacAllister last night."

"Okay, Lieutenant, as you seem so sure, my people will check this out. I'd like to thank you and Captain Smithers for giving me so much of your time. You've both been very helpful. Just leave this with me. Please look at the rest of the photos of inactive mercenaries, and if you don't recognize any others, you'll be free to go."

Captain Smithers and Lieutenant Ridley left as soon as Ridley had finished going through the pictures, and Scott Frawley sat at his desk, thinking quickly. Based on reports from his own people, he had personally authorized that George Wilkinson be put in the inactive mercenary file. And he thought, young Ridley seemed so positive that this was the man he saw with the major, that maybe he himself had made an error in judgment about Wilkinson. Scott Frawley was willing to admit to himself that he had made a mistake, but he wouldn't wish others outside the department to know about it. He would have to have this checked out very quickly. He got John Miles on the phone and instructed him to have a field agent investigate, right away, George Wilkinson's rented house in Marlow.

As Frawley sat staring at the photograph and the fact sheet, he wondered how George Wilkinson would have gotten mixed up in the hijacking of missiles and the kidnapping of a British major in England. It seemed totally out of character when compared with all his previous activities, which had always occurred overseas. In fact, Scott noticed that the Wilkinson file emphasized the fact that Wilkinson had never been known to break a single law in England.

At that point, an awful realization slowly crept into Scott Frawley's mind. He recalled several conversations in the past seven or eight months with Major MacAllister about various mercenaries, and, in particular, he remembered telling the major about George Wilkinson and MI5's assumption that he had now retired. Scott could even recall saying to Kevin that now they had one less mercenary to keep tabs on. Scott felt embarrassed, but luckily he knew there were no witnesses to his conversations with Major MacAllister. Scott began to realize that he might have unwittingly supplied Major MacAllister with important information without any idea of its ultimate implications. Then he thought, *It must be pure coincidence. After all, I mustn't jump to conclusions.* The phone call to Sir Ian certainly made it look as if the major had been kidnapped. But where did George Wilkinson fit in? Scott didn't have any answers.

It was nearly ten o'clock when Scott Frawley got the report that George Wilkinson had not been in the rented house in Marlow for several weeks. An MI5 agent had actually broken into the house to investigate, and a careful search of the house and the condition of the food in the refrigerator seemed to confirm that Wilkinson hadn't been there for at least three weeks. Scott Frawley was very disturbed at this news. On the one hand, it would appear that some faction of the IRA was behind the kidnapping of the major and the hijacking of the missiles, yet he felt sure that Lieutenant Ridley had not made a mistake in identification, putting George Wilkinson also at the scene of the hijacking. He decided to put out an all-points bulletin for Wilkinson, which would cover every port and airport in the country.

Shortly afterward, he got a call from Scotland Yard to the effect that a customs officer in Fishguard, Wales, had reported to his local police station that he thought he had seen Major MacAllister getting aboard the ferry the previous night. On learning this, Scott immediately put a call through to the local police in Fishguard and was connected with a Sergeant Jones. The sergeant confirmed that they'd had a report from a customs officer who was watching the six o'clock news while eating his dinner that evening, before going on night shift at the dock. Apparently, he had seen a man who resembled Major MacAllister, with his wife and child, board the ferry in a car the previous night. He couldn't recall the car and wasn't 100 percent sure that it was the major, but when he saw the photograph on TV, he thought there was a resemblance.

Scott thanked the sergeant for the information and hung up.

He wasn't convinced that the reported sighting was indeed valid but couldn't rule it out. But if the major had been kidnapped, how could he have been boarding the ferry to Ireland with a supposed wife and child? He made additional notes on his pad. It was already ten thirty, so Scott decided he had better make his final report of the day to the prime minister before she went to bed.

Once he gave his name, he was connected right away to Muriel Hobson. He gave her a brief report of what he had discovered to that point in time, including the fact that a known mercenary could be involved. He omitted any mention of his private speculations about Major MacAllister. He also advised the PM about the expected call to Sir Ian Sinders the following morning at seven o'clock. He said it was too early to be sure that the IRA was indeed involved. The PM asked him to give her another report as soon after the expected morning call from the terrorists as possible, and then she bid Scott good night.

Scott felt there was little more he could do that night, but he wanted to stay awake until after midnight, as by then he felt it wouldn't be unreasonable to call Paul Laster, his old friend at the CIA, at his home. Given the nature of the crisis, he felt Paul would certainly forgive him if Scott woke him up between five and five thirty in the morning his time. It was already eleven thirty, and Scott had plenty to occupy his mind, so the time passed quickly.

At midnight, the chimes of Big Ben, just a couple of blocks from his office, broke the silence of the night as Scott sat, perched fourteen floors above the quiet streets of London. For Scott Frawley, Big Ben had always had a certain significance, for to him it represented the watchtower over Parliament and the surrounding government buildings, from which all power emanated. As Scott sat studiously arranging each piece of the puzzle and each bit of new information, a possible picture of what had actually happened was forming in his mind, but he couldn't be sure, and he had to be very certain. Everything he knew at that point suggested two possible scenarios: one had his friend Major MacAllister as the victim, and the other as the mastermind.

Finally at twelve thirty, feeling tired and perplexed, he decided he could now safely call Paul Laster. The last time he'd spoken to

Paul was several weeks earlier when Paul was named CIA Chief for European Operations. He picked up the phone and dialed a long string of numbers to reach Paul at his home in Virginia. It seemed to ring forever before a sleepy man's voice answered.

"Hello. Paul Laster here. Who's calling?"

"Sorry to wake you up, Paul, old chap. Scott Frawley here."

"Good God, Scott, do you know what time it is?"

"Yes, about five thirty. I am sorry to wake you, Paul, but this couldn't wait."

"Jesus Christ, Scott. It'd better be damn good!"

"It is. We have two nuclear missiles missing—we suspect hijacked by the IRA, but we're not sure. Could be the Libyans or the Palestinians."

There was silence from Paul for a moment or two, but the voice that came back on the line was suddenly wide awake. "Did I hear you correctly, Scott? Are you saying the British have gone and lost two goddamn nuclear missiles?"

"Yes." Scott Frawley spent the next five minutes giving Paul Laster a very concise version of all that had happened since the previous evening. Frawley knew that the fact that Major MacAllister was kidnapped along with the missiles would strike a personal note with Paul, Jenny Laster's ex-husband.

Paul let out a long, low whistle before he responded, "So, from what you say, there's no real danger, as without the firing mechanisms they're inoperable?"

"Yes, that appears to be the case, according to Sir Ian Sinders. But I'm not totally convinced. It is possible that the firing mechanisms were duplicated."

"What you suggest would mean an inside job."

Scott smiled and said, "Yes, there is always that possibility. But at this point, I can't really determine that for sure. Paul, the reason I'm calling you is that I may need some help on this, and some information from your agents in the field throughout Europe. But at this stage, this has to remain an unofficial request, and confidential between two old friends. On no account must you mention anything to your superiors or anything that might reach the president of the US. Naturally, if we should learn that these missiles can be launched, I will notify you immediately, and our PM will notify your president."

"Does Jenny know that the major is missing?"

"Yes, actually, I spoke with her myself just a few hours ago. Obviously, she is not aware that nuclear missiles were stolen."

"Putting the missiles aside for a moment, Scott, you know as well as I that Kevin MacAllister also has top clearance here in Washington and has access to a lot of information about our nuclear capability and our dispositions. If he is grilled by the wrong side, this could have serious repercussions here in the US. You do realize that, don't you?"

"Of course, old chap. That's partly why I'm letting you know now. Though, if it is indeed the IRA who got him, I don't think they're going to do anything to harm American interests."

"That may be true, but even then, the fact that any terrorist group of whatever persuasion is holding someone who has had access to US secrets is going to cause quite an uproar in Washington and the Pentagon. We have a couple of well-placed agents in the Republic of Ireland. As soon as you get off, I will contact them right away and see what they may be able to dig up."

"That would be damn decent of you, Paul. I'm spending the night at my office, and you have the number, so you can reach me any time. I'll keep you posted on any new developments here, and I sure appreciate your help. Just remember, Paul, at this point this has to be unofficial and between us only. Cheerio then. And again, sorry for having to wake you up, but I knew you'd want to know."

"You're damn right, Scott. I'm glad you called. Looks like we'll both have busy days ahead. Good night. Try to catch some sleep. Talk to you later."

Scott was glad he had called Paul Laster, as he needed all the help he could get on this one. He stared at the notepad on his desk, but everything was getting blurry, so he turned off the light over his desk and decided to call it a night. He went into the small room right off his office, which contained a compact bathroom and a single bed, a nightstand, and a couple of telephones. He looked at the bedside alarm clock, which read 12:45 a.m. He really was tired, and after taking off his suit, he lay down on the bed in his shirt and shorts. The last thing he remembered as he drifted off to sleep was the solitary chime of Big Ben.

CHAPTER *10*

IT WAS TUESDAY, SEPTEMBER 7, six o'clock in the evening, and the bells of Saint Paul's had just stopped ringing. Jeremy Sands, one of the most dedicated investigative journalists in England, was sitting back in his chair with his feet up on his desk, watching the news on the TV in the corner of his office, which was located on the fifth floor of the Sentinel Building at the corner of Fleet Street and Shoe Lane. At six feet two, Jeremy was known affectionately by his close friends as L. J., short for Lanky Jeremy.

As he sat watching the evening news, he had been looking for some major issue on which to test the new government's willingness to change. He took his feet off the desk and sat bolt upright as the newscaster reported from the Ministry of Defense that a certain Major Kevin MacAllister was missing after an accident near the Salisbury Plain and was believed to be suffering from amnesia. As he studied the photographs flashed on the screen—one of the major in uniform and one of him in civilian clothes—Jeremy wracked his memory to recall where he had met the major, for he was sure they had met. Suddenly it came to him, and he recalled the occasion as if it were just the other day. It had actually been two years earlier at Southampton, when the navy was launching a new class of nuclear cruiser. Sands had been introduced to the major along with Sir Ian Sinders, the head of the joint chiefs of staff. Jeremy remembered being curious as to why an army major seemed to be so close to Sir Ian and in attendance at a navy launching. By chatting with various people at the event, he had learned that Major

MacAllister appeared to hold an important position relating to the maintenance of Britain's independent nuclear deterrent.

Afterward, Jeremy had done some research on the major and had found out about his brilliant university record in nuclear weaponry. He had tucked the information away at the back of his mind, his journalistic instincts convinced that someday the information might be useful. The newscaster had moved on to another topic, but Jeremy tuned it out as he sat back in his chair, thinking. He smelled the possibility of a story here; he wasn't sure what, but he thought the Ministry of Defense press release sounded a little too neat and compact.

Jeremy knew that the British Army had begun four days of military exercises that morning in Salisbury Plain, and he felt sure that a senior officer couldn't have had an accident and then supposedly disappeared with amnesia without anyone being able to find him. With so many troops in the area, it just didn't add up. He also realized that, as things had been rather quiet over the last several weeks, he might be grasping for a story where there was none. He needed something juicy to sink his teeth into and to get his adrenaline running again. In any case, he made up his mind to look into this further.

Jeremy flicked the switch on the remote and turned off the television, then made a couple of phone calls to his sources within the government, one of whom was in the Ministry of Defense. His first call didn't yield much, but he did learn that the military exercises had been suspended for several hours that morning as troops were used to search for Major MacAllister. The exercises had been resumed though they hadn't found the major.

Jeremy was not satisfied and needed to know more, but then he remembered that there was a young woman from the typing pool called Emily Jones who often joined a bunch of them from the paper in the pub around the corner. Single, friendly, and fond of her gin and tonics, she had let slip that her first cousin was a corporal attached to a certain major at the Ministry. It didn't take Jeremy much persuasion to get his phone number from Emily. So his next call was a lot more fruitful, as he learned from a Corporal Jones, who sometimes served as a driver for Major MacAllister, that in the late afternoon there had been a private meeting at Downing Street between the prime minister, the home secretary, the foreign secretary, MI5, and Sir Ian Sinders. This information intrigued Jeremy, as he didn't think a simple disappearance would warrant the attention of the prime minister unless more was involved. Right now there was no way he could find out what had transpired at the Downing Street meeting, but he figured the more people in government who got involved in the supposed disappearance of Major MacAllister, the better his chances of being able to learn something. Jeremy decided that for now, the best he could do would be to put a couple of junior reporters on it. He told them to keep a lookout at the Ministry of Defense, around 10 Downing Street, and possibly at the government office building that housed MI5, to keep an eye out for any unusual activity that might give him a lead.

After his call to Corporal Jones, he took out a fresh notepad and began to scribble some notes. He decided he might just have enough to at least write a few short paragraphs for the front page of tomorrow morning's edition of the *Daily Sentinel*. He enjoyed writing short, suggestive articles that might well smoke out the government's position and lead to him learning more.

In the world of British journalism, Jeremy Sands was considered a master craftsman at wording articles just right, without being libelous or downright untrue. When he had finished making his notes, Jeremy turned on his PC and spent the next half hour putting together a short article. He then called the night editor and explained that he had a short piece for the next morning's front page and was faxing it right over.

It was about seven thirty when Sands finally left his office and walked out into the night air of Fleet Street. As was customary for him, he first went to a nearby restaurant, a journalists' haunt, to have some dinner. Afterward, he began to hit the various pubs in and around Fleet Street, where he would meet colleagues and acquaintances from other newspapers and see if he could learn anything new on the story of the missing major. He found no one who knew even as much as he already knew, and by ten o'clock, feeling a bit disappointed, he made his way over to a couple of pubs around Whitehall. There he heard the usual political gossip, but the issue of the missing major wasn't discussed at all. In fact, Jeremy sensed that the government officials and workers who frequented those pubs were studiously avoiding the topic.

Finally, at around a quarter after eleven, having enjoyed a good many scotches but still feeling quite clearheaded, Jeremy Sands took the Tube home to his flat in Islington. As he sat on the train going home, Jeremy couldn't help but believe that his hunch was correct and there was more to all of this than met the eye. When he got into his dark, empty flat, the first thing he did was check his answering machine, as always. There were several messages, none of them very important, but the last one caught his attention immediately. It was from Emily's cousin, Corporal Jones in the Ministry of Defense; Jones had left his home number with the request that Jeremy call him as soon as he got in.

First, Jeremy poured himself a stiff scotch and settled into the comfortable chair by the phone. He dialed the number, and Jones answered right away as if waiting for his call. Jeremy was startled to learn that apparently two nuclear missiles on an MML were missing but considered completely inoperable because of Ministry procedures controlling the disposition of the firing mechanisms. Jones was not aware of whom the government suspected of taking the missiles and the major, but he assured Jeremy that should he find out that information or establish that the government had been contacted by anyone, he would certainly get back to Jeremy. The entire call lasted less than forty seconds, as Jones was concerned with the risk of his phone being tapped.

Suddenly, Jeremy Sands felt almost stone-cold sober. This was a startling development and very frightening—in fact, so damned scary that he took no consolation from the fact that his hunch was right. This was certainly more than the simple disappearance of a senior army officer. Jeremy poured himself another scotch as he considered this revelation in light of what he had already learned. His first assumption was, quite naturally, that terrorists must be behind the whole affair, and he speculated as to which group it might be. Next, he wondered if and when the government would admit that two nuclear missiles had been hijacked. Jeremy's own conviction was that they would admit nothing, and he knew he would have to tread very carefully, as this indeed was a matter of national security and would certainly be covered by the

Official Secrets Act. But depending on what he discovered the next morning, it may also be a matter where the public had a right to know, and he wouldn't hesitate to report on it if he felt that was the case. He turned on the late news on the telly, just in case any new developments were announced, although he was now pretty certain there would be nothing. He was right; the late news merely carried a repeat of what he had seen on the six o'clock broadcast. There was nothing further he could find out that night, and he thought he'd better catch a few hours of sleep, as he planned to make a very early start in the morning. He set his clock for five o'clock, for he wanted to make it to his office before six. Jeremy had never been a man who needed a lot of sleep, and as he lay in the dark, his mind was hyperactive as he explored all the possibilities. One thing he was sure of: this could well turn out to be one major story—and maybe even the biggest story of his entire career. As he finally drifted off to sleep, Jeremy felt a growing sense of anticipation and a strong conviction that the next day would be an exciting one.

CHAPTER *11*

I T WAS ONLY FIVE THIRTY in the morning, Wednesday, September 8, when Sir Ian finally got up. He had lain awake for the past hour, and although the bed in his small room at the Ministry was comfortable enough, he simply had too much on his mind to sleep properly.

After he shaved and showered, Sir Ian put on a clean uniform and decided he needed some fresh air before the arrival of Scott Frawley. It was ten minutes past six as he left the Ministry and walked down toward the embankment; the sun had already risen, and in the gray dawn there was a chilly wind blowing off the river. It was just what Sir Ian needed after a restless night in the cramped bedroom at the Ministry. He walked for about fifteen minutes and was just going back into the Ministry building when he caught sight of Scott Frawley coming around the corner of Richmond Terrace from Parliament Street. Sir Ian waited on the steps; Frawley sped up to catch up with him and arrived puffing and panting. The two men entered the Ministry building together and went up to Sir Ian's office. Once there, they settled down to wait in two comfortable chairs near the telephone. Sir Ian was the first to break the strained silence.

"We've still got twenty-five minutes to wait. Would you care for some tea and toast?"

"Yes, I would like that."

Sir Ian called down to the Ministry cafeteria and requested that tea and toast for two be sent up right away. Within a few minutes, it arrived. Then, as the two men sipped their tea and munched on their toast, they tried to make a little conversation to help pass the time.

"Well, Scott, I take it there were no more developments last night?"

"No, there really weren't any developments, as such. One possible sighting of the major at the Fishguard ferry was reported, but on looking into it, it appears that it can't be substantiated at this point. I did have Lieutenant Ridley review a lot of file photographs of known IRA terrorists, and indeed some mercenaries, most of whom are ex-British Army. However, he didn't recognize any of the IRA as being the people with the major on the night he disappeared. But he did make a tentative identification of a mercenary whom he thought looked like the captain who accompanied the major on Monday night. My people are investigating this further now, and if I find out anything concrete, I'll certainly let you know."

Sir Ian had known Scott Frawley for many years, and he quickly realized that the devious man sitting beside him probably already knew a lot more that he was letting on. That made Sir Ian feel a little uneasy. Even though he, personally, had a clear conscience, he knew that because of his position, any blame for the current bloody mess would be laid at his doorstep. Feeling uncomfortable, Sir Ian got up and paced back and forth by the window.

Finally, right at seven o'clock, Sir Ian's private phone began ringing. He reached out nervously and picked it up while simultaneously Scott Frawley picked up an extension close by. The recorder was noiselessly and automatically activated by the ringing. Cautiously, but in a strong voice, Sir Ian asked, "Who is it?" He immediately recognized the voice with the strong Northern Irish accent from the previous evening. He confirmed that he was indeed Sir Ian Sinders, and the voice at the other end told him to listen carefully to everything he was going to say and not to interrupt, as he would say it only once. Sir Ian looked over at Scott Frawley, who nodded, and then Sir Ian said, "Okay, I'm listening."

The caller said, "We are the Green September group for a united Ireland. We demand that the British government announce on all radio and television stations the immediate withdrawal of all British troops from Northern Ireland and make a public commitment to a six-month timetable for the full unification of Northern Ireland's six counties into the Republic of Ireland. If this announcement is not made by

2:00 p.m. tomorrow, Thursday, September 9, we will launch a nuclear missile shortly afterward, targeted for London. As you don't believe we have the ability to activate the nuclear warheads, we will give you a demonstration this afternoon. You have until 2:00 p.m. today to clear the area within a two-hundred-mile radius of the point of longitude sixteen degrees west and latitude sixty degrees north, which is just northwest of the George Bligh Bank in the North Atlantic. We will launch our first missile into this target area this afternoon." He paused. "There will be no further warnings. You'd better meet our demands; the alternative is the destruction of London and millions of people. We will also kill the major."

After the caller was finished with his entire message, he hung up immediately. Sir Ian hit the replay button, and both men listened intently to the voice. Sir Ian and Scott Frawley looked at each other, almost in a state of shock. They could hardly believe what they had just heard. Scott Frawley immediately rewound the tape in the recorder and set it again to playback. The two men sat very quietly and for a second time listened carefully to the playback of the message, every word burnt into them.

Before Scott Frawley could even open his mouth, Sir Ian nearly exploded. "Who the bloody hell is the Green September group, Scott? I've never heard that name before. Are they yet another bloody splinter group from the IRA? Talk to me, man! Your department is supposed to keep tabs on all these terrorist groups. Who the hell are they?"

"I'll be perfectly frank with you, Sir Ian. I have no idea who they are. This is the first time I've ever heard of the Green September group. They may or may not have a connection with the IRA. But let me ask you, Sir Ian, how can they possibly launch those missiles without the firing mechanisms? Or how could they have managed to duplicate them? Even Major MacAllister's expertise can't create the firing mechanisms without the originals to copy. Isn't that the case? Or at least that's what you led me to believe yesterday."

At that moment in Sir Ian's office, one could have cut the atmosphere with a knife. Sir Ian clearly recognized Frawley's tactics in turning the more critical question back on him. He phrased his answer carefully.

"Indeed, Scott, as I told you yesterday, to the best of my knowledge, the missiles cannot be activated without the original firing mechanisms or precise duplicates. I'm not a technical man; the major always assured me of that fact. It almost sounds as if you are implying that somehow they could have been duplicated by the major, which would suggest that this whole affair is an inside job. I don't believe that, and I think their threats of launching the missiles with the nuclear warheads activated are a big bluff."

Scott Frawley didn't respond right away, but then the ringing of the phone interrupted them. Sir Ian picked it up and handed it to Frawley, saying, "It's for you." Half a minute later, Frawley hung up and turned back to Sir Ian. "That was my people who were trying to trace the call. Unfortunately, the caller wasn't on long enough for them to trace the exact source, but they were able to establish with a high degree of certainty that the call came from somewhere in the Republic of Ireland. That would seem to confirm that the missiles and the major are being held somewhere in Ireland. Now back to your question of a few moments ago, Sir Ian. I'm not necessarily suggesting that it was an inside job here at the Ministry. I know the main firing mechanisms are kept at each regimental post and that only the duplicates are kept here at the Ministry vaults. That opens up the possibility that somehow duplicates may have been made from the master firing mechanisms held at the regimental HQs. At least that's a possibility, and I'll look into it. On the other point, your suggestion that it's a bluff is also a possibility, but I'm inclined to believe it's a very real threat. Otherwise, why would this Green September group commit themselves to firing one missile into the North Atlantic as a demonstration of their ability to explode the nuclear warheads? If they actually succeed in doing that, then I believe the threat to London is very real. Wouldn't you agree?"

At that moment, Sir Ian's private secretary, Jane Hawley, arrived early at the office and, popping her head around the door, asked them if they would like fresh cups of tea. The two men nodded. A minute later, she came back with the tea and left them alone to get on with their discussion. Sir Ian was feeling increasingly beleaguered, as he could see the sense of what Scott Frawley was saying, but he hated to admit to himself that somehow this Green September group had obtained duplicate firing mechanisms. He decided that as soon as Frawley had left, he would independently check out the security surrounding the firing mechanisms held at regimental headquarters for the Royal Welsh Guards. He turned to Frawley and said, "At this point, we are only speculating. I guess we must wait and see what happens this afternoon. But our first priority, I believe, must be to notify the minister and the prime minister and to see about clearing that area in the North Atlantic."

"You're right, Sir Ian. Why don't you leave it with me to set up a meeting with the prime minister? As it is already a quarter to eight, what I suggest is that we both try to get in and see her at eight thirty. I'll go back to my office now and set it up. That will give me a little time to look into some other aspects before we met at 10 Downing Street. I'll have my secretary call Jane to confirm the time, as I don't know the PM's schedule."

Sir Ian nodded his agreement while Scott Frawley drained the last of his cup of tea and then got up to leave.

"Cheerio, Sir Ian. See you later at Downing Street."

When Scott Frawley had gone, Sir Ian sat for several minutes, thinking. In many ways, he now felt helpless and powerless, as he knew he wasn't trained to fight the invisible enemy. And in his mind, that was how he saw this Green September group. Sir Ian was particularly disturbed by the suggestions from Scott Frawley that somehow or other his friend and colleague, Major Kevin MacAllister, might be implicated in the whole rotten business. But, as there was absolutely nothing concrete to suggest that the major was indeed involved personally, Sir Ian decided to put that whole aspect of the matter out of his mind. He put a call through to the regimental commander of the Royal Welsh Guards, who was still down in the Salisbury Plain area. He learned that the regimental CO was in the field and would have to be located and would call back. By eight fifteen, Sir Ian got the call and, to his dismay, learned that there was no possible way that the firing mechanisms maintained at regimental HQ could have been removed at any point. Everything, he was assured, had been double-checked, and there had been no leak at that end.

Right after he hung up, Jane came in to say that Scott Frawley's office had called to confirm the meeting with the prime minister at eight thirty. A few minutes later, Sir Ian left for the meeting. He felt a little more cheerful on the five-minute walk over to Downing Street, as the earlier cloud cover had lifted, and the day was now clear and sunny.

Sir Ian arrived just a little early, at a few minutes before eight thirty, but on this occasion, he was not left waiting but was shown into the prime minister's private office at once. He was a little surprised and annoyed to find that Scott Frawley was already there, along with the same cast of characters as at the previous afternoon's meeting, with the exception of Sir Hugh Blake.

Again, Prime Minister Muriel Hobson was flanked by Ernest Brooking, the home secretary, and Charles Mills, the secretary of state for foreign affairs. Of course, her confidential secretary, Jack Larson, was in attendance. This time, the minister of defense, Gordon Hargreaves, sat to the side of the prime minister's desk.

"Glad you're here, Sir Ian. We just got started a few minutes ago. Do have a seat."

Sir Ian picked a comfortable armchair alongside Charles Mills and opposite his boss, Gordon Hargreaves. Scott Frawley was sitting in the middle on the opposite side of the desk from the prime minister. He was decidedly uncomfortable as he felt the prime minister's penetrating gaze fixed on him. He noticed the somewhat pinched expression on her face, and she addressed him rather tersely. "Well, Sir Ian, Scott here has already brought us up to date on all the latest developments and, in particular, on the phone call you and he just had from this so-called Green September group. And despite your assurances that none of the firing mechanisms are missing and that they are unlikely to have been duplicated, we've reached a consensus here to take the threatened launch of the missile this afternoon seriously. So, what remains to be decided at this meeting is how we proceed to clear the area of all shipping with a minimum of fuss and as tactfully as possible."

Charles Mills, sitting to Sir Ian's right, was the first to speak. "I believe that we must inform the Americans at once and enlist their help. Firstly, they can help us clear ships in the area by informing their allies on the other side of the Atlantic. Secondly, I believe we should have Scott here liaison with their CIA, who may be able to help track down this Green September group. Thirdly, if the need should arise, the American government may be able to exert more influence on the Irish government than we ourselves can. Likewise, I believe we must inform the Russians because, if indeed a missile is launched and does successfully create a nuclear blast, we don't think we can be quite as frank with them as we should be with the Americans. So I suggest we concoct a suitable story that there is a risk of a nuclear explosion this afternoon at that point on the North Atlantic. And rather than having my department contact West European governments, I would suggest that Gordy here contact NATO ministers."

"I think that's very well put, Charles. I agree that we should do as you suggest. For the moment, let's put to one side the issue of a suitable cover story for those we can't take into our confidence about the missiles. Gordy, is that okay with you? Do you think you can handle it with the various ministers of the NATO countries?"

"No problem. I'll take care of notifying NATO countries."

"Charles, as soon as you have officially notified the Americans, please advise Scott immediately so that he can begin working with the CIA. And you, Sir Ian, can you insure that the Royal Navy will set up patrols around the entire area to make certain that no commercial ships or navies from other countries enter the targeted area?"

"Certainly, Prime Minister, I will issue instructions to that effect the moment I get back to the Ministry. I was just thinking that if indeed a missile is successfully launched this afternoon, we may be able to pinpoint exactly from where it is launched. Let me explain. You may be aware that the Americans have a series of satellites circling the globe whose sole task is to keep an eye on activity around the world; these satellites carry highly sensitive infrared cameras that should be able to pinpoint the emissions from any missile launch. I'll contact the US Military in the Pentagon to cover this aspect. However, their system of satellites does not provide 100 percent coverage, as there are several one- to two-minute periods out of every twenty-four hours when different parts of the globe are not covered. To compensate for these windows, as we call them in the military, I'll have four of our high-altitude RAF reconnaissance planes cover the length and breadth of Ireland so that we can't possibly miss the point of origin of any missile launch."

"That's an excellent consideration, Sir Ian. Please proceed with it the moment you're back in the Ministry. So, now to the big issue, gentlemen. How do we provide a good cover story in case there's any leak of this to the media?"

Ernest Brooking, the home secretary, spoke for the first time. "You know, I've been thinking over this aspect of it; let me throw out my idea and see what you all think. What if we were to say that we've been conducting a geological survey on the ocean floor in the targeted area, and we're scheduling some blasts for this afternoon—blasts that may create some seismic activity in the area and some possible fallout, depending on local atmospheric conditions. To me, this would seem plausible, and if we were to use it, we could in fact give out this information to the radio stations to be included with shipping weather forecasts for the area. And if Fleet Street should get wind of anything, we could stick to the same story. Besides, I think it could be an adequate story to give the Russians."

Everyone in the room was silent for a minute or two, thinking over Ernest Brooking's proposed idea. Finally, the prime minister said, "Unless anyone disagrees or can think of a good reason why this wouldn't be plausible, I think Ernest has a damn good idea." The PM paused a moment and looked around the room. When everyone nodded, she said, "Okay, so let's use that story, where appropriate. But, Ernest, your proposal does raise another question in my mind, and I believe, Sir Ian, your people should be asked to resolve it. My point is, if there actually is a nuclear explosion, what will the likely fallout consequences be? How far will a high level of radioactivity spread? Please have this checked out, also, and let me know."

"I will do so, Prime Minister, but it's my understanding that that far out in the Atlantic, whatever fallout occurs should be mostly dissipated before it reaches any land mass. But I will have it confirmed."

The prime minister's face now appeared to relax a little, as they were making progress. She looked at them and said, "Gentlemen, as you know, I was scheduled to have my first meeting with Charles Cassidy, the premier of the Irish Republic, at Checquers this weekend. Obviously, right now the Irish government may be the most important one that we have to deal with, as it looks as if both the missiles and the major have been taken to Ireland. So, I have decided that I'll call Charles Cassidy and apprise him of the situation and solicit the help of the Irish authorities in tracking down the so-called Green September group. I suggest we meet again this afternoon at about four o'clock, depending on what happens earlier in the afternoon. But I do want to be kept advised of any significant developments during the course of the day. At this point, Sir Ian and Scott, if you would be good enough to leave us, I have some other issues to discuss with my ministers." Sir Ian and Frawley departed.

As soon as the door closed behind them, Muriel Hobson said, "Gentlemen, we're facing a very serious crisis, not only from the standpoint of our fight against terrorism but also from a purely political point of view, as I have no doubt you have already realized. First of all, there's no way we can give in to blackmail from a group of terrorists, even those who may be holding a nuclear ace up their sleeves. And that stand which we must take gives rise to another very serious problem— the public's right to know. As you're all well aware, we were elected partly on our position that we would support a more open government and less use of the Official Secrets Act. You can all recall when we were in opposition how we repeatedly fought the previous government's increasing use of the Official Secrets Act to suppress information. And we know that the previous government never faced a crisis as serious as that which we are now facing. So we're in a classic dilemma, because any public announcements at this point on even the remotest threat of a nuclear missile hitting London would create absolute panic in the streets, and we'd play right into the hands of the terrorists. Even within our own ranks, we have to be careful. That is why I have kept these meetings as closed sessions and will continue to do so, as we could have major political problems if it went to a full cabinet meeting. And certainly we don't want awkward questions in the House of Commons.

Consider the fact that in our cabinet and as a leading member of our Labor Party, we would have to contend with Harry Roberts, who is an avowed antinuclear pacifist and the acknowledged leader of the left wing of our party. In addition to that, we have to consider the two Liberal Party members in our cabinet, whose stand is also most likely antinuclear, and the defection of the Liberals from us on this issue would lead to the fall of the government. Therefore, we have to continue maintaining the utmost secrecy on everything surrounding this crisis; otherwise our own political futures and that of our party could be in serious jeopardy. If indeed a nuclear explosion does occur this afternoon, we'll have to discuss this issue further, as our ability to keep a lid on the terrorists' demands may be severely strained. But until then, let's carry on with the tasks we decided on earlier and see if we can somehow resolve this crisis before it gets totally out of hand. That's it for now, gentlemen. Thank you very much."

Everyone got up to leave to return to their respective ministries. But the prime minister asked her confidential secretary, Jack Larson, to stay with her while she telephoned the Irish premier. As soon as the others were gone, Muriel Hobson, never a woman to waste a minute, turned to Jack Larson. "Okay, Jack, give me your opinion as to how we should best play it with the Irish government. We know they're a touchy lot over there."

"Well, I think we have to be reasonably straight and honest with them, as no matter what we think of them, over the long term we need their help and cooperation if we're ever to rid ourselves of the Northern Ireland problems. Clearly, telling them about the missiles increases the risk of a leak, as I don't believe their security on information is as tight as ours. And many of those in government over there are probably, at heart, sympathizers with the IRA in principle, if not in method. So I would consider it a high risk that anything we tell them will end up in the wrong hands. But in the present circumstances we really don't have much choice, as we do need their full cooperation to help us recover the missiles and find the Green September group before there is serious damage to our national interests."

"I'm afraid you're right, Jack; we really have no choice. And although I realize it increases our risks in some ways, I'll take the open approach with Charles Cassidy. Okay, Jack, see if you can get him on the line for me."

Muriel Hobson composed her thoughts while she waited for Jack Larson to get the Irish premier on the phone. A few minutes later, Jack handed the phone to the prime minister, who put the receiver to her ear and waited.

"Good morning, Charles, I'm so glad I could reach you right away, and I won't beat about the bush. The fact is, Charles, we have a major crisis on our hands."

"Good morning. As we're still meeting on the weekend at your country residence, couldn't it possibly hold until then? Like yourselves, you know, we also have a coalition government and have got a very important vote coming up in the Dail this morning, and I've got to be there very shortly to muster the votes. But if it can't wait, perhaps you can tell me very briefly what this is all about."

Muriel Hobson spent the next five minutes outlining, as succinctly as possible, the essence of the crisis as it had developed so far. When she was done, there was a long silence from the Irish premier.

"Are you still there, Charles?"

"Yes, I am. It's just that this could also be an explosive issue for our government, if you'll forgive my use of that word."

"But, Charles, can I count on your cooperation in tracking down this so-called Green September group? We have to move swiftly if we're to have any hope of preventing a major disaster."

"You have to understand, Muriel, that for me to organize a search for the Green September group in the time frame that we have, it has to be handled very delicately. So you'll have to be patient. But I do promise you my cooperation and that of the Irish government, army, and police force. It would help if you'd have a personal courier bring photographs of the missing major and any other useful information or descriptions that you can supply, to me in Dublin immediately. You realize you are asking me to organize Irish authorities to search for and bring to justice Irishmen who have kidnapped a British major. That may appear to you to be a simple task, but politically, it could stir up mixed emotions in my country here."

Muriel drummed her fingers on the desk impatiently. "I appreciate your cooperation. We'd be happy to send over some of our best people who are specialists in dealing with terrorists, if you wish."

"Absolutely not! That would only aggravate a very delicate situation. I'm sorry, but I'm sure you can understand that."

Muriel Hobson decided not to push for any more; she felt relieved that she had a reasonable assurance that they would get some cooperation from the Irish government—just how much she wasn't sure. Like her grandfather, Lloyd George, she didn't really understand the intricacies of Irish politics. "Yes, I understand. We deeply appreciate your cooperation, and I'll personally keep you advised on any new developments from this end. And if you could do the same, it would be very helpful."

"So that's settled. I have to run now. No doubt we'll talk later in the day. Good-bye."

"Cheerio, Charles, and thanks." Muriel Hobson put down the phone, looked at Jack Larson, and said, "The Irish are certainly a complex people, but I believe that Charles Cassidy will make every effort to have the Green September group found. Whether they'll act fast enough, I have my doubts. We should be thinking of some direct action ourselves. Although I realize that route is fraught with danger, as there would be a bloody outcry from the Americans and the United Nations if we bypassed Irish sovereignty in any way. Perhaps if we can pinpoint the location of the terrorists, we may be able to use a lightning raid by the SAS. Anyway, for now we'll let the Irish government handle it. But it behooves us to keep our options open and to consider other alternatives."

Jack offered her a mirthless smile and said, "That would certainly be a serious step to take. I agree that it would be best to leave any consideration of such a step at least until this evening when we can see what develops this afternoon. Now, just to remind you, you have to be in the House in ten minutes. I have your papers all ready."

"Good, then we'd best be on our way." A couple of minutes later, they left Downing Street for the House of Commons.

CHAPTER *12*

I T WAS ABOUT ELEVEN THIRTY in the morning on that Wednesday, September 8, when Charles Cassidy got back to his office in Leinster House, a building that also housed the Dail, the Irish Parliament. He was greeted by his secretary, Seamus Ryan, who was holding a big package that had arrived about ten minutes before by courier from the British prime minister. With the two doors to his private office closed, alone with Seamus Ryan, Charles Cassidy quickly tore open the package. It contained photographs of Major Kevin MacAllister in both military uniform and civilian clothes, also a photograph of a certain George Wilkinson, described as a mercenary and reportedly involved in the hijacking of the missiles. The last item in the package was a brief, technical description of an MML. That was all. It crossed Charles Cassidy's mind that the Brits weren't giving away too much. He laid the photographs out on his desk neatly while Seamus Ryan looked at them over his shoulder.

In his early fifties, Charles Cassidy represented the new breed in Irish politics. He was a pragmatist who grappled with Ireland's many economic problems and had little time for the politics of the past. A fairly trim man about 5'10" in height, with black hair going slightly gray, dark blue eyes, fine features, and carefully manicured hands, he was a lawyer by profession. He was certainly more educated than previous Irish premiers, with a more polished style than any of his predecessors. Charles Cassidy had emerged seven years earlier as the leader of the Fine Gael Party, which had its roots in the pro-treaty party of 1922 when Ireland gained independence. He led a coalition government that comprised his own Fine Gael Party and the minority Irish Labor Party. They had been in power now for three years. It was only during the past fifteen years that his party had been in government on three different occasions; the previous fifty years had been dominated by the Fianna Fail Party, whose roots went back to the anti-treaty party of 1922. It was mainly the impact of the troubles in Northern Ireland that had increased the volatility of politics in the Dublin government over the past twenty years. And while publicly both of the major parties were for the unification of Ireland, in private many members of each party believed it was now impractical, and given the high level of unemployment and the faltering economy of the Republic of Ireland, many believed the Republic couldn't even afford to take over the six counties of Northern Ireland. Charles Cassidy was one of those who believed this, though he would never admit it in a public forum.

Charles Cassidy now felt that the biggest dilemma of his career had been foisted on him by the British prime minister. For even though successive Irish governments had come out strongly against the tactics of the IRA and other terrorist groups in Northern Ireland, Charles Cassidy realized that there was still a romantic sympathy among the people of Ireland for the cause. He realized that while his party was voted into power by the Irish people acting on the major economic issues facing the country, if the issue of the unification of Ireland had been put to them in an emotional appeal, he may well not be sitting in this office today.

Cassidy also believed that if you scratch beneath the surface of any Irishman living in Ireland, England, or America, even one several generations removed, one would find a deep romantic conviction that Ireland must be unified. So for him to instigate the search for a group that just might succeed in blackmailing the British government to accede to its demands could almost cast him in the light of a traitor in the eyes of his Irish people. Yet his government must also maintain law and order, and even if it meant cooperation with the British government, the Irish government had to be seen by the rest of the world as pursuing terrorists just as diligently as anyone else would. Whatever he did,

Charles Cassidy knew he would be walking a fine line, and it would take all his skills to stay on top of the situation.

After consulting with Seamus Ryan, Charles Cassidy decided his first call should be to Des O'Houlihan, his minister for internal affairs, who was in charge of both the Gardai, Ireland's police force, and also Special Branch. He agreed with Des that the photographs should be duplicated and distributed to every Gardai station throughout the country, within the next couple of hours, and that no mention would be made to anyone about the missiles. But Des told Charles that it would be necessary for him to brief more fully his head of Special Branch, Jim MacAllister, as Special Branch was a small specialist force that was the equivalent of MI5 in England. They would pursue the Green September group independently. The two men agreed that Des O'Houlihan would get everything rolling as soon as he got the photographs and that he would work out a plan of action with Jim MacAllister right away. Des promised to keep Charles Cassidy informed of his progress.

Cassidy's next call was to Jerry O'Toole, the minister of defense. When Charles called, Jerry just happened to have the Irish Army chief, General Dan MacEoin, sitting in his office. Charles's instructions to them were clear: no mention of the missiles should go beyond the two of them, and they should remain ready to have troops from the southern and western commands committed to the search just as soon as Charles gave the word. With that settled, Charles decided to wait to see if indeed a missile was launched in the afternoon, before utilizing the Irish Army in the search for the Green September group. He was sure that the British prime minister wouldn't be very happy that he was delaying his commitment of troops to the search, but she would have to accept it; it was his choice. His final call was to Thomas Flynn, the minister for external affairs and an old friend whom he trusted implicitly. He discussed the problem with Thomas even though no action was required of his department at that time. He needed Thomas's advice and opinion. Thomas Flynn agreed that Charles had done all he could.

Charles Cassidy turned to Seamus Ryan. "Well, Seamus, I know we can rely on the boys to play their parts. But what do you think of it all? I wonder who the hell the Green September group really is. Do you think they're a splinter group from one of the IRA groups?"

"Sure, it's quite a puzzle. It's hard to keep track these days of all the IRA groups. It probably is another splinter group, but it doesn't seem typical of their style. But what if this Green September group actually succeeds?"

"That's a frightening thought! It's one thing to have a nuclear explosion go off in the middle of the Atlantic where it probably won't harm anyone, but it's quite another if a group claiming to be Irish drops a nuclear bomb on London. That could lead to a terrible state of affairs for all of us."

"But, Charlie, what if after the first missile goes off, the British government actually gives in to their demands rather than risk a bomb droppin' on London? That'd be a whole different story, wouldn't it?"

"That's very unlikely, as there's no way the British government could be seen to give in to terrorists' demands, no matter what's at stake. I certainly wouldn't like to be in their shoes. But we've got our own problems. What if we don't find this group in time? The Brits will probably want to send in their secret SAS group, and that would put us in a very difficult spot. You know the opposition in the Dail would make a big fuckin' deal about the fact of me allowing a British sniper team on Irish soil, and it would surely leak out! Indeed, they'd be sure to accuse me of weakening Irish sovereignty and giving in to our ancient enemies!"

"I know," Seamus said sympathetically. "But if we use our own special forces, there'll be hell to pay with many of our countrymen who still support the aims of the old IRA."

Charlie let out a long sigh and said, "So we'd end up between a rock and a hard place, with no way out."

The ringing of the phone interrupted them; Seamus automatically picked it up.

"It's Des for you, Charlie."

"What's up, Des?"

"First, thanks for the photos. They'll be on their way out around the country within the hour. But I've just been talking with Jim MacAllister, and believe it or not, this Major Kevin MacAllister is Jim's first cousin. They used to spend a lot of holidays together over in Galway and down in Kerry. Anyway, it appears they were pretty close as children and teenagers but haven't seen much of each other in the past few years. Despite his personal interest in this, unless you disagree, I'm still letting Jim direct Special Branch's efforts in the search for the Green September group who have allegedly kidnapped his cousin."

"That'll be okay. I don't think it will hurt. In fact, with his cousin's life at stake, Jim will probably make an all-out effort to find him, and so find the terrorists. Anything else?"

"No, that's all for now."

After hanging up, Charles explained this new wrinkle to Seamus Ryan.

"So it's certainly a small world, isn't it? Anyway, we have about forty-five minutes before my next meeting, so how about goin' around the corner to Doyle's Bar and grabbin' a pint of Guinness and some oysters?"

"Sure, that's just what we need to give us strength after this mornin'."

It was one thirty in the afternoon on Wednesday, September 8. Rory McDevitt, the commander of the IRA in Belfast, looked out the window of a farmhouse, noting several of the armed men surrounding it. His counterpart, Padraig Flannery, commander of the Provisional IRA in Derry, sat across from him at an old kitchen table. Flannery said, "Rory, I don't know what to make of it. But I can absolutely assure you that it's none of our people involved."

McDevitt clenched his fist. "Well, it's not our boys either, so then who the fuck could it be? I mean, we've got to keep some bloody discipline and coordination, or we'll never beat back the Brits."

"Listen, my sources down in Dublin say that a British mercenary by the name of George Wilkinson is involved. Some o' the old boys in Derry tell me that he used to be a captain in the Royal Fusiliers and served here in Northern Ireland back in the early seventies. Apparently he's a Scotsman and appears to be a fair man but tough, and he didn't like how the British Army was handling some things here, so after two tours of duty, he resigned and has been a mercenary ever since, serving around the world. It would strike me as unlikely that such a man would be involved in kidnapping a British major from the Ministry of Defense and a couple of nuclear missiles. There has to be more to all this than meets the eye. The fact that he was a mercenary suggests to me that somebody's footin' the bill for this."

McDevitt sighed and sat silent for a moment, looking up as if the answer were on the ceiling. "You could be right at that because I can't think of any of our lads who would be enterprising enough to organize this on his own. But what's this I've heard that you and the Provos are lookin' to get your hands on a demonstrator model of a British surface-to-air missile for South Africa in exchange for new weapons? Is it true?"

Flannery looked out the window for a moment and grinned. He said, "It could be, but I can assure you nothing's happened about it yet, and it may never happen. Jesus, it's bloody difficult to get our hands on any British missile. That's what's so puzzlin' about what I'm hearin' from down south."

McDevitt sighed and put his head in his hands. "So the bottom line is that we don't know who's behind it. And besides, we're not even sure that this so-called Green September group really has nuclear missiles. But by Christ, if they do, it's gonna be damn bloody interesting to see what happens today. So your sources are tellin' ya that the first of the two missiles is gonna be fired into the Atlantic today to demonstrate to the Brits that they can arm the nuclear warheads?"

Flannery's eyes were sparkling as he said, "That's what I'm hearin', but we'll soon see if it's true. If it happens, then you and I have gotta decide what we're gonna do about it. Do we claim that this Green September group is part of our organization, or is there a better way we could exploit the situation? I'm almost wishin' it's true and that they blast bloody London to hell!"

Troubled by Flannery's excitement, McDevitt sighed again and said, "I don't know, but you know the way the Brits think—they'll automatically blame us, so maybe we should take the glory for it. But there's another possibility." He leaned forward and said, "If indeed there's a nuclear blast today, maybe it'll scare the pants off the Brits, and they'll actually back down rather than risk a nuclear bomb fallin' on them in London."

"I doubt that. Think back a few years ago when we tried to bomb them in Brighton. All it did was make the bloody Tory government tougher. 'Course, if this threat is true, we're not talkin' about any old car bomb or a bit o' plastics; we're talking about a great big bloody nuclear bang!"

At this, McDevitt stood up. "Listen, we're not gonna solve anything right now, and you know if we spend too long together, the Brits may find us here. So for now, let's agree that whatever we do, we'll present a united front on this. I would say our best bet is to wait and see if there really is a nuclear blast this afternoon. What do you say?"

Standing, Flannery said, "You're right. We'd better keep on the move and get the hell out of here. Let's meet tonight again about seven at the old place near Ballymena. Okay then?"

"Right. I'll see you then." The two men shook hands and went outside together, each joining his own group of men. Within minutes, each group got into several different cars and went off in opposite directions.

It was only 7:00 a.m. local time on Wednesday, September 8, when Paul Laster arrived at Colonel Gary Marshall's office at the Pentagon. Laster had requested the meeting. At 6:05 a.m., he had gotten the official word from the State Department about the kidnapping of Major Kevin MacAllister and the hijacking of the two nuclear missiles. As Paul had promised Scott Frawley on the phone the evening before, he had acted as if that were the first time he had heard of the incident. Colonel Gary Marshall was in charge of the coordination of the Unites States' entire nuclear arsenal across the four services, roughly the equivalent role that Major Kevin MacAllister played for the British Armed Forces. Paul Laster knew that just two weeks earlier, Major MacAllister had spent four days in Washington, DC, working with the colonel on the American position for nuclear arms reduction talks with the Russians. Paul had known Colonel Marshall for many years and had a very high regard for him.

Paul spent the next twenty minutes giving the colonel a detailed account of everything he knew about events in Britain over the past thirty hours. When he finished, the colonel finally said, "This is extremely serious, Paul. As you know, the major has become a very good friend of mine, and I'm concerned for his safety in the hands of terrorists. Obviously, I'm also very concerned that any information he has in his head doesn't get into the hands of the Russians. From what you say, that would appear unlikely, if indeed it is some faction of the IRA that has kidnapped him and taken the missiles. The IRA, even though I'm aware that the Provos certainly have Marxist leanings, wouldn't tend to do anything against American interests that would destroy support they get from Irish Americans in this country. Anyway, Paul, that's just my gut reaction, for what it's worth. But tell me, what can I do to help?"

Paul had decided to steer clear of any insinuation that Major MacAllister might have been involved in orchestrating this, as Scott Frawley had hinted to him on the phone, so he proceeded tactfully.

"Well, did you think there was anything bothering the major when he spent a few days here with you?"

The colonel got up and took time to pour them both some coffee before he answered. He sat back down, passed a cup over to Paul, and said, "No, there wasn't really anything I noticed; in fact, he seemed to be in rather good form. When it came to business, he was his usual serious self, and, in fact, he made several useful suggestions, which we are incorporating into our proposals for the next round of talks with the Russians. You know, he really is brilliant when it comes to tactical nuclear weapons. I certainly hope that it's the IRA behind this for their own purposes and not acting as agents for the Libyans, the PLO, or the Russians. Do you think that the British are reasonably certain that the IRA is behind this?"

Paul shrugged. "Well, you know Scott Frawley, their key man in MI5, seems to be quite sure that it is some faction within the IRA. But he isn't definite. For now, we can only work on that assumption, until something comes out to the contrary. You know the major had Irish parents, don't you?"

"Yes, I did, as a matter of fact; though to talk to him, he came across as pure British."

"Did he ever talk about Ireland much with you?"

"Not very often." The colonel spread his hands in a wide, sweeping gesture and said, "As you know, I've visited Ireland a couple of times, and we talked about good spots for fishing. I think he was very fond of Ireland in that regard."

"So, bottom line in your opinion—the major didn't seem to be under any undue stress or appear to have anything troubling him?"

"That's right. I'm sorry I can't be more helpful. But there is one thing I just thought of that may help the British in this crisis. If a missile is launched into the North Atlantic, proving they can activate the second one, we have a new gadget that can pick up missiles after they've been launched and redirect them. We haven't finished testing it, but it's worth a thought. Here in the Pentagon, we've dubbed it the MTA, short for missile target alternator. What do you think?"

"That might prove invaluable, if it works. Anyway, the British are our closest allies, and I certainly think we should offer it to them. I'll leave it with you to arrange, as it really is a military matter rather than my department."

"Good, I'll talk with the chief of staff when he gets in and arrange it. Perhaps we can get it and a couple of our experts on the early afternoon Concorde flight to London. Then they should have it by this evening, their time. I know that's too late for the first missile, but it may be crucial for the second. Well, if there isn't anything else I can do for you now, I'd better get moving on this idea."

"No, I guess that's about it for now. And thanks again for coming in so early. By the way, you won't mind if I mention this MTA device to Scott Frawley, will you?"

"No, that'll be fine. But I'll arrange this with their chief of staff, Sir Ian Sinders. Keep me posted of any new developments."

After leaving the colonel's office, Paul began to wonder why Scott Frawley seemed to be hung up on implicating Major MacAllister in the hijacking of the missiles. Perhaps that was the only solution he could think of as to how the terrorists could have the firing mechanisms, if they did. It seemed there had to be someone on the inside. But the major? Paul Laster doubted that his MI5 colleague was on the right track. He left the Pentagon and drove back to his office in Langley.

It was already three o'clock in the afternoon on that same day in Moscow, when Paul Laster had started his meeting with Colonel Marshall in Washington. Anatoli Kouznetsov, head of the FSB, was sitting in his office on the fifth floor of FSB headquarters overlooking Red Square. He had just returned from a meeting with the foreign minister and was now waiting for Sergei Rastvorov, his chief of European operations, to come and meet with him. As he sat, he thought about what the foreign minister had told him. Apparently, the British foreign secretary had contacted the Russian Federation in advance so that none of its navy vessels or fishing trawlers would be in the area. The British had also requested that Moscow advise their East European allies who might have shipping in the area. The Russian foreign minister said he had called in Anatoli Kouznetsov because, at best, he was skeptical of the British reasons for clearing the area of shipping. He said he had assured the British foreign secretary that they would clear the area but had demanded a fuller explanation of what was going to occur. The British foreign secretary had been acutely diplomatic about it all and had said that there was a chance that there might be no problems from what the geological expedition was doing but that they just wanted to play things safe. Kouznetsov shared the same opinion as the Russian foreign minister and felt certain that there was a lot more to this. Finally, Sergei Rastvorov arrived in his office.

"Sit down, Sergei. I have just come from our foreign minister's office, where I learned that the British appear to be up to something very odd."

Kouznetsov quickly outlined what he had learned, and Rastvorov seemed genuinely surprised at what his boss was telling him. Rastvorov said, "I can assure you that my people in Western Europe keep track of everything of significance that goes on. And I was not aware of any British geological survey going on anywhere in the North Atlantic. You're right; there must be more to this."

"Yes, I'm certain I'm right. So I want to know what the British are really up to. You are to get reports from our agents in England right away. Report back to me in one hour."

"It will be done."

When Rastvorov left his office, Kouznetsov thought that the deadline to clear shipping from that area of the North Atlantic was five in the evening Moscow time, so he should know more before then if Sergei was successful in finding out something. Anatoli Kouznetsov was an impatient man and a ruthless one. He believed that information was power. He paced around his office, anxious to know what the British were really doing. Half an hour later, at a quarter to four, Sergei Rastvorov returned with a wide smile.

"You are looking very pleased, Sergei. What have you found out?"

Rastvorov sat in the chair in front of Kouznetsov's desk. "You were certainly right. There is a lot more, and it's most interesting. As you know, this week the British are holding military maneuvers on the Salisbury Plain. Some of our London agents have been in the area, observing them. And it would appear that a Major MacAllister, who is their senior officer at the Ministry of Defense, responsible for coordination of Britain's nuclear forces, has disappeared. They're saying it is a kidnapping. But here is the best news of all: two short-range nuclear missiles on a mobile missile carrier have also disappeared. And from phone conversations that we tapped in London, it seems that some Irish terrorist group calling themselves Green September are believed to have the British major and the missiles somewhere in Ireland. That is most interesting, no?"

Kouznetsov leaned forward, smiling, and said, "That is excellent, but it may not be so good that a terrorist group has nuclear missiles. In fact, it could be very dangerous; it may not be in Russian interests. I still don't see the connection between that event and the clearing of the shipping in the North Atlantic. We need more information. Please make immediate contact with our agents in Northern Ireland, as perhaps the Marxist-oriented IRA Provos have a better idea of what's really going on."

Rastvorov stood and said, "I'll see to it right now. With luck, it may take only half an hour, and I'll be back."

Alone again, Kouznetsov was very intrigued with this new information. For two reasons, he was very, very interested. One, if they could get their hands on this Major MacAllister, they would be able to get a lot of information on not only the British nuclear forces but also about the Americans' forces. And two, it would be the grand coup of his career if it were at all possible for him and his people to get even one of the missiles, intact, back to Russia, as he knew the Russian Army would love to be able to examine the technology used in a British nuclear missile. Kouznetsov, who rarely smiled, now grinned a little to himself at the thought of what a superb achievement that would be. Kouznetsov's fantasies were interrupted twenty minutes later when Sergei Rastvorov returned once again, and Kouznetsov begrudgingly admitted to himself that Rastvorov was being unusually efficient today. "What new information have you managed to obtain, Sergei?" he asked.

Rastvorov sat down across the desk from Kouznetsov. "It becomes even more interesting. Our sources in Northern Ireland have informed me that even the IRA, both the regulars and the Provos, are not aware of the Green September group, who have taken the British major and the missiles. In fact, they're wondering how to exploit the situation for their own ends. What they've learned is that the British government was at first skeptical of the ability of this group to arm the nuclear warheads of the missiles because of their internal security controls on the firing mechanisms. But apparently, the group who has the missiles claimed that they can activate the nuclear warheads and will demonstrate by launching one into that zone in the North Atlantic today, some time after two o'clock their time. This group's demands from the British government are for immediate withdrawal of British troops from Northern Ireland and a public announcement with a timetable for the unification of Ireland. Otherwise, they threaten to launch the second missile on London itself."

Kouznetsov frowned. "How would you like this idea? Perhaps we might be so kind as to save London from that second missile, if we could get our hands on it for ourselves."

Rastvorov broke into a huge smile. "That would be a stroke of genius. But the time frame is very short. If indeed this Green September group demonstrates that it can activate the nuclear warheads, there is less than twenty-four hours until the launch of the second missile. That would leave very little time for us to find them, even with the help of the IRA."

Kouznetsov spread his hands in a sweeping gesture. "But what if we simply follow the Irish government in its search for the terrorists? I have no doubt that the British government will already have requested that they seek out this Green September group. Maybe the Irish Army and police force will lead us to them. It certainly is an idea worth considering. But in the meantime, we'd better wait and see what develops."

It was shortly before two thirty, Wednesday, September 8, and Scott Frawley was just finishing up a late lunch of a roast beef sandwich and a glass of milk at the desk in his office. Scott had been going nonstop since he'd gotten back to his office at nine fifteen that morning after the early meeting with the prime minister. As he sat trying to digest his lunch, his ever-busy mind was summarizing all that he had learned in the past few hours.

One significant development during the morning was that he had confirmation from the Fishguard police that Ron Trelford, the customs inspector who thought he had seen Major MacAllister board the Fishguard ferry late on Monday night, had now made a positive identification based on several different photographs of the major that Scott's department had sent overnight. This fact disturbed Frawley deeply, as it seemed to indicate that Major MacAllister had crossed to Ireland of his own free will with a woman and child as cover. He couldn't quite figure out how, if terrorists were involved, they could have persuaded him to do that other than by holding either his wife or Jenny Laster as hostages.

He had decided not to inform anyone else of this confirmation because the implications would be extremely difficult for anyone else to yet grasp or understand. Scott had not liked the prime minister's decision to be so open with the Irish government, as he didn't have a high regard for their security. He felt sure that the information would leak out somewhere from that source. He was also rather surprised that there hadn't been any claims from either the IRA, the Provos, or from any other splinter group, aside from the phone call that morning from the Green September group.

Scott was also concerned on several other fronts, as he already had word that some reporters from the *Daily Sentinel* had been observed snooping around Downing Street and in the vicinity of the Salisbury Plain. And just in the last half hour, he had received a report that known Russian agents were believed to be in the Salisbury Plain area also. He knew that the minute the British foreign secretary contacted the Russians about clearing shipping out of that area of the North Atlantic, they would have immediately contacted the FSB to investigate. Even while he had sat in the prime minister's office that morning, Scott could have foreseen that, but it wouldn't have been appropriate for him to cast skepticism on the agreed-upon cover story to the Russians and others.

Scott Frawley was acutely aware of MI5's embarrassing failure to penetrate either the IRA or the Provos to any significant extent. The most MI5 agents were ever able to pick up was very peripheral information, which didn't allow MI5 to ever take any preventative action against IRA activities in Britain or Northern Ireland. So Scott had been very relieved when he had talked to Paul Laster at the CIA in Langley about an hour earlier. The CIA's agents in Ireland were certainly in a much better position than MI5's to find out information.

Paul had told him that the CIA agents had learned only that it appeared neither the IRA or Provos were involved in kidnapping the major and hijacking the missiles. He'd said that this was just an initial report from his agents in the field, and he wasn't yet prepared to say conclusively that that was indeed the case. For Scott, this was very worrisome, as it could blow his theories about IRA involvement and would again open up other even darker possibilities. Likewise, Paul Laster wasn't very happy with that report because if some group other than the IRA or other Irish-connected group was involved, the risk to US national security was much greater. Paul had also brought him up to date on his early morning meeting with Colonel Gary Marshall, Kevin MacAllister's opposite number in the Pentagon, and had told him he was pretty sure that Gary Marshall had been unable to shed any new light on the major's disappearance. But Scott had been relieved to learn of the Pentagon's offer to send over the MTA to the British military. He advised Paul Laster of the increased activity by Russian agents in the Salisbury Plain area. Before wrapping up his phone conversation with Paul Laster, he had raised the sensitive issue of whether Paul, through his colleagues in the FBI, could help him obtain an immediate copy of the will of Kevin MacAllister's granduncle, which was apparently with a New York law firm. Paul hadn't been able to give Scott much hope that they would be able to do anything about that, but he said they would try.

During the course of the morning, Scott had talked with Sir Ian Sinders, Gordy Hargreaves, and the other ministers and knew that everything that had been agreed to at the morning meeting with the PM had been carried out. He had called the PM just a short time ago and informed her of where everything stood. He wasn't able to give her any new developments from his department but expressed a high degree of confidence that he was putting more pieces of the puzzle in place. It irked him to admit it to himself, but he knew there was nothing else he could do before the time when the first nuclear missile was scheduled to go off in the North Atlantic.

Just before three o'clock, Scott Frawley got up from his desk and went to stand by the window. He rolled up the blinds and gazed out at the wide-open skies, even though he knew nothing would be visible from this far away. He stood quietly and was thinking that all his colleagues in the British government who knew what was about to happen were probably doing the same thing right then. Though it wasn't particularly warm in his office, Scott Frawley began to sweat. The Green September group had been very careful not to divulge the precise moment of the impact, but Captain Smithers learned that after 2:00 p.m., the first open window without satellite coverage would occur at approximately 2:59 p.m., and depending where the missile was launched, he had estimated that it should hit that area of the North Atlantic at approximately 3:15, based on the fact that the Penguin-class missiles travelled at Mach 3 or roughly 2,100 miles per hour. Scott Frawley began mentally to count down.

CHAPTER *13*

O N WEDNESDAY, SEPTEMBER 8, WHILE Terry had something to eat and some hot fresh-brewed tea from the little camper stove, Kevin stood at the entrance to the cave, observing the weather. The early morning mist had burned off, and instead of the gray, rainy day more typical to this part of the country, the day had turned beautiful with clear skies and sun. That didn't please Kevin. George and Tom joined him.

"You look concerned again, Mac. What's up?"

"It's the bloody weather, George. I figured the odds were good that it would be nice and gray and misty out, thus reducing the chance of anyone seeing the flash from the missile when it's launched."

George frowned and said, "But I thought that with it being launched from inside the cave, there was very little likelihood the liftoff could be seen from land?"

"No, that's not entirely true, as there'll be a visible exhaust from the rocket engine as it climbs."

"Oh, I see. That's a bit of a problem, isn't it? But in any case, no matter what the weather, am I not correct in thinking that the infrared cameras on board any circling satellites or reconnaissance planes will see the launch?"

"Yes, but at any point on the globe, there's a one- to two-minute gap in coverage, about three times a day. That is why I selected 2:59 p.m. today as the blast-off time for the first missile. At that point, from this spot on the earth, there's a one-minute, twelve-second window when there will be no coverage directly overhead. But I'm damn sure the Royal Air Force will have its high-altitude reconnaissance planes with their infrared cameras wide open, blanketing Ireland. So we'll be extremely lucky if the liftoff is not detected. The best I'm hoping for is that with the initial heat source from the blastoff being dissipated back down through the cave, what will register on any infrared camera may be vague enough to make it impossible for them to pinpoint exactly where we are. I have no doubt they'll track the path of the missile after it's launched and will be able to gauge its exact speed, and may, through calculating the distance traveled and speed and time, be able to come within a few square miles of the launch site."

Tom asked, "So, Major, this control pad thingy is like a kind of baby computer, and when you insert it into the open slot of the guidance system, it sorta takes control, and the coordinates you already input take control of the missile. Is that right?"

"Yep, Tom, just like a computer."

Kevin explained enough to satisfy Tom's curiosity but judiciously avoided telling him too much. When it came to these missiles, Kevin ultimately trusted no one, not even George.

"All this technical stuff is way over my head," Terry chimed in, "but what I do understand is that when it does explode, it will surely make one God almighty huge fuckin' bang!"

"You got that right. In fact, each missile will have the explosive impact of the equivalent of four hundred thousand tons of TNT."

Terry appeared gobsmacked and then broke into a huge grin as he said, "Be the Jesus, Major, I would love to ram a missile right up the arse of Muriel Hobson and blow her to kingdom come!"

Kevin looked at Terry in mock surprise and said, "You don't like the British prime minister then?"

"No, I like her fine. I just think the old biddy needs a good fucking in the rear!"

George finally joined in and said sarcastically, "Well, Terry, there's no mistaking what you think of the PM."

It was only twenty minutes after noon, and the day, unfortunately, was still bright and sunny. Kevin was feeling restless and suggested to George that the two of them take a walk down the mountain to the farmhouse and check in with Ned, Sean, and Pat. George jumped at the suggestion. The two men set off down the mountain, leaving Tom and Terry to keep watch in the cave. They found Ned feeling pretty relaxed; he seemed to be at home in these mountains and didn't appear to be giving too much thought to the launching of the missile. A short while later, they reached Sean, who seemed decidedly on edge, and after a little probing, George learned that with so much time on his hands, Sean had been worrying about his sick mother. George and Kevin did their best to reassure the young man and to put it in perspective. Kevin told him it wouldn't be that much longer before this was all over and he would be able to slip away to see his mother. At the same time, George took the opportunity to remind Sean that if he dare desert his post, there would be no money, and he might be killed.

When they got to the farmhouse, they found Pat Feeney alert and ready for action. Pat appeared to be in his element. George checked with Pat to make sure he had enough food, ammunition, and anything else he might need, including cigarettes. Just before they left him, George asked Pat to keep a sharp eye out also to the rear, to make certain that Sean Morrissey didn't get any crazy notions about skipping out on them. Pat assured George that he would have no hesitation in killing Sean if he thought Sean was running out, jeopardizing the whole operation. Kevin overheard this, and although he said nothing, it sent a shudder down his spine. As he had gotten to know each of these men, he really didn't want to see any of them die as a result of this operation.

At one fifteen, they left Pat alone in the old farmhouse and took a longer route back by the lake to their cave in the mountains. In many ways, Kevin found the waiting unbearable. He was relieved to see that there was absolutely no trace of the piano truck they had ditched in the lake the previous afternoon and that there was no sight or sound of any wandering tourist or fisherman.

As they made their way around the shore of the lake, they came upon an outcropping of rocks that rose far above the surrounding shoreline and almost looked as if the earth had coughed it up and thrown all the rocks together on the edge of the lake. They decided to scramble up to the highest rock and sat there for a few minutes, quietly, just soaking up the scenery. For a few brief moments, Kevin felt tranquil and almost intoxicated by the wild, natural beauty of the mountains and picturesque landscape. Then Kevin saw a vague hint of mist on the horizon and prayed fervently that it would close in on the mountain before the launch. As he gazed about, Kevin found that the splendor of the surrounding countryside reinforced in him the conviction that this fair land must once again be united and belong to all Irishmen.

As they climbed down from the rocks to the shoreline, Kevin again felt the strong conviction that what he was about to do was the only thing that could be done, to finally free all of Ireland of any British presence, for all time.

It was about twenty-five minutes past two when George and Kevin got back to the cave. Tom and Terry had almost completed the task of removing their equipment and belongings from the inside of the cave and stowing them neatly in the undergrowth around the mouth of the cave. They were doing this on instructions from George, who'd feared that if they left anything inside, it might ignite and be destroyed by the rocket's emission as it launched. Max seemed particularly pleased to see his master back again. Everything was being set up for the launch, and with the cave cleared, George sent Terry forward to join Pat Feeney at the farmhouse. He told Tom that immediately after the launch, he was to set out and join Sean Morrissey at the second lookout point.

At exactly 2:30 p.m. everything was ready for the launch except for the final programming of the guidance system in the missile. Kevin stood at the mouth of the cave, looking out, and was immensely relieved to see a thick mist rolling in fast, beneath low clouds from Dingle Bay. He felt his prayers had been heard.

Kevin decided it was time to do the final programming of the missile. He opened the little trapdoor on the side of the missile guidance system as George and Tom looked on. First, he set the coordinates for precisely sixteen degrees west and sixty degrees north, and then he set the target distance at exactly 550 miles. Finally, he set the speed at 2,100 miles per hour. He had earlier set the trajectory so that the missile would rise to 40,000 feet and would travel at that height until it reached the target area, when it would nose-dive to the target zone. Finally, after checking his watch against the time from George and Tom, he set the launch time for exactly 2:59 p.m. That was it. The countdown began.

Above the countdown meter, he pointed out to Tom and George the readout that showed the time between launch and hitting the target area as exactly 15 minutes, 42.86 seconds. That would put the time of the nuclear explosion in the North Atlantic at exactly 3:14:43. Kevin closed the trapdoor on the side of the missile guidance system, and all was set for the launch. George finally raised the question that must have been on everyone's mind, which Kevin had anticipated. "Mac, can you explain to me about the fallout from the nuclear blast and where you expect it will drift?"

"I'm glad you asked. The reason I picked those particular coordinates in the North Atlantic is that the location is far enough away from any landmass to minimize serious fallout risks. But most importantly, the main wind pattern there is westerly to southwesterly, meaning that the fallout will be carried in a northeasterly direction beyond the northernmost tip of Scotland and to the south of Iceland, toward the Arctic Circle. By the time any fallout is blown over land, the radioactive intensity will be so dissipated as to be barely noticeable. The real danger level from radioactivity is in a very short radius around the core of the blast area. Of course, ultimately, the radioactive fallout is carried by the winds around the entire globe. But as in the French nuclear tests in the South Pacific and the other nuclear tests in the past forty years, the radioactive fallout dissipates around the globe and doesn't raise appreciably the overall level of radioactivity in our atmosphere. Not unless there was a large number of nuclear blasts simultaneously."

George and Tom seemed comfortable with that explanation. There were still twenty minutes until launch time. The three of them again lapsed into silence, and each seemed to look at his watch every few seconds.

To help distract them, Kevin began to regale George and Tom with a bit of Irish history he had learned from Granduncle Bertie. He told them about Thomas Davis, a Protestant barrister, writer, and poet who had been born in Mallow, County Cork, in 1814, the son of an English Army surgeon and an Irish mother. "Even though Davis died in 1845, in his short life he had a dramatic impact on the development of Irish nationalism. He was one of the three founders of a newspaper, the *Nation*, which first appeared on October 8, 1842. Within a very short time, this newspaper reached a higher circulation than any other paper in Ireland at that time. Thomas Davis produced most of the editorial writing, and he became one of the key formative figures in the development of a true Irish nationalism." Kevin looked up to make sure they were interested, and they appeared to be. He said, "Let me quote from one of Davis's essays in that early Irish newspaper: 'Nationality is no longer an unmeaning or despised name among us. It is welcomed by the higher ranks, it is the inspiration of the bold, and the hope of the people.'" Kevin paused to let that sink in, and then he said, "My granduncle taught me a poem by Thomas Davis that ran like this:

'A nation's voice, a nation's voice—
        It is a solemn thing!
It bids the bondage-sick rejoice—
        'Tis stronger than a king.
'Tis like the light of many stars,
        The sound of many waves;
Which brightly look through prison-bars;
        And sweetly sound in caves.
Yet is it noblest, godliest known,
        When righteous triumph swells its tone.

A nation's flag, a nation's flag—
        If wickedly unrolled,
May foes in adverse battle drag
        Its every fold from fold.
But, in the cause of Liberty,
        Guard it 'gainst Earth and Hell;
Guard it 'til Death or Victory—
        Look you, you guard it well!
No saint or king has tomb so proud,
        As he whose flag becomes his shroud.

A nation's right, a nation's right—
    God gave it; and gave, too,
A nation's sword, a nation's might,
    Danger to guard it through.
'Tis freedom from a foreign yoke,
    'Tis just and equal laws,
Which deal unto the humblest folk,
    As in a noble's cause.
On nations fixed in right and truth,
    God would bestow eternal youth.

May Ireland's voice be ever heard
    Amid the world's applause!
And never be her flag-staff stirred,
    But in an honest cause!
May freedom be her very breath,
    Be Justice ever dear;
And never an ennobled death
    May son of Ireland fear!
So the Lord God will ever smile,
    With guardian grace, upon our isle.'"

When Kevin had finished reciting the poem, he looked at his watch—four minutes and fifteen seconds until the launch. He said, "It's time for us to get out of the cave." After he put the leash on Max, they all left. Tom started his descent toward Ned and on to Sean Morrissey, whom he wouldn't reach until after the launch. George and Kevin went about fifty yards to the left of the cave, facing the ocean side of the mountain, which was now invisible in the thick, darkening mist. There, the two men crouched in the undergrowth, and Kevin, shortening the leash on Max, clutched him close as they lay on the ground.

Kevin stared at his watch. Thirty seconds before 2:59 p.m. Twenty seconds. Fifteen seconds. Kevin and George could hear the ignition fire on the rockets. Ten seconds. The noise intensified. Nine, eight, seven, six, five, four, three, two, one. It was launched and soared like a streak of lightning up through the mist and out of sight. The deadly payload was on its way to the target zone in the North Atlantic, and Kevin fervently and silently prayed that the British government had heeded their warning and that there were no ships within a hundred miles of the target.

CHAPTER *14*

IT WAS THREE THIRTY IN the afternoon on that Wednesday, September 8, when one after another, the sleek high-altitude reconnaissance planes with their swept-back wings landed at the RAF base at Farnborough, just thirty miles southwest of London. The planes taxied one behind the other to a hangar on the western perimeter of the airfield. An RAF helicopter stood by with its rotors already whirring. Captain Smithers from the Ministry of Defense was standing by the open door of the helicopter; the pilot, sitting at the controls, was awaiting his word to lift off. Each of the four pilots from the reconnaissance planes brought to Captain Smithers a square black diskette that he had just removed from his plane's computer-aided infrared photographic equipment. Captain Smithers took each one and dropped it into an envelope without a word. As he slammed the door behind him, he told the pilot to make haste back to the Ministry. With Major MacAllister out of the picture, Captain Smithers was now reporting directly to Sir Ian Sinders, and Sir Ian had sent him down to Farnborough to await the return of the reconnaissance planes. They already had gotten the radioed reports that indeed the missile launched had created a nuclear blast at the exact spot in the North Atlantic where the Green September group had warned them it would take place.

It was only a fifteen-minute flight back to the rooftop of the Ministry of Defense. Captain Smithers's mind was in total turmoil. The events of the past twenty minutes now proved conclusively that this Green September group had somehow duplicated the firing mechanisms and were able to activate the nuclear warhead of the missiles. He knew Sir Ian Sinders was in an absolute rage at what had happened, and he couldn't fail to realize the implications of the nuclear blast.

Everything now pointed to the fact that Major MacAllister was the only person who could possibly have had the firing mechanisms duplicated, and the original duplicates replaced in the Ministry vaults without anyone knowing. For Rodney Smithers, this was a shattering realization, as he had always looked up to Major Kevin MacAllister and in his wildest dreams could never have imagined that the major would do something like this. For Sir Ian Sinders, it was even worse; apart from feeling a sense of personal betrayal and shock, as the head of the joint chiefs of staff, he knew that he and he alone must now accept full responsibility for the breakdown in the internal security of the Ministry. And Sir Ian knew that no matter what happened in the next twenty-four hours, when it was all over and if he were still alive, the government would demand his resignation.

The helicopter touched down on the roof of the Ministry, and Captain Smithers almost jumped out as he dashed to the open doorway and took the elevator down to the Strategic Analysis Department. The head of that department, Reg Cooper, was waiting for Rodney, and when Rodney handed him the envelope with the four diskettes inside, Reg immediately distributed them to four waiting analysts, each of whom sat in front of a blank computer screen. The diskettes were rapidly loaded into the computers, and the difficult process of reviewing the data and computer-generated maps, grid by grid, commenced. Before Captain Smithers left to go upstairs to report to Sir Ian, he stressed again to Reg Cooper that the initial analysis be completed as swiftly as possible and the results reported to him up in Sir Ian's office.

Two minutes later, Captain Smithers strode into Sir Ian's office and couldn't believe that the man behind the desk was the same man he had seen only a couple of hours earlier. Sir Ian was slouched over the desk, his face a sickly ash color, and the patrician look of command in his features appeared to have evaporated. Rodney saluted smartly. "Just sit down, Captain Smithers, and tell me what has happened."

"Sir, the diskettes are now in Strategic Analysis, and I should be getting an initial report within ten minutes."

"You realize, Smithers, the gravity of the situation we now face. We have less than twenty-four hours to find the Green September group and prevent the launching of the second nuclear missile on London. I'm meeting with the prime minister around four fifteen. We must have some answers before then, as it is imperative that we pinpoint the location of Major MacAllister and the other terrorists."

It struck Rodney Smithers that in that last sentence Sir Ian was now including Major Kevin MacAllister in the terrorist group, rather than as their victim. Rodney wished there were some other explanation for the major having duplicated the firing mechanisms and cooperated with the terrorists. Sir Ian broke in on his thoughts.

It was five minutes to four when Jane Hawley came in to inform Sir Ian that the prime minister's office had called to say that the meeting would commence at 4:15 sharp. As Sir Ian nodded his acknowledgment to Jane Hawley, Smithers noticed the expression on his face. It was as if the man were about to face a firing squad. Rodney actually felt sorry for him, as he knew Sir Ian to be a true gentleman of the old school, and he understood how difficult it was for Sir Ian to comprehend what had happened. As they waited impatiently for the strategic analysts' initial reports, Rodney made a gallant effort to cheer up Sir Ian.

"At least, sir, we have that new-fangled missile target alternator, or MTA, as they call it, arriving from the States with a couple of experts on this afternoon's Concorde flight. It should arrive in at Heathrow just before six o'clock. That may be our one hope of diverting the missile, if by some chance we don't locate it before tomorrow afternoon."

Sir Ian's face did brighten for just a moment, before quickly lapsing back into a worried look as he responded, "That may be true, Smithers, but I don't place a lot of hope in new, unproven technology such as this MTA thing. Besides, as I understand it, it has been designed primarily based on US-made missiles, and later improvements will be made to work on Soviet missiles, if they can obtain enough information about them to do so."

At that point, Reg Cooper, the head of the Strategic Analysis

Department, carrying several large printouts, was ushered in by Jane Hawley. "Excuse me, Sir Ian and Captain Smithers, but I know you gentlemen are waiting to see these right away."

Reg Cooper spread on the table six large computer printouts that showed a computer-generated map of different sections of Ireland, laid out in grids. Sir Ian and Captain Smithers had both gotten up, and Reg had placed the printouts so that they were facing toward Sir Ian, while Captain Smithers, who was leaning over Reg's shoulder, would see them upside down. Reg began to point out what the different grids represented and used a pencil to pinpoint various features of the map. Reg explained that the grids represented the western portion of Ireland from latitude fifty-one degrees, thirty minutes north to fifty-four degrees, thirty minutes north and from longitude nine degrees west to ten degrees, thirty minutes west.

"If you look here, gentlemen, I've circled in red three points that initially look as though they could be the launch locations for the missile. However, further analysis eliminated one of these as being caused by atmospheric disturbance, leaving two to analyze further. One lies exactly on the fifty-third degree and thirty minutes north parallel and just west of nine degrees, thirty minutes west. The second one is in the vicinity of the fifty-second parallel where it intersects the longitude ten degrees west. Only one of these can be correct, but it is possible from the high altitude from which these were shot that a flash of lightning could create a similar impact. Right now my people are enlarging these two segments further and are analyzing in detail what we call the ripple lines, to ascertain which represents the launch point for the missile and to provide an explanation of the other heat source."

Sir Ian and Captain Smithers nodded, but Sir Ian was anxiously looking at his watch, as it was already five minutes past four. They waited, but no one came. Reg Cooper called down to his department and learned that his analysts were as yet unable to pinpoint with certainty which of the two locations was the source of the missile launch. Sir Ian seemed extremely upset at this news, but there was nothing he could do about it, as he simply had to leave right then for his meeting. He told Reg that he would take the two grid printouts showing the location of both possible areas; he folded them neatly and put them in his attaché case and left.

When he was out of earshot, Smithers explained, "Sir Ian is under terrible pressure right now. I'd appreciate if you could let me know the moment your people can confirm the launch site. That will enable us to work something out with the Irish government, to take some action."

"Okay, Captain Smithers, I do understand. We'll do everything we possibly can to isolate the correct location. But I must warn you that there are rare occasions when two different physical events that happen simultaneously show up in the same way in this form of high-altitude aerial photography. However, we may also be able to determine which is the most likely launch point by studying the photographs taken of the trajectory of the missile, the distance traveled, and the approximate time taken. I'll call you in your office the moment I know anything for certain. You can rely on us; we'll work through the night, if necessary. That's the best we can do, Captain."

The two men left Sir Ian's office together and parted at the elevator as Smithers went back to his own office.

Sir Ian arrived at the front door of 10 Downing Street at exactly 4:13 p.m. It was drizzling from darkening gray skies, which matched his mood. He was shown in right away to the prime minister's private office. As he entered, Sir Ian mused that he had seen more of 10 Downing Street in the past two days than he had in the previous two years, and he really didn't like it. Sir Ian was greeted rather curtly by the prime minister and was asked to have a seat. He looked around, and with the exception of the home secretary, Ernest Brooking, everyone who had attended the morning meeting was already there. But this time, the seating arrangements were a little different. Only Jack Larson sat to one side of the prime minister, near her desk. The other chairs were arranged in a semicircle in front of her desk, almost as if the prime minister were putting distance between herself and everyone else in the room other than Jack Larson. It crossed Sir Ian's mind that he may not be the only one to fall as a result of this crisis. There were only two empty chairs left; Sir Ian chose to sit beside Scott Frawley, leaving the center chair for the home secretary when he arrived. Off to Sir Ian's right sat Charles Mills, the secretary of state for foreign affairs, flanked by Gordy Hargreaves, the minister of defense. The atmosphere in the room was ten times tenser than at the morning session. At that moment, Ernest Brooking burst in, out of breath and panting. He apologized for his lateness, saying he had just come from the House of Commons, having been delayed during the afternoon question time by some issues raised by an impudent young Tory MP from Devon.

Once Ernest Brooking sat down, Prime Minister Muriel Hobson said, "Well, gentlemen, now there's no doubt. Obviously, the Green September group has the means of activating the nuclear warheads of the missiles they hijacked. Fortunately, there have been no reports of any casualties from any stray ships in the area. As of right now, the only thing we can congratulate ourselves for is that Gordy and Sir Ian here ensured that the area was kept clear by the Royal Navy.

"Now we come to the real crisis: clearly this Green September group can deliver on their threat to hit London with an armed nuclear missile, unless we can get to them first. Please give us the latest information from the reconnaissance planes."

There was no mistaking the terse tone of the prime minister's voice and the desperate gravity of the situation. Everyone shuffled in their seats in the uncomfortable atmosphere, and all eyes focused on Sir Ian, awaiting his response.

"Well, Prime Minister, I have here the blowups of the computer-aided aerial photography from the reconnaissance planes, with the initial analysis from the Strategic Analysis Department, which I just got less than ten minutes ago."

Sir Ian paused as he got up and brought the two relevant printouts to Muriel Hobson's desk and laid them out in front of her. That acted as a general signal for everyone to gather around the desk, looking over each other's shoulders at the grid maps. Very briefly, Sir Ian indicated the two most likely areas from where the missile was probably launched. "I expect, Prime Minister, to have absolute confirmation from Reg Cooper within the hour, as to which of these two locations was the actual launch site. I think you can all see from these grids that both of these locations are in very mountainous regions on the western seaboard of Ireland."

"Yes, Sir Ian, I believe we can all see that. But what do we do next?" There was no mistaking the impatience and frustration in Muriel Hobson's voice, and everyone returned to their seats, including Sir Ian, who left the maps in front of the prime minister. Gordy Hargreaves was the first to speak.

"I believe we have only two options. We can provide this information to the Irish government right away and rely on them to find the terrorists before the second missile can be fired. Or we can send two units from the Special Air Service Regiment to each of these locations and have them track down and take the terrorists and recover the missile. I realize this second alternative will have to be a clandestine operation, as any suggestion of British soldiers in uniform being found on Irish soil, no matter what the circumstances, will create a major international incident—clearly a case of usurping Irish sovereignty. Either way, those would appear to be the only two options at this point, and perhaps we should use a combination of the two."

There was silence in the room, and Sir Ian guessed everyone was thinking the same thing. The risks of relying on the Irish government alone to find the terrorists could be too great. While use of the Special Air Service Regiment was risky from an international point of view, it was probably less so from a purely military point of view. For Sir Ian, this was a difficult moment as the Special Air Service Regiment, more commonly known as the SAS, was one of the few bones of contention he had had with the previous Tory government. He had understood very well the need to establish an elite force, the equivalent of the United States Delta Force and the Russian Spetsnaz. But he would have preferred that its formation occur under the auspices of either MI5 or Special Branch, rather than as part of the British military structure. However, Sir Ian had eventually agreed, and the regiment was established several years earlier. The entire SAS Regiment numbered no more then 450 troops but soon gained a reputation for its effectiveness and for not taking prisoners. The actions of the SAS had, over the past several years, gained frequent media attention as they were often successful against the IRA because of their willingness to take the battle to the terrorists on their home ground in Northern Ireland, rather than to wait passively for them to strike. This media attention culminated most recently in the first public hearing over the execution-style killings of three IRA members in Gibraltar carried out by a small SAS unit. As a result of the hearing, there was a public outcry from civil liberties groups insinuating that the British government had gone too far in the use of the elite SAS Regiment. Since then, use of the SAS had been kept very low-key, and he knew their use being proposed now by Gordon Hargreaves struck a chord with everyone sitting in the room. The prime minister said, "Gordy, you've hit the nail on the head. There are only two options, and if there is no disagreement, I propose we exercise both those options. First, I will again talk with Charles Cassidy and impress on him the seriousness of the situation and that he must use all resources at his disposal to track down the terrorists by noon tomorrow. Secondly, Gordy, you and Sir Ian will prepare plans to have two crack units of the SAS flown out to two navy frigates off the coast of Ireland, close to the two areas indicated on the map. Both units will carry out commando-type raids on the areas indicated, no uniforms will be worn, and no identification carried that will indicate that the troops involved are members of the SAS. If need be, you will select volunteers for this mission. Is that clear?"

Before Sir Ian could even open his mouth to agree, Gordy Hargreaves had already assented.

"One last thing before we leave the military aspects of this crisis. Sir Ian, I understand from Gordy here that the Americans are sending you a new piece of technology that can supposedly divert missiles. Can you tell me a little more about it?"

"Yes, Prime Minister. In fact, I expect the missile target alternator, as it is called, and the experts to arrive shortly before six o'clock. As I understand it, the MTA has not yet proven 100 percent reliable in tests, and I wouldn't like to stake the lives of millions of people here in London on its use. However, if all else fails and we haven't located the remaining missile in time, we'll have to attempt to use the MTA."

"I agree, Sir Ian. Clearly the MTA will only be a last resort, and it would seem a desperate gamble at that. Now, Scott, what progress has MI5 made in pinpointing what happened and perhaps in being able to establish the nature of this Green September group?"

Sir Ian suppressed a smile because now it was Scott Frawley's turn to squirm in his chair and to feel the penetrating gaze of the prime minister.

"Well, we have now established for certain that Major MacAllister crossed to Ireland, in the small hours of Tuesday morning, on the ferry from Fishguard to Rosslare. By virtue of that, and the fact that the Green September group obviously has duplicate firing mechanisms, it is now clear that Major MacAllister is the man who obtained the duplicates. As to whether he did it of his own free will, and we haven't been able to establish any motives for that as of yet, or indeed if he was somehow forced into going along with the Green September group, we cannot establish with any certainty. As of this moment, my colleagues in the CIA have also been unable to uncover anything relevant to the major's actions, but their contacts and penetration of the IRA is continuing, and I do hope to have some more concrete news later this evening."

Scott Frawley paused for breath before continuing, "All security checks have been run on his family background and on the major himself, and there was no hint whatsoever that the major could have any possible link with, or sympathy for, the IRA. In fact, on the contrary, he was frequently heard to condemn the violence and atrocities committed by the IRA. There was never an inkling, throughout his exemplary years of service to the British Army and the Ministry of Defense, that he might harbor a deep-rooted desire for a united Ireland. I now have some indications that the major had never even contemplated the hijacking of nuclear missiles until the past year or so. And I am now in the process of trying to establish what events or incidents in his life may have triggered the major to do what he has apparently done. Right now, the answer may lie in a will in a New York lawyer's office, and I have enlisted the help of the FBI to get me a copy of that will."

The prime minister frowned and said, "It would appear, Scott, that somehow our security system has broken down, just as much as it did in the cases of Philby, Burgess, and McLean. And perhaps with even more dire consequences than their acts of treason. But you must do whatever you have to do to get a copy of that will, as I don't yet have the warm, close relationship with the current American president that my predecessor had, and so I cannot intercede in that quarter. Now we come to one of the most crucial aspects of this entire crisis: the public's right to know. The issue before us, gentlemen, is do we issue public warnings of the possible impending nuclear missile attack on London tomorrow afternoon? Obviously, to do that would create more panic and more chaos than the city of London—or any city in the history of mankind—has ever seen. So clearly we cannot warn the public. Besides, no evacuation plans in the world could accommodate five to six million people in less than twenty-four hours. So the question becomes, who should we warn? Members of our government? Key military personnel? Who? If we warn too many people in the government or in senior military positions, we do run the risk of a leak to the media, despite the Official Secrets Act, and I have no doubt that the media is already probing the major's disappearance, in particular the *Daily Sentinel.* I assume you all saw that short but insidious article on the front page this morning. Do we warn the queen and other members of the royal family, or do we insist that they are evacuated? Anyone got any suggestions?"

There was no rush to answer the prime minister, as the whole issue of what warnings, if any, the public was entitled to was one of the thorniest issues facing modern governments around the world. The previous government had come under attack for withholding from the public a warning sent to airlines and airports about terrorist bombs in radio cassette players, precisely the kind of bomb that investigators later said brought down a Pan Am jet in Scotland the previous year. In turn, when this information was released in America, there was a public outcry against the US government's handling of those warnings. Everyone in the room was acutely aware of the difficulties of warning the public about any terrorist actions or threatened actions. And in this case, each and every one of them was uncomfortably reaching the same decision: it was a practical impossibility to warn five or six million Londoners and to be able to do anything about evacuating them in time.

Finally, Ernest Brooking, the home secretary, spoke up. "I concur absolutely with what you say—we don't have any choice. Clearly our main objective must be to have ourselves in a position to provide continuity in government and law and order in the event nuclear disaster hits. We have right below this building a series of nuclear shelters from which we can continue to run the government. Likewise, the Ministry of Defense has its nuclear shelters from which to run the military. I suggest that those of us in this room compile a list of all key government and military personnel who would be needed after a disaster. As for the royal family, I believe I have a possible solution to getting them out of London. As you are all aware, the queen and many of the royal family go to Balmoral Castle in Scotland next week and normally attend the Royal Highland gathering in Braemar. According to the royal calendar, the queen and her family are scheduled to leave London next Monday. I believe we could make a change in that calendar so that, in fact, they leave London tonight. Hopefully, the media will not make too big a deal of that."

The prime minister smiled. "Excellent suggestions. We'll certainly compile the list before we end this meeting. As for the royal family, that is an absolutely marvelous idea. And when I explain the circumstances to the queen herself, we should be able to ensure that all key members of the royal family, including the queen mother, are safely out of London by tonight. To minimize the risk of media attention to the changes in the plans, I'll suggest to the queen that those members of the royal family who have public engagements in the northern part of the country should still keep them. However, any of them with engagements in and around the London area and the southeast should cancel them. I'll also suggest to Her Majesty that these changes not be announced until sometime later tomorrow. I think that covers all the fundamental issues, so let's get on with compiling the list so that everyone can get moving on what needs to be done."

The list was compiled in about ten minutes, and Muriel Hobson broke up the meeting quickly, explaining she wished to get on the telephone to the Irish premier right away. Sir Ian reluctantly accompanied Gordon Hargreaves back to the Ministry.

Once there, Sir Ian very quickly had orders out to two of the frigates from the strike zone in the North Atlantic to steam to positions off the west and southwest coasts of Ireland. Instructions were issued for two units from the SAS Regiment to be dispatched to each frigate, with detailed operational orders not to be given until they were on board. Captain Smithers informed Sir Ian that Reg Cooper and the Strategic Analysis team had still been unable to pinpoint the missile launch site. However, from their study of the photographs taken of the missile traveling to the target zone, their opinion was that the point on the map near the southwest of Ireland was more than likely the missile launch site. But they couldn't yet state that categorically.

With all instructions issued, Sir Ian sat alone in his office, waiting for the arrival of the American experts and their MTA. Sir Ian realized that the decisions they'd reached at the meeting with the prime minister were the only options left to the British government for dealing with this impending disaster. In London, all they could do now was to settle down to a long period of anxious, nervous waiting.

The church bells were ringing in unison across Dublin, an old tradition at six o'clock, calling people to evening prayer. Charles Cassidy, the Irish premier, and his secretary, Seamus Ryan, were sitting in his office in Leinster House with the windows open, overlooking Kildare Street. It was an hour since the British prime minister had called him on that fateful Wednesday. The call had been brief and to the point, providing Charles with the locations of the two possible missile launch sites and little else.

In the past hour, Charles had given the information to Jerry O'Toole, his minister of defense, who had promised immediate mobilization of army units from barracks in Cork, Limerick, Galway, and Athlone. He had then talked with Des O'Houlihan, his minister for internal affairs, to organize the Gardai and Special Branch to focus their efforts in assisting the army in the two areas indicated. There was nothing more he could do. Both Charles and Seamus were stunned at the incredible thought that there was still one nuclear missile on Irish soil. The nuclear blast in the North Atlantic earlier that afternoon had really brought home to both men the fact that they were in a state of extreme crisis, and they were totally flabbergasted that terrorists had actually managed to hijack British nuclear missiles.

"Seamus, I have this uneasy feeling that the Brits are up to something else and are not relying on us to find the terrorists. It strikes me as very curious that Muriel Hobson made absolutely no offers of help when she called a while ago, whereas this morning when she first called, she was most anxious that I accept some help from British resources such as the SAS. What do you think?"

"I'm sure you're right. I wouldn't trust those Brits as far as I could throw them. The thing about it is we'll never know for sure, as I doubt they would send in anyone wearing British uniforms. They're smart enough to know that no matter what the circumstances, that would cause a hell of a fuss on the international scene. But no matter what they do, the main thing is for our boys in the army and the Gardai to find this Green September group before anyone else does. That will be a real feather in our caps!"

"You're right of course, but the big question is, can we find them in time? It's almost nightfall, and any search of the wild and rugged mountains in Galway and Kerry will be severely hampered by darkness. The best we can hope for is that our troops and Gardai will be in place and ready to move quickly at the crack of dawn tomorrow."

"Yea, Charlie, it's going to be a long night."

"You know, Seamus, now that the British reconnaissance planes have narrowed the search for the Green September group to two possible areas, it would almost seem inevitable that we find them. But I worry when I remember the old saying, 'In Ireland, the inevitable never happens, but the unexpected often occurs.' Let's hope on this occasion that we surprise both ourselves and the British and that the inevitable occurs and we actually find them in time."

Both men settled down to the long wait ahead of them, knowing full well that they would be burning the midnight oil that night, along with many others in Ireland.

Just after seven that evening, Rory McDevitt was again sitting across from Padraig Flannery. It was too dark for Rory to see the lake outside the country cottage, which was only five miles from Ballymena in County Antrim, Northern Ireland. He couldn't even see any of the armed IRA or Provos guards in the yard. Two other men had joined them for this meeting, Ronan Cleary, the local Ballymena IRA commander, and Lieutenant-Colonel Nikolai Dorovin of the FSB, who handled FSB operations in Northern Ireland under the alias Nicky Dwyer. Like the other two IRA commanders, Ronan Cleary was also in his early thirties, but Nicky Dwyer was a man in his midforties, with gray hair and a bushy black mustache. Nikolai Dorovin had a remarkable ability to adopt the lilting Northern Ireland accent almost at will, and when he spoke in his role as the principal FSB agent in Northern Ireland, it would have been difficult for anyone to detect that he was actually a Russian. Nicky Dwyer had now spent almost five years in Northern Ireland, based in Derry where he operated closely with the Marxist-oriented Provos. Over the years, he had arranged for a significant number of arms shipments to the Provos from Czechoslovakia and East Germany, for which Russia had never requested payment.

"So, from what you're tellin' me, Padraig," McDevitt said as he pushed his hair back from his forehead, "your people in Dublin have confirmed the nuclear explosion out in the North Atlantic this afternoon, and so it would seem the second missile is also armed with a nuclear warhead. What your good friend Nikolai here is suggesting is that we join forces to capture this missile for the Russians. You lads put me in a very difficult situation, as such an action would certainly make the Americans mighty upset. How do you propose we get around that one?"

Flannery started to speak, but before he could answer, Nicky Dwyer said, "If I may, I think I can best answer that. Here's my basic proposition. If we can succeed in obtaining the second missile intact, Moscow has authorized me to pay US $5 million to both yourselves and the Provos, along with several major arms shipments, which will include some of the latest Russian weapons, among them tactical nonnuclear missile launchers. The Russian weapons are superior to the Czechoslovakian weapons you're currently using. Now as for the dilemma of your support from America. What I suggest is that we organize this operation as if only the Provos were responsible, so that any word that filters back to your Irish-American support groups in the States or to the CIA will not involve the IRA regulars. What do you think of that, Rory?"

Rory McDevitt was quiet for a few moments as he studied Nicky's face and then Padraig Flannery's. At last, he said, "Okay, Nikolai, you can count the IRA in."

Flannery smiled and said, "That's just great. I'm very glad we can both agree with Nicky here. Now down to business. My sources tell me that the Brits have supplied the Dublin government with two possible locations from which today's missile was launched. What I suggest we do is this. We'll take nine of your best lads and nine of mine, and we'll intermingle them between two groups, one of which you will lead, the other to be led by me. That means we should only need two cars for each group. Nicky here will accompany my group, and we'll go after the possible site in Kerry while you and your group go to the site in Galway. If you agree with this, Nicky will arrange for two Russian fishing trawlers to be in international waters off the coast of both locations. Each group will establish radio communications with those trawlers, and when we have the missile, the nearest one will launch a small boat to come in to the coast and pick it up. Does that seem fair to you?"

"Yes, that should work fine."

"Good. So let's work out the details and the timing quickly so that we can get moving."

Padraig Flannery took out a map of Ireland and circled the two approximate locations where the other missile might be. As he drew the rough circles on the map, he said, "Our lads in London concluded this piece of intelligence by keeping their ears to the ground and picking up the whispers around Whitehall and the pubs of Fleet Street."

The four men studied the map and made detailed plans of how they would go about seeking the missile. McDevitt was very aware that both those areas were going to be crawling with the Irish Army and the Gardai. He threw in the possibility that the Brits would somehow be using the SAS as well, without the Dublin government knowing it. The operational details were worked out very quickly, and the men selected from both the Provos and the IRA regulars. The men chosen were already in the vicinity. The meeting lasted only forty-five minutes, and with their plans set, the small groups quickly dispersed.

Later that evening, once back in Derry, Nikolai Dorovin communicated with his boss, Sergei Rastvorov, at FSB headquarters in Moscow. His superior was extremely pleased, and everything was put in motion to ensure that the two Russian trawlers would be off the west and southwest coasts of Ireland on time. Meanwhile, the two IRA groups were already traveling south under cover of darkness. As he left for his late rendezvous with Padraig Flannery in the south of Ireland, Nikloai Dorovin was extremely pleased with his evening's work and felt certain that if this operation were successful, he would undoubtedly get a promotion to full colonel of the FSB.

Although already seven in the evening in London, it was only two in the afternoon in Washington, DC, when Paul Laster accompanied Dave Wharton Jr., the director of the CIA, to a short, private meeting with President Glenn Anderson at the White House. Paul Laster, having recently been promoted to head of CIA operations in Europe, felt somewhat awed as they were shown into the Oval Office, as this was his first visit. The president was alone except for his chief national security adviser, Roger Helms. Paul already knew Roger Helms quite well, and it was Helms who said, "Paul, may I introduce you to Glenn Anderson, president of the United States." The president extended his hand, and Paul shook it, enjoying the surreal feel of the moment. Then they all sat down.

Before Paul could get over the handshake, Dave said, "Mr. President, as no doubt Roger has already told you, it appears that this Green September terrorist group successfully launched a nuclear missile this afternoon in the North Atlantic and created a nuclear explosion. So, it is the opinion of the British government and their intelligence services that the second missile taken by the terrorist group and aimed at London can indeed create a nuclear explosion. The CIA concurs with this assessment."

The president said, "You all realize, of course, that if a nuclear missile is allowed to destroy London, the repercussions will be disastrous for the entire world. So every possible action must be taken to prevent that from happening."

"Yes, Mr. President, and those steps are already being taken. The British government has already requested that the Irish government organize its army and police force in a search for the Green September group. The British reconnaissance planes have already pinpointed two possible locations. Additionally, but unbeknownst to the Irish government, we understand that they are mobilizing two units of their elite SAS Regiment to carry out clandestine operations off the coast of Ireland. While we can't publicly sanction that, as a practical matter, we must support them. Additionally the Pentagon has sent over the prototype of our missile target alternator, along with two experts who should have landed in London about an hour ago. They will be used in the event that the terrorists are not reached in time. But the most disturbing development of all is that we suspect the Russians may be showing an interest in the situation. As you are well aware, they provide weapons to the IRA Provos who have definite Marxist leanings and who operate separately and often at odds with the IRA regulars. So despite Glasnost, it is our assessment that the Russians may view this as too good an opportunity to miss, and we have no doubt that they may make an effort through the IRA Provos to obtain the missile for themselves."

The president frowned and scribbled a note on a pad on his desk. "That would be a very serious turn of events, and we must do everything possible to prevent that. But do you really believe they would do it? As Roger tells me, the British penguin class nuclear missiles are not much more sophisticated than some of their own. For your information, Dave, one other aspect of this that I discussed with Roger before you came in is that we're mobilizing a part of the Atlantic Fleet to take up position in St. George's channel, between England and Ireland. So that as a last resort, if the Green September group succeeds in launching the nuclear armed missile toward London, we can shoot it down in the upper atmosphere. At least the fallout from that explosion will not have nearly as severe an impact on either the British or Irish populations as would a nuclear explosion in the heart of London."

"I'm certainly glad to hear that, Mr. President, as we are now in a race against time. I would like to respectfully suggest that as you have already met the Irish premier, Charles Cassidy, perhaps you could give him a phone call. And impress on him again that given their close ties with our government, he must do all in his power to capture the Green September group and prevent the missile being launched. As you're aware, the relationship between Dublin and London is very touchy at times."

"I'll be happy to do that, Dave, and will, as soon as we're finished with this meeting. As you know, I haven't yet met the new British prime minister, Muriel Hobson, and as her brand of socialist politics is so different from my own, I'm not sure it would do any good for me to talk to her. But perhaps a phone call of personal support wouldn't hurt our special relationship with the British. There doesn't appear to be anything else we can do at this point, but please keep Roger here advised of any developments at any time in the next twelve to sixteen hours. Good day, gentlemen."

With that, Dave Wharton Jr. and Paul Laster left the Oval Office. The meeting had lasted only ten minutes. As they left the White House and went out into the bright afternoon sunshine, the main topic of conversation between the two men was what angle the Russians would take in all of this.

It was five o'clock on that Wednesday afternoon, September 8, when the submarine broke the surface of the dark gray North Atlantic. It emerged between two surface ships that were poised about a mile apart. It was the flagship submarine AS *Rosario* of the admiral of the Argentinian Atlantic fleet. The two waiting surface ships were the AS *Cordoba* and the AS *Olavarria*. The AS *Cordoba* also served as the admiral's flagship for Argentina's Atlantic fleet when he was not aboard his submarine. Both were Evita-class battleships from Argentina's navy. Aboard the AS *Cordoba*, Captain Raul Martinez was standing on the bridge with his binoculars focused on the submarine. Now that the sub had fully emerged from the depths, he saw the hatch in the conning tower swing open and several people climb out. Without putting down his binoculars, he gave instructions to set course for the submarine.

Within five minutes, they were alongside, and once anchored, Captain Martinez left the bridge and went down to the starboard side of his ship to welcome aboard his commanding officer, Admiral Enrico De La Cortes. The two men immediately went below, and the AS *Cordoba* cast off from the submarine.

"You know my first love is submarines," Cortes said. "I had planned to spend at least half of our monthlong exercises aboard the sub if the events of the past few hours hadn't changed my plans."

"Better you than me," Martinez said. "I get claustrophobic in those subs." Martinez had just set sail ten days earlier with Argentina's Atlantic fleet from its home port of Mar del Plata. He had arrived in the North Atlantic two days earlier. It was the previous evening when the wireless message came through to the AS *Cordoba* from the Americans, requesting that they stay clear of a certain area in the North Atlantic this afternoon.

Admiral De La Cortes had instructed all the ships and submarines in his Atlantic fleet to stay out of the danger area. "How close did the *Rosario* actually get to the launch site?" Martinez asked.

"We were within 150 miles, and the equipment aboard our submarine was able to record the extent of the explosion a little after three o'clock this afternoon. The seismic readings gave strong indications that it was probably a nuclear explosion." Cortes raised an eyebrow and said, "I wonder what the British are really up to."

"I don't know, sir, but we got those long-range photographs of the danger zone that you wanted." Martinez pointed to his desk, where several large photographs in black and white were laid out. Cortes walked over and studied them for a moment.

"Well, Captain, what do you make of these?"

"It's hard to know, Admiral. But one thing is clear. The explosion, which occurred at a great depth, did cause minor tidal waves; however, due to the distance we were from the explosion and the increasing cloud cover, it was hard to determine for sure that it was a nuclear explosion. As you can see from these photographs, there is no clear mushroom-type cloud above the point of impact, as one would expect. But that is not to say it isn't there, as it may have been partially hidden by cloud cover."

"Well, Captain, from the seismic readings aboard our submarine, I believe it most definitely was of the magnitude of a nuclear explosion. But that's not a normal area of the ocean for underwater tests, so I'm really puzzled as to what the British are doing. I believe it would be useful if we keep the fleet in this vicinity for a couple of days and see what develops. You never know; we may learn something useful."

"I agree, Admiral. It's certainly worth waiting around. I'll have signals sent to the other ships in the fleet."

The admiral's face creased into a broad smile, and he said, "You never know; we may even learn something that may be useful in the next Malvinas war!"

Martinez knew the admiral had served his country well in its war against the British on the Falkland Islands, and although they lost that round, most Argentinians considered it just that—the first battle of a war they would eventually win. Most Argentinians believed their time would come to recover the Malvinas Islands, which they believed rightfully belonged to Argentina. In any case, the admiral seemed pleased at the turn of events, as it provided some distraction from the routine series of naval exercises they were conducting.

The five submarines and eight surface ships that made up Argentina's Atlantic fleet were now steaming closer to the Irish coastline. As the forecast was for some heavy weather to build up in the area in which they had just rendezvoused, the closer they moved to the Irish coast, the more of the storm they would miss.

CHAPTER *15*

IT WAS ONLY FIVE IN the morning on Wednesday, September 8, and still pitch-black outside when the shrill clanging of the alarm clock quickly woke up Jeremy Sands. He had managed to catch about four hours of sleep, and that was enough for him. Despite the many scotches he had had the night before, once he had that first cup of coffee, he was wide awake, and the events of the previous evening came flooding back into his mind. As he sat there with a cigarette in one hand and a cup of coffee in the other, thinking, what disturbed him most of all was the brief phone call from his source in the Ministry of Defense the previous night. That source had informed him that not only was a certain Major MacAllister missing but also two nuclear missiles on an MML. As one of Britain's most dedicated investigative journalists, Jeremy Sands had decided it was his duty to get to the bottom of this whole affair, no matter what it took to find out the truth.

Jeremy reached his fifth floor office in the Sentinel Building on Fleet Street by six o'clock. The night staff, who were now winding down, were not surprised to see him, as he was well known to be into the office very early, particularly if he was working on a major story. Even as a chain smoker, Jeremy always hated the first whiff of stale smoke that hit him when he entered his office each morning. Of course, as he lit up yet another cigarette, he didn't notice it any longer.

As he got his office coffeepot going, Jeremy sat down and went through the pile of telexes and wire service cuttings that the night staff had laid on his desk. Then he noticed to one side, circled in red, a hard copy of the early morning shipping forecast from the BBC Home Service. He picked it up and read through it quickly to the last paragraph, which was highlighted in yellow. It requested shipping to stay clear of a large area in the North Atlantic from two o'clock on that afternoon, due to some tests by a British research team. This really intrigued Jeremy as, knowing about the nuclear missiles, he was struck by the fact that such a large area of the North Atlantic had to be cleared of shipping for possible seismic activity from tests that a British research team was supposedly carrying out. Not that Jeremy knew much about what British researchers might be doing, but he would have it checked out by one of the night staffers and find out if there could be any truth in it. After he called up one of the night staffers to look into it, Jeremy shuffled through the rest of the wire service items and didn't find anything particularly interesting. But then it would have to have been awfully good to distract his mind from the missing nuclear missiles and the major. Half an hour later, he got the report back from the night staffer saying there was no record anywhere of a British research project going on in that part of the North Atlantic.

Jeremy hung up the phone. *Just as I thought.* He sat back in his chair and concentrated on the problem of the two missing missiles, for he realized he couldn't yet disclose this information to anyone, as it was most definitely subject to the Official Secrets Act. He debated whether he could even bring it up to his editor, Donald Mortimer, as they had both had injunctions slapped on them by the courts under the previous government, and of course Jeremy had gotten a small taste of Brixton Prison. He needed more information, and he considered contacting his friend Harry Roberts, who served in the cabinet as minister of transport and power but who also was the leader of the left wing of the Labor Party and was a vocal proponent of unilateral nuclear disarmament for Britain. But then he realized that even for Harry Roberts to make an issue of something with the government in which he was serving would be very difficult without more concrete facts, or at least strong suspicions. And Jeremy didn't feel he really had enough information yet. He considered that his Ministry source might be mistaken about the missiles since he hadn't been able to get corroboration from another source, though on reflection his inside source had never been wrong in the past. But there was always a first time.

The morning dragged on as he tried to focus on other stories he was working on. But try as he could, the issue of the missing nuclear missiles and the requested clearance of the large area in the North Atlantic kept coming back into his mind. During the course of the morning, he got reports of unusual activity around 10 Downing Street, the Ministry of Defense, the Home Office, and even at the nondescript government offices opposite the Home Office, which he knew housed MI5. His instincts told him there was definitely something big happening, which reinforced in his mind that two nuclear missiles were indeed missing. *If that isn't bloody big, what is?* But he couldn't quite link together that fact and the clearing of the North Atlantic. If some terrorist group had successfully managed to hijack two nuclear missiles, why the hell would they want to detonate them in the North Atlantic? It wasn't yet making sense, but Jeremy was confident he would get to the bottom of it. He came to one conclusion, and that was that the government, in particular the prime minister, appeared to be playing this crisis very close to their chests, as all the information he received indicated that there had definitely been no full cabinet meeting. In fact, the only ministers reported frequenting Downing Street in the last couple of days were the minister of defense, the home secretary, the foreign secretary, and Sir Ian Sinders, the chief of staff. Based on that, Jeremy felt sure that the other cabinet ministers were being kept in the dark. He was itching to put together a suggestive piece for one of the afternoon editions of the *Evening Sentinel*, but he still felt some uncertainty about just how pointed he could be without running afoul of the Official Secrets Act once again.

At lunchtime, Jeremy decided that he would visit a couple of his favorite pubs along Fleet Street and see what he might learn from some of his fellow reporters. He first went to the Red Lion Pub around the corner, where he had a pork pie and a beer, followed by a scotch and chatted with a few colleagues from other newspapers.

First he collared George from the *Times,* but he only had soccer on his mind as the Cup quarter-finals were only days away.

"So, Jeremy, who are your favorites to make it through to the semis?"

"Haven't given it much thought yet; got other things on my mind. Probably Chelsea or Arsenal."

Jeremy quickly got the impression that nobody else had picked up on the unusual activity around Downing Street, and he heard only one comment about the supposed tests to take place this afternoon in the North Atlantic. Jeremy was a little surprised, and he thought everyone else must have their heads in the sand, or perhaps he was reading more into events than he should. Even already, the reported disappearance of the major appeared to be second-rate news. In fact, most reporters seemed to be speculating on the results of the upcoming by-election at Bexley, scheduled for the following Tuesday. It was seen by many as a test for the Labor/Liberal coalition.

Feeling disappointed, Jeremy left the Red Lion and ambled up Fleet Street toward the law court and went into the Lord Ranelagh Pub, another favorite haunt of his that usually had a good mix of reporters, lawyers, and politicians hanging about at lunchtime. Not seeing anyone he particularly wanted to talk to, Jeremy went straight up to the bar and ordered himself a scotch. He was just stuffing his change in his pocket when he felt a tap on his shoulder. He swung around to see Harry Roberts standing there, grinning at him.

"L. J., you old rascal, what are you up to then? Filling your hollow leg? Good to see you, old friend! Haven't seen you in several weeks, old chap!"

"Oh you know me, Harry. I'm always here and there and about the place. But tell me, what's new with you? You'll have a drink with me, won't you?"

"I'm afraid I can't, old chap; I have to get back to the House. We have the first reading of my new transportation bill this afternoon, so I have to be there on time. Perhaps later we can get together for a drink?"

"Actually, Harry, I wanted a word with you anyway. It'll only take five minutes. So you'll stop for one drink, won't you? Your usual scotch?"

Harry Roberts nodded. A broad shouldered, stocky man, he was a good deal shorter than Jeremy, and although in his early fifties, he had thick brown hair without a trace of gray. Jeremy ordered two scotches, and while they waited for their drinks, Harry asked, "So what is it you want to talk to me about that couldn't wait till later, L. J.?"

"Oh, just idle curiosity, actually. What have you heard about the testing that's supposed to happen in the North Atlantic this afternoon? Apparently all shipping is being cleared out of the area."

Their drinks came, and Harry said, "Oh, I haven't heard anything different from you, L. J. I expect it's some useless research, a carryover program from the previous government. If you want my opinion, the money would be better spent on housing and public transport for the working classes. So why your idle curiosity about something so insignificant?"

Jeremy Sands hesitated a moment or two before he answered, as he certainly couldn't yet mention anything about the missing nuclear missiles. But it would do no harm to plant a couple of seeds in Harry Roberts's mind.

"Oh I don't know, Harry, must be a slow news day. There was just something about the report that caught my fancy. Something about seismic activity. I usually associate that with either earthquakes or nuclear explosions. But then, as you know, I don't have a very scientific mind. Just forget I asked."

"Well, L. J., old chap, you fox, there's probably nothing in it. Will you be around later this evening? I could meet you here if you have time for a decent few drinks with an old friend. I expect I'll be through in the Commons about six or seven."

"Oh, I'll be about, Harry. That'd be super. I'll see you here this evening then. Cheerio."

"Well, aren't you going to wish me luck on the first reading of my new bill?"

Jeremy smiled and asked, "When have you ever needed luck, Harry? If I know you, you always get your way, and you'll bulldoze this bill through like you do everything else. But for what it's worth, good luck, Harry!"

Both men were grinning as they left the pub together. Harry grabbed a taxi to get back to the Commons, and Jeremy strolled back to his office. Jeremy was feeling pleased with himself because, if he knew his old friend, he had no doubt that Harry Roberts's curiosity was aroused. So he looked forward to learning something useful that evening. It was two thirty when Jeremy got back to his office, and despite his good fortune in running into Harry, he was otherwise feeling frustrated that he didn't really have a good, juicy story to put on the front pages of the earlier editions of the *Evening Sentinel*. But he told himself he still had time—to his mind, the day was still young, and there were several more editions before the final one hit the street at eight o'clock that evening. Jeremy sat down behind his desk and started flicking through the various phone messages piled high beside his phone, and all the other bits and pieces of information that had been left on his desk while he was out at lunch. There was all the usual kind of stuff, including a few items on other stories he was working on. Right then, they didn't interest him; what caught his eye was a phone message from an old friend in Dublin whom he hadn't heard from in quite a while—Stephen Scanlon, a well-connected businessman who also happened to be a TD in the Irish Dail, the equivalent of a British MP in the House of Commons. Jeremy selected this as his first call.

"Hi, Stephen. Just got your message. What's up?"

"I just found out something I thought would interest you. The British prime minister has requested the help of the Irish government in locating both Major MacAllister and two missing nuclear missiles. The kicker is that the Irish government has been notified of threats by a terrorist group called Green September to launch a nuclear missile at London. But first they proposed a demonstration of their ability to do so by launching the first missile this afternoon into that much-talked-about area of the North Atlantic."

Jeremy sat back in his chair and let out a low whistle. He could hardly believe what he'd heard, but he knew Stephen Scanlon was 100 percent reliable, and however he'd gotten the information, he knew it would be factual. "Christ almighty," Jeremy said, "this is the biggest crisis the country has faced, probably ever in its history, and the goddamned government is keeping mum about it." He paused, then remembering his manners, said, "Thanks for letting me know. Is there more?"

"No, that's all I have."

"Well, thanks again. Sorry, but I've got to go." Jeremy began to think slowly and carefully about the implications of what he'd just learned. Could it really happen? Surely the Ministry of Defense must have some security measures that would have rendered these missiles inoperable except with proper authorization and procedures. Then it dawned on him, the government had probably operated on the assumption that the nuclear missiles were useless in the hands of this terrorist group. But it would seem the terrorists anticipated the initial reaction of the government and were going to demonstrate their ability to detonate the nuclear warhead on the missile this very afternoon. *My God,* Jeremy thought as he looked at his watch and realized that if Stephen Scanlon's timing was correct, it may have already gone off. It was already five minutes past three.

Jeremy sat there in a state of shock, and he almost expected to feel or hear something. Of course, he didn't. But he continued to sit there almost in a trance, and his vivid imagination began to conjure up images of London totally destroyed by a nuclear blast. The sheer horror of that imagery convinced Jeremy that no matter what the risks to himself, he had to do something.

It was after four o'clock when the first reports started drifting in. There was a report from a TWA pilot flying a 747 from New York to London that some sort of blast in the North Atlantic had created an intense flash of light and had caused his instruments to malfunction for a good minute. TWA offices in London had issued a statement to the press to that effect, after the plane had landed safely at London's Heathrow airport. Next came a weather report that said that shipping in the vicinity of the North Atlantic had experienced minor tidal waves. Although no damages or injuries were reported, it was stated to be the result of some unusual seismic activity in a part of the North Atlantic. But what Jeremy found most interesting was that there were no public statements from any government officials on the matter. It was almost as if they ignored it, no one would take any notice. But Jeremy was piecing together these first two reports as a basis for a front-page story.

For him, the real clincher came at a few minutes after five o'clock when he received a copy of a report put out by a major weather and radar tracking installation at Tromso, in northern Norway. It reported a higher than normal level of radioactivity in the atmosphere in their vicinity. The report included a comment that the radioactive level recorded was close to or slightly above the level recorded after the accident at Chernobyl. Jeremy was delighted, as this last report gave him a means of focusing his article on a possible nuclear explosion and the consequent radioactive fallout, without having to reveal his secret knowledge of the missing nuclear missiles. Jeremy was now convinced that this terrorist group had indeed proven that they could arm and detonate the nuclear warhead on the missiles they had hijacked.

The *Evening Sentinel* was published approximately every hour from eleven in the morning onward, until the last edition at eight o'clock at night. The bulk of the evening newspaper remained the same in each edition; however, at a minimum, the front and back pages changed to reflect the latest breaking news, sports, and racing results. Jeremy worked feverishly to finish a front-page spread that he wanted in the six o'clock edition. He called his editor, Donald Mortimer, to get the okay on the headline he proposed to use. The headline read, in big, heavy print: "Mystery Explosion in North Atlantic!" Underneath, in smaller print, it read: "High Level of Radioactivity Reported off the Coast of Norway." At this point, Jeremy didn't take his editor into his confidence about the missiles. He decided to save that shocker for later.

When the six o'clock edition hit the streets, it brought an immediate reaction from the media. Television, radio, and newspaper reporters descended on 10 Downing Street, clamoring for an official government explanation. Jeremy sent a junior reporter from the *Sentinel* down to join them, while he himself stayed in his office, glued to the television news. Finally, at six thirty in the evening, the news media were met by a spokesman who came out of 10 Downing Street and issued a short statement that, in effect, there was a test explosion in the North Atlantic that afternoon, carried out by the government, the nature of which could not be disclosed, as it was a matter of national security. The spokesman went on to say that there was no possible danger from this explosion and that what little fallout occurred would spread into the upper atmosphere harmlessly. That was the end of the statement.

As he watched it live on the television, Jeremy thought that it was so typical of the British government; the statement really said little or nothing other than to acknowledge what others had reported. He was now convinced that the prime minister and her closely associated ministers, who were obviously in on this, were determined not to let the public know anything about what had happened in the past forty-eight hours. Jeremy turned off the television and, checking his watch, decided he'd better go up the street to the Lord Ranelagh Pub to meet Harry Roberts, as he had promised earlier.

Just as he was leaving the office, his phone rang. Jeremy hesitated a moment in the doorway, quickly debating whether to answer it or not. He decided he'd better. It was his editor, Donald Mortimer, asking him if he would come up to his office for a couple of minutes. He hung up without saying why. Jeremy put the phone back in the cradle, wondering what Mortimer could want, although he had a good suspicion what it might be. Jeremy headed off down the long corridor beside the newsroom, hearing the clicking of many reporters' computers keyboards as they worked on stories for tomorrow's *Daily Sentinel*. Donald Mortimer's door was open, so Jeremy walked right in. The editor was sitting behind his desk and had a serious expression on his face.

"So what's up, Don?"

"Why don't you sit down, Jeremy. This won't take long."

Jeremy sat down in a comfortable armchair opposite his boss, knowing full well that when Donald Mortimer asked one to sit down, it was going to be something very serious indeed, as usually he left people to stand and never detained them for more than a minute or two. Jeremy sat expectantly.

"Well, L. J., it looks like you've done it again! Your lead story on the front page of the six o'clock edition certainly caused quite a stir over at Downing Street. I'm sure you were watching the evening news also. To cut a long story short, it looks like the government wants to put a muzzle on us again. I just had a call a few minutes ago from the home secretary, Ernest Brooking. And he suggested quite bluntly that we shouldn't publish any more about this explosion in the North Atlantic unless we are absolutely sure of our facts, and that any insinuations would be treated as a breach of the Official Secrets Act. He stated categorically that the explosion was quite simply the result of some tests being carried out by the government that involve national security, and he basically said, 'Hands off.'"

"Sod them! Those lying bastards! They're proving they're no better than the previous government. There's a hell of a lot more to this than meets the eye, Don. And I know enough already to sink this bloody government!"

"What exactly do you mean, L. J.?"

Jeremy wondered if he'd gone too far, but then he decided that the time had come to tell Donald Mortimer most of what he knew. Jeremy gave his boss a concise overview of everything he was aware of and finished by saying, "And just when you called, I was on my way to meet Harry Roberts. If anybody can stir this up, he certainly can."

Donald Mortimer was looking at him aghast, hardly able to believe his ears. "This is absolutely incredible! But if you're to avoid going to jail again, somehow you have to get an independent verification of what your source at the Ministry told you. Otherwise, the government is going to invoke the Official Secrets Act, and this time, I wouldn't be at all surprised if they tried to shut us down. If you can get that verification, I'll back you all the way. You're right; this is potentially the biggest story we've ever had. Now you'd better be on your way to meet Harry Roberts!"

Jeremy got up to leave, and just as he reached the doorway, Donald Mortimer called after him, "L. J., I am going to put a hold on the front page for tomorrow morning's *Daily Sentinel* until the last possible minute. I'll be in my office until late, very late probably. If you can come up with something solid that we can print, then we will give it a front-page splash! Good luck."

"Thanks, Don. See you later."

It was a little after seven when Jeremy finally left the Sentinel Building. It was already dark outside and slightly foggy, so Jeremy buttoned his overcoat around his neck to keep warm in the chilly, damp night air. He was preoccupied as he walked slowly up Fleet Street, and his lanky frame cast long shadows from the street lighting.

CHAPTER *16*

I T WAS CLOSE TO MIDNIGHT, Wednesday, September 8, and Scott Frawley sat alone in his office on the fourteenth floor of the Government Office Building on King Charles Street. He was standing by the window, and despite the pounding rain outside, he could see lights still burning in the Foreign Office and the Home Office on the opposite side of the street. Scott had been in his office since a little after five o'clock that evening, when he got back from the last meeting with the prime minister. He was still angry from the comments made by the prime minister that the breach of security by Major MacAllister was just as severe, if not more so, than the breaches by Burgess, MacLean, and Philby. Most of all, he was angry at himself because in his heart he knew that what she said was absolutely true.

For the umpteenth time on that long dreary evening, Scott stopped pacing by the windows and went back to his desk and sat down. Scott Frawley admitted only to himself that he and MI5 were to blame for not having prevented this act of treason by Major Kevin MacAllister. Scott kept thinking, if only he had noticed something in the previous few months and had had the major followed and watched, this would never have happened. But it was too late for any of that now. The horse had bolted, as they say. As he sat there, Scott was also bristling at the fact that once the missiles had actually been hijacked, there was little that MI5 itself could do to recover them, particularly as the south of Ireland was one of the weakest links in MI6 operations outside of Britain. He couldn't argue with the fact that any possible recovery of the remaining missile had become a military matter. And the best he had been able to negotiate since leaving Downing Street earlier that evening was that the two SAS teams that would be sent in at dawn the next morning would each be accompanied by an agent from MI5.

Scott now had to content himself with building up an ironclad case of treason against Major MacAllister, George Wilkinson, and whoever else might be involved, but he was focusing on MacAllister and Wilkinson. Scott took some comfort from the fact that MI5 had made some progress in establishing what had happened after the two missiles had been hijacked. With the help of local police and inquiries through a wide area, they had discovered the deserted farmhouse and barn at Sherbourne Farm near Devizes, and from this they had reconstructed the possible route the terrorists took to the ferry in Fishguard. MI5 had figured that some sort of truck had to be involved in transporting the missiles but hadn't yet discovered conclusively what kind of truck it was. But Scott considered this progress purely routine and the least that could be expected of even a regular police force, whereas Scott's vision of MI5 was to prevent events or to actively shape events.

The phone rang, interrupting his thoughts, and when Scott picked up, Paul Laster greeted him. "Hi, Paul," Scott said. "How are you holding up?"

"Well, as I'm sure you know, it's been a long day. It appears that the Russians, through their agent in Northern Ireland and their regular support of the Provos, seem to be taking a big interest in the missing British missiles."

Scott frowned and said, "That's not good. We can't let them find them first." He paused and asked, "By the way, have you made any headway on getting a copy of MacAllister's granduncle's will?"

"Not yet. Even using the FBI, it will take at least a couple of days to get the necessary legal okays to be able to demand files from the lawyer's office in New York."

"Can't you find a way to get it without the legal okays?" Scott asked.

Paul laughed and said, "Sorry, but since the Watergate scandal, any break-ins or anything along those lines, particularly against lawyers, are out of vogue in America." They talked a few more minutes, though

Scott wasn't actively listening but rather planning how to expedite getting the will. "Thanks for your efforts," he said before they hung up.

Scott decided to take action himself. MI6 had two first-class agents residing in the New York City area, who acted as British watchdogs and verified anything that the British learned from the Americans through normal channels. Their cover was a very successful travel agency, right on Fifth Avenue in Manhattan, called British Tours, Inc.

Immediately after his call from Paul Laster, Scott called Herb Ready and Greg Ansell in their New York office. "I need you to do something for me as soon as it's nightfall," he said. "First, break into the offices of Driscoll, Hanrahan, and Moynihan, located on the corner of Fifty-Seventh Street and Park Avenue. Seek out the file relating to Bertie MacAllister, the granduncle of Kevin MacAllister. I need a copy of his will. If you're unsuccessful in locating anything in the law office, break into Mike Driscoll's home out in Rye, Westchester County, just north of the city. I need that will as soon as possible."

Scott fully expected that they would soon have all the proof and evidence he needed to show what Major MacAllister's motivation was in hijacking the nuclear missiles.

Scott was still very disturbed that the Russians had interest in the missing British missiles. This information from the CIA was alarming, though admittedly, if it were a choice between having the missile dropped in London and the resulting devastation and loss of life, and the Russians getting it, Scott would definitely opt for the Russians having the missile. But in reality, both of those possible outcomes had to be prevented at all costs. Scott realized that any Russian interference using the IRA Provos would seriously complicate matters. But he certainly didn't want to advise the prime minister of a possible Russian attempt to get their hands on the missile. Then he would have to admit to another failure in MI5, namely that they had never been able to pinpoint the principal FSB agent operating in Northern Ireland. Scott knew there were several FSB agents operating there. But he also knew that there was one in particular who was highly placed but seemed to be buried behind a smokescreen in tight connection with the IRA Provos, whom MI5 had never really been able to penetrate, although MI5 had had some minor successes in penetrating the IRA regulars. So far, Scott had been unable to tie in either the Provos or the IRA regulars with this so-called Green September group. And beyond the major and George Wilkinson, the rest of the members of the group still remained a mystery to him.

Since the previous evening, Scott had made sure that MI5 had put wiretaps on the telephones of Sheila MacAllister and Jenny Laster. He also had agents tailing Jenny and Sheila. Another major factor was the British press, in particular, the *Daily Sentinel* and the *Evening Sentinel*, and that goddamned reporter Jeremy Sands. Scott Frawley viewed Sands as almost a communist, given his record for national security. After the six o'clock edition of the *Evening Sentinel* had hit the streets, the prime minister had called him and instructed him to have someone keep an eye on Jeremy Sands.

Later in the evening, he had gotten a report that Jeremy Sands had met Harry Roberts, the radical minister for transport and power, in a pub on Fleet Street. Scott was very concerned about this meeting because Jeremy Sands had better contacts in Dublin and in Northern Ireland than even MI5. If he had learned the whole truth of what was going on and passed it on to Harry Roberts, there was going to be big political trouble, and Scott had no doubt that Muriel Hobson would lay the blame at his door. He knew Harry Roberts was an ardent antinuclear activist and that if he got wind of the full extent of the current crisis, he would exploit it to full advantage.

Nearby, Big Ben had just finished striking midnight when another call came in.

"Hello, Scott Frawley here."

"Hello, Scott. Greg Ansell speaking."

"I thought you'd call sooner," Scott said.

"Hang on to your hair, old chap. It's not like London here. People often work late in their offices. We had to wait until 6:00 p.m. when the last person left the law offices. Then we gave it another half hour to be absolutely sure the coast was clear. Besides, there were janitors running around the building, cleaning."

Scott Frawley interrupted him impatiently. "Okay, Greg, I don't need a whole bloody history of how you went about it. I need to know what you found out."

"Okay, old chap, don't get your dander up! I think we found out what you wanted to know. We found the will. Turns out our Major Kevin MacAllister inherited something over $17 million." Greg Ansell paused a second. "Anyway, there were also some handwritten notes in the file that seemed to indicate that the inheritance, which had mainly been in stocks and bonds, was liquidated into cash proceeds between March and July of this year. There was also another handwritten note on a scrap of paper—a real puzzle. It simply said 'Place new will in box, keep key at home.' We're not sure what to make of that."

"That's excellent, Greg. Now I want you and Herb Ready to see what you can discover at this lawyer Driscoll's home. How long do you think that might take?"

"That's a tall order, old chap, as first of all he lives in Rye, which is about forty-five minutes out of Manhattan. The other problem is that it's only a little after seven in the evening here, and unless he and his wife go out for the evening, it's going to be very difficult for us to break into his home and do a thorough search. But we'll see what we can do. By the way, I will be faxing over a copy of the will to you very shortly, but let me quote you the last sentence in the will, which is rather intriguing. 'With this money, I request Kevin to find a way of using a part of it to further the cause of 'A Nation Once Again.' So what do you make of that, Scott?"

"That's very interesting, Greg, and as for breaking into the lawyer's home, I don't care what time of the night it is here when you get back to me, as I probably won't sleep much anyway. But I'll be expecting your fax shortly then! Thanks."

"Okay, old chap, if there's nothing else, then Herb and I better get a move on out to Rye."

"That's it for now, Greg, and again, well done."

Scott Frawley hung up the phone, seeing both Major MacAllister's motivation and means to carry out this operation. But for what MacAllister had done, and worse, for what he might do to London the next day, he felt he could cheerfully snap his neck in half.

In the middle of everything else on that busy evening, Scott

Frawley had managed to coordinate with the home secretary, Ernest Brooking, and Special Branch, to ensure that the royal family had gotten out of London. Everything went smoothly as far as Buckingham and Kensington Palaces were concerned, but the aging queen mother, when told of the pending threat to her beloved London, refused to leave her residence, much to the consternation of the home secretary. Scott actually admired the stand the old lady had taken and really couldn't fault her logic, as she felt her place was with her people. But apparently the queen mother fully understood the need for the duke of Edinburgh and other members of the royal family to evacuate the city, and she actually encouraged them to leave without delay. Everything had been managed speedily and discreetly, and the home secretary had remarked to Scott afterward that he believed the media couldn't possibly have gotten wind of the departure of the royal family from London.

As it approached twelve thirty in the morning, Scott Frawley decided he would go and lie down in the small bedroom next to his office. He felt weary but knew he still wouldn't sleep. He didn't even bother to undress and just lay there in the dark, fully clothed, alone with his thoughts. Although he and most of his top operatives were all on the list to move to the bomb shelters the following morning, he somehow couldn't really believe that the end of London was near. And although he could hardly bear to think of the total destruction of London, he barely gave a thought to the five to six million people who would probably perish in such a disaster. He dealt with that possibility in an abstract way, telling himself how important it was that the authorities survive to go on governing and running the country. In a rather cold-blooded way, he equated the need for the authorities to survive as being important for the remaining 90 percent of Britain's population that would exist even if five to six million people were wiped out in London. He really looked on it dispassionately, as a matter of percentages. And not being in fear for his own life, Scott Frawley could, with a cool and calculating mind, consider the odds of the missile hitting London tomorrow, as fifty-fifty. As he dozed off, uppermost in Frawley's mind was that somehow or other, he had to emerge from this crisis as the top dog of all British intelligence services.

It was two thirty in the morning when the phone by the bed rang and Scott Frawley, who had only been dozing fitfully, was immediately wide awake as he picked up the phone. It was Greg Ansell again, calling from New York. Ansell reported to him that they'd been lucky, that apparently the lawyer Driscoll and his wife had gone out for the evening, and he and Herb Ready had been able to get inside the house and carry out a thorough, systematic search. But they'd found nothing. Scott was angry at him at first, but when his anger subsided, he said that overall they had done well but for them to continue probing and see if there was anything else they could find out about MacAllister's affairs with that lawyer. Before he rang off, he did thank Ansell and Ready again for what they had done.

He had barely hung up the phone when he remembered Ansell's promised fax transmission and went to see if it had arrived. He found it and began reading the copy of the last will and testament of the late Bertie MacAllister. When he was done, Scott Frawley turned off the light and closed his eyes to try to catch some sleep. And as he drifted off, an image of an old man he had never met came into his mind, uttering the last words of the will he had just read. For Scott Frawley, there was no further doubt. This will clearly indicted Kevin MacAllister, having provided him with both the motive and the means to carry out this deadly operation of nuclear blackmail. That was the last thing Scott Frawley remembered as he finally fell asleep.

CHAPTER 17

I T WAS THREE THIRTY IN the morning on Thursday, September 9, and Collins Barracks in Cork City, Ireland, was a hive of activity. Colonel Paddy O'Brien, the senior ranking officer in charge, had received his instructions directly from General Dan MacEoin, chief of staff, the previous evening. The instructions had been clear: the colonel was to mobilize every last man in the two battalions stationed at Collins Barracks, slightly over two thousand men. Colonel Paddy O'Brien had been flabbergasted at the instructions, for nothing like that had ever happened in the thirty years he had spent in the Irish Army. Besides, he knew Collins Barracks didn't even have enough army transport trucks to move that number of soldiers. The general was well aware of that fact and had said he was sending down twenty additional trucks from Dublin, which, when added to the forty trucks already stationed at Collins Barracks, should be adequate to move all the soldiers over to the area in County Kerry to be searched. The extra trucks from Dublin had arrived at a little after midnight.

The next part of the instructions was equally clear: the colonel was to rendezvous at five thirty in the morning with a third battalion that was being moved south from Sarsfield Barracks in Limerick, under the command of Captain Basil Dougherty. The rendezvous point was in open country two miles south of Farranfore in County Kerry, just eight miles north of Killarney. This point was roughly sixty-two or sixty-three miles from both Limerick and Cork and represented an ideal launching point for searching the entire mountainous area known as the MacGillycuddy's Reeks. The general had expressed his confidence to the colonel that with three thousand men at his disposal, he should be able to complete a thorough search of the entire region by ten in the morning.

The final part of the instructions concerned the Green September group. The colonel had received many copies of the photographs of both British Major Kevin MacAllister and the mercenary, ex-Captain George Wilkinson. A set of these photographs was made available to every single squad of men involved in the search, from all three battalions. The two targeted men and any other members of the group were to be taken alive, if possible, and any equipment they may have with them was to be taken intact. Instructions were explicit that only small arms fire up to and including machine guns were to be utilized. No mortars or hand grenades. The general had gone on that any infringement of these explicit orders would have serious repercussions. Colonel Paddy O'Brien was somewhat puzzled at the instructions concerning mortars and hand grenades, but given the general's tone and the massive mobilization of men involved, he realized this was a major operation and he shouldn't question his orders. In turn, the colonel had relayed all these instructions to Captain Basil Dougherty at Sarsfield Barracks in Limerick, and all arrangements were made.

Now, exactly at 3:30 a.m., Colonel Paddy O'Brien got into his staff car and gave instructions to the large convoy of sixty trucks to start rolling down the winding, steep hill that led down to Patrick Street in Cork City. The long convoy rumbled through the sleeping city of Cork and out onto the western road in the direction of Killarney. At the same time, thirty trucks were leaving through the south side of Limerick city, also in the direction of Killarney.

Meanwhile, at approximately the same time, another battalion was moving out of its barracks in Athlone, right in the middle of Ireland, and heading in the direction of Galway. There, they would join two battalions of the western command based in Renmore Barracks for the search of that area's Maumturk Mountains. Their instructions were similar, the only difference being that given its convenient location, the Renmore Barracks would serve as field headquarters for the search in that area.

The previous night, Jim MacAllister and ten of his best men from Special Branch in Dublin had driven down and settled in for the night in a small country hotel just north of Killarney on the Farranfore Road. After their arrival, Jim and his men had held a joint briefing session with the local superintendent of Gardai at Gardai headquarters in Killarney. Jim and his men didn't get to bed until well after midnight and now had been up again since four in the morning and enjoyed a hearty breakfast at four thirty. They then got ready to await the arrival of the army. By five o'clock, Jim and his Special Branch team were out in their cars at the side of the Farranfore Road, awaiting the army convoy. They didn't have long to wait, as about ten minutes later the first trucks came into sight from the direction of Killarney. Jim got out of his car and approached the staff car carrying Colonel Paddy O'Brien. After the two men had conferred for several minutes, it was agreed that Jim and his men should join the convoy to where the colonel was going to set up his field headquarters, two miles south of Farranfore.

By twenty minutes to six, the field headquarters had already been established in a tent and Jim MacAllister was reviewing detailed maps of the entire area with Colonel Paddy O'Brien as they both sipped hot mugs of coffee on a chilly autumn morning. The major roads that circled the mountainous area of the MacGillycuddy's Reeks also happened to be the major tourist route, known as the Ring of Kerry. The only other paved road in the area actually ran over the mountain range from Killorglin, on the north side of the Ring of Kerry, to Waterville on the southwest corner. Colonel O'Brien said, "The general ordered me to cooperate fully with you and your Special Branch team, and I'm happy to do so. I agree that strategic roadblocks should be set up periodically all around the Ring of Kerry and on any roads leading to the area. Captain Basil Dougherty, second in command, was given the task of assigning the three thousand men from the three battalions to spread out over the entire mountain range area. They'll take the trucks as far as they can go and then split into small groups of six to eight men to start the long and arduous search across the entire mountain range."

"Very good, sir," Jim MacAllister said.

By six in the morning, the units to establish the roadblocks had already been dispatched, and the first units were being sent to the farthermost points of the Ring of Kerry to start the search of MacGillycuddy's Reeks.

The search strategy adopted called for a two-pronged approach to the mountainous region. Roughly 1,400 men would be spread out between Kenmare to the south and New Chapel Cross to the southwest, while another 1,400 men would approach the mountains in a line from Killorglin to New Chapel Cross. In this way, the two arms would form a pincer that would meet roughly in the middle of the MacGillycuddy's Reeks. Initial instructions to the men were to proceed with caution, and when the location of the terrorists had been clearly identified, they were on no account to engage in an open gunfight with them. As soon as the terrorists' location had been pinpointed and surrounded, they were to await further orders.

By seven o'clock, as the sun began to rise behind them, the area of the field headquarters was almost deserted except for a few trucks and a couple of armored cars. The full-scale search was underway, and Colonel Paddy O'Brien finally relaxed a little, feeling that now it was only a matter of time.

At a quarter to two that same morning, two cars had been parked at the side of the road just south of the small town of Gort in County Galway. Padraig Flannery, Derry leader of the IRA Provos, leaned up against the front car, smoking a cigarette and looking anxiously at his watch. In the second car, Padraig had four of his best sharpshooters along for backup. Nicky Dwyer was to have met him at this very spot at least five minutes earlier. Padraig was feeling a little bit concerned, for when they had passed through Galway City earlier, they had noticed a lot of activity around the Renmore army barracks. It was in Galway that he and his men had separated from Rory McDevitt, the IRA leader in Belfast who was taking the other group to cover the possible missile location in the mountains to the west of Galway city. Finally, in the distance to the north of him, Padraig Flannery could see the lights of an approaching car. But as he wasn't yet sure if it was Nicky Dwyer, he moved closer to the hedge at the side of the road, and undoing his fly, he pretended to take a leak, in case the car contained some nosy plainclothes Gardai or other curious people.

In the event they stopped, Padraig had concocted a good cover story—he and the lads in the two cars traveling south were part of a bigger contingent on their way from County Donegal to play a big hurling match that weekend in Kerry. For that reason, all arms and radio transmitters were well concealed, and the trunk of each car appeared to contain only hurling sticks, sporting gear and a few clothes for overnight.

The lights of the car were now drawing closer and closer, until finally the car came into full view and appeared to be slowing. Padraig could feel his neck muscles tighten, and while he kept one hand down, his other hand slipped inside his jacket pocket and clutched a hidden revolver for friendly reassurance. The car stopped alongside, and with a flood of relief, Padraig saw that it was Nicky Dwyer. He quickly zipped up his fly and went over to Nicky. "I was gettin' worried," Padraig said.

"Small delay because of military traffic in the area," Nicky said.

It was quickly agreed that Nicky would transfer into the front car with Padraig while two of the lads from that car would get into Nicky's car and take up the rear in third place.

The three cars now continued their journey southward, reaching Limerick City just a little before three o'clock in the morning. Padraig deliberately chose a route through the city that took them past the Sarsfield Barracks, and there his suspicions were confirmed, as he could see a lot of activity, which indicated that the army there was also about to set out. Padraig commented to Nicky that they had just made it in time, for once the convoy of troops got on the road out of Limerick, it would have been very difficult for the three cars to pass them. And the alternate routes were literally dirt tracks that would have slowed down their progress considerably. After passing through Limerick, their drive on the deserted roads was uneventful.

It was a quarter to five in the morning by Padraig Flannery's watch as they took the right-hand fork in Farranfore toward Killorglin. From Farranfore, it was another forty miles to their destination of Cahirciveen on the northwest corner of the Ring of Kerry. Having passed through

Killorglin and beyond Glenbeigh, the road began to get narrower and twisty, and a driving rain-like mist was sweeping in off Dingle Bay. Padraig and the other two carloads of Provos didn't reach Cahirciveen until a little after six in the morning.

Just south of Cahirciveen, which was still shrouded in misty darkness, Padraig took a turn to the left, up an unmarked road, followed by the other two cars. The three cars traveled about five miles along the bumpy dirt track before coming to a stop outside the ruins of an old abbey. The abbey didn't look any different from any other twelfth-century ruin in the area, but in actual fact, it was one of the Provos' principal safe houses in the republic, and the ruin concealed many twentieth-century conveniences. It was surrounded by an old disused moat, the walls of most of the moat having tumbled down over the centuries. Padraig, in the first car, driving very slowly, led the way over the grassy, uneven ground down into the moat area and about halfway around the moat, into what looked like a huge tunnel, partly blocked from view by a rotting doorway hanging over it. The other two cars followed close behind, until eventually the lights of Padraig's car showed a big cave a couple of hundred yards in from the entrance of the moat. Here, there was enough room for the cars to turn around on the rocky floor of the cavern and to face out toward the exit. Padraig switched off the engine of his car, and the others followed suit. Nicky Dwyer expressed surprise at what an excellent hiding place the Provos had, as did some of the men from Rory McDevitt's command in Belfast, who obviously had never seen the place before.

Everyone had his task to carry out and set about it right away. Radio equipment and eavesdropping equipment were quickly removed from concealed areas in the three cars. "Can you tell me about the history of this place?" Nicky Dwyer asked.

While the men were busy with their tasks, Padraig explained, "I first learned of the place from my grandfather in the early 1960s, as apparently his grandfather and other Republicans had used it on and off during the Troubles between 1916 and 1923. Legend has it that in earlier centuries, when the moat and cavern were filled with water, it had on occasion been used as a drowning pool, where chieftains in the area would get rid of their enemies."

"A dark history," Nicky mused. "I like that."

"Me, too," Padraig said, scratching his ear. "The abbey itself was sacked in the 1600s by marauding soldiers from Cromwell's armies. Some time after that, a nearby river was diverted so that the moat and the cavern gradually dried out. In later centuries, the cavern was used as a hiding place for priests on the run from the British authorities. On occasion, the cavern was even used to hold masses for the surrounding country folk. Over the years, it became deserted and forgotten by most people until my grandfather and others started to use it during the Troubles."

Padraig then showed Nicky Dwyer two smaller caves that led off from the main cavern in different directions, which, while quite large at their entryways, were soon reduced to crawling tunnels, each of which came out in a different place in the MacGillycuddy's Reeks more than a mile away. Padraig explained, "This provided two safe escape routes in case people couldn't get out the way they came in." Then Padraig proudly displayed the Provos' masterpiece of improvisation, leading him to one side of the cavern toward what looked like a mass of rocks. Padraig walked around behind the rocks and began to push the whole pile of rocks forward. It turned out they were plaster of Paris, very realistically done and mounted on a wooden frame on wheels. "They can be positioned about halfway down the main tunnel through which we came in, and they fit so exactly that anyone entering from the moat, on reaching these rocks, would assume they had reached the end of the cave. This took a couple of years to build."

As the radio equipment had now been set up and all guns and weapons checked, Padraig gave orders to two of his men to wheel the fake rocks toward the middle of the tunnel from the moat. They left just a small enough gap for one of the men to go forward to the moat entrance and stand guard. Padraig's plan was to wait until the searching Irish soldiers had passed them overhead and then to follow them until the Irish troops found the Green September group and the nuclear missile. His informants in Dublin had advised him that the Irish Army was being accompanied by a unit from Special Branch and that orders had been given to restrain from a shootout with the Green September group. Apparently the objective of the Irish government was to capture alive as many of the terrorists as possible, and the missile intact. Padraig had been delighted on hearing this, as that allowed him to let the Irish troops and Special Branch do the searching, and then while they were standing by, he and his lads would slip in through their lines and get the missile for themselves.

That is, Padraig thought to himself, *assuming the bloody missile is here and not up in the mountains west of Galway.* But Padraig had chosen to cover this area for the good reason, which he didn't tell Rory McDevitt, that his sources in Dublin assured him that the British government was almost sure that the missile was located in this region. But given the danger, they had still requested the Dublin government to cover the mountains in county Galway just as thoroughly.

By eight o'clock, Padraig's group of lads had everything in readiness, and now all they could do was wait for the searching Irish soldiers to pass them overhead. As the minutes slowly dragged by, there was an air of increasing tension and nervousness among the men in the cavern, as each one knew that this was going to be a rough operation and they may not survive the day. But there was a hell of a lot at stake, and everyone felt it was worth the gamble. As Padraig thought about the sophisticated weapons and the money they would get from the Russians if they pulled this off, he smiled.

At about a quarter to nine in the morning, the forward lookout at the entrance in the moat came back, out of breath, to report that it sounded as if the Irish soldiers were finally in the area. The entrance to the cavern was quickly sealed off with a final push forward of the fake rock mass in the middle of the tunnel. Three men stood behind it very quietly, listening.

About five minutes later, they could hear the distinctive sound of army hobnailed boots clamoring around the rocky floor of the first half of the tunnel. By now, the men in the cavern were scarcely breathing, as the slightest sound would carry and reverberate through the tunnel. Many different sets of footsteps were heard clearly by everyone. And then the poking of gravel by gun butts. Muffled voices could be heard from the other side of the fake rocks, and gradually, the footsteps faded away as the Irish soldiers were departing. Everyone in the cavern let out a big sigh of relief but still remained very quiet for another few minutes. Finally, the three men who stood behind the rock facade, holding it securely in place, gradually pulled it back a little, leaving enough space for one man to go ahead. That man was wearing rubber-soled shoes and moved very cautiously to the cave entrance in the moat. Soon, he returned to the cavern to give the all clear.

Padraig selected three men, two from his own Derry Provos and one of the Belfast lads, to stay behind in the cavern with the cars and equipment. One of the men staying behind was constantly to monitor any field radio communications in the area and to notify Padraig on the single two-way radio that he would carry. Nicky Dwyer didn't normally participate in Provo operations in Northern Ireland, but on this occasion he insisted on accompanying Padraig and his men. The potential prize was too great for him not to be present himself. And so, at about ten minutes past nine, Padraig set out with the six other men and Nicky Dwyer, all wearing army flack jackets and sturdy rubber-soled shoes for the rocky climb ahead. Each man was armed with two revolvers with silencers and extra ammunition, along with an extra-sharp hunting knife. The eight men set out stealthily toward the moat, and the entrance to the cavern was closed off behind them.

Emerging into the morning light, Padraig was pleased to see that the area was still blanketed by a swirling mist, which was so typical. The men paused for a couple of minutes in the middle of the old ruins while Padraig quietly ascended a crumbling old watchtower to see if he could gauge how far ahead the Irish soldiers were. When he got to the top, he strained his eyes to see if he could spot anyone through the mist. He focused on one spot about a mile away, as there was an occasional gap in the mist. Nobody was in sight, so he returned to join the other men. "We must be at least a mile and a half behind the Irish soldiers," he said. "A safe distance, I would think." With that, he gave the signal for them to move out, and the race was on to capture the nuclear missile before the Irish soldiers did.

CHAPTER *18*

I T WAS STILL ONLY SEVEN in the morning, Thursday, September 9, but the Ministry of Defense was abuzz with activity. Sir Ian Sinders's office was as busy as Piccadilly Circus at rush hour. His secretary, Jane Hawley, had come in at a little before six to help coordinate all the activity. Margaret Bloomington, Major MacAllister's secretary, had also come in early to help Captain Smithers organize the move of Section Q11, the nuclear liaison group, to the bomb shelter beneath the Ministry Building. Captain James Harscombe, Sir Ian's adjutant, was also dashing around. Helicopters had been landing and taking off from the Ministry roof every few minutes since five thirty, ferrying in key officers and personnel from around the United Kingdom. Each person selected had a key task to perform as part of the nuclear emergency military headquarters, in the bomb shelter about a thousand feet below the Ministry Building.

Gordy Hargreaves, the minister of defense, came in and greeted Sir Ian. Then he said, "We'll be joining the prime minister and other ministers and civil servants in the nuclear bomb shelter buried below 10 Downing Street. That shelter is connected by a long tunnel to the emergency command center below the Ministry. Those not privy to the activities of the Green September group were told that this is purely an emergency exercise."

Sir Ian knew the purpose was to see how rapidly command operations could be transferred to the nuclear bomb shelter in the event of a nuclear attack. He knew that even Jane Hawley and Margaret

Bloomington, who had top security clearances, would have been told the same story because of concerns that the more junior members on the Ministry staff might panic and leave the building or notify their families and in that way spread panic in the streets of London. It had been decided that only after the complete evacuation of all the people in the Ministry to the nuclear bomb shelter would everyone be told the truth. At that point, they would have no way to communicate with people on the outside, except through authorized channels, which the senior officers would control.

Sir Ian had seen himself in the bathroom mirror that morning and thought he looked as if he had aged ten years in the last twenty-four hours. He hadn't had a wink of sleep all night. Throughout the night, he had overseen emergency removal of all troops from barracks around the London area to outlying army camps. All RAF airfields in the southern part of England had been put on standby alert and were ordered to be ready to scramble all planes into the air within minutes. All ships in the British fleet based in ports in and around the southeast of England were ordered to sea during the night. The two SAS units had also been transferred to two British frigates off the southwest coast of England. In fact, as Sir Ian checked his watch and saw that it was ten minutes past seven, he realized they were already on their way to the west and southwest Irish coasts, having been scheduled to leave at seven o'clock, a little before daybreak.

At seven thirty, Captain Harscombe came in. "Sir Ian," he said, "the last helicopter bringing in key personnel has already landed and taken off again. Everything else is in place for the final move down to the emergency operations center in the nuclear bomb shelter later this morning."

"Thanks for letting me know," Sir Ian said. "You're dismissed." He sat back in his chair, feeling weary and totally disillusioned. He had never really believed he would live to see the day when there would be an actual threat of a nuclear attack on London. The American experts, who had arrived with the prototype MTA, had been dispatched with an army escort to a remote part of Cornwall, where they would set up the MTA and be ready to latch onto the missile's flight path as it headed from Ireland to London.

Through the night on their long drive down to Cornwall, the two US experts were given all the manuals covering the operations of the Penguin-class nuclear missiles. Sir Ian desperately hoped that these two men would learn enough to be successful with the MTA, but he was skeptical. However, he had been impressed when he'd met the two men, as they had explained the technology behind the MTA and their game plan: if they could lock into the guidance system in the missile heading for London, they would be able to divert it into the upper atmosphere and explode it there relatively harmlessly. It was about an hour earlier when he had received confirmation that they were in place in Cornwall and all ready to go. Everything had been arranged for them to be notified immediately by the high-altitude reconnaissance aircraft that the RAF would be flying over Ireland all morning long.

Sir Ian had also been informed that part of the US Atlantic fleet was now positioned in St. George's Channel and was ready to shoot the missile out of the air if the MTA should fail. Sir Ian took more comfort from this, as he believed it had a fifty-fifty chance of success.

But even with all military aspects of the crisis now under control, Sir Ian couldn't help feeling that the prime minister was making a big mistake in not at least considering giving in to the demands of the Green September group. In his heart, Sir Ian couldn't believe that retaining a million and a half people in Northern Ireland was worth risking five to six million people in London. Sir Ian despised terrorism in any shape or form. He began to feel that maybe it really was time that the Irish problem was settled once and for all. Sir Ian even acknowledged to himself that despite all the historical circumstances that gave rise to a divided Ireland, it really was an unnatural state of affairs. And if only the politicians had had the sense to resolve it in the last seventy years, then this crisis would never have happened.

As Sir Ian contemplated all these things, Jane Hawley interrupted his thoughts. "Excuse me, Sir Ian," she said, "here's a signal from HMS *York*, the frigate now standing in international waters off the southwest coast of Ireland." Sir Ian read the signal, which had been sent to him simply to confirm that both SAS units had left on time and should now be nearing the coastline of Ireland. When they had any word from the landing parties, they would notify Sir Ian immediately. Sir Ian then called down to the minister to let him know that everything was in readiness. Gordon Hargreaves thanked him and hung up, as he was due at 10 Downing Street at eight in the morning for a full cabinet meeting, summoned by the prime minister.

For his part, Sir Ian was relieved not to have to visit 10 Downing Street again and felt that all he could do at this point was to do his duty for queen and country to the best of his ability. When it was all over and no matter what the outcome was, he would resign.

Gordon Hargreaves also had not slept the night before, and though feeling fatigued from the intense strain of the crisis, five minutes after the phone call from Sir Ian, he was on his way over to 10 Downing Street. When he arrived there at five minutes to eight, he noticed several members of the press hanging around, and a couple even tried to stop him with questions. But he ignored them and was admitted immediately into Number 10. He felt relieved when the door closed behind him.

Inside the front hallway of Number 10, Gordy noticed many senior civil servants scurrying around and quickly made his way to the doorway into the main cabinet meeting room. Inside, most ministers of government had already gathered, and when Gordy appeared, he was surrounded by several of the ministers hurling questions at him about what the latest news was from a military point of view. By that time, all the ministers in the cabinet had been informed of the nature of the crisis, but little more information was given to them at that point.

When Gordy had talked with the prime minister on the telephone early that morning, they had agreed that he would not give out any further information until the full cabinet meeting was in session. Gordy Hargreaves spied out his old friend, Ron Butler, the minister of state for Northern Ireland, at the far side of the room. He weaved his way through the crowded room to join him. It was now two minutes to eight, and everyone began to take their places around the long table. There were twenty-two ministers serving in the full cabinet, in addition to the prime minister herself. As everyone settled in their seats, Sir Hugh

Blake, the permanent cabinet secretary, who sat to the rear of the empty chair for the prime minister, called the meeting to order.

At exactly eight o'clock, Muriel Hobson came out of her private office at the far end of the cabinet meeting room, followed by her private secretary. Her face looked grim, and the bags under her eyes were witness to the fact that she, also, had not slept the previous night. She took her place in the chair at the head of the table, and Jack Larson sat down behind her. There was a hush in the room, and all eyes turned to the prime minister as she cleared her throat rather noisily.

"You all know why we are gathered here this morning, as we face the most severe crisis that this country has ever faced—indeed, even more grave than that faced by Winston Churchill in the darkest days of the Battle of Britain in World War II. I've spent the entire night wrestling with the problem of what we must ultimately do. To this point, I've taken only a handful of you into my confidence. The reasons for this are now plain to understand, as doing otherwise would have increased the risk of word getting out and causing a panic here in London."

As Muriel Hobson paused for breath, a few in the room looked quite incensed that the prime minister could think one of them might have leaked the information, even unwittingly. Harry Roberts's eyes narrowed perceptibly as he stared coldly at the prime minister. She resumed.

"In any case, I've now decided to put the whole matter to a vote of the full cabinet. Simply stated, the issue to be decided is, do we give in to nuclear blackmail and this Green September terrorist group and make a public announcement before two o'clock today that we will put forward a plan to reunite Ireland or do we take a hard line approach of no negotiations whatsoever with the terrorists, and by doing so, risk the devastation of London and the annihilation of five to six million people?" She paused and looked around at the men before her. "I know some of you would say that the choice is an easy one and that we cannot risk such an enormous loss of life in London. But I say we cannot afford to give in to terrorists' demands no matter what the risk to the civilian population. Because if we were to give in on this occasion, who knows what demands we may face in the future as a result. It could be that

Wales may demand separation from the United Kingdom, or Scotland might. What would we do then? As the legitimately elected government of all the people of the United Kingdom, we must do what is best for the long-term stability of this great nation of ours."

Muriel Hobson paused again for breath. Hargreaves noticed that both ministers of state for Welsh and Scottish affairs had visibly winced at her words. And by now, there was definitely an uncomfortable atmosphere in the room. With Sir Hugh diligently taking notes of every word spoken, Hargreaves wondered if Muriel Hobson was very conscious that history might look on this cabinet meeting as a moment of infamy or as a moment of great strength by the British government.

She seemed aware that it was an absolute gamble to either shoot down or divert the missile, if launched, a fifty-fifty chance. He knew that Muriel Hobson fervently hoped that it wouldn't come to that and that somehow, for once in their lives, the Irish authorities would manage to perform effectively and efficiently and capture both the terrorists and the missile before it was ever launched.

The prime minister went on, "So the time has come to make our choice between the two options, and I recommend that we take a tough line. It simply isn't good to give into the demands of terrorists. We'll now have a twenty-minute discussion period, and then we'll take a vote by a show of hands."

Immediately, heated discussion broke out up and down the long table. Muriel Hobson was flanked by strong supporters of her position. On her right sat Ernest Brooking, the home secretary, and Charles Mills, the foreign secretary. On her left were Gordy Hargreaves and Ron Butler. These men fielded many of the questions directed at the prime minister's end of the table.

As she sat there, Hargreaves wondered if she had begun to realize it would be a tight vote. Those with antinuclear sentiments tended to gravitate toward Harry Roberts's position, which basically called for capitulation to the terrorists and finally granting unification to Ireland. Hargreaves figured that Harry Roberts could count on the support of the three Liberal Party members in the cabinet and probably also on the chancellor of the Exchequer who, while tough on fiscal matters, was perceived as antinuclear in his sentiments. As the minutes ticked by, the noise level in the cabinet meeting room rose rapidly.

Sir Hugh Blake, who had been glancing at the clock on the table beside him, finally stood up and called the meeting back to order. He announced that the twenty minutes were up and that they should now proceed to take a vote. As the discussion ended, all was quiet again. Sir Hugh explained that a raised hand would imply agreement with the prime minister's position. All others would be registering their position to negotiate with the terrorists and to prepare plans for the reunification of Ireland over a period of time.

The prime minister sat, stony-faced, at the head of the table and slowly scanned every single person sitting at the table. Sir Hugh was standing beside her to her right and appeared to be very slowly and deliberately taking a count of the raised hands around the table. He counted only eleven raised hands, which meant a tie, as eleven were opposed. As was customary, Sir Hugh announced the outcome as a dead heat. All eyes now turned to the prime minister.

She sat, unflinching, for a good minute, as the silence in the room almost screamed for an outcome, and history would now record that the ultimate decision was made by her alone. In keeping with the strict practice of cabinet meeting procedures, Muriel Hobson, the prime minister, raised her right hand and said softly, "So be it."

Those three simple words broke the tension in the room and possibly sealed the fate of five to six million Londoners. Hargreaves saw Harry Roberts catch the prime minister's gaze. He figured that no matter what the outcome, she could expect a major political challenge from him. With the decision made, the atmosphere in the room was now very subdued, and as no other business had been scheduled for this special cabinet meeting, the meeting was officially declared closed by Sir Hugh Blake. Now each minister had to prepare for the evacuation of his ministry and key personnel to the nuclear bomb shelter far below Downing Street.

Even though the government supposedly had until two o'clock that afternoon in which to respond to the demands of the Green September group, it had been generally agreed between all members of the cabinet that all evacuations would be completed by noon.

CHAPTER *19*

I T WAS ALREADY A QUARTER past seven on Wednesday evening, September 8, when Jeremy Sands reached the Lord Ranelagh Pub. Inside, he anxiously looked around the crowded bar, trying to find Harry Roberts. There was no sign of him. He slowly made his way through the crowd, up to the bar, and ordered himself a scotch. When the barman brought his drink, Jeremy asked if there were any messages for him. Jeremy, or L. J. as he was generally called, was well known by all the barmen in the pubs around Fleet Street, so the barman answered promptly.

"Actually, L. J., there was a call for you about twenty minutes ago from a Harry Roberts. His message was sorry he couldn't make it, but he's been delayed in the Commons. Says he'll call you in your office no later than ten o'clock. That was it. Sorry."

"Thanks, Bruce. But now that I'm here, I might as well stick around for a while."

Grinning, Bruce left him to serve another customer. Jeremy took a sip of his scotch and stood with his back to the counter to have a look around the crowded pub and see whom he might talk to. Not seeing anyone in particular he wanted to chat with, he soon fell into conversation with two reporters from the rival and more conservative *London Recorder* newspaper. Next, Jeremy ran into a couple of barristers he knew well, who seemed more eager to discuss the big murder trial going on at the Old Bailey than the nuclear explosion that afternoon in the North Atlantic.

After a while, Jeremy drifted over to join a couple of conservative politicians who were now in the opposition. They were eager to talk about the nuclear explosion but only from the point of view that they were delighted at the government's embarrassment over the whole issue. But they expressed no doubt that it simply was some government testing of new nuclear weapons. They were particularly pleased that the relatively new Labor government was finding itself in a position where it also had to invoke the Official Secrets Act, just as the Conservative Party did when in power.

By about nine o'clock, while sipping his seventh scotch and having talked to many more people, Jeremy decided he should be getting out of there. He was totally amazed that nearly everyone he talked to seemed quite willing to accept the government's explanation for what had happened that afternoon. And automatically assuming it was a matter of national security, they didn't seem willing to question or probe it further. Jeremy thought to himself, *My God, their heads are so deep in the sand! If I were to stand up this minute on a chair and tell all of them what might happen tomorrow, they would probably laugh me out of the pub and say that L. J. has finally lost his mind!*

Jeremy knocked back his last mouthful of scotch and went out into the chilly night air. He walked briskly down Fleet Street to the Sentinel offices, for it was one of those evenings when, although not particularly cold, the damp, slightly foggy air made it seem chillier than it really was.

It was just about nine fifteen at night when Jeremy reached his office on the fifth floor. He was feeling unusually sober and very disappointed that he hadn't yet spoken with Harry Roberts. That meant that the time was running out for him to be able to have an explosive front-page story for tomorrow morning's edition of the *Daily Sentinel*. Ten o'clock at night was the absolute latest deadline for having detailed front-page cover stories sent to typesetting in time to be included in the first editions of the next day's paper, which would leave the printing offices for national distribution by three o'clock the following morning.

Jeremy stood by the big window opposite his desk, overlooking Fleet Street below. He gazed out at nothing in particular, and his mind was in turmoil. He was thinking this might be the last night he would ever look out on the now almost deserted street. Only an occasional well-lit double-decker bus gave any indication of life. Jeremy thought, *This very spot where I am standing and the entire surrounding area could well be a bloody enormous radioactive crater by tomorrow afternoon.* The shrill ringing of the old-fashioned phone on his desk broke into his thoughts. He was so lost in thought of unspeakable horror and destruction that the mundane reality of the phone ringing nearly made him jump out of his skin in fright. Getting a grip, Jeremy reached the phone in two swift strides and picked it up. It was Harry Roberts.

"Harry, old friend, where have you been? I've been going frantic waiting for your call. We need to talk. Did you talk with the prime minister?"

"Good heavens, L. J., you seem to be in a rare state of agitation this evening! What's the matter? I'm sorry, but I was delayed in the Commons until ten minutes ago. Unexpected, long-winded opposition to my new transportation bill from the Conservatives. It finally passed its first reading but only after a lot of exasperating, unnecessary discussion by the bloody Tories. And no, I didn't get a chance to talk with the prime minister. In fact, come to think of it, she seemed to be avoiding me this evening. Is that nuclear test in the North Atlantic this afternoon that has you all riled up?"

"You're damn bloody right it is. But it's not what it seems."

Jeremy then proceeded to give Harry Roberts a succinct and rapid overview of everything he had learned about the hijacking of the missiles by the terrorists and their threats. From the noises at the other end of the phone line, he could tell he had Harry Roberts's rapt attention. When he had finished, there was dead silence on the other end.

"Harry, are you still there?" Jeremy paused a moment. He could hear an audible gulp as Harry Roberts swallowed and the faint sound of Harry Roberts clearing his throat. "Now you can understand why I was so frantic to talk to you."

"Yes, I do. This is the biggest bloody cock-up in British history. Can you meet me in fifteen minutes?"

Harry almost spat out the words; Jeremy's old friend was very angry indeed.

"Absolutely! Where?"

"Let's meet in the snug at the Essex Arms, on the corner of Chandos Place and Bedford Street—you know the one, just up from the Strand. Let's say ten o'clock. It's almost quarter of ten now. Okay?"

"Fine. I'll see you then."

"Bye!"

Harry Roberts had hung up without another word, and slowly Jeremy put the phone back in the cradle. He thought, *Boy, old Harry must be angry if he thought I needed directions to the Essex Arms.* Jeremy prided himself on knowing almost every pub in central London, and although he hadn't been in the Essex Arms for quite some time, he certainly knew it as well as most. Still leaning against the front of his desk, Jeremy dialed the extension of his editor, Donald Mortimer. It was answered instantly.

"Hello, Don. Jeremy here. I'm afraid I'm not going to have any front-page story for the *Daily Sentinel*. So no need to hold the presses any longer."

"So you didn't get confirmation from Harry Roberts about what your sources told you?"

"No, I haven't met with Harry yet, but I'll be seeing him in fifteen minutes. However, to cut a long story short, he doesn't know any more than I do at this point. But we may need to talk about it. Where can I reach you if I need to?"

"That's too bad, but best see what Harry has to say, in any case. I'll be at my flat in Knightsbridge tonight. I'll be leaving shortly and should be back in the morning by about seven o'clock. You have the number, don't you?"

Jeremy detected the relief in Donald Mortimer's voice and realized that his editor was walking a fine line between freedom of the press and running afoul of the government again. "Yes," he said, "and if you need to reach me for any reason, after I meet with Harry Roberts, I'll be coming back here to spend the night."

"Fine. By the way, Jeremy, I just learned from a couple of sources that it appears the entire royal family, with the exception of the queen mother, have left London, apparently bound for Balmoral in Scotland.

I thought it would interest you, as it probably ties in with the nuclear threat against London. According to the court calendar, they shouldn't have left until later next week."

"Thanks, Don. That just reinforces my conviction that the threat is very real. Well, if there's nothing else, I've got to dash and meet Harry. Cheerio-bye."

"Cheerio, Jeremy, and good luck."

Jeremy hung up, flicked off the light in his office, and almost ran down to the elevator. When he got to the street, he started walking in the direction of the Strand, keeping an eye out for a taxi. He'd gone about a block when he finally flagged one down. Jeremy checked his watch as he got into the cab; it was already eight minutes to ten. The traffic was light, and he made it to the doors of the pub at exactly one minute to ten.

As he was paying the taxi driver, another taxi pulled up behind him, and Harry Roberts jumped out. The two men entered the pub together and headed straight into the snug. As it was a Wednesday night, the snug was deserted except for a young couple canoodling at a table in the corner. While Jeremy went up to the bar and ordered two double scotches, Harry sat down at a table in the corner opposite the smooching couple. When Jeremy brought the drinks to the table, each of them took a large gulp before Harry Roberts spoke.

"By Jove, I'm ashamed to be a member of this government!" Harry said, thumping his fist on the table. "You know, I tried to call Muriel Hobson right after I talked with you, and that sod Jack Larson told me she wasn't available but that my presence was requested at an emergency session of the full cabinet at eight o'clock in the morning at Downing Street. When I asked him what the agenda was, he curtly told me, 'Special business.' Damn right it is, when you're going to discuss the possible destruction of London and five or six million people. Mark my words, L. J., if we survive tomorrow, somehow I'll make Muriel Hobson pay. And I may even topple my own bloody government."

"Okay, Harry, just calm down a little. If it's any consolation, if we do come through tomorrow, you can count on my support and that of the *Sentinel* newspapers in whatever you propose to do. Anyway, Harry,

I think we can safely assume that everything I told you from my sources is true. And your emergency cabinet meeting in the morning would seem to confirm that. But also, just a few minutes before I came down here to join you, I learned that all the royal family have left London, with the exception of the queen mother."

"I'd lay odds on that was the work of the home secretary, Ernest Brooking. It wouldn't surprise me if the queen mother actually refused to go, as she's a gutsy old lady and the one member of the royal family who has the common touch and a deep love for the ordinary folk of London. So, bloody Muriel Hobson and her cronies are probably patting themselves on the backs for evacuating the royal family. But what about all the Londoners, the millions of people who could die? What are we going to do about them?"

Jeremy took a slug of his drink and said, "I don't have the answer to that one. I've been thinking of nothing else all afternoon and evening. At this late stage in the game, I can't see a viable way of warning the people without causing a panic. I've even debated whether it would be worth saving even a handful of people from the catastrophe that may befall them. Mind you, I could still do it and use the midmorning edition of the *Evening Sentinel*, but then I worry about the consequences if the panic that could ensue might, of itself, kill people. That would look particularly bad if somehow or other the government does manage to thwart the efforts of the terrorists to launch the second missile against London. You do see my dilemma, Harry?"

Harry nodded. "Perfectly. If only we had more time, I might even have been able to persuade my old friend Tom Williams, the leader of the National Transport Workers' Union, to have called a one-day strike of British Rail and London Transport and so stop all Tubes, trains, and buses. That would have forced a majority of workers to stay out of central London tomorrow. But I know from past experience in the Mine Workers' Union that it would take a good twenty-four hours to organize a massive, total walkout. So that rules out that possibility. But maybe the *Sentinel* should publish some kind of warning in the morning and see what develops. It won't matter much if none of us survives. On the other hand, if we do survive, it will play a very critical part in the future course of events for this country. But I will be able to advise you better after tomorrow morning's cabinet meeting."

"You may be right at that, Harry. But what if some people get killed in the panic that would follow our warning in the newspaper?"

"I think that's a risk we may have to take, but we'll see. None of this could have happened if the Irish Question had been resolved a long time ago, as it should have been. It's my opinion that they should be one country, and Northern Ireland is nothing but a cash drain on the British treasury and a complete waste of money. But then, the previous Tory government, in power for so long with a big majority in Parliament, squandered the opportunity to settle the Irish issue once and for all. They stubbornly followed the old policy, as if Northern Ireland were an integral part of the UK. But that's a load of political hogwash, and of course, if we were a nuclear-free country, we wouldn't have any bloody missiles to be hijacked in the first place, for whatever reason."

Jeremy and Harry stayed in the snug until closing time at eleven and downed many more scotches while they earnestly discussed all the possibilities that the future might hold. No one else had come in after they had arrived, and the young couple opposite them had continued to smooch, apparently oblivious to anything the two men were saying. Jeremy managed to get the last couple of scotches from the barman just as he was calling, "Time, gents, please!" The young couple was first to leave, at a few minutes after eleven. Harry remarked to Jeremy with a wink that he knew what they would be up to that night.

At ten minutes past eleven, the two men left the pub and strolled down toward the Strand to get taxis in different directions. Harry told Jeremy that he would be spending the night at his London "digs", as he called it, which was actually a small bachelor-sized flat in Westminster, though he still kept his main home in Yorkshire, where his wife and family spent most of their time. Harry hailed the first taxi that came along, and the two men shook hands firmly, not sure they would ever see each other again. As Harry's taxi headed off in the direction of Westminster, Jeremy decided he really wanted to walk back to Fleet Street despite the chilly, damp night air.

As Jeremy strolled down the Strand toward Fleet Street, he couldn't help thinking that this might be the last time he would walk along these famous old streets of London, a city that had become so much a part of him over the years. But as he was so preoccupied, he hardly noticed his surroundings and still found his way back to the *Sentinel* offices by instinct.

By a quarter to twelve, Jeremy was going up the steps to the main entrance to the Sentinel offices when he noticed, out of the corner of his eye, a couple of men lurking on the opposite side of the street, facing the Sentinel Building. He had seen the same men earlier in the evening and was now convinced that they were from MI5. He wondered if he had been followed to the Essex Arms and seen with Harry Roberts. Jeremy went on in and said good night to the night porter as he walked over to the elevators. A couple of minutes later, he was back in his fifth-floor office and stood for a while in the dark, looking out his window at the two men on the opposite side of the street below.

Big Ben struck midnight in the distance, and Jeremy decided there was nothing more he could do that night. Taking off his jacket and tie, he decided he would bed down on the long sleeper sofa in the corner of his office. Before settling down for the night, he called the night operator to let her know he was in the office but didn't want to be disturbed unless it was absolutely urgent. Sleep didn't come easily to Jeremy that night, but he finally drifted off into fitful dozing at about one o'clock.

Jeremy woke up at five thirty but lay there thinking and didn't finally get up until about a quarter to seven as the black night sky gave way to a gray, rainy, murky dawn. He felt stiff all over, and his throat was dry. His tongue felt like sandpiper in his mouth. As he got up, he was thinking, *Today is Thursday, September 9, and this day may become as famous to future generations in Britain as the Battle of Hastings in 1066.* Once he was up and had stretched a bit, Jeremy felt a little better, and he put on his coffeepot to brew some fresh coffee. He wandered over to the window, and his eyes automatically focused on a doorway opposite. There were still two men standing there in the rain, with hats on and coats pulled up around their necks. But they were different men from the two he had seen the night before.

After he had his first cup of coffee, Jeremy got his spare shaving kit from his desk drawer and went down the corridor to the men's room to shave and have a good washup. When he got back to his office, he took a fresh shirt and suit out of the closet and removed them from their dry cleaner's bags. By the time he had changed, Jeremy looked his usual immaculate self, and nobody would ever have known he had spent the night in his office, sleeping in his clothes. It was a quarter to eight, and Jeremy couldn't focus on anything other than the nuclear threat, so he decided he would pop around the corner to a little restaurant and grab some breakfast.

Jeremy was back in his office by eight thirty, and, feeling like a caged animal, he couldn't do anything but pace, occasionally glancing out the window to see if the two men were still in the doorway opposite. They were. At about ten minutes to nine, the phone rang, and Jeremy almost jumped on it, as if about to attack it. It was Harry Roberts. The conversation was brief. Harry very quickly gave Jeremy an outline of what had transpired at the 8:00 a.m. cabinet meeting, which had just broken up ten minutes earlier. The two men agreed that Jeremy should disclose all in a front-page exclusive in the first edition of the *Evening Sentinel*, due on the streets at eleven o'clock that morning.

As soon as he hung up, Jeremy sat down at his desktop computer and typed feverishly for the next forty minutes. The words tumbled out of him almost faster than he could type. As soon as he was done, he printed it out and, almost running, went to Donald Mortimer's office. Luckily, the editor was alone as Jeremy barged in. Jeremy quickly brought Donald Mortimer up to speed on everything he had learned from Harry Roberts and then handed his proposed front-page layout to Mortimer.

As chief editor of both *Sentinel* newspapers, Donald Mortimer had to make the final decision whether to go to press or not. As Mortimer read the story, Jeremy paced back and forth in front of his desk, impatiently. When the editor was done, he looked at Jeremy long and hard and finally said, "Okay, we'll run with it, and may God help us all. I've circled a couple of minor word changes, but otherwise, it's fine, and let's get it down to the presses."

"Believe me, Don, we're doing the right thing, no matter what the outcome. Thanks."

Without another word, Jeremy rushed back to his own office. He made the corrections. Ten minutes later, the whole story was down in electronic typesetting. The headlines were to be topped by a photograph from their archives, showing the mushroom cloud of a nuclear blast at the French test sites in the Pacific. Now, all Jeremy could do was wait.

At ten minutes to eleven, the eleven o'clock edition of the *Evening Sentinel* was delivered to Jeremy's office. He looked at the headline over the story he had written, and it sent a shudder down his spine. The headline ran, in heavy black print underneath the photograph: "Nuclear Threat to London Imminent Today."

Jeremy walked over to his side window and stared down below until the first delivery truck emerged from the bottom of the building. He knew that inside, it was stacked high with the first of that day's editions of the *Evening Sentinel*, carrying his story. It was customary for the first delivery truck to supply the newspaper vendors along Fleet Street and then the surrounding streets in the direction of the city, as that first edition also focused on latest breaking news in the financial markets and was generally snapped up by business people. He moved to his front window to watch what was happening below. The first bundle of the *Evening Sentinel* had been dropped off at the vendor right at the corner below. He watched that vendor unwrap his bundle and put the headline print in front of his stand. A line of Londoners quickly formed, snapping up the newspapers. Then one of the two men from the doorway opposite rushed over and bought a paper and took it back to his companion. They looked at each other, apparently horrified, and the one who had gotten the newspaper sent the other one off, running. Jeremy saw him head to a public phone booth, and instantly Jeremy realized what was going to happen.

Within minutes, people seemed to be running around Fleet Street in all directions. And many more people started to pour out of surrounding office buildings as the word spread like wildfire. Even the Sentinel Building itself wasn't immune, as many of the clerical workers and junior staff members poured out of the front door five floors below him. As the panic spread, the swelling crowd surged out into the street, and traffic was brought to a complete halt. People were running frantically in the direction of the nearest Tube stations at Blackfriars, Temple, Chancery Lane, Mansion House, and the British rail stations at Blackfriars and Cannon Street. Jeremy had some misgivings as he observed the spreading panic, but the damage was done, and he consoled himself with the thought that at least some of these people might actually escape London. Ten minutes later, several carloads of plainclothes police and MI5 agents battled their way through the crowd, toward the Sentinel Building. Within minutes, Jeremy was confronted by Donald Mortimer, accompanied by several senior officers from the Special Branch. They were informed that they were being placed under close arrest and would be held in this building, and that all further deliveries of that fateful first edition of the *Evening Sentinel* were being impounded by the government under the powers of the Official Secrets Act. Jeremy didn't mind, for he knew he had done what he had to do, and if he were to die that day, he would die happy, knowing he'd done his best.

CHAPTER *20*

I T WAS ABOUT SEVEN IN the morning on Thursday, September 9. Kevin MacAllister was sitting among the rocks just outside the entrance to the cave where the missile was located. Dawn was slowly breaking across the eastern skies behind him as he gazed out toward the ocean. Everything around him was enveloped in the endless swirling mists off Dingle Bay. Kevin felt tense, as the final day of his long-planned operation was dawning. He had already been sitting there for about half an hour after spending a sleepless night tossing and turning in a sleeping bag on the cold, damp floor of the main cave. And despite encouragement from George Wilkinson that he should sleep, Kevin's efforts at sleep were thwarted by vivid visions of the photograph of Hiroshima that hung in his office in the Ministry. Every time he shut his eyes, that vision came into his mind.

Kevin was amazed that George Wilkinson had managed to catch several hours of sleep, as had each of the other men at their respective posts while they took turns keeping watch.

Late the previous night, Kevin had gone forward to each lookout point to talk with the men and made a final stop at the farmhouse where Pat Feeney represented the first line of defense and was now accompanied by young Terry O'Neill. Kevin noticed that each man displayed, in a different way, the mounting tension felt by each and every one of them. They all knew that the next few hours were critical. Kevin found each of the men to be proud and pleased with the success of the previous afternoon's demonstration. Tom Fallon had monitored

274

the BBC's news reports on the radio the previous evening and relayed the stories to the others. One and all were convinced that the nuclear blast in the North Atlantic must have put the wind up the British government, good and proper. But Kevin had suspected that behind the brave words, perhaps each man, or at least some of them, secretly harbored a hope that the British government would capitulate to their demands so there would be no need to fire the second nuclear missile at London.

Kevin and George, at least, shared the belief that, while it was unlikely that the British government would stand down, even in the face of a nuclear threat, they may have by some miracle come up with some diversionary tactic. But in the final analysis, both men couldn't conceive of them not pulling a "Kruschev" and backing down at the very last possible moment, as happened in the Cuban Missile Crisis of 1962.

After his harrowing night and recurring visions of a nuclear holocaust, Kevin had to admit to himself that in his heart he also cherished a vague hope that the British government would back down. At the same time, Kevin knew he would do what he had to do, out of a sense of duty to a united Ireland and, of course, to his much loved granduncle Bertie.

As he sat there, Kevin was growing increasingly jumpy, and his imagination was playing tricks on him, for with every sound he heard he imagined someone coming to get him. And then he would realize that what he heard were the normal early morning sounds of the mountainside coming alive, as birds went about their business, rabbits came out of their burrows to explore the early morning terrain, and brooks continued their swift run down the side of the mountain. All this time, his beloved and faithful Max was sitting by his side. Kevin watched Max's ears and heard the low growls rising in his throat and put an arm around him to keep him from dashing into the undergrowth to get at the rabbits.

To take his mind off what lay ahead, Kevin conjured up loving images of his adorable Jenny. He thought about all the wonderful times he had enjoyed with her over the last five years. Kevin could recall every precious minute of their recent time in New York and every word they'd spoken to each other. It now seemed to have been in another world and another time. In those few days, he and Jenny had become closer than ever before. They had reached new heights of pleasure in their lovemaking, and he could recall clearly every loving, tender moment of that wonderful shower on their first night in New York. The mere thought of that night sent a tingle down his spine and caused a throbbing urge between his legs. Kevin thought, *What the hell am I doing here when I could be with the most wonderful woman in the world?*

Kevin's eyes clouded over, and for a moment, he clutched Max so tightly that he almost hurt him. He looked down at Max apologetically, brushing away a few tears from his eyes. In that instant, if anybody had asked Kevin MacAllister what was his biggest sacrifice in doing what he was for a united Ireland, he would not have listed wife, job, or money but Jenny Laster. He wondered how Jenny must be taking all of this and hoped and prayed she was still safely up in Norwich, far away from London. Sitting there alone with his dog, Kevin vowed that if somehow he should survive this day and live in freedom in some unknown land, he would find Jenny and ask her to spend the rest of her life with him. But with what he was about to do, he wondered if she could still feel the same about him.

Kevin thought about his wife, Sheila, and felt sorry for her. He knew that if he were to live, he could not spend the rest of his life with her; he had already stayed with her too long. His eyes misted again as he thought of his dead son, Owen, plucked from this world at the tender age of three. Kevin got out his wallet and fished out the several photographs of Owen. As Kevin looked at them, his eyes welled up in tears. He thought what might have been with Owen alive but never was. His hands trembled, and he dropped the photos. As he picked them up, he noticed a photograph of his best friends, Peter and Lois Royston, and their two children, Angela and Ross.

Looking at the photo of the Roystons brought back many happy memories for Kevin. He had known them both for over twelve years, and their children from the day they were born. He was more like a favorite uncle to Angela and Ross rather than mommy's and daddy's good friend. He felt relieved that Peter and Lois were safely out of the country and away in Portugal on their annual vacation, and the children were safe in boarding school down in Devon, far enough away from London to be out of danger. Kevin would never wish to be the cause of anything bad happening to his dearest friends. As he looked through the photos one last time, Kevin barely gave a second glance to a picture of Sheila, who happened to be in one of the photos with his son, Owen. He thought to himself how strange it was that he no longer felt any love for the wife he'd lived with for so long—all he could feel for her was pity. Kevin put away the photos and stuffed his wallet back in his pocket. He thought, *I have to get a grip and carry on.* Kevin stood up and attached the leash to Max's collar as he gave him one last short walk to relieve himself. Max stretched himself backward and forward and shook his whole body as if he had gotten cramped from sitting so still and close to Kevin for almost two hours. Kevin looked out in the direction of Dingle Bay, and for a few moments, the mist parted and gave him a tremendous view of the sea. This view recalled to his mind the immortal description of West Kerry, written in an essay by John Millington Synge in 1907, and appropriately called "In West Kerry":

> One wonders in these places why anyone is left
> in Dublin, or London, or Paris,
> when it would be better, one would think,
> to live in a tent or hut
> with this magnificent sea and sky,
> and to breathe this wonderful air,
> which is like wine in one's teeth.

Kevin's Granduncle Bertie had quoted those words to him so often that they were engraved on his mind. And as Kevin stood on the side of this mountain, he had a fleeting glimpse of why John Millington Synge had written those words in 1907. *Really, nothing has changed,* Kevin thought. *This is one of the most timeless places on earth.*

When Max had answered nature's call, Kevin turned and went back into the cave, as the almost ever-present mists were swirling again, blocking out his wonderful view.

It was almost eight thirty when Kevin and Max got back to the front of the cave where the missile was located. George was up and had been joined by Ned, who had been replaced at his lookout post by Tom Fallon, leaving Sean Morrissey on his own. Ned was busy brewing tea and making cheese sandwiches for everybody, so that at least they would have some food in them before the fight. Kevin thought both George and Ned looked tired and strained, their eyes underlined by circles. None of them had shaved since Monday, and the growing stubble on their faces served to emphasize their weary, rough looks. Kevin felt his chin and realized he probably looked as bad as they did, or worse. Normally he was clean-shaven and scrupulous about his appearance. George was the first to speak as he looked at his watch.

"Where've you been then? You've been gone a long time, as I've been up since seven fifteen, and you'd already gone. I was beginning to get a little concerned about you; I thought you might have gone and left us for good!" George laughed, but it wasn't his usual hearty laugh; it was as if he were forcing it.

My God, Kevin thought, *maybe he really did think that I might leave them. Or maybe even tough old George is getting nervous.* That thought unnerved Kevin, but he wasn't one to show it.

"I hardly think you need to worry about that, George. After all, this is my show, and we're all going to see it through to the bitter end."

"Oh, I wasn't serious, Mac, but I was getting a little concerned. You realize the Irish government probably has troops out looking for us right now. And if your assessment is correct—the British government probably had high-altitude reconnaissance planes flying over Ireland yesterday afternoon. They must have at least a rough idea from what part of Ireland the missile was launched. Even though this is a large mountainous area, if they started the search at dawn this morning, which would make sense from a military point of view, then it's only a matter of hours before they reach us."

"You're right—I do realize that. And we may have to launch the missile earlier than planned, if they get too close. I know that wouldn't be living up to our warning to the British that we wouldn't launch it before two o'clock, but let's be honest with ourselves; the chances that the British government will announce acceptance of our demands over the radio are slim to none. By the way, have you heard anything new and interesting on the radio news while I was gone?"

"No, I haven't. Except that the full news at 8:00 a.m. did carry a repeat of the statement issued by Downing Street that we heard last night. It's almost as if nothing happened, or the British government simply blacked out any further news reports about it. There wasn't even a reference to it on the Irish radio. I would give my right arm to see if there is any flap about it in the newspapers. Because if I know Fleet Street, they'll find a way to make news about yesterday's explosion. And I'm sure there are reporters hanging around Downing Street to make it embarrassing for the government."

"You're probably right, but perhaps we're better off at this point not knowing what's in the newspapers."

While Kevin and George had been talking, Ned had been busy with his sandwich making and was now giving Max some kibble and some warm milky tea in another dish.

"Tea's up, gents! Come and get it while it's hot."

Ned handed the two men mugs of hot tea and thick cheese sandwiches that looked more like doorsteps, and he kept one for himself. The three men ate in silence; nobody was particularly hungry, but each ate as if he were. Kevin figured the same thought was probably on all their minds: who knew when they would get their next meal? Max, having quickly wolfed down his kibble, was already doing the rounds and managing to get some cheese scraps from each of them in turn. Kevin smiled as he thought of that beautiful sunny Saturday in Bedford, New York, when he and Jenny stayed at her family home, and her dog, Jeepers, attached himself to him and scrounged lots of cheese tidbits.

When they finished eating, Ned gathered up four more big cheese sandwiches, put them in a brown paper bag, and filled a large thermos with hot tea. He took his leave of Kevin and George and set off down the mountain to bring the food and tea to the other four men. George yelled after him, "Ned, tell the others I'll be down shortly for a last look around." Then George turned back into the cave and spoke to Kevin. "You know, Ned is really an amazing man. Nothing seems to faze him.

I've known him many years, and he has served me in many foreign operations, and the night before we begin an operation, he'll have the jitters as good as the next man. But once we get going on something, he's as steady as a rock, and I can always rely on him to the end. We're lucky to have him on this operation."

"You're absolutely right there. In fact, I think they're all good men in their way. And the credit is all yours for picking them."

About fifteen minutes after Ned left, the field phone rang in the cave, and George grabbed it up immediately. And as George's face clouded over in apparent anger, Kevin became very concerned. George hung up and said that Ned had radioed back to Tom from Sean Morrissey's lookout post halfway down the mountain to say that he couldn't find any sign of Sean but that he'd found his submachine gun lying at the spot where he was supposed to be. Ned told Tom that he would search for him and radio back the minute he knew anything. George nearly exploded as he said to Kevin, "If Sean has gone and bolted, I'll find him and kill him!"

"Come on, George, he wouldn't do that. Besides, there's no possible way he could have heard anything about his mother."

"You know as well as I do that anyone who's on his own for hours on end can have his imagination play tricks on him. And somehow, he may have gotten it into his head that his mother was getting worse and decided to disappear. If that's the case, no matter what happens, he's as good as dead. If I can't do it myself, I'll hire someone to track him down and kill him."

"I just can't believe—" The ringing of the field telephone interrupted Kevin, and George grabbed it up once more. Kevin felt a flood of relief as George's face relaxed a little and he said, "Well, have Ned tell him that he bloody well better not wander off again, or I'll have his guts for garters!" George slammed down the phone.

"Can you believe it, Mac? The flaming idiot decided to take an early morning stroll over to the lake to enjoy the view! He must think we're on a bloody pleasure trip here! Anyway, Ned has his ways, and I'm sure when he gets through talking to Sean Morrissey, Sean won't even think of leaving his post again. But in his defense, Sean claims to have heard something land on the other side of the lake, said he thought it sounded like a helicopter, so he went to check it out, but with the mist, he couldn't be sure. Ned's going to check further when he gets to the farmhouse and talks to Pat and Terry. But you know, if the Irish government already has soldiers on the other side of the lake, it's only going to be a matter of two to three hours before they reach this mountain."

"If that's the case, George, then we've got less time than we thought. I'd better get cracking on programming this missile and leave myself flexible on the launch time."

Captain Leslie Caldwell was sitting in the bow of what looked like a small fishing boat. Six men manned three oars on each side of the boat, and they moved swiftly toward land. Les, as he was generally known, was a veteran captain of Britain's elite force, the SAS, and was now in command of a small unit of British commandos under orders to destroy the Green September group and, if possible, to capture Major Kevin MacAllister and ex-captain George Wilkinson alive. Their number-one priority was to disable the missile before it was launched on London. Les had handpicked the eight men accompanying him, and several of them, like himself, were veterans of previous attacks on IRA terrorists. With these experienced commandos in his unit, Les was feeling confident that he could successfully complete the mission he was given. He glanced at his watch; it was already close to eight o'clock as the boat rapidly drew closer to the shoreline.

They quickly disembarked and hid the boat as best they could among the rocks. Captain Leslie Caldwell led the men about a mile inland until they reached a narrow, winding road at the foot of the MacGillycuddy's Reeks. They crossed the deserted road, and, checking his compass, Les led the men west across the rocky terrain, gradually leaving the road far behind them. It was slow-going, and no one spoke as each man concentrated on the path ahead of him to avoid tripping or spraining an ankle.

None of the men wore military uniforms or carried any identification that would link them with the SAS. No two men were dressed alike;

they wore a motley assortment of tweed jackets and heavy pants or jeans. The only thing they all had in common were the heavy-duty, rubber-soled boots they wore. Their weapons consisted of an assortment of high-velocity automatic rifles and revolvers with silencers and hunting knives. Three of the men wore backpacks filled with hand grenades and plastic explosives. From a distance, they would pass as game hunters.

After heading due west for approximately three miles, Les called a short halt to split the group into three groups of three. He would lead the way with two men, and the other two groups were instructed to follow at roughly two-hundred-yard intervals. It was closing in on ten thirty, and Les was growing concerned that they hadn't seen or heard anything yet.

As they set off again, the terrain began to get rockier, and soon they were climbing steadily up the side of a mountain. They had gone only a half mile or so when Les stopped and signaled to the two groups behind to halt, as he thought he heard gunfire in the distance. He took out his compass and focused on the direction where he thought the gunfire originated. It seemed to be roughly southeast of them. He would guess that the gunfire was about a mile and a half away. Staying where he was, Les signaled the other two groups to join them. As the nine men crouched between the rocks, they again heard several more rounds of gunfire. As they listened, Les made his decision and led the men cautiously in the direction of the gunfire. After they had gone about half a mile, the gunfire stopped, and silence reigned around them. By now, they were higher up on the mountain and in a good location to look back to see if they were being approached from the rear. Les decided they would stay put and see what developed. Checking his watch, he saw it was already nine minutes past eleven o'clock.

At about twenty past nine, George left Kevin alone with the missile, and he began to descend the mountain and make his last inspection of the men. At Kevin's suggestion, he took Max with him on the leash. While he was gone, Kevin got everything ready on the missile, programming the guidance system so that this missile would fly at the maximum trajectory level of 50,000 feet at a speed of 2,100 miles per hour. He entered the distance as 480 miles, which he had carefully calculated so that the missile was targeted to hit the very center of London, using Big Ben as the focal point. Based on this, Kevin estimated that from time of launch, the missile would take thirteen minutes and forty-three seconds to reach the target. Quickly, he had everything set except the launch time. That he would leave until the last possible minute.

While waiting for George to return, Kevin sat by the mouth of the cave, staring at the cold, black steel of the missile. Kevin thought, *It almost looks like a shiny new toy, and yet it carries such a lethal payload.*

George was back by twenty-five past ten, and Kevin told him that everything was set to go. Likewise, George reported that the men were ready for action and that Ned was already back in place at the nearest lookout point. George explained that he had given strict instructions to Pat Feeney and Terry O'Neill to fall back if it looked like trouble was near. George also told Kevin that neither Pat nor Terry had seen anything unusual all morning, and so he had come to the conclusion that Sean Morrissey may just have been imagining that he saw a helicopter in the distance. But Kevin wasn't so sure and fervently hoped that the mist would keep any helicopters away from the mountain. Both men were quiet for a while, each lost in thoughts of what lay ahead. Kevin's mind was wandering back to Granduncle Bertie again, and as he sat there, the words of some of the poems and ballads of Thomas Davis, which he had heard so often from Bertie, began to come back to him. He decided to share some of them with George and so help distract his mind.

"You know, George, when I was on the other side of the mountain this morning with Max, gazing out at the ocean, a poem came into my mind, written by the early nineteenth-century poet, Thomas Davis, whom I told you about yesterday. I felt it was so true of Ireland, a poem called 'This Native Land of Mine,' and I would like to recite a few verses for you.

> She's not a dull or cold land;
> No! she's a warm and bold land;
> Oh! she's a true and old land—
> This native land of mine.

Could beauty ever guard her,
And virtue still reward her,
No foe would cross her border—
No friend within it pine!

Oh, she's a fresh and fair land;
Oh, she's a true and rare land!
Yes, she's a rare and fair land—
This native land of mine."

George seemed to relax a little as he listened to Kevin's recitation of the poem. Kevin was pleased, as he could tell that George was one of those rare professional soldiers who also had an appreciation for poetry and the arts.

"Those were beautiful and simple words. Although I have only been in Ireland on a few short occasions before, this country always struck me as a place of great natural beauty and not unlike my native Scotland. And from what little I've seen of this part of the world, this is certainly one of the grandest. Do you have any more interesting verses by this Thomas Davis?"

"As a matter of fact, I have several. Let me give you the first verse of another great poem he wrote called 'Self-Reliance.'

Though savage force and subtle schemes
And alien rule, through ages lasting,
Have swept your land like lava streams,
Its wealth, and name, and nature blasting,
Rot not, therefore, in dull despair,
Nor moan at destiny in far lands:
Face not your foe with bosom bare,
Nor hide your chains in pleasure's garlands:
The wise man arms to combat wrong,
The brave man clears a den of lions,
The true man spurns the Helot's song;
The free man's friend is Self-Reliance!"

"That strikes me like a capsule of Irish history in just a few words. This Thomas Davis clearly had the soul and heart of Ireland."

"You're right. It really does capture the spirit of how Ireland has felt about foreign rule down through the centuries. But perhaps one of the most inspiring and enduring ballads that Thomas Davis ever wrote is one called 'A Nation Once Again.' One of my favorite verses runs like this:

> It whispered, too, that freedom's ark
> And service high and holy,
> Would be profaned by feelings dark
> And passions vain or lowly;
> For freedom comes from God's right hand,
> And needs a godly train;
> And righteous men must make our land
> A nation once again."

"You know, Kevin, I think those words sum up the driving force behind this whole operation. I believe you have just revealed to me your ultimate motivation to see a united Ireland."

"Yes, I will admit it inspires me just as it has inspired many Irish patriots and leaders in the 150-odd years since it was written."

Both men lapsed into silence and settled down for a tense wait as Max lay down between them. But Kevin had a feeling in his bones that they wouldn't have to wait very long.

CHAPTER *21*

I T WAS A QUARTER AFTER ten in the morning, and an atmosphere of frustration and anger prevailed at the Irish Army field headquarters just south of Farranfore. Everyone in the headquarters was very much aware that General MacEoin's deadline to have the search of MacGillycuddy's Reeks completed had not been met. Colonel Paddy O'Brien, the officer in charge of the search, was pacing and muttering to himself. His second in command, Captain Basil Dougherty, was keeping himself busy monitoring communications with the troops in the field conducting the search. He had a group of soldiers manning a bank of field telephones on tables in the corner of the tent. Meanwhile, in the opposite corner of the large tent serving as field headquarters, Jim MacAllister and his ten men from Special Branch in Dublin were sitting around a large table drinking mugs of tea and giving the appearance of being deep in conversation.

In the middle of the tent, alongside where the colonel was pacing, sat the young Lieutenant Martin Maloney, who served as the colonel's adjutant. The lieutenant sat hunched over a table and appeared to be glancing through some papers, as if he wanted to avoid eye contact with his boss, the colonel. The phone on the table rang shrilly. Even as the lieutenant went to answer it, the colonel beat him to it and grabbed the receiver.

"Colonel O'Brien here," he barked in his strong Cork accent. "Yes, General. No, General. Yes, General, the very second I know anything, I'll call you right away." The Colonel slammed the receiver back in its cradle and, talking out loud to nobody in particular, said, "Be da'jesus! I can't control the fucking weather!"

The colonel then resumed pacing. And nobody said a word.

Padraig Flannery, Nicky Dwyer, and the other six men crouched in a dried-up riverbed behind some trees, waiting for the Irish soldiers about a half mile ahead of them to move forward. Padraig glanced at his watch. Already twenty-five minutes before eleven, and nothing so far. Padraig was disappointed and feeling discouraged at the slow pace of the search. Padraig thought to himself that maybe his informants in Dublin got the story wrong, and perhaps the missile was up in the Galway area after all. Padraig thought, *If that happens, I'm going to be really pissed if the Belfast contingent of the IRA and Rory McDevitt get their hands on the missile, rather than my Provos.* Padraig flicked on his two-way radio back to his lads in the cavern who were monitoring all other signals in the area. He had left Dermot McHugh in charge, and Dermot's voice now came over his radio.

"Hello, have you picked up any hint yet that suggests the Irish Army has found anything?"

"No, no news yet. Oh, lotsa chatter goin' on all right on the airwaves this morning, but nothing that suggests they've found anything yet. But don't be worryin'. I'll contact you the minute I hear anything."

Padraig flicked off his radio immediately, to lessen the chance that their signal might be picked up. The Provos always used a low band on the short-range frequency—one that was never used by either the Irish Army or the Gardai, but Padraig was a cautious man and never liked to take unnecessary risks. He was just reaching for his binoculars when he noticed that one of Rory McDevitts's lads from Belfast had lit up a cigarette.

"You fucking idiot! What are you trying to do, get us all killed? Put it out this instant, or I'll shoot your balls off!" The man did as he was told.

Padraig Flannery now trained his binoculars through a gap in the trees and focused in on a group of Irish soldiers a little over half a mile away. He realized they had now reached the southeast corner of Mount

Coomacarrea and were, he estimated, about a mile from the base of it. As he observed the soldiers through the binoculars, he got the impression that the soldiers were deciding to move northward around the other side of the mountain. As the southern face of Mount Coomacarrea was pretty sheer, he guessed that the soldiers considered it unlikely that anyone could be hiding on that side of the mountain. Before he lowered the binoculars, he could see the soldiers moving farther northward and fading into the distance. At that moment, Padraig made up his mind that they could be making a mistake and decided that when he and his men reached the point the soldiers had just left, he would position two men to cover the southern face of the mountain. Padraig gave the signal to move out, and, quietly, all eight men headed northward by the east side of the mountain, following the Irish soldiers.

After they'd gone about a mile, Padraig called a halt. The terrain of trees and wild bushes had given way to a more rocky landscape with sparse undergrowth, and Padraig gathered the men around him behind a cluster of rocks, giving them cover from any Irish soldiers who might still be close by. Padraig gave instructions to two of the men—one of his own Provos and one from the Belfast IRA—and told them to stay in this position and watch the southern face of the mountain for any activity.

He again took out his binoculars and scanned the horizon ahead of them. At first, he didn't catch sight of anyone and, for a moment, thought he may have lost sight of the Irish soldiers they had been tracking. Just then, toward the northwest corner of his view, he spotted several Irish soldiers setting up guns behind some rocks. He raised the level of his binoculars above their heads and saw an old, dilapidated farmhouse about another quarter of a mile on. He focused the glasses carefully on the farmhouse and slowly scanned the windows and doorways of the old building.

Just as Padraig thought he'd detected a slight movement at one of the windows, he heard the first sound of gunfire. Slowly, he again scanned the entire side of the farmhouse that was facing in his direction, but he couldn't tell where the sound originated. Then he realized that it must be coming from the north side of the farmhouse, for as he moved the binoculars off to the right, he could see another distant group of Irish soldiers coming from the northeast toward the farmhouse. He quickly brought the binoculars back into focus on the Irish soldiers he had first noticed behind the rocks about a half mile forward from him. Just then, that group of soldiers also came under fire from the southern side of the farmhouse, and he could see the soldiers position their rifles over the rocks toward the farmhouse, and they began returning the fire.

Putting away his binoculars, Padraig crouched down again behind the rocks and explained to the others what he'd seen. He told the two men who were to stay there and cover the southern side of the mountain that they should also provide cover for them as they moved forward in the direction of the gunfire. Before moving out, Padraig quickly raised Dermot McHugh back in the cavern and let him know what was happening. Then, Padraig, Nicky, and the four other men edged out from the rocks and cautiously moved forward, crouching low. After about two hundred yards, they stopped again, and Padraig said he was sure that the Irish soldiers were engaging the Green September group in gunfire, but he doubted very much that the missile and the entire group were in that farmhouse. It was Padraig's opinion that the farmhouse was merely serving as a lookout and that the missile was almost certainly well hidden somewhere higher up in the mountain. Nicky agreed. At that moment, the little red light on Padraig's two-way radio began flashing, and he flicked it on. Dermot McHugh's voice came crackling over excitedly, saying he had just picked up a radio message from the troops around the farmhouse that suggested they had finally found the Green September group and requested backup troops and helicopter support. Padraig replied, "Yes, we know. Thanks." And Padraig turned off the radio. Slowly, the six men began to inch closer to the Irish soldiers and the farmhouse.

Padraig Flannery was peering through his binoculars, still focused on the farmhouse. He kept scanning the length of the farmhouse and the attached outhouses. There hadn't been any gunfire for several minutes now, and then he noticed two men slipping out a door at the far end of the outhouses at the point furthest away from the Irish soldiers. They moved quickly across the short open space and were soon lost to sight in thick undergrowth and rocks. He kept his binoculars trained in the direction he thought they must be headed. Quietly he watched for several minutes, and then through a gap in the trees, he thought he caught sight of the two men again, briefly. He decided to make his move.

Padraig quickly explained to Nicky and the other men that he intended to follow these two members of the Green September group, as he was certain they would lead them to the missile.

Quietly, they left their hiding place behind the rocks and, crouching low, followed Padraig and began the slow climb in the direction of the north face of the mountain. They had gone only about a half mile when they came under fire from a rocky ledge about a hundred yards away from them, on higher ground. The men ducked for cover behind some rocks and rapidly returned fire. Padraig focused his binoculars on the spot where the gunfire originated and could now make out at least three people aiming at them from that high ledge.

After a five-minute exchange of intense gunfire, Padraig had already lost two of his men, one from Derry and one from Belfast. Both had been shot in the head, which convinced him that there was at least one good marksman on that ledge. But he and Nicky had gotten in a couple of licks of their own and were sure they had killed at least one, maybe two of the men on the ledge above them. For a moment, all was quiet. Then Padraig heard gunfire farther away to the northwest of the ledge and higher up the mountain. He wondered what the hell that could be all about, as he was convinced there was no way the Irish soldiers could have gotten that far.

Padraig knew that they couldn't stay where they were, because he had no doubt that their short gun battle with the men on the ledge would probably bring the Irish Army running after them. So he decided that he and Nicky and the remaining few men should climb farther up the mountain in the direction of the new gunfire.

With some regret, Padraig left the two dead men behind but not until he removed their weapons and gave them to the other men. Checking his watch, he saw it was already twenty minutes past eleven as they headed off in the direction of the new gunfire.

Colonel Paddy O'Brien had resumed pacing, having just finished his sixth conversation with the general in Dublin in the last hour. He felt like he was living in a pressure chamber, although he realized that the general, too, was under intense pressure from the Irish prime minister. At that moment, he heard a yell from the corner where the banks of field telephones were and turned to see what was going on. Captain Basil Dougherty strode over and explained, "At last, Colonel, the Green September group has been located in an old farmhouse about a mile and a half southeast of the village of Glenbeigh and a few hundred yards from Lough Caragh. Our soldiers have come under gunfire from this farmhouse, but they estimate that there are only two or, at most, three men inside. They're returning fire but have made no move to take the farmhouse and are waiting for orders."

"Great! You stay here and take command. I'll take MacAllister and his men and Lieutenant Maloney with me up to that area. Have one of the helicopters rev up and stand by. Get a concentration of troops by that farmhouse ASAP and call the general with the news."

"Understood, loud and clear, Colonel!"

The atmosphere in the tent changed dramatically, from doom and gloom to an air of intense excitement. Within seconds, Captain Dougherty had the men on the field telephones contacting all the nearest units. In less than a minute, Colonel Paddy O'Brien, the young lieutenant, and Jim MacAllister and his Special Branch men were boarding the helicopter. It was a roomy twenty-seater, battle-class Westland, with four machine gun nests manned by gunners who were already aboard. Lieutenant Maloney gave the pilot the coordinates for the location of the farmhouse, and the pilot set a westerly by southwesterly course. Their target area was about eighteen miles away as the crow flies, and the pilot told the lieutenant it would take them approximately thirteen to fourteen minutes to reach it. The colonel turned to Jim MacAllister and briefly outlined to him his planned operation.

"Jim, if you look down there to the left, you'll see the farmhouse about three-quarters of a mile ahead. It is just discernable in that break in the mist."

The pilot maneuvered the helicopter so that they would land in a clearing near the edge of the lake, about 250 yards northwest of the farmhouse. As soon as they were firmly on the ground, the colonel was first to be out of the helicopter and hurried over to a group of waiting soldiers.

A sergeant stepped forward to greet them. Colonel O'Brien immediately recognized the bulky form of Sergeant Joe Mulligan from his own barracks in Cork.

"Good morning, Sergeant. Who's in charge here right now?"

"Well, Colonel, sir, I suppose I must be, sir, as there's no other NCO hereabouts."

"Well, Sergeant, then you can tell me what's going on around here. Do you still have the terrorists bottled up in the farmhouse?"

"Well, sir, as far as we know, they're in there, though we haven't exchanged any fire in the last five minutes or so. Also, there are a lot more soldiers coming into the area, and I'm not quite sure what you'd like me to do with them, sir."

"You mean to tell me, sergeant, that the farmhouse isn't completely surrounded? Good God, man, they may have gotten away already!"

"Well, Colonel, sir, beggin' your pardon, sir, you know some of the soldiers who have just arrived are from the Limerick barracks, and I don't have any authority over them, do I? Besides, we've been holding down the farmhouse from the north and northeast sides, and, until a few minutes ago, they were shooting at us and pinning us down."

Turning to Lieutenant Martin Maloney, he instructed him to take the sergeant and to make sure that all soldiers in the area were now aware who was in command and that the farmhouse was completely surrounded right away. Then the lieutenant was to report back to him the minute that had been done. As the lieutenant and the sergeant hurried off to carry out the colonel's orders, the colonel turned to Jim MacAllister.

"Jim, I think it's best if you and I and your men take up position behind those trees over yonder and wait there until the farmhouse is completely surrounded. Then we'll decide whether to take the farmhouse or not."

Jim nodded agreement and gave instructions to his men to accompany him and the colonel over to the clump of trees about 150 yards from the north side of the farmhouse. Within a couple of minutes, the lieutenant came back, puffing as if he'd been running hard. He reported that over one hundred soldiers had now surrounded the farmhouse and the outbuildings, and there was no way for anyone to get out. The colonel instructed the lieutenant to order the men to start approaching the farmhouse slowly with guns at the ready. And he reiterated his instructions to take the terrorists alive if at all possible. Jim MacAllister's men fanned out among the soldiers as they started approaching the farmhouse, and Jim accompanied the colonel. Both had revolvers drawn and ready.

As they closed in on the farmhouse, Colonel O'Brien thought it very odd that they had not been fired upon, and he grew increasingly uneasy, suspecting that their prey may already have flown the coop. Sergeant Mulligan was the first through the farmhouse doors with several soldiers following him. Thirty seconds later, he yelled back to the colonel that there wasn't a soul inside. The colonel cursed and swore under his breath, "Too bloody fucking late! Jesus! The general will have my balls in a sling!"

Jim MacAllister was the first to speak. "All is not lost, Colonel! We know they still have to be in the area, and given the position of the soldiers when we arrived, there's only one possible route they could have taken, and that is a southwesterly route by the lake and up toward the mountain."

"You're right, of course, Jim. But still, it would have been nice to catch one or two of the buggers now. Perhaps they'd have talked. Anyway, let's take a look around and see what traces they left behind. Maybe that'll tell us something."

Jim, the colonel, and several of the other Special Branch men went into the farmhouse. There was still the smell of fresh cigarette smoke in the air and lots of grounded-out butts on the floor near the window. In fact, one butt was still smoldering, which suggested that whoever had been there had only left in the last five or ten minutes. A thorough search of the farmhouse turned up nothing more than some litter, food wrappings, spent shells, and empty cigarette packs. Everyone went outside. The search of the outbuildings turned up only two cars in the barn. On learning this, Jim MacAllister immediately asked the colonel to make sure that his soldiers didn't touch anything inside or outside the cars. Jim would have two of his men dust the cars for fingerprints and for any other signs that might help identify the terrorists.

The colonel and Jim MacAllister set up a temporary headquarters in the farmhouse while they decided what to do next. More soldiers were pouring into the area, and in the yard outside, Lieutenant Maloney and Sergeant Mulligan were organizing them into the units while they waited for the colonel's orders.

An outburst of gunfire broke out somewhere to the south of them, and the two men immediately ran out in the yard. The colonel ordered all troops in the direction of the gunfire.

After they'd given the order for Pat and Terry to abandon the farmhouse, Kevin turned and said, "Clearly, George, we're now going to have to launch earlier than we'd originally planned."

About another three or four minutes had gone by when Ned called back again on the field telephone. In three minutes, the phone rang again, and shortly after George answered it, Kevin heard him say, "Ah, fuck! Tell the lads to fight and not let anyone get near the cave." He turned to Kevin and said, "They've come under fire by some other unknown group."

Kevin was stunned. "Who the hell could it be? The SAS? The IRA? The Russians?"

"I've no idea, Kevin, but I'd lay odds on it that it'll bring on the Irish Army faster than anything."

They were pretty certain that they were not Irish soldiers, and they wondered what the hell was going on. George swore and told Ned to tell the lads to fight and not to let anyone get any nearer to the cave. George slammed down the phone and filled Kevin in. Kevin was stunned; he had expected the Irish Army to be after him, but now he wondered who these other gunmen were.

He turned to George and asked, "Who the hell could these gunmen be? Do you think the British government has sent in the SAS? Or could it be the IRA? Or could it be some Russian group out to get the missile? Just who the hell are they?"

"I've absolutely no idea, Kevin. Your guess is as good as mine. But it certainly adds a new wrinkle. And I would lay odds that it will bring the Irish Army in this direction faster than anything. But at the same time, whoever they are, they will either melt away when the Irish Army approaches or they'll turn and take on the army for us."

Both men lapsed into silence again, and by now Max was cowering deeper in the cave, near George, as the sound of gunfire grew louder and closer. Then, during a short lull in the gunfire, both men heard the sound; there was no mistaking it. It was definitely a helicopter in the distance. Kevin used his binoculars to scan the horizon in the direction of the farmhouse but in vain. Mist covered everything below him.

Captain Leslie Caldwell and the eight men of his crack SAS unit were still crouched in the same position, higher up on the mountain. Having waited for several minutes as the sound of gunfire died down in the distance, he decided it was time to move in that direction and find out what was going on. His experience told him that they must be near their target. Gingerly, Les led his men farther up the mountain, moving cautiously, for the rocky terrain provided little cover, and the sparse undergrowth was almost useless. The nine men had gone about a quarter of a mile when a single shot rang out. As they ducked for cover, Les looked behind him and saw one of the men fall, shot in the chest, apparently dead instantly.

For several moments, they crouched in the dirt, behind rocks, and all was quiet. Finally, Les gave the signal to carefully edge forward, but crawling between the rocks, they were exposed. Another shot rang out and caught one of the men in the shoulder. This time Les caught a glimpse of where the shot had come from—several hundred yards farther on and still higher up on the mountain—but it was difficult for him to be sure with the mist swirling around. A little farther on, to the left he noticed a small stand of stunted trees that could provide them with some cover, so Les made every effort to get his men there safely. But as they made their way, a third man was hit in the leg.

Once Les and the men reached the relative safety of the trees, they set up gun positions and began to return fire. As Les studied the terrain through his binoculars, he realized that whoever was firing at them was in an almost unassailable position, and it would be difficult for his men to find their target. He decided to send two of them with hand grenades to skirt around to the right and climb above the position they were being fired from, to hopefully wipe it out. As they came under heavy fire in the trees, he sent the two men down the mountain to circle around the long way, out of range.

Les checked his watch as the two men left, crawling down behind him; it was 11:30 a.m. It was going to take them at least ten if not fifteen minutes to complete their mission. Moments after they left, Les and his remaining few men, two of whom were wounded, came under attack from the rear. Now under intense fire from the front and the rear, Les began to wonder if he'd led his men into a trap in unfamiliar terrain. The mist was growing thicker, which didn't help matters, and Les wondered if the other two men would make it. He thought, *At least that would take the heat off us on one side.*

Les assumed he was under fire from two contingents of the Green September group until suddenly he noticed that some of the shots from the group to his rear now seemed to be aimed at the higher spot on the mountain. Les was confused, and it slowly dawned on him that somehow or other, he and his men were caught in a three-way fight.

Kevin's face was grim as he listened to the latest news from George. Sean Morrissey was killed by someone other than Irish soldiers; Pat Feeney had been badly wounded in the left shoulder; luckily, Terry O'Neill and Tom Fallon were still okay. And Ned had just been fired upon from an entirely different direction by yet another unidentified group. George thought that they were probably Irish soldiers who were coming in from the west. With Kevin's full agreement, George had just told Tom and Terry to help get Pat Feeney back to Ned's lookout post and to leave Sean Morrissey's dead body behind but to take his weapons and anything else that might help identify him.

It was already 11:35 a.m., and Kevin put Max on the leash as he walked toward the missile for at least the twentieth time and debated aloud with himself when he should launch. At that point, George left him, saying he would go down to give Ned support until the others could reach him. Alone with Max and the missile, Kevin grew increasingly nervous and anxious. Kevin thought, *It would be Sean who would be killed—the one man who so desperately needed the money to help his mother. If any of us survives the next half hour and gets out of this mess, I must make sure George takes care of Sean's mother financially. I wonder who else we'll lose before this battle is done.*

George came running into the cave with blood streaming from the side of his head, but when Kevin registered his concern, George brushed it off and said it was only a graze from a bullet and nothing serious.

"Kevin, I think you'd better get ready to launch. It's complete confusion below. Terry and Tom made it okay with Pat Feeney, and Pat isn't too badly injured—at least he's still able to use a rifle. Anyway, the lads are holding their own for now against the attack from the west. But while I was still there, the strangest thing happened: the group attacking the lads came under attack themselves, from the rear, from the northeast! Then that same group started firing on us. I just don't know what the hell is going on!"

"Sounds like a right bloody mess down there, George. You're right. I'm going to set the timer right now. It's already 11:40. I'll set it to lift off at 11:45."

Kevin deftly set the timer for 11:45 a.m. George held Max close to him on a short leash while Kevin was setting the timer. By the time Kevin was done, both men looked up to see Ned come running into the cave, closely followed by Tom Fallon and Terry O'Neill. Sweat poured off all three of them, and Ned was screaming, "Major, Captain, we're gonna have to get the hell out of here!" He then got better control of himself and said, "Things are getting hot below. Pat insisted that he would hold them off. I've never seen such a look in the eyes of a man. I think he's hell-bent on dying after he takes a few of them with him. But there was no shakin' him, and he insisted that me and the lads get the hell out of there."

Before Kevin could say a word, George responded for both of them.

"You did right, Ned. The missile will be launched in only two minutes, so I want you and Tom and Terry here to hold off at the mouth of the cave until then. Then we're all on our own to get the hell out of here as best we can. Right?"

"Understood, Captain. We can manage that. With the fine job Pat Feeney is doing down below, there should be no problem."

George tugged urgently at Kevin and said, "Mac, we need to join the three lads outside the mouth of the cave, too, and crouch down on the ledge to avoid the exhaust backfire from the missile as it launces in a minute or two. Do you want me to hold on to Max?"

"No, thanks, George, I'll hold him tight to my heart," Kevin said as they withdrew from the cave. Kevin knew in his heart that the end was near for his most loyal companion Max.

Everyone was deadly quiet, and the silence of the next two minutes was punctuated occasionally only by the sound of sporadic gunfire. Kevin watched the second hand on his watch as he hugged his beloved Max closer to him. He began the countdown—*Five, four, three, two, one … it's off!* The roar in the cave was deafening as the missile shot straight up into the air. With the exhaust from the rockets glowing brightly, it cut like a silver knife through the mist, on its way to the total destruction of London.

CHAPTER 22

AFTER THE CABINET MEETING CONCLUDED on that fateful Thursday morning, a directive had gone out to all ministers to activate the Armageddon Protocol. The aptly named Armageddon Protocol had been put in place in the late 1960s under the then Harold Wilson Labor government. Throughout the 1950s and 1960s, the threat of nuclear war was perceived to be very real, and many governments put in place plans to attempt to carry on in the event of a nuclear conflict. The Armageddon Protocol called for the construction of a nuclear bombproof bunker at least a half mile below the Ministry of Defense and 10 Downing Street and was to be able to house at least four thousand government ministers, support personnel, and key members of the military command structure. The bunker project was code-named Pindar and presented enormous engineering challenges, as below ground London was an absolute maze of tunnels for trains, sewers, utilities, and so on—some going back centuries. It took over twenty years to construct, at a cost in excess of half a billion pounds. All systems were updated annually to reflect the very latest technology. Pindar was designed to be totally sealed from the outside world and to be self-sustaining in all aspects of life for a minimum of five years like a model mini-city. The Pindar bunker had also included the construction of 5.7 miles of nuclear bombproofed tunnels that extended from 10 Downing Street and the Ministry of Defense to other key centers of government.

By eleven in the morning, the evacuation of key personnel to the bunker had been completed, and ministers were already gathering in the underground cabinet meeting room. The room in many respects resembled the cabinet meeting room at 10 Downing Street, except there were no windows. At exactly 11:30 a.m., Muriel Hobson, the prime minister, along with her minister of defense, Gordy Hargreaves, entered the room. A hushed silence fell on the room. Gordy Hargreaves was the first to speak.

"I'm pleased to announce that all military operations are in place, with full working communications and computer systems. We're in direct and immediate contact with both special SAS forces that are now closing in on where the missile launcher has been located in the mountains of Kerry in southwest Ireland, and with RAF reconnaissance planes that are circling over the southwest of Ireland. At this juncture, the prime minister has asked me to turn the meeting open to questions or suggestions so that we get everybody's views on what the next steps should be."

Then in his usual position at the opposite end of the table to Muriel Hobson, Harry Roberts spoke up. "Prime Minister, do you believe it was fair to give government workers only one hour advance notice that we were shutting offices for the day and that they could return home, before the information hit the streets in the *Evening Sentinel* at eleven o'clock?"

With a reproachful look on her face, Muriel Hobson looked Harry Roberts straight in the eye and said, "Harry, we had no way of knowing that Jeremy Sands was going to release a story like this in the first edition of the day at the *Evening Sentinel*. Clearly there must have been a leak somewhere within our government, and I intend to get to the bottom of it."

Harry Roberts responded sharply, "With respect, Prime Minster, Jeremy Sands happens to be one of the smartest, best reporters on Fleet Street. I believe that he simply put two and two together and got four."

"Instead, he has single-handedly managed to cause widespread panic on the streets above us. The latest police reports coming in indicate that the word has spread like wildfire throughout the West End and as far out as the Square Mile in the East End of London. People seem to be exiting office buildings and stores in droves and heading for overcrowded train stations, buses, cars, or any sort of transport they can find to get out of central London. So a nice job Mr. Sands has done."

Before he had a chance to respond, Gordy Hargreaves got up out of his chair and yelled for quiet. Looking at his watch, Gordy then announced, "It's right on the dot of 11:40 a.m., and I just got word that everything is in place in Cornwall with this newfangled American missile target alternator, and they are in direct contact with those ships of the US Atlantic fleet that are now trolling the waters in St. George's Channel. So, from a military perspective, we have two alternatives to stop this missile reaching London. Either the new American technology in the laser-based MTA works or in the worst-case scenario, they have a high-tech conventional missile destroyer ready to launch a missile that can blow the nuke up in the high atmosphere."

Discussion erupted around the table again while a messenger slipped into the room and handed Muriel Hobson a folded note, which she opened. Her face went white when she read it.

Muriel Hobson began banging her fist on the table and yelled, "Please, please, everybody, just shut up and listen. This is crucial. I've just received confirmation from one of the RAF reconnaissance planes that at precisely 11:45 a.m.—that's just one minute ago—the second nuclear missile was launched and appears to be headed in the direction of London. I'm advised that its travel time to the heart of London is thirteen minutes and forty-three seconds, which means that we should be ready for a missile strike at precisely 11:58:43.

A frightened hush fell on the room as the ministers looked at each other with grim faces and mouths open in horror at the thought of what was a mere twelve minutes away.

Meanwhile, on the fifth floor of the Sentinel Building on Fleet Street, Jeremy Sands and Donald Mortimer stood looking out the window of Donald's corner office. Having been placed under close house arrest just about half an hour earlier, they were watched closely by two agents from MI5 and three senior officers from Special Branch. They stood there quietly watching the scenes of panic in the streets below as people hurried to get away from London. The TV in Mortimer's office was tuned in to BBC Channel 4 News where the news team still had two helicopters flying low over London. The cameras in these helicopters were showing office buildings and stores dumping out thousands of people onto the jammed streets of London from the West End to the East End. The reporters commented that the majority of people were heading for train stations, underground stations, buses, cars, and taxis. But a considerable number of people were gathering in places like Hyde Park and Trafalgar Square, and it was reported that all churches, temples, and even one or two mosques that lay within the central London area had filled up with capacity crowds. Jeremy and Donald turned away from the street scenes below and looked at the television screen as the BBC reporters in exemplary fashion remained calm and soothing in reporting events as they saw them. Then the screen filled with images of the tens of thousands of people who had linked arms in jammed Trafalgar Square and were singing, "We Shall Overcome." For a few moments, the reporter said nothing but let the sounds of people united in fear rise above all else. Then one reporter commented, "There has not been a scene like this in Trafalgar Square since the end of World War II, on VE Day."

As the helicopter camera scanned the crowd and the surrounding buildings, it paused momentarily on the church clock tower at St. Martins in the Fields, which now read ten minutes to twelve. Jeremy and Donald and their five guards stood rooted to the spot, staring at the television screen.

Less than ten seconds had passed since the rocket left the mouth of the cave. Kevin and George crouched side by side with their hands over their heads and ears, hugging the side of the mountain to the right of the cave, and Kevin was still holding on tight to the trembling Max. On the other side, Ned and the rest of the men did the same. For a split second, with his eyes closed tightly, Kevin realized what he had just done and in his mind's eye could see a vivid vision of London destroyed and burning beneath him. He recoiled in horror as George tugged at his arm urgently, shouting, "Mac! We've got to get the hell out of here!

Whoever's coming after us is closing in. There's gunfire coming from all directions. We've got to get back inside the cave. Ned and the boys are gonna hold off anyone coming up the mountain from the ledge in front of the cave entrance for as long as they can."

As Kevin and George raced into the tunnel, Ned yelled after them, "Tom, Terry, and I should be able to hold out for at least five minutes and then come after you and meet at our agreed rendezvous point on the other side of the mountain. Gunfire's getting closer, and I fear Pat must be dead by now. But knowing him, he probably took at least a half a dozen down with him."

As they clattered deeper into the cave, Kevin looked at George and said, "I didn't catch that last part, George. What did you say about Max?"

"Mac, I truly hate to say this, but the time has come for Max, as agreed all along."

"I know, George. My heart is breaking, and I think Max senses his end is near as he is now moaning with a whimper." Kevin got his handgun ready. He had already added a silencer earlier in anticipation of what he must do. Kevin's hand trembled as he gently held Max and placed his gun to Max's head, looked into his eyes, and faltered. George firmly took Kevin's gun from his hand and fired. In a split second, it was all over, and Max lay still on the ground.

"Thanks, George," Kevin murmured, holding back his tears.

"I am so sorry, Mac, but you know we don't have a minute to spare!"

"George, if you or I ever get out of this alive, you have my word that I will take care of the surviving families of all those killed. And I know you will, too, if I don't make it."

As the sound of gunfire grew more and more distant, George and Kevin were now down to a slow pace, and for the last couple hundred yards were crawling on their bellies to get to the end of the cave on the other side of the mountain. George went first as they exited the cave and paused to scan in all directions to see if he could see any movement or hear any gunfire. He didn't and beckoned Mac to follow him. Together they slithered downhill through the undergrowth to the bay below and slowly disappeared from sight.

Meanwhile, on the other side of the mountain, Captain Les Caldwell and the remaining four members of the SAS team decided it was time to get the hell out of there, as they seemed to be under heavy gunfire both from the cave and from off to their left on the east side of the mountain. With the missile already gone, he had failed in his mission and now owed it to the remaining men to try to get them out of there in one piece. Les knew if he could make it to the dinghy, they could get out to the waiting submarine.

On the east side of the cave, Padraig Flannery, Nicky Dwyer, and the remaining two men from the Provos knew it was all over once that missile had fired. It was critical that they try to get back to the safety of their cavern hiding place in the ruins of the castle before the Irish Army caught them.

Jim MacAllister and his men watched as Colonel Paddy O'Brien and his men made their way to the ledge and found two dead bodies. He and three of his team from Special Branch came up behind him. The colonel turned, and Jim looked him in the eye and said, "I've already lost twenty men to some super marksman up on the ridge."

"So, no Major MacAllister or Captain Wilkinson? I guess they got away."

"Maybe not," the colonel said. "I've ordered every single soldier we have to scour every square inch of this mountain on all sides. We'll find them."

Jim nodded, but he was thinking that not one of these soldiers would know these mountains like his cousin Kevin, and he felt relieved that he wouldn't have to confront his cousin in a life-or-death situation. And yet the colonel and the Irish government would see him as having done his job. On the other hand, Jim felt kind of sorry for the colonel, as he would take one hell of a bollocking from the general over not getting there in time to prevent the launch of the missile.

They moved on to the cave, and Jim smelled the strong, acrid rocket fuel as they poked around in the cave. A quick search of the rucksacks and equipment left behind in the cave revealed absolutely nothing.

CHAPTER *23*

I T WAS JUST ABOUT TEN minutes past eight in the morning when the British Army helicopter landed at the far corner of the Penzance Training Camp in southwest Cornwall. The firing range at the camp extended almost from the little town of Penzance on the south coast of Cornwall to the even smaller town of St. Ives on the other side of the peninsula. Captain Rodney Smithers stepped out of the helicopter and was greeted by Sergeant Rex Jones, who commanded a squad of twelve men from the Royal Welsh Guards, which was one of a handful of nuclear-ready regiments in the British Army, and they had also recently participated in the military exercises on Salisbury Plain. Sergeant Jones saluted the captain smartly and said, "Good morning, sir! The two Yanks are already here and all set up, ready to go."

"Thank you, Jones. Yes, they said they would study the manuals of our Penguin-class MMLs all night long and get totally up to speed on them."

"That they did, sir." Jones chuckled. "They probably know more about those missiles now than we do, sir."

"Okay, good, good. Take me to them. Thanks."

Jones led the way to the concrete bunker half-built into the hill overlooking the ocean far below, one of many remaining on the British coast since World War II when a Nazi invasion was feared. Inside, Captain Smithers was greeted with the smell of coffee brewing. *Probably in honor of the Yanks*, he figured. The two Americans were busy at a fairly large computer they had set up in the corner of the bunker. Captain

Smithers strode over to join them, and they both got up and introduced themselves.

"Hi, Captain. My name is Harry Palmer, and this is my partner, Randy Hollis. I hail from Atlanta, and Randy hails from Boston."

Randy gave a big smile and said, "Glad to meet you, Captain. This is a tough situation you Brits are facing here."

Rodney bantered a little more with the friendly Yanks and said, "So you think you know more about the Penguin class of nuclear missiles now than I do, right?"

Harry Palmer was quick to answer, "No, no, Captain. I think we've learned a lot through the night, but we still defer to you as the expert. In fact, I want to run this by you."

While the Americans explained a quirk in the master program, which they planned to use to retarget the Penguin-class missile in midair by using their computer-integrated laser prototype, they had some technical issues for Rodney and proceeded to pepper him with questions in rapid order.

Sergeant Jones got one of the men to bring over three steaming mugs of coffee to the captain and the two Yanks. As the captain finished his huddled discussions with the Americans in the corner, he got up and said to Sergeant Jones, "How about you see if you can rustle up a good old-style english breakfast for our two guests and myself."

"Right away, sir. I'll get one of the men right on it. The bunker comes equipped with a full field kitchen, and so we're good to go."

Half an hour later, they were all tucking away an english fry-up of bacon, eggs, sausages, black pudding, and english baked beans, washed down with strong tea. By ten o'clock, everything was prepared, and the two Yanks were all set to initiate their new program called the missile target alternator and transmit it to the incoming missile by laser beam.

Rodney suggested that the exhausted Americans, who had worked through the entire night, catch a quick hour of sleep. Two of the soldiers brought in a couple of standard army cots and set them up in the corner near the computer. Gratefully, Harry and Randy lay down and were sound asleep in less than a minute.

Rodney decided to take a walk along the cliffs. He could see a couple of the American missile destroyers off in the distance. At exactly 11:00 a.m., Rodney woke the Americans, and one of the soldiers brought them two cups of hot, strong coffee. Rodney was now beginning to feel the mounting tension as he addressed the Americans, saying, "We now need to be on standby and ready to launch the program at a moment's notice. Two of Jones's men are out on the cliff tops with very powerful binoculars, scanning the horizon and the skies above it." Fortunately, in Cornwall the sky was clear and blue.

As Rodney paced nervously, time was ticking. It was already after eleven thirty.

At 11:47 precisely, the field telephone in the other corner of the bunker rang shrilly. Sergeant Jones answered it and immediately drew to full attention. He said, "Captain, it's for you."

Rodney raced over and took the phone. It was Sir Ian Sinders, who said tersely, "This is it, Rodney. They launched the missile early, at precisely 11:45. It's following the exact trajectory we expected and should be over Cornwall in about seven minutes. You and the Americans need to be ready to see if the MTA will work."

"Yes, sir. We're absolutely ready to go." He hung up.

Rodney told the Americans about the early launch, and they immediately set the computer's tracking device to pick up the exact path of the missile. They got a lock on the position. American specialist Harry Palmer set the program to release at exactly 11:54 when it was calculated the missile would be almost directly overhead. Randy's right index finger hovered over the Enter button on the keyboard, ready to execute the release of the laser program that should immediately connect with the missile's computer overhead and reprogram it. The MTA program called for the missile to be redirected to go eighty thousand feet above the Arctic Circle and explode, where it was believed that the prevailing winds should disperse the radiation into the outer atmosphere with minimal damage to earth.

There was a tense silence in the bunker, and all eyes were riveted to the standard army clock on the wall as it ticked away the seconds toward 11:54.

At precisely 11:54, Randy Hollis pressed firmly down on the Enter button, and the program was released on a laser beam that passed right through the bunker ceiling as if it didn't exist. Seconds later, the two soldiers who had been scanning with binoculars rushed into the bunkers. One of them yelled, "Amazing! Bloody amazing! In an instant, the missile visibly changed its trajectory and headed higher due north. I've never seen anything like this!"

Sergeant Jones smiled proudly as Rodney and the two Americans jumped up and down wildly with their arms around each other. "Oh my God, we've saved London!" Hollis shouted. "We've saved London!"

Rodney told Sergeant Jones to get Sir Ian Sinders on the phone to give him the news. "Sir Ian, it worked. It's incredibly unbelievable. The MTA actually worked. American computer technology is unsurpassed. It's incredible."

The second he hung up on Rodney, Sir Ian Sinders rushed right into the cabinet room without as much as a single knock on the door and yelled, "The American MTA worked! Unbelievable! Simply astounding!"

The prime minister stared blankly at him and then, dropping all decorum in front of her cabinet ministers, jumped up and down and yelled at the top of her voice, "Incredible! Astonishing!"

The room erupted into screams of joy and jubilation that likely could have been heard half a mile above on the streets of London.

CHAPTER 24

O N THE OTHER SIDE OF the mountain, Kevin spotted Ned approaching the cove just in time to join him and George and get the boat out of the cave and into the water.

"Thank heavens, Ned, you made it!" he said, greeting him like a long-lost brother.

"I did, Captain, but I'm the only one left alive."

With the mist thicker than ever, they were almost invisible. The three of them got into the boat and quietly slid out to sea. Rowing with muffled oars, the three men made their escape out to the open waters at the mouth of Dingle Bay. Ned's plan had been that they make their way to Little Scully Island, an uninhabited but wooded island off the coast of Waterville. With the aid of a compass, they headed in that direction. The open seas were a good deal rougher than they had expected, and suddenly they hit a rock that tore a good-sized hole in the side of the boat. They immediately took on water and could not bail quickly enough to save the boat from capsizing. In the confusion, Ned got tossed out of the boat and was quickly lost to sight in the thick fog. As the boat overturned, Kevin and George clung to it for dear life and scanned what little of the horizon they could see through the thick banks of fog, trying to locate Ned. They called his name but got no answer.

"Mac, I now have to confess I knew Ned's one dark secret in life: he never learned how to swim! So my guess is that he has already gone to a watery grave."

Kevin looked away with a tear in his eye. With the compass and everything else but the clothes they were in gone, Kevin and George now had no idea where they were and how far they had drifted. The tide was pulling them farther out to sea, and the water was getting choppier by the minute.

"You know, George, sharks are known to frequent these waters. I'm told they swim up here with the Gulf Stream." Kevin clung to the boat tighter and hoped there were no sharks around. "Let's tie ourselves together so we don't get separated," he suggested. "I could cut off strips off my shirt and—" He stopped when he saw George taking a length of rope out of his coat pocket. After tying the ends around their belts, they were sure of always being within ten feet of each other.

"It'll get dark soon," Kevin said as he stared out beyond George. Then he saw something he could hardly believe through a break in the mist. "There must be a God," he whispered.

"What is it, Mac?" George asked.

"A ship. I saw a ship."

"You're shitting me," George said, looking over his shoulder as a wave washed over them. "Well, by God, you're right … British?" he asked.

"No, I don't think so," Kevin said after spitting seawater from his mouth. "Maybe Argentine. The tide's taking us toward it. Let's kick our legs and push this boat and try to get as near as we can."

George lifted his left shoulder in a half shrug. "There's not much chance they'll spot us, you know."

"Come on," Kevin said. "We've been lucky so far. I think they may be our ticket out of here."

"Surely our best bet," George said.

ABOUT THE AUTHOR

BORN IN GOREY, CO. WEXFORD (a.k.a. Kennedy Country) south of Dublin, Ireland, Ray Vernon is the youngest of eight children. He grew up in Ireland, and after graduating from Cork University, he moved to London. He has also lived in Hanover, Germany, and Milan, Italy. For the past forty-one years, he has lived in the United States—first in California, then New York, and now Plymouth, Massachussetts. His corporate career in sales and marketing took him to more than eighty countries and gave him the opportunity to experience lots of adventures in his many travels.

Ray is still Irish to the core, a history buff who loves all music, from hard rock to classical, and is a consummate conversationalist on any topic, ranging from world affairs to politics. Currently, Ray is a very active and successful real estate broker serving Boston's South Shore and Cape Cod. He readily admits that he is passionate about writing and real estate and loves meeting new people.

Ray lives in Plymouth with his wife; they have a daughter and son, with five wonderful grandchildren who he calls the "absolute delights of [his] life."

Printed in the United States
By Bookmasters